A CLASH OF STEEL

A Treasure Island Remix

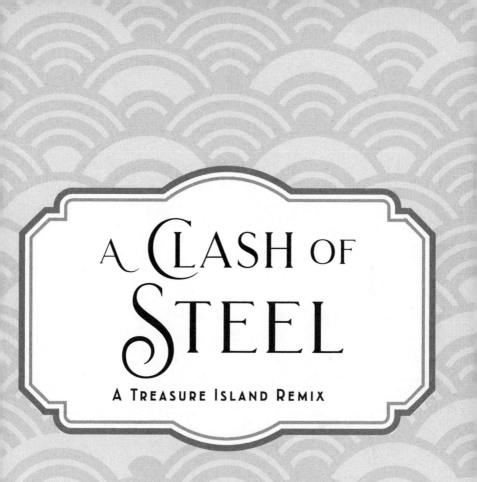

A CLASH OF STEEL

A TREASURE ISLAND REMIX

C.B. LEE

FEIWEL AND FRIENDS
New York

A FEIWEL AND FRIENDS BOOK
An imprint of Macmillan Publishing Group, LLC
120 Broadway, New York, NY 10271
fiercereads.com

Our books may be purchased in bulk for promotional, educational, or business use.
Please contact your local bookseller or the Macmillan Corporate and Premium Sales
Department at (800) 221-7945 ext. 5442 or by email at
MacmillanSpecialMarkets@macmillan.com.

Library of Congress Cataloging-in-Publication Data is available.
First edition, 2021
Jacket design by Rich Deas
Interior design by Angela Jun
Feiwel and Friends logo designed by Filomena Tuosto

Printed in the United States of America.
ISBN 978-1-250-75037-2 (hardcover)

10 9 8 7 6 5 4 3 2 1

For anyone who has ever wanted *more*.

Lời nói gió bay, truyện chép chuyền đời.

Words may disappear like the wind; a story is passed on forever.

端雲霞落淵洋日
彼岸花兮盼遠方
遙遙行者尋何志
寅虎丑時泪莹光

When sunset clouds fall
    into the deep ocean blue
The place where the spider-lilies bloom
    longing for distant vistas
Weary traveler, for what aspiration
    do you come?
The tiger's tears shine brightly
    at the second watch of night.

1818
The South China Sea

THE WILD STORM SEEMS TO HAVE NO END, THE HEAVENS above unleashing a relentless torrent as the sea rises and falls in response. The wind howls, screeching as it cuts through the torrential rain, snapping at every item that had the misfortune to be left loose. The small fishing vessel is not built for this type of onslaught at all, and it tumbles in the rising waves like a child's toy.

A shrieking gale knocks open a loose hatch and sends a deluge of rain below deck. The storm's rough waves send all the empty hammocks swinging. A chubby hand reaches for the edge of one of the two hammocks whose owners should be sleeping. Her eyes blink wide awake.

The girl is but eight years old, grinning wide enough to rival yesterday's shining crescent moon. A particularly ferocious wave crashes against the hull, knocking her grip loose and sending the hammock swinging. She tumbles to the rough-hewn floor in a heap, but rights herself quickly, her bare feet plopping against the wet planks.

She climbs above deck, and immediately her hair whips behind her with the sheer force of the wind. The crew is shouting, barely audible over the roar of the wind and the rain. She can hear her mother barking orders, something about avoiding the shoals and more complicated directions lost in the wind.

The ship heels perilously to one side, and she laughs when she almost falls, skidding to the right to keep her balance. It's like a dance—the moon trying to peek out behind the clouds, the rains making all the surfaces as slick as if they've been coated with oil, the ship's deck approaching vertical as crew members desperately hang onto something, anything, to avoid being thrown into the sea.

"Anh! Get back below deck! This storm is no joke!"

"I can help, Mẹ!" Anh calls out to her mother.

"The halyard line is twisted! It won't pass through the eye!" Bác Tu shouts. A particularly fierce gust wrenches the line out of his hands, and the wind whips it up into the air before he seizes it again.

"I'll get it, Bác Tu! Don't worry!" Anh races forward, her hands trailing along the rail as she makes her way to the mast. Anh delights in the challenge, her hands and feet finding their place on the swaying lacings. She climbs the drenched, slippery mast, ignoring the commotion below.

Her uncle shouts at her something incomprehensible, but

Anh gets the gist of it; he wants her back down on deck immediately. But she is almost there, and no one else would have done it—or could, she guesses, as she's smaller and faster than anyone, except maybe Auntie Ling, who outraced her across the deck the other day.

Anh concentrates on holding tight, using the lacings for balance as she makes it to the top. She finds the tangle and shakes it loose, and immediately the line pulls taut with the force of the wind, passing through the eye easily.

Anh slides back down to the deck from the mast, and for a second it feels like she's flying, a small act of defiance against the storm as she falls toward the deck. The surface rises up to meet her sooner than she anticipates. Her cheek smarts from where her face smacks against the wet wooden planks of the deck; she curls up into a ball and rolls just as an errant wave sends the ship toppling in the other direction.

"Anh!" Mẹ shouts out in horror.

"I'm fine!" Anh declares, getting up. She races over to where her mother is pulling her line and joins her, her arms straining with effort as they pull. Together they manage to furl the sail in a few moments. Anh barely has time to be proud before her mother picks her up and starts carrying her below deck.

"Hey!" Anh struggles, wiggling playfully.

"Do not ever do that again," Mẹ says.

"But I helped," Anh insists.

"It's too dangerous in a storm. The mast is no place to climb," Mẹ says, setting her down. "Go back to sleep."

"But I want to be up top!"

"Stop acting like a wet fish!" Mẹ snaps, holding her still.

Anh frowns; usually her mother joins her in the game, teasing and tickling her.

"It's safer down here. You can help above deck another time, when the sea can't take you away from me."

Anh nods and makes her way back toward her hammock. She listens to the footsteps on the deck above, the crew's shouts.

A shrill cry rises up from the hammock next to hers. Her little brother is awake.

Anh peers over the edge of the swaying fabric, looking down at his little face scrunched up and covered in tears. He cries even harder, reaching for comfort.

"It's just a storm, Thanh, it'll pass," she says. She reaches out, and he takes her hand, his stubby fingers closing around her own, but he only bawls louder.

Her mother climbs down the ladder and wrings out her shirtsleeves, dripping water onto the floor as she approaches them.

"Hush, hush, it's fine, it'll be over soon," Mẹ says, coming up to Thanh's hammock. She picks up Thanh, and he presses his face against her neck.

"When?" he sobs.

"That is not for us to know or decide. All we must do is endure it. And all you can do right now, little one, is to go back to sleep."

4

Anh settles into her hammock and watches her mother sit down, gently holding Thanh and making soothing noises. With her foot, she reaches out and steadies Anh's hammock as well. Anh smiles, listening to the storm rage on.

Thanh fusses, continuing to cry.

"What about a story?" Mẹ asks with a soft smile.

Thanh sniffles and nods, wiping at his face.

Voices shout from above deck. "Captain! Should we try to make for the lee of the island to weather the storm?"

"I'll be there in a moment! Go ahead!" Mẹ calls out. "All right, little ones. A story."

"One with treasure!" Thanh gurgles, breaking into a smile.

"Zheng Yi Sao," Anh presses. One of her favorites. She knows the story of this formidable woman by heart, but she loves the way her mother tells it.

"Yes, yes," Thanh mumbles. "Tell us about the treasure again."

Her mother snorts and smiles. "Again? Well. Let me see if I remember."

"The thousands and thousands of ships!" Anh chirps. "The great Dragon Fleet!"

Her mother smiles at Anh, stroking Thanh's hair as her voice slips into a familiar cadence. "Many years ago, before you both were born, these seas were ruled by pirates. Seeing another sail on the horizon would be worse than seeing a rising storm. You didn't know what you were chancing when you set out for a haul; it could be your ship, your entire livelihood, your life itself. Most fishers went upriver instead, going inland instead of facing the pirates."

"But you and Ba didn't, Mẹ!" Thanh gurgles excitedly.

"Yes, well, many called us fools. But we took our chances, and we caught fish and crabs and prawns and continued to make our living. See, the pirates hardly bothered with us. In fact, the few times a ship would come alongside they would perhaps intimidate us a bit, but mostly it was to convince us to join their fleet. The pirates were so bold, they set out for only the most desirable of prizes—traders from distant lands, kings' galleons filled with precious spices, lumber and oil, gold and jade, riches you could only dream of."

Anh sighs as she settles into the familiar story, thinking of the daring feats of the pirates. She's heard so many stories of their sieges, how they fought against the Qing emperor's navy when no one else dared to. The sounds of the storm fade away as she listens to her mother's story.

"The waters were soon impassable without the seal of protection from the great Dragon Fleet, a massive confederation of pirates who sailed under the command of one woman, a fierce and ruthless leader who commanded thousands and thousands of ships. For years they controlled all the travel in these waters, the entire coast of Việt Nam and the south of China, and were so fearsome that the Qing even enlisted help from the British and the Portuguese. But their massive ships could not maneuver the narrow channels and bays, especially in the archipelago of Hạ Long Bay."

Anh nods sleepily, thinking of the small floating fishing villages adrift on makeshift docks, and the scores of tiny places tucked inside the coves. She's never seen a large imperial warship like the ones in Mẹ's stories, but she can imagine how silly it might look, trying to wedge between the tall narrow passages of cliffs rising up in the bay, the shallow rivers that led inland toward hidden coves and clusters of villages.

"Zheng Yi Sao had a colossal ship, and all her lieutenants had these beasts that were practically like floating cities. The Dragon Fleet was a massive organization—many squadrons sailed under their banner with thousands of ships, including the Red, Yellow, Blue, and Black Banner Squadrons, only united under Zheng Yi Sao's command. Cheung Po Tsai, the lieutenant of the Red Banner Squadron, had a temple constructed on his, but the majority of the vessels that made up the bulk of the ships were small junks, flat-bottomed ships—"

"Like ours!" Anh says, excited.

Mẹ smiles. "Do you want to tell the story, or should I?"

Anh ducks her head sheepishly and waits for her mother to continue.

"Yes, ships like ours could easily sail upriver without any trouble. There were many fishing vessels that joined the fleets, local fishing folk looking to try their luck at something more." Mẹ shrugs and smiles, lost in a distant memory. "And then as more ships did the same, and the stories of Zheng Yi Sao and the Dragon Fleet grew and spread, the

Qing Emperor grew tired of the pirates challenging him and humiliating his navy, but try as he could he could not best their cunning. She and her pirates would lay waste to his ships, ruthlessly seizing any goods he tried to distribute or those of foreigners hoping to do trade with his empire. A whole ship laden with gold, jade, and jewels headed for the kingdom of Siam fell to her once, and her sights grew even higher.

"Zheng Yi Sao had done what no other pirate in the South China Sea had before—she had united multiple squadrons into an army, amassing enough wealth and power to draw the attention of multiple empires . . . at least until the emperor could take no more."

"What happened?" Thanh asks sleepily.

"At first, he attempted to eradicate the pirates. The Liangguang governor-general of the Guangdong province and the Qing navy, however, were helpless against the might of the fleet. The Chinese, the Portuguese, the British— even in their attempts to work together to fight the Dragon Fleet—could not defeat Zheng Yi Sao and her pirate army. They attempted to corner her, but she held the entire port of Canton under siege, her Red Banner Squadron blocking all trade until the Liangguang governor-general surren- dered to her terms. They issued pardons to all the pirates, and many of the skilled lieutenants and captains were recruited into the navy and given official positions of their own. The rest of the pirates, pardoned but with nowhere to go, went back to their lives—fishers and merchants, struggling to get along."

Thanh is asleep now, and Mẹ rises up slowly from his hammock, giving him a soft smile.

"And Zheng Yi Sao? What happened to her?" Anh asks, gripping the edge of her hammock.

Mẹ smiles, lowering her voice. "No one knows. She disappeared. Some say she took a position in the navy, or that she died in that battle. And some say she still commands a ship to this day, and you can see the shadow of it on nights like these, riding a wild storm."

"And the treasure?"

"Lost forever. The loot of thousands of ships, plunder from different kingdoms, collected over her reign when she commanded these waters. Some say it was hidden so cleverly that she must have summoned dark magic to help hide the island where it was buried. That the island itself is only visible on the night of a full moon, and that no one could sail there without the blessing of the sea gods, or the ghost of Zheng Yi Sao herself guiding the way."

Anh gapes. "What kind of treasure?"

"Everything you can think of. Imagine crates filled with precious jewels and jade, so lustrous and green, polished and perfect. Gold and silver cash from the Qing imperials who thought they were above their own people. Barrels of expensive spices and rich lumber harvested from deep inland. Luxuries from faraway lands, silks . . .

"Enough wealth you would need to use multiple lifetimes to spend it all," Mẹ says.

"Do you think it's still out there?" Anh wonders out loud, her eyelids starting to droop. "It's real, right? It's not just a story?"

"Of course it's real, little one. Here, take this."

Mẹ hands her something cold and worn, something that almost looks like a cash coin with the square hole in the center—except instead of being engraved with the emperor's seal, it has a long dragon coiling around the center, with clouds swirling around it. The dragon's long whiskers hook around its face, and the eyes look right up at the beholder, as if issuing a challenge.

Anh closes her eyes and clutches the coin tight, falling asleep with a dream in her hand.

CHAPTER ONE

THE ARRIVAL

1826

Guangdong province, the empire of China

THE HORIZON GLITTERS AS IT DISAPPEARS INTO THAT UNIMAGinable place where sea meets sky. I've been watching this ship for over an hour, ever since it left its port. From here, Canton is just a suggestion of buildings, a smudge of shadows barely visible on the gleaming delta. Through my spyglass I can barely see the movement of ships. I can only imagine what it must be like: sailors laughing boisterously as they approach land, singing songs, departing crews shouting as they heave the sails and set out into the world beyond.

This particular junk I've been watching must be massive. But now with the ship drifting out to sea, it is but a pinprick between my fingers. The ship disappears over the horizon, off to lands I can only dream of.

Soft puffs of clouds are scattered across that bright blue expanse above, drifting along the playful spring wind. The breeze kisses my face, and I take a deep breath, wondering if this same wind is the one that lifted someone's lucky sails.

I close my book, whispering the words of the poem I've committed to memory, each verse filled with a longing I've never truly understood: "Once you've experienced ocean, nothing else is considered water."

Yuan Zhen's words have always spoken to me; this particular poem filled with longing is no exception. There's something about describing a feeling that is so magnificent it may never come again, a love that is irreplaceable, that captures my imagination. I sigh, wondering what that would feel like.

I readjust my position in the tree, stretching before settling back into the forked crook of the trunk, a perfect spot for curling up in, the bark worn from many lazy afternoons. It would be easy to miss me, just a slight youth hidden in the trees—and indeed that is my intention, as I have been shirking my duties.

I trekked half the morning to get to this particular spot on the peak of the cragged mountain, where the cliff directly faces south toward the delta of the Pearl River, offering a glimpse of one of the ports of Canton and the ships leaving it.

I am sixteen, and I have never left the village. I've never

even been to the bustling metropolis of Canton, despite my mother owning another teahouse there—even more successful and busy than the one in the village. Mother has always said the city is no place for a young girl.

I sigh, dreaming of the stories that the travelers there must tell, the distant places they've been, music and foods from other lands. I can only imagine the taste of honeyed dates, the feel of finely spun silks from Siam, the heat of those famed spicy noodles from the Sichuan province, juicy tropical fruits from faraway lands.

I've only glimpsed these other worlds beyond my small riverside village in my scrolls and books, precious rare luxuries, stories and poems collected from Master Feng's collection or gifts from Mother's travels.

Down in the valley, I can see the sloped tiles of the village's roofs surrounded by sparkling streams as they cross the delta in delicate threads before they meet the Pearl. The great river sparkles, deceptively calm in this afternoon light. I lose sight of it past the fields of terraced rice paddies and catch it again beyond the rising green cliffs in the distance, twisting and turning like its namesake's dragon tail.

Approaching footsteps pull me out of my daydreams. I climb a bit higher, hidden in the leafy canopy. The path up to the top of this peak isn't well known, and there's nothing of interest up here other than the view. There are far better trails on the other side of the river, yielding fruit-bearing trees, tall stalks of bamboo, and better hunting. The rising rocks on this particular steep slope make it too precarious for a casual walk.

An amused voice huffs. "Xiang! I see you, you know."

I laugh, tucking myself farther into the tree, taking another steady step on the branch above me. I can hardly believe Master Feng trekked all the way up here, but sure enough, I can see the edge of my tutor's familiar robes coming around the last switchback. His hair has slipped out of its usual careful topknot and is loose around his face, sweat lining his brow. He winces as he stretches, arching his back as he reaches for the sky.

"And how was the walk, old man?"

Master Feng scoffs at me, standing up taller. "The disrespect!" he scolds, but the tone holds no heat and his eyes are dancing with amusement.

Despite his preference for boring texts and badgering me about proper calligraphy and stodginess with forming characters, my tutor has always listened patiently to my rambles and indulged me in stories of his former travels when he was a scholar.

I laugh again. "Are you not forty years?"

He gingerly walks over to me, picking his way toward the ledge where the tree is clinging to the edge of the mountaintop, and follows my gaze. He sighs. "Sometimes I feel much older, as if I have lived many lifetimes."

I can barely imagine Master Feng as the way the elderly villagers describe him as a young boy growing up here. Old

Man Lo always would say, "That Feng Zhanli, so smart, makes us all so proud." He scored high enough in the imperial examinations to study at the university in Beijing, and then traveled extensively before returning—finding his fortunes in Canton, traveling the sweeping hills of Siam, visiting ancient temples in Cambodia, and making friends in every port. Everyone is always talking about how it's a shame he never married, but he's the darling of the village, an eccentric academic regarded with fondness.

I never tire of his stories, especially those from when he worked as an accountant on several merchant ships, helping traders keep their ledgers and run their businesses. Master Feng has traveled to so many kingdoms in his work, and even more when he started working for my parents. Now that I'm thinking about it, I want to ask more about what they were like back then—especially my father—but I know it'll just put him in an unnecessarily despondent mood.

His eyes turn from the horizon and then back up to the tree. "Have you been here all day? Watching ships again?"

"No," I lie, and with a glance below me I realize it's too late to hide the pile of discarded banana leaves carelessly strewn on the ground, sticky rice residue still clinging to the shiny wrappers from my meal earlier. There are even a few strips dangling from the branch below me. I wince. Orange peels are scattered exactly where I dropped them, seeds shining with juice in little trails on the ground—and to my horror, there's even one on the scroll sticking out of my bag.

Master Feng's mouth falls open in shock when he sees it. He huffs toward me, plucking the peel off. He unwinds the scroll to inspect it before rolling it back up and securing it tightly. "I thought I said not to take these out of the library," he chides. He wipes the outer edge carefully with the sleeve of his robe, apparently appeased the contents haven't been damaged.

"I am expanding my mind, as you directed me this morning. Continuing my studies. You never said *where* to do it."

Master Feng makes a noise of disapproval. "These texts would be impossible to replace."

"I was careful, I promise!"

His expression softens as his fingers linger over the bound cover of my favorite title. "Stories again?"

"I'm done with all my lessons," I say.

It is true. I spent half the morning copying prayers for the new shrine for the Xuan family at Master Feng's request and even redoing them when he complained that I was being too hasty, forming the characters incorrectly. My fingers are stained with ink from the practice. I hate calligraphy, and I can't see any point in making the words pretty as long as the reader understands what I have to say. In any case, Mother is not here to criticize my work. The past two weeks I have savored this time to myself, easily slipping away from everyone who is supposed to be minding me in favor of spending time drifting down the rivers in my sampan boat and climbing up here to watch the distant port.

Master Feng humphs, but I can tell he's amused. "I

16

thought you might want to know your mother returns home today. I set out looking for you as soon as her messenger arrived."

I sit up so quickly my woven hat tumbles to the ground, along with the rest of the ripe oranges I'd collected for my afternoon of watching the ships. "She said she wouldn't return for another month!"

He points to the river, and for a second it's just the winding green cutting through the mountains as it always has. I follow his gesture and spot the red tinge of a sail slowly drifting into view as it rounds the bend, an impressive vessel with three sails that can traverse the river with ease.

I gasp and lose my balance, nearly falling out of the tree; I barely grab the branch above me in time. I hoist myself higher and pull out my spyglass again. The junk could be a merchant ship on its way upriver toward the larger cities, but I can see it turning onto one of the tributaries leading directly to our village.

I scramble down from my perch. The branches catch on my bare arms, my heart pounding with panic. It could only be Mother's ship.

There's no time to waste. I must be home immediately.

I jump too soon from the lowest branch, my pendant slipping out of my shirt with the movement, and the ground rises up to meet me faster than I expect. I tumble right into Master Feng and cough, spluttering dust as he helps me up to my feet, laughing.

"Thank you!" I call over my shoulder, already on my way down the path, my heart pounding with panic.

"There is no need to run!" Master Feng shouts after me. "The ship is still quite far off. Xiang! Slow down, you're going to hurt yourself. Nightfall, I believe is what she said—"

The dirt trail is hot under my sandals as I race down the mountain, the sound of Master Feng's voice already fading away. The steep trail is covered in rocks and roots—it took about two treacherous hours to reach the peak, but it should only take half the time to descend. I know every dip and bend of the path, every place where the rocks are loose, which branches are worn smooth by my fingers reaching for handholds.

Birds flutter and squawk as I startle them from the trees, my footsteps thundering as I jump, my blood pounding in my ears. My hair flies free from the loose braid I gathered it in this morning, and I have no time to care.

Finally, the path evens out as I meet the soft green of the fields below and the stream where my sampan boat is waiting. I gulp, wondering if I should take the time to stash it back in the rushes. The sampan is technically a secret—Mother would disapprove. Getting this one took months of planning and hassle and stockpiling silks in order to trade Elder Xuan for it. But it had been worth it for the freedom to explore downriver, to get away from Lan Nai Nai's harsh lectures and the monotony of the teahouse.

I chance a look at the sun already dipping low behind the mountains, casting long shadows in the golden afternoon light. Behind me, Mother's ship is prominently visible now, all red sails and polished teak amid a sea of green fields. I can come back tomorrow to fetch the sampan. Going upriver will be slower than on foot, and I will need time to get ready for Mother.

I settle into a steady pace, already exhausted from the trek down, but I have to make it before Mother gets home. My golden pendant bounces against my chest, and I tuck the small piece back under my shirt. The shape is familiar against my skin, the width and length of my smallest finger, like a tiny scroll, a comfort tucked close to my heart.

I race along the small river that flows past our village, waving at Yao the vegetable seller and her boat filled with fresh produce. More sampans are filled with fishermen checking their traps, and other vegetable sellers and rice carriers lingering together and trading gossip.

Leaving my boat behind means I still have to cross the river, and I can just imagine Lan Nai Nai's face if I were to arrive at the teahouse dripping water and covered in mud.

I make a quick decision and jump onto the nearest sampan boat. "Pardon me! Coming through!" A head of cabbage threatens to roll off into the water as the boat jostles, and I catch it neatly, throwing it back onto the boat.

"Always in a hurry," Old Man Lo mumbles in distaste.

He's perpetually sour, grumpy no matter the weather. "So rude!"

Dashing across the floating market, I jump from boat to boat, keeping to the edges as I traverse the small river. A few sellers laugh and shake their heads, and I call out apologies as I scramble across the sampans laden with vegetables, sacks of rice and other goods.

"That Shi Xiang is so strange and wild, always running off into the woods," Lo mutters.

"She could have been your daughter-in-law!" one of the fishermen teases. "You could be resting in that teahouse right now instead of working so hard every day."

"Ha! Madam Shi would have never approved," Lo retorts. "In any case, my boy came to his senses quickly before he could properly make a proposal. He's got a better match in the next village anyway."

Their comments sting, but I don't let them know that I can hear them and keep running. I know I'm a mess, my hair loose and flying down my back, my clothes streaked in dirt.

Most of the village finds me odd and avoids me, likely because of Mother's strange city ways or because of my own lack of decorum. I used to have close friends, like Lo Qian. Perhaps that's why the vegetable seller dislikes me so much; he always thought I was a bad influence on his daughter. Qian and I used to play together as children, running in the fields and laughing and taking quiet naps in the marshes, tickling each other with the long grasses.

I shake my head. Qian is long gone, married off to a blacksmith two villages away. Best not to dwell on the time we had spent together, no matter how much I miss it.

Even though the other villagers still view Mother with suspicion, they would never say anything outright to her; she's the only reason lumber and many other resources make it to this backwater. Before I was born, Mother arrived in the village with her retinue and had the teahouse built like Father always wanted, so she has always told me. He grew up here, in this quiet village with the mountains rising behind it like islands on a sea of rice fields.

A quiet life, a good life, she always had said was what he wanted for us.

Living at the teahouse, there isn't any need for me to be in the fields or gathering up in the mountains, so I suppose people expect me to stay and help manage the business. But with so few patrons, it's barely enough to keep Lan Nai Nai busy. Plus, she hates me underfoot in the kitchen. I'm a terrible cook. I've even burned rice.

I bob and weave through the main village street, brushing as much dirt off my clothes as I can before I get home. There's a small, sleek-looking rowboat moored in the waterway by the teahouse—Mother's messenger, no doubt.

The teahouse is the finest building in the modest village, standing proudly on the edge of one of the main waterways. The carved and polished dark wood gleams in the light of the setting sun. Oiled paper brightening the windows speaks to the comforts we offer—a warm cup of tea and a place to gather with friends, a simple and delicious meal, a quiet place to rest your head for the night.

Lan Nai Nai said the villagers had scoffed when Mother wanted to build the teahouse here, thinking it would never draw enough patrons to justify the business, but she seemed not to care. It still stands quietly on the banks of the waterway, humble and inviting.

I carefully slide open the screen door and step inside. A few patrons look up from their meals as I close the door behind me, their conversation pausing as they take in my disheveled appearance.

I duck my head sheepishly and dart past them. I don't know all their names, but they're familiar enough, rice carriers and merchants who stop by our village to sell their goods and rest before making their way upstream. A woman with wild eyes sitting alone in the corner gives me a calculating look as smoke drifts from her pipe. She looks to be about forty, her skin browned with sun and her clothes aged with wear. Strange streaks of white crust the sleeves of her jacket, and I realize it must be salt from her time at sea.

"Shi Mei-Mei," she says, nodding at me.

I remember now—I met her several months ago, on one of Mother's last visits. I had bumped into her, and she'd merely glared at me until I backed away. She's an intimidating figure, someone the villagers gossip about endlessly, about everything from her crude demeanor to the nature of her employment.

"Hello, Yang Jie-Jie." I bow my head respectfully, mumbling over what I think is her name and enunciating the honorific. I don't want her to report back to Mother that I was rude.

She laughs, smoke billowing from her mouth. "It's Kang."

I nod with embarrassment, fumbling past her table toward the kitchen.

Lan Nai Nai gives me a disapproving look as she sets down a tray of tea. She isn't actually my grandmother, and she takes care to remind me of that every time I call her that nickname. She gives a placating smile to the merchants before walking over to me swiftly, her skirts rustling against the smooth tiled floor. She looks worried, her eyebrows knitting together as I follow her into the kitchen.

"Aiyah!" she huffs as soon as we're out of the dining room, slapping at the dirt on my clothes. "You're a mess! Where have you been all day? Master Feng went out looking for you once the messenger arrived! Madam will be home tonight, and you look like some common street urchin!"

"I know, I know," I say, bobbing my head in apology. "I came as quickly as I could."

The kitchen is bursting with the scents and chaotic bustle of cooking. Lan Nai Nai stokes the coals, and a sweet, savory smell drifts from the steaming pot—a black bean sauce for the fresh fish on the chopping block. It looks like they've been preparing extra food all day for Mother and her retinue.

I duck under baskets of rushes and spring onions gracefully swaying in the soft breeze that is drifting through the open door. I offer a quick prayer at the small kitchen shrine next to the doorway. *Kitchen God, please let Mother see me favorably tonight*, I pray fervently. The incense is burning low in the pot overflowing with ashes, and I breathe in the familiar scent as I try to focus on what's to come.

I turn back to Lan Nai Nai. "I did find these for you on my walk," I say hastily, pulling from the deep pocket of my trousers a handful of herbs and offering it to her. Lan Nai Nai has been complaining for a few days about how it's practically impossible to find any dìhuáng root near our village. "For your back."

Lan Nai Nai shakes her head but takes the herbs. "Where is Master Feng?"

"He found me at the top of the mountain. I ran on ahead; he's probably still on his way."

She sweeps her hands at me, the same exasperated gesture she would use to shoo me back to my lessons whenever I would wander into the kitchens as a child. "Aiyah, you need to change! There's not enough time to boil water for a hot bath, but I can bring you some fresh water to wash with."

"Thank you!" I call out gratefully as I race through the small courtyard and wave hello at Lan Nai Nai's husband, Lan Zhai, as he turns a slab of roast pork over the open courtyard firepit. He must have been stoking those hot coals all day.

"Hello, Lan Yéye!"

"Xiang." He waves at me. "Oh my, you look—"

"I know!" I bound up the wooden steps of the inner courtyard staircase and sprint down the walkway past the guest rooms and toward my own. I fling open the screen doors, scrambling out of my plain trousers and shirt. I kick the coarse cotton clothes away and stumble toward the washbasin, nearly tripping over yesterday's dirty clothes as I make my way to the wooden washbasin and step inside. The cold water is numbing, but I scrub hastily at my face and body, shivering as I adjust to the temperature.

The door slides open and closed behind me, and Lan Nai Nai enters with a bucket of fresh water that she pours in the basin. I yelp as she ladles it over my hair, making disapproving noises as she plucks leaves from the tangles.

"If you had been home hours ago you would have had ample time to get ready with a *hot* bath," Lan Nai Nai says.

My teeth chatter together as another ladle sends a stream of inky black hair over my eyes like a curtain. I splutter and shift it away from my eyes. "I like my walks."

Lan Nai Nai carefully combs my hair as she clucks at me. "You could be such a pretty girl. One of these days you'll be married and will have to manage a household of your own. You won't be able to go running off lost in your own head anymore."

I scowl. The topic has been brought up before, but Mother has refused any of the would-be suitors in the village. She said they were more interested in my dowry and the teahouse, and she would procure a better match in the future. I hope that day will never come; I can't imagine it at all.

"Don't make that face, Xiang. You can't stay here forever." Lan Nai Nai empties her bucket on my head and begins washing my hair.

The teahouse and this tiny village are all I've ever known. I do not wish to stay, but to be married to some man I hardly know? I can't imagine that, either. I want to see the world, see the places in my stories, distant coasts and faraway lands.

Lan Nai Nai hands me a thick robe to dry off with as she rummages through the chest of finer clothing that I only wear for Mother's visits. She glances at my gold pendant, a slight frown pursed on her lips. "You should take off that ugly old thing. What about this instead?" She pulls out a simple jade pendant from my keepsake box and smiles at me. "A lady who matches her jewelry with her clothing is seen to be demure and intelligent."

Lan Nai Nai is always sighing at me to wear more of these delicate things, but I have no patience to be dressed up like a doll when Mother isn't home.

I shake my head at the pretty jade piece as Lan Nai Nai

dangles it from its fine gold chain. I play with the pendant on my neck, sighing. This simple gold piece has always been my favorite. My fingers trace the inscription on it: 永愛. My fingers know each clumsy stroke by heart. Mother gave it to me when I was a child.

Back then, Mother would spend weeks at a time in the village. I remember her carrying me and singing to me in the courtyard, and I would follow her on long walks in the woods, clinging to her knee. After pestering her for stories about Father, Mother finally presented me with the pendant. I realize now it was most likely to placate my constant babbling, but I love it anyway.

I like to think Father saved up for this piece of gold and had it shaped but couldn't afford for the artisan to engrave it, so he did it himself, concentrating as he declared his promise of enduring love. Since he was lost at sea, it is the only tangible thing I have left of him. There aren't any paintings or likenesses of him in our home. He left no journals, no treasured items that once belonged to him. We don't even have an altar for him, or any of my ancestors for that matter. Father's family is all gone, their shrines lost in a storm many years back. Mother's parents died when she was young, and she never speaks of the people who raised her. I suppose they were cruel to her or treated her as a servant, whoever they were. No matter. I light incense in my unknown ancestors' memories and place it in the central shrine in the courtyard. I do love having this reminder of him with me always, though.

I know little of my father. Only that he and Mother were fairly successful salt merchants, but a storm capsized his ship on one of his journeys. Mother only speaks of him sparingly, her face a stone wall that is impossible to break. I stopped asking Master Feng about him when I was quite young as well because it always threw him into a dark mood, a shadow of pain cast behind his eyes; I suppose they were quite close friends and losing him must have been devastating.

I wonder if Father would be proud of my accomplishments. I feel like I've been trying my whole life to make Mother proud, but she is always leaving.

As I got older, the visits got shorter and farther between. Lan Nai Nai always said it was because I was too rambunctious, laughing and running wild, and Mother disapproved of my clinging need for affection. I taught myself to hold still, like the calm waters of a lake, hoping Mother would like me, would want to spend time here. I worked hard in my studies, learning from Master Feng and Lan Nai Nai: calligraphy, history, penmanship, sums, embroidery, painting, cooking. Some of these skills came easier than others—while I devoured all of Master Feng's textbooks and scrolls, clamoring for more philosophy and history, the more practical tasks eluded me. But I would still try my hardest.

But Mother's visits grew only rarer, sometimes with weeks, months, or even longer spells between them, her disapproving stare only deepening when I tried to show her my accomplishments: a cluster of steamed leek buns or painstakingly detailed embroidery work.

Once my fingers had ached for days when I tried to copy the delicate pattern of lotuses on a jacket Mother had brought me from her last trip. But neither Lan Nai Nai nor anyone in the village was an expert in the craft beyond simple sewing and mending, and I had no one to teach me. I remember presenting the scrap of fabric to Mother and receiving only a disdainful sniff at the clumsy attempt. After that I focused on the studies I did enjoy, histories and accounts of travelers, poetry and riddles, and filled my mind with hopes and dreams. After all these years Mother is still a mystery, but it doesn't stop me from trying my best to impress her.

Lan Nai Nai holds up a jacket with delicate golden detailing on bright blue silk. "What about this?"

"I haven't worn that since one of Mother's visits last year. It's too tight around the chest."

Lan Nai Nai grumbles, her wrinkled face twisting in a scowl. "You're a young woman now. You come from a good family and would have the best marriage in the village if your mother wasn't so picky with suitors. You need to stop dressing like you have nothing."

I wince at the reminder. It was easier to have friends in the village when I was little. There is no one my age to speak with now—everyone left is either much older or younger, my childhood friends all gone off to marry or seek their fortunes elsewhere.

"I can let it out one of these days when it's not so busy. Maybe next time." Lan Nai Nai sighs. "I might as well be managing this business, for all the time Madam spends here. She swans in and out of here like we're a brood of carp in a pond she feeds once in a while."

By the time Master Feng gets back, his face red with exhaustion, I've been scrubbed clean and am wearing a stiff brocaded silk jacket embroidered with peonies and matching trousers. With Lan Nai Nai's help, my hair has been arranged into a simple and elegant knot and decorated with a heavy brooch carved from teak that is setting me off balance, but I manage to keep my head upright. The jade pendant dangles outside my jacket, and I sit in the courtyard with one of Master Feng's books. It's a precious thing, crafted with delicate pages sealed and bound in leather that has been worn smooth by my hands over the years as I've read and reread the stories within.

"Quick work," he remarks with approval. "I hate that mountain. Why do you go up there so often?"

"It's the only place with a view of Canton."

Master Feng tilts his head ever so slightly; a look of understanding passes between us. He hands me the woven hat, a few bruised oranges gathered inside. "You forgot this."

"Thank you," I say sheepishly.

"Are you ready?" he asks. He knows how anxious I get whenever Mother visits.

I swallow nervously. It doesn't matter if I am ready or not. A red sail peeks over the rooftop of the teahouse.

Mother has arrived.

CHAPTER TWO
TRIALS AND PREPARATIONS

RAUCOUS LAUGHTER ERUPTS FROM THE TABLES NEXT TO US. Tonight, I'm not serving anyone in the teahouse, and I'm not eating with Master Feng or Lan Nai Nai in the kitchen or alone under the lanterns in the courtyard. I'm tempted to scratch at the stiff collar around my neck, but I resist and hold my head up high.

Every table in our dining room is full, the ship's crew squeezed onto extra chairs and makeshift stools of barrels and crates, drinking voraciously from the cups of rice wine that Lan Nai Nai keeps nervously refilling. I glance at them, trying to take in all the details. The sheer amount of colors and mismatched styles in our dining room is almost over-whelming. Some of them wear worn silks and brocades, once fine but weathered with time. Some have the same con-ical woven hats as the farmers and fishermen here wear, but most keep their heads wrapped in turbans or head scarves in a style I've only seen on sailors used to long days in the sun, the fabric loosely covering their ears and neck.

There are even more people on the ship still that Lan Nai Nai dropped off food for earlier. Only the higher-ranking officers of the ship are eating in the dining room tonight— the captain, the helmsmen and their wives, laughing as they talk about their last port. There's a tense energy I feel between those of us who are usually here: me, the Lans, the merchant patrons, with the presence of these strangers to the village. Mother and the crew seem not to notice or care. After they've paid their respects to Lan Nai Nai and Lan Yéye, Mother and the crew are wrapped up in conversation and inside jokes and business talk that I can tell make the merchants at the far table uneasy.

Mother's face is hard but regal, her hair coiffed up in an elegant style. A single jade brooch is pinned in her hair, a modest display of her success as a merchant. The commanding air she wears around her like a cloak, her damask dark blue jacket ornamented with cranes. Glittering rings sparkle on her fingers as she flips through a ledger, ignoring the array of delicacies Lan Nai Nai has prepared for this visit, only the best choice in fish and game and the freshest vegetables from the market upriver. The rich array of food is stunning after weeks of plain rice, steamed vegetables, and fish.

Hot steam rises from the dishes, and the tantalizing smells make my mouth water, but I am still. The crew is engaged in conversation with one another while keeping an eye on Mother. She doesn't pay any of us mind, and I'm sure she can hear my grumbling stomach, along with everyone else's, but she is still wrapped in conversation with a round-faced man who is rapidly taking notes, his brush quick as he listens intently.

"Lao Ping, once we are back in Canton, set up another meeting with that foul-mouthed charlatan," Mother says, glancing over his shoulder at the open ledger propped onto the table.

"Yes," Lao Ping says, writing so fast that ink flecks onto his face. "Do you mean Chen Tao or Chen Rui—"

Mother sniffs disdainfully. "They're both despicable. This price for salt is unacceptable, and tell Captain Guo not to take any Chen merchandise onto his ship until they accept the terms. Remind him that their goods can't be sold without my ships and no one else in this town will work with him if I decree it."

"Zhanli! You're still here!" one of the sailors roars, clapping Master Feng on the back.

"I live here, Minggang," Master Feng says.

Minggang, a stocky man already on his third cup of wine, lets out a hearty laugh. "Come have a drink, tell me about . . ."

"Poetry," another snickers, his face already red with wine.

"Certainly," Master Feng says coolly. "Should I recite an old favorite? Perhaps a selection of poems on decorum."

I can't figure out the relationship the sailors have with Master Feng; some of them treat him like an old friend, but there's a patronizing air about it, like they find him silly.

I strain my ears, trying to listen to their stories, picking up on their excitement about a new type of rice wine they'd sampled in Changping. There's some talk of trading opium and how they'd be earning twice as much silver, but it dies down quickly after a harsh look from Mother.

"Well, certainly we will take the bribe from the governor-general to report on any activities of any suspected White Lotus meetings at the Pearl House," Mother says, still wrapped in business talk. "Remember to double the fee for any private rooms requested by White Lotus members to ensure their anonymity from the city officials."

I turn my attention to the sailors' conversations, trying to follow along as best I can without seeming too eager. One of the women who was only introduced by surname— Leung—is drinking as well, her face red as she regales her listeners with a story about how Lao Ping had once attempted to wrestle a turtle onto the deck of the *Jīn Lǐyú*.

"But, Captain—"

Captain? I had thought she was the captain's wife, but now as I observe closer I see that the people at the other table seem to defer to her, waiting for her to finish her story and refilling her cup of wine from the pitcher Lan Nai Nai had left on their table.

I want to hear more about what it's like in Canton with so many people, about kingdoms all over the world and what life is like at sea, but the conversation keeps jumping from topic to topic.

Lan Nai Nai places a platter of roasted pork on our table, the crowning dish to our meal, and serves the first portion onto Mother's plate. This is what Lan Yéye had started roasting early this morning, painstakingly tending to it all day. My mouth waters. It's glazed with the precious sugar and spices Kang must have brought earlier. She's sitting at the same table in the corner, joined by more of the crew members as they look our way, waiting for their share.

Our table falls silent as we all wait with bated breath for Mother's approval. She takes a bite of the pork and nods at Lan Nai Nai, who heaves a sigh of relief. Mother begins to eat, plucking her choice of the delicacies on the table. Lan Nai Nai, finished with bringing out food for the rest of the tables, sits down at the end of ours. I notice that no one else from the ship's crew is eating, as if they are all waiting for Mother to fill her plate before reaching for their own.

I hold my head higher, wondering if I could one day command such respect. They must have worked with Mother for many years. I recognize a few familiar faces, but I've never been formally introduced to the crew she sails with, and only rarely has she had them dine with us like this. The crew always seems to give Mother much more regard than a merchant they are simply ferrying home. It must be how successful she is, working through the bustling and competitive trade scene in Canton. They don't just trade salt, I infer, but it is their most profitable cargo other than ginseng and lumber.

I'm fascinated as they talk business—supplies and ships, what is needed for repairs, crews, wages, and ports. I drink it all in, the places they speak of, the ports from Thăng Long to Nha Trang to Macao, and of course Canton, where it all begins. I savor the conversation and the food, the crunch of the crispy pork skin and the savory taste of the meat, roasted in its own fat and caramelized soy sauce. I let it linger on my tongue. The platter is already empty, portions of the meat served to everyone in the dining room. I take the serving spoon and pour the remainder of the sauce on my rice to soak in the flavor and catch Lan Nai Nai shaking her head in disappointment at me.

Oh, right. Manners.

I slink back, but no one else appears to have noticed, and Mother's deep in conversation with Master Feng.

"I've reviewed the ledger, and everything seems in order," Mother says. "Rice, liquor, tea leaves—everything from this supply run should last you half the year." She glances at Master Feng, some sort of amusement sparkling in her eyes. "And I've brought you more books. These are from the university in Beijing. There's another account of one of Zheng He's voyages for you."

"Ah, thank you," Master Feng says, bowing his head gratefully, and he smiles broadly at her.

Mother gives him a slight nod in return, and my stomach

falls a little. Mother has barely looked my way the entire dinner.

Master Feng glances at me, raising his eyebrows in the slightest acknowledgment of our shared secret: *I'm* the one who voraciously reads all the accounts of Zheng He's adventures and keeps clamoring for more.

I pretend to eat slowly for a chance to sit at the table longer. Ever since Lan Nai Nai brought up the question of my future earlier, it has been dancing on my lips. Since last year's debacle with Lo Zhan, surely Mother wouldn't approve any marriage to a local boy—I wouldn't want to, either.

A sudden idea springs to my mind, and the small cup of wine I've been allowed emboldens me, my face flushed with excitement as Captain Leung talks about purchasing new sails for her ship. Surely if Mother chose a woman as a trusted travel companion and business partner, she could approve of *me* working in the business as well.

Finally the talk of money and supplies for the teahouse subsides. Mother has hardly said a word to me since the stiff-lipped nod she gave me when she arrived at the house, her figure sweeping off the massive deck of the *Jīn Lǐyú*. The junk's enormous red sails loom just outside, the screen open to let the night breeze in to quell the rising humidity. The ship dwarfs the expanse of the building itself, the sails reaching higher than the rooftops, and all other junks and sampans had to clear out to make room. It's clearly a seaworthy vessel, its ironwood planks and rugged sails having seen many storms.

"Mother, how were your travels?" I ask politely.

She glances at me, her eyes flickering from my face to my elaborate hairstyle to the clothing carefully chosen for her approval. I feel a bit too polished, like a delicate porcelain doll, but Lan Nai Nai always insists on dressing me in my best, to show that they've been taking good care of me while Mother is away.

"Quite successful," she says.

"I hear that opium has now surpassed salt as the highest-grossing trade product out of Canton," I say.

Captain Leung laughs. "I'd say it has! And the price is only getting higher. Opium's worth its weight in gold."

Mother glances at her, and the captain falls quiet. "Clever girl, although I'm surprised the news reached this far upriver."

I drink in the word *clever*, at the brief moment Mother took to acknowledge my question, pleased with myself. I hide my smile and look at my plate; I always pester any travelers who come through the teahouse for news, any information that would make me seem more cosmopolitan and interesting to Mother, and this past month's gleanings have netted me a rare compliment.

"And, Master Feng, she's been doing well in her lessons?"

"Very well," he replies. "Excelling in her studies."

"Being obedient and dutiful?" Mother asks, turning to Lan Nai Nai.

"Yes," Lan Nai Nai says—even though just the other day

she scolded me for an hour about tracking mud through the teahouse.

I need to take advantage of this slight attention on me. "I wanted to talk with you about my future," I start hesitantly. "As you know, I've completed all the lessons in history and sums, and Lan Nai Nai has praised my household work as well as my abilities with the lute and embroidery."

"She's quite accomplished," Lan Nai Nai says after a moment, biting her lip.

I'm grateful she doesn't elaborate on my clumsy needlework or how the birds fly away in protest anytime I pick up the stringed instrument. Lan Nai Nai's never told Mother any of my mishaps in the kitchen, either, saving the lectures for when we're alone. She knows that her job here is only secure so long as it includes taking care of me, and she could be easily replaced if Mother deems her no longer useful. We have an understanding, a loyalty of sorts, where she speaks not of my wandering or my sampan boat, and I don't talk about the cooking and household lessons that stopped a few years ago after I nearly burned down the teahouse attempting to cook a meal on my own.

I swallow, taking a deep breath. If I don't ask now, she'll be gone for another month—perhaps longer. "I wanted to ask you . . . if you're returning to Canton, perhaps you could bring me with you. There are other women who work in the business with you, and like Lan

Nai Nai, I could manage one of the teahouses as well. If I lived in the city with you for a while, I could learn—"

Mother cuts me off with a stern, quick voice: "Absolutely not."

Master Feng's eyes twinkle at me, and he gives me a proud look. "It's a fantastic idea. I believe with her studies she would have the business acumen to run a teahouse efficiently, and Xiang has always wanted to see Canton."

The other conversation at the other tables comes to a stop, the sailors' interested eyes turning to Mother. I wonder how well they know Mother, to see her every day, to know her moods so intricately. I've been seeking her approval my whole life, and to have this group of strangers seem to know her better than I ever could is jarring.

I nod hopefully, thankful Master Feng believes in me.

"Running a business requires many skills," Mother says, taking a sip of her wine. "And if you don't know the city—"

"How can I know the city if I've never been?" I blurt out.

Immediately everyone looks at me, and I drop my eyes to my empty plate and mutter, "I apologize, Mother. I meant no disrespect."

"The girl speaks her mind," Captain Leung roars in approval with a knowing grin.

Mother lets out a small humph, but her face is unreadable. Is she angry? Disappointed? Proud? I don't know. But as a widow, she's done far more than any other woman I've ever known in this village.

She glances at me and picks up the pitcher of wine, refilling my cup. "Did you try the pork, Xiang?"

"Yes, it was delicious. The spices really bring out the flavor."

Mother tilts her head, regarding me with the full intensity of her stare.

I try to sit up a little taller.

The corner of her mouth quirks up in a rare smile. I can't tell if it's amusement or if I should be offended that she might be laughing at me, but my heart leaps at the acknowledgment all the same.

"You have good taste. There's a spice blend used in another dish where the pork is minced so fine and then cooked quickly in roasted garlic, and it's absolutely delectable. But you must eat it immediately after it is cooked to get the full aroma. I don't believe we brought any on this trip, but I'll save some on our next trip for you." Mother takes the serving spoon and picks out the best part of the braised fish—the soft tender meat of the cheek—and places it on my plate. "Of course, the city is home to many foods that would not travel well. There's an inn in the eastern district in Canton where they make minced pork buns with a flaky crust—it's not a bao made with rice flour, but another grain the Europeans use, with fat ground into the dough, making it flaky and quite delicious."

My mouth waters from just the description, but my mind is spinning. *Where is she going with this if not to accept my proposal and to bring me to Canton?*

"How is the village this time of year?" she asks.

"Quiet, as always," I say.

"Mm. The life your father wanted for you."

Master Feng stares at his empty cup of wine. "A safe life, where she would have everything she needed. But she also has dreams of her own. Surely he would empathize with her wanting to see more of the world. Wouldn't you?"

Mother raises her eyebrow at me. "Is this true, Xiang? You dream of Canton?"

"I would do my best to make you proud, wherever I am," I say quietly.

"Hmm." Mother's thoughtful noise draws out as she looks between Lan Nai Nai and Master Feng.

"She has your spirit," Master Feng interjects.

Mother laughs. "Are you sure?"

I bite my lip, trying not to let the hurt I'm feeling show on my face. The smile earlier, the derisive tone of her laughter; she still sees me as a child. The painful reminder unseats any eloquent words I could have said to try to convince her otherwise.

"I suppose we can discuss this further. Let us take tea in the courtyard." Mother nods at Lan Nai Nai, and I follow her outside.

Lanterns twinkle as she regards me in the early evening light.

"Are you happy here, my treasure?"

I almost blush at the nickname; she hasn't called me that since I was very young. It reminds me of when she would carry me and sing to me softly in the courtyard, brushing my hair as if I were a doll.

I take a deep breath, drinking in her voice and the way she is looking at me now, her eyes softened a little. She must have been waiting for us to be alone. The cold regard she had toward me at dinner is just who she is when she's talking business; she is like that to everyone, but here with just the two of us, she can be open about how she truly cares about me.

"Xiang?"

Oh right, she asked me a question.

I falter at the word *happy*; Lan Nai Nai is always talking about expectation, and building a life out of what you are given. That the gods are merciless and we are subject to their whims and can only do so much with the fate we are given.

But Lan Nai Nai grew up here in this village and has always been working for others. It's been strange, living in the teahouse as a merchant's daughter. If I were the daughter of a farmer or a fisher, I would learn the skills to work in the fields or in the rivers. I'd be more invested in learning how to manage a house and keep a family fed. But Lan Nai Nai always only expected me to marry well, though even with the teahouse and a higher dowry than most, I haven't received many proposals, and Mother has rejected all of them anyway.

No one has met my standards, either, but I don't know what I'm looking for. Surely a companion who I could contentedly spend my days with.

For a brief moment, I think about Lo Qian, my childhood friend who got married last summer. Her smile lingers in my mind, the way we would spend each day together, the way she would laugh when dragonflies landed in my hair and how she would gently shoo them away. She would know how to answer the question, always ready with a smile and eager to see the bright side of any situation.

Am I happy?

The question hangs in the air as I struggle to answer. It feels like some sort of trick to catch me being ungrateful, which I'm not. Mother's business abroad does well enough to make up for the lack of patrons at the teahouse in the village, but we certainly aren't in a position for her to be able to send me to court in the Forbidden City, even if I had wanted to go. I'm lucky to live here in this peaceful village, safe from storms or the troubles I hear that plague larger cities, like bandits and disease.

What kind of answer does Mother want here? What would make her most likely to acquiesce to my desire to leave the village?

"Of course," I finally manage. Positioning myself to want more would be unseemly.

"But you long to live in the city." Mother sighs. "I can see it, too, the restlessness in your eyes. Perhaps the city would be good for you. And you could be safe in Canton, with the right husband and the right protection."

Husband?!

"Oh." I'm elated Mother is taking my request into

consideration, but this was not the direction I had thought it would take. "What about managing the teahouse?"

Mother looks at me, her eyes scrutinizing. "The Pearl House is not like the teahouse here," she says finally. "Lan Chun's duties, however well you've learned them, would be a fraction of what you would have to be responsible for if you wanted to manage the business in Canton."

"I'm sure with you as a teacher I would be able to perfect those skills in time," I say, hoping the flattery will appeal to her.

Mother glances away. "You should know that city can swallow people whole, and many easily succumb to the ease of opium and other pleasures. There are those who would take advantage of you, a naive youth from the country. And to succeed as a business owner, you would need to be ruthless, to make allies, to drive hard bargains."

I let Old Man Lo overcharge me for bean sprouts the other day because I didn't want to argue with him. I muster all the confidence I have and say, "I can do all that."

Well, I could learn.

"I keep an office at the teahouse, but I have other affairs to tend to—the trade, the merchant ships. You know this. I would not be able to stay in Canton long to mentor you. I would be more comfortable if I knew you were protected."

"Perhaps Master Feng could come," I suggest. "He could chaperone me."

"Hm."

Mother doesn't say anything for a long moment, and I nervously take a sip of my tea.

"You speak of the future, and to be honest I have been thinking of it as well," she finally says. "I want you to be safe and secure, and Canton could be a good place for you to learn some skills under the proper circumstances. And to perhaps find a good husband for you. Given the slim and disappointing proposals I've received in this village I think that may be the best course of action . . ."

"I—" I bite my tongue. I don't want to travel to Canton just to find a husband. I love the freedom I have now, to wander and daydream and climb the mountains here to my heart's content. And I want it somewhere new, where I could see more than what I've ever known, experience things I've only dreamed of. None of these include a husband and a household or children or the things that Lan Nai Nai always assured me my future would include.

"Living closer to Canton could be a good life, I think." Mother glances at me with a soft smile. "You would have servants and people who could accompany you to the city, and you could be as safe as you are here."

I look up to the stars and take a deep breath. In another lifetime I must have seen the world, slaked this thirst for more, and I can't help but think this is a lonely compromise, to settle for a life I do not want.

I muster up my courage, my heart in my throat. "Let me prove to you that I can run the business and I can handle being on my own in the city. Please."

Mother regards me for a long moment. She has always been difficult to read, but years of seeing her only sporadically has taught me to look for the smallest betrayal of emotion in her expression; the twitch of her eyebrows, the way her eyes may dart back and forth as she thinks, calculating all the options. She's doing that now, her features still and impassive, and she must come to some sort of conclusion as a hint of a smile quirks on the corner of her mouth.

"I will bring you to Canton, and Master Feng will accompany you while you are learning the responsibilities necessary. I will introduce you to any suitors I deem fit, and I will determine whether you can handle both Canton and the Pearl House, husband or not."

It isn't a no.

I can't fight the grin that leaps onto my face. I want to embrace Mother, but I get my emotions under control and I settle for clasping my hands together. "Thank you," I say, barely able to keep the excitement from my voice.

Whatever is to come, it would be in the city. It would be new. It would be different.

"We leave tomorrow," Mother says. "To your new life."

I exhale, thinking of the river and sights unseen. "Yes. Tomorrow."

CHAPTER THREE
DOWN THE RIVER

THE *JĪN LǏYÚ* IS STEADY UNDER MY FEET AS I CLIMB ABOARD, and the massive vessel seems almost unmovable, like a great house floating in this humble waterway. I look back as the plank is raised high and stowed away. Master Feng stands next to me, his presence a familiar comfort as we regard the teahouse and the village.

It looks so small and dusty from here; the deck of the ship is higher than any of the buildings in the village, including even the teahouse. A small crowd of people—practically everyone in the village—has come out to see us off. Mother's ships are always a spectacle that people gossip about for weeks. I can't help but smile, thinking about how I would watch with everyone else, trying to hide how much I wanted to be leaving as well.

And now I'm here.

The last sacks of salt and other cargo are unloaded, a neat pile by the waterway's edge. The Lans stand by the supplies, and Lan Nai Nai looks taken aback when I wave at her.

"Good luck," she calls out gruffly.

"Thank you," I say respectfully, a reluctant fondness seeping through me. "Goodbye, Lan Nai Nai and Lan Yéye." Despite her constant badgering and insistence of how annoying she finds me underfoot and her never-ending lectures, I think I might miss her. As distant as they both were, I never thought of them with much affection, but now I may never see them again.

I am saying goodbye to them as much as I am saying goodbye to the village, and while some part of me is sad, it is dwarfed by the excitement for what is to come.

"Are you nervous?" Master Feng asks.

A stray lock of hair escapes my loosely tied bun and falls into my face. With a flick of my head I toss it backward, and I laugh. "Not at all."

Lan Nai Nai at first had wanted to dress me up as she usually did for Mother's visits, but we had compromised. She packed the peony jacket and trousers for me, along with my everyday wear, the sturdy tunics and trousers I'm accustomed to. I'm glad that I insisted on bringing them; I don't feel quite as out of place next to the sailors in their varied ensembles.

I watch with interest as the crew gets to work, every

person with a duty. The deck of the junk is a litany of the clatter of feet and the rhythmic thump of ropes. Captain Leung is relaying directions to her quartermaster, Lao Ping. There are people everywhere—at the helm, at various places on the deck, tying and unfurling ropes. Men with long bamboo pikes push the boat away from the edge of the waterway, and then two rowboats begin the long task of towing the *Jīn Lǐyú*. We drift slowly along the narrow tributary that leads to the Pearl River, the hulky merchant ship too large and unwieldy to raise sails just yet. Long oars extend from the rowboats as the crew heaves together in a steady rhythm to get us out and then we're on the great river.

The mountains rise up alongside us like cragged islands reaching toward the sky, buoyed on calm inner seas of green. The fields murmur with the wind, and in the distance, I lose track of which mountain peak was once mine. How strange it is to be looking back as I draw closer and closer to the ocean.

The Pearl drifts and turns, ten times wider than any waterway I've navigated myself. Soon we aren't the only ones on the river, this lifeline toward the interior of the kingdom of China. I'm impressed by the strength of the people in the smaller rowboats making their way past us, remembering how my arms would ache from rowing my own sampan boat. A twinge of regret flows through me; I'd left it by the tributary.

But it doesn't matter. I'm finally going to Canton.

Canton is a bustling port city, a spectacular metropolis that I have only heard about from stories, the gateway to the Middle Kingdom. It'll take a week to reach in Mother's great ship.

After a day's journey, we take on steady wind directly toward Canton. Two other vessels sail behind us, smaller junks for ferrying messages or supplies swiftly back and forth to the great ship.

Mother's cabin is filled with strange artifacts that I'm sure bear many stories. I try to take in as many details as possible: the trinkets sitting on the shelf, the expensive chests carved from teak, the fragrant sandalwood figurines. I knew that Mother traveled often, but these quarters look more like a home than her chamber back in the village ever did. It feels personal—the way a jacket is carelessly draped over a stool, the scrolls unfurled next to her bed, the chests open to reveal journals, ink, and brushes.

After so many years of such sporadic contact, the opportunity for an extended amount of time with her is strange. Although, in the days since we left the village, we've had only a few stilted conversations over tea in her cabin—she's almost always busy in meetings with Captain Leung or other crew members, or alone in her cabin working on the details of her business.

Or perhaps, a sniveling voice inside me would remind me, *it is because she does not prefer my company.*

I've wanted my whole life for Mother to see me, to be proud of me and acknowledge me. Now that she's here, across from me at this small table, it's all I can do to stare at the gently bobbing tea left in my cup, wondering if she would find it impertinent if I asked all the questions on the tip of my tongue. I spotted what looked like a poem that she hastily rolled up and stuffed away before setting out the tea, and I've steeled myself to ask about it the entire time, wondering what poet could have written it. Perhaps we have a favorite in common. But instead I am afraid, scared of losing whatever progress I've made toward her approval so far, and we sit in a long, drawn-out silence until Captain Leung interrupts us.

Somehow, despite being on a ship with more people than the entire village houses, I've never felt more alone. The crew gives me curious looks when I venture above deck, and the first few days I watch avidly—asking questions about the sails, how the steering mechanism works, idly playing with a piece of rope and trying to mimic a knot. One of the sailors, Lu Fen, seems to find that especially annoying, and glares at me before grumbling that he needs it to secure a sail.

Lao Ping seems amused by my curiosity, answering some of my questions at first and then cocking his head and glancing behind him. On the far end of the ship, Mother's disapproving stare hardens, but I press on. "What does it mean, *stern*?"

"Ah, that's the back of the ship, and the bow is the front.

But you don't need to know all that, miss. Don't you worry about it; we'll get you to Canton safe and sound. Best place for you to wait is in your cabin."

"Oh. Right." I have the distinct feeling I'm unwelcome on deck, so I retreat to the cabin that had been set aside for me.

It's a small space, barely wide enough for the firm cot and my trunk, but it's away from the scrutiny of everyone else. From here I can hear the crew talking and laughing, sometimes shouting orders to one another. I am too afraid of being underfoot, or for Mother to realize that I'm not cut out for this life after all.

There are a few other cabins. The largest one is reserved for Captain Leung, and there are some for the other higher-ranking officers. And of course, Mother's and mine. The rest of the crew sleeps in hammocks slung in a large general area that are stowed away and replaced with makeshift tables and stools at mealtimes. I can hear them talking late through the night, and I wonder what it must be like to live in and out of ports like this.

The river gets wider and wider, and we pass by villages in the distance, larger than I've ever seen before. We pass a floating market that rivals even the size of my village back home, sampan boats piled high with fruits and vegetables, bold merchants paddling up to the edges of the *Jīn Lǐyú*, holding up their wares and bartering with Lao Ping.

It takes time to get used to the rocking of the ship, the sound of constant water rushing by, the constant movement and noise of the crew working. I can't even bring myself to enjoy the collection of books Mother has given me to pass the time, unable to focus on anything except the unknown to come.

We're drawing close to Canton, and the anticipation starts to bubble up inside me, like a buoyant, living thing.

I toss and turn in my cot and try to get some rest; we're due to arrive in the city tomorrow, but I can't sleep. The ship is quiet, a rare thing; it must be the middle of the night.

I creak open the cabin door and tiptoe past sleeping crew members in their hammocks. Kang is snoring, her grip tightening on a long knife even in her sleep. I climb up toward the deck, and the cool night air greets me.

Stars glint above me, and I step toward the empty deck; an unyielding breeze keeps us steady, and Lu Fen nods at me from his night watch post. Other than Lao Ping relieving himself over the side of the ship, the deck is empty, a stark contrast to the uproar of usual activity.

I walk to the other side of the ship, not envying Lao Ping in that precarious position, holding on to the edge of the ship to relieve his bowels. I've only used the chamber pot left for me in my room, embarrassed about the cavalier attitude the rest of the sailors have about their bodily functions. Even Captain Leung has done it, deftly climbing over the side and squatting before jumping back onto the ship.

I can't imagine being comfortable enough with a group of people just to laugh about things like that.

The moonlight softly reflects off the water in pale glimmers, broken up by the wake of the ships traveling through. I watch the landscape go by much longer than I would have dared in the daytime, when the whole ship is awake and moving and my self-consciousness pulls me back. In the distance, just past the mountains, I see something sparkle, something that isn't just the haze of the clouds beyond.

I gasp as the horizon comes into view, and beyond the mouth of the river, the glittering ocean approaches. Hundreds of flickering lights gleam from streets unseen, softly glowing against stone, and distantly I can make out the cheerful red of lanterns and banners streaming from buildings. There's the border of a massive stone wall, ambling as it tracks through the forest, and clusters of buildings rising up on the hills leading to the ocean. I can see the shadows of ships' masts and the outline of docks, just barely.

Canton.

Knowing that we've been moving toward this place is one thing, and actually *seeing* it is another. My heart pounds nervously. I want to shout with joy, to gleefully declare our arrival, but there's no one beside me; Lao Ping is long gone, and Lu Fen is high above in the crow's nest. I'm alone, and I whisper the city's name to myself like a promise.

I watch the lanterns ahead as we draw closer, agonizingly slow, to the city and my future. Finally Kang climbs up on deck from below, and she and Lu Fen exchange a heady conversation about rice wine, cutting my musing short.

My water flagon is empty, and I regret not filling it before I'd retired to my cabin for the night, because now my throat is parched. I quietly creep back below deck and toward the galley.

The sliding door to Mother's cabin is closed, but I can see a lantern is flickering inside, casting shadows against the wooden frame and illuminating the sheer oiled paper screen.

Mother is still awake.

"Yeung, I don't understand," comes a man's hushed voice on the other side of the screen. "This is all so quick . . . The Liu family seems well intentioned, but the son can hardly make conversation, as far as I remember."

Master Feng? In Mother's quarters?

When I was a young child, I used to believe that Master Feng was my father. I'd asked him as much, and he'd laugh every time before swinging me into the air, telling me he would only be so honored. Of course, that was before I truly understood that my father had perished at sea.

Mother sighs. "Xiang knows she is to meet suitors. Liu Mingbao can provide her with a life of comfort and security. She could have all the books she'll ever read, and she won't have to work at the Pearl House."

Master Feng humphs. "You led her to believe you would teach her to manage the business. That's all she wants. She doesn't need a husband for that."

"Every day the officials make my job harder," Mother huffs. "The business is not as it was, and there are new trade bosses every day to contend with, new rivals, new tariffs, more officials to bribe. Running the Pearl House, let alone the trade and all my interests abroad, keeping it afloat, keeping my employees paid—it's difficult enough with all these new gangs and those insufferable triads to keep track of."

Master Feng makes a soft *hmm* noise, and I can imagine him nodding intensely.

"I don't have enough people in Canton I can trust to just . . . speak my mind like this. You're a rare gem, Zhanli." The admission is almost imperceptible.

"Of course, Yeung. You know I—I respect you. I'm always here to listen. Provide counsel, should you need it. You can always stay longer, if you need to unwind from the pressure of . . . everything."

Mother sighs. "I'm needed too often in the city. I cannot imagine the chaos that would ensue without me. Who would enforce my policies? Keep prices fair? It is too much for Xiang. She's better off in the village. It is safe there. Canton is not. You know as well as I what this city is like."

"Ah, Canton." Master Feng chuckles, like there's some secret joke between them.

"We were young there," Mother says, her voice warm with some memory.

"I was so handsome," Master Feng says.

"You're still handsome," Mother replies. I've never heard her sound like this . . . almost loving.

Master Feng chuckles again. "It's been a while since I've sailed with you."

Mother's tone softens. "I know."

"Perhaps once Xiang gets settled, I could come along on your next route. We could go to Sumatra, or even—"

The hopefulness in his voice is uplifting, and I can't help but hope Mother will say yes. During her visits, she would always spend time going over the teahouse accounts with Master Feng, but I recall a few times they would take all the ledgers and spend the whole day on a walk somewhere. The fresh air was a change of pace, Mother would say, but I can't imagine spending the entire day just going over the numbers. Master Feng would pack an entire sampan boat full of food and drink, and he'd be in a great mood for days even after Mother left.

"Zhanli." The name is both affectionate and firm. A warning, perhaps. "You know the business is to be my priority. I will not have time for distraction."

"Of course." Master Feng sighs. "You know, Xiang could be good at running the business. Aren't you always saying you're shorthanded at the Pearl House? Xiang's sharp, quick on her feet. And she has your spirit."

Mother laughs. "I hardly think so. You're just soft on the child. You think she could do no wrong."

"Xiang just wants to live in the city. She wants to be useful. She wants to make you proud. She wants to be *you*."

My heart leaps into my throat. I've always been fond of my tutor, but I've never heard him voice such sincere, unwavering belief in me.

"She could never be me. I've worked this hard so she never would have to! It's final. I'm having a messenger post the letter tonight with my response."

"Don't, Yeung, please—"

"Stop challenging me. You have no right to—"

"You don't understand," Master Feng presses. "I know Xiang. She would see this as a betrayal after you promised her a choice. She would resent you. You can't do this to her—"

"She is *not* your daughter!"

I can't remember ever hearing Mother raise her voice. Harsh criticisms, a thin, pursed lip, and stern expressions were my most dreaded reactions, but this cold, final tone turns my insides to ice.

There's a long silence, and I can't imagine the expression on Master Feng's face. I want to open the screen door to see, but I'm afraid that would only reveal my presence. As it is, I can only see the outlines of Master Feng's profile in the limited expanse of the window as he stares back at Mother.

When he speaks again, Master Feng's voice shakes with an anger I have never heard in him before. "She might as well be! Haven't I raised her? Taught her sums and history? I have been living in that village for sixteen years because *you asked me to*! I have never asked you for anything until now. Give her a chance. She will not want to marry this boy."

"Chances," Mother scoffs. "Choices. What choices did I have when I was her age?"

Master Feng doesn't say anything for a long moment, and when he does, his voice crackles with emotion. "We do not get to choose the hand we are dealt, and yet you have made a life for yourself many would envy," Master Feng says. "And now you would choose for your daughter, despite hating others making decisions for you."

Mother doesn't say anything at first. "A choice, then, as I promised," she finally says. "I will show her the Pearl House, and she will meet the Liu family. And when she chooses marriage and safety, you will learn that all people are the same. Why risk a hard life when you can have an easy one?"

CHAPTER FOUR

CANTON

I MAKE SURE MY FACE IS STONE THE NEXT DAY AT BREAKFAST when I join Mother in her cabin. We eat grilled fresh fish, delicate chunks flaking into my green scallion rice porridge, and Mother is looking over a long scroll that appears to be some sort of shipping manifest.

I'm still hurt by what I overheard last night. But it doesn't matter, not when she still plans to present me with that choice. I'm ready to prove that I'm not only capable of being the head of the business but also that I do have Mother's spirit, just like Master Feng believes.

"We will arrive by noon today," Mother says. "Make sure all your things are packed and ready, and tonight we'll be at my home in Canton. Your new home."

"I can't wait." I give her a calculated smile, careful and in control, like a challenger picking up a sword.

Our ship snakes along the river around the edge of the city, where we pass through the outer stone walls and the expansive fields of rice and other crops I cannot identify. After we pass the inner walls, the river's traffic starts to swell.

I cannot help but be transfixed by the sight as we approach my future. Canton is a contradiction, a strange juxtaposition of humble buildings and the impossibly luxurious, everything built atop itself. Even from the widening river I can hear horses and the clatter of carriages and people in the streets. There are grand houses with sloping roofs and gardens, stone structures with thatched roofs, and scaffolding everywhere, like the city itself is racing toward the sky, trying to grow as it breathes with the thousands of people living in it.

We emerge from the mouth of the river, where the Pearl meets the inner sea, and I can hardly breathe as I can see clear to the ocean for the first time.

And ships.

Ships as far as the eye can see.

There are some ships so large I would not have thought it possible. Familiar-looking junks with massive red sails, and many ships with tall masts and square sails, flying banners from unfamiliar kingdoms, and even more ships with no banners at all, no claim to any empire. Peculiar ships with curious sculptures carved into their masts, ships with many cream-colored sails and unfamiliar shapes made of wood. There are ships that I have no name for, ships with rows and rows of solemn-looking cannons, ships made of dark and sleek mahogany, ships made of fragrant sandalwood and teak, ships that defy imagination.

The sailors move together in an easy rhythm, guiding our junk as we maneuver to avoid the others we encounter, some of them shouting greetings to one another.

"Tariffs are high today, brother, watch out."

"Only carrying fish today," Lao Ping says from where he's sitting on the railing, feet dangling, but he nods in appreciation as we pass the other merchant ship. The other sailor waves companionably as they set out to sea. "Good luck to you."

"And to you in port! If you're planning to visit Jingyi at the Moon House you should forget it! She'll be too lovelorn over my departure!"

Lao Ping laughs. "She'll never prefer you, my friend, when she can have me!"

The rest of the sailors seem to be in a jovial mood to be returning to Canton, and the deck is a flurry of activity as we pull into the docks properly to settle and berth the ship.

There's so much happening on the docks I don't know where to look first. I want to climb higher to see all of it at once. But I stay still as our ship pulls into the harbor, folding my hands quietly as the crew prepares for us to drop anchor. The activity on our own ship is nothing compared to the jostle ahead, people and horses and carriages and rickshaws clamoring for room on what little I can see of the city streets beyond the harbor. As we come to a stop I can hear ships creaking, oars slapping against the water, people shouting, and the din of crates and barrels shifting as they're loaded or unloaded. Smaller rowboats and junks crowd right up next to the larger ships, carrying sweaty sailors toward the shore along with their cargo.

I climb down into a bobbing longboat. Fen Quai, one of the older sailors, offers me his hand as I step inside. Even this vessel to ferry us to shore is larger than any rowboat I've ever steered at home.

Mother is already sitting stately at the helm of the boat. She nods at me, seeing me seated, and then jerks her head to Lu Fen, who begins rowing us to shore.

We butt up against other smaller crafts as we draw closer to the docks, and now on the water I have to look up to see the rest of the massive ships as we thread our way through.

There's one ship whose sails appear to have been mended multiple times, a ratty-looking junk next to the other impressive ships in the harbor. This area of the docks looks unkempt as well, planks haphazardly stacked upon one another without clear design, as if the need for more berths grew too quickly for Canton to build proper ones fast enough.

But the figure perched atop the tallest sail, watching the crowds below like a hawk, is what draws my attention. It's a bright-eyed youth clad in a motley collection of clothes, and as I draw closer, I see more clearly the faded bright brocade of colorful silks, a mismatched combination of a green embroidered jacket undone at the neck, revealing an expanse of warm brown skin, and another colorful shirt.

Our eyes meet for a single moment, and I feel a trickle of camaraderie: How many times have I wistfully looked out to the far unknown from my mountaintop perch?

A cross-looking man on the deck calls up at her in a melodic language I do not know; he's similarly dressed in a strange combination of clothes. He regards the youth with a put-upon look and heaves a heavy-looking basket of gleaming fish upon his shoulders.

A woman carrying a barrel rolls her eyes. "Get down from there, Mei-Mei! We only have until sundown to make this delivery."

The girl—either her younger sister or other family member, judging from the honorific, although she looks nothing like the slight woman on the deck—laughs at the two of them.

"Coming," she singsongs back at them. Her Cantonese has a bit of an accent, the words fitting in her mouth with an amused lilt.

They must be a fishing vessel. I've never seen such a large ship for what I thought was a humble venture. Back home, fishers would travel by rowboat downriver or spend time on the riverbank shores, catching enough to sell at the floating market. But the sheer number of nets stowed along the rails suggest this one junk could catch more fish in one haul than my village sees in a year.

I watch as the girl deftly swings herself off the sail, gliding down the mast as if it were nothing, and then gracefully leaps down to the deck. She doesn't look like any girl I've ever seen—her hair is loose, floating about her shoulders, her eyes dancing wild with merriment. I would have mistaken her for a boy had it not been for the honorific, and I watch her, fascinated now by the capable way she maneuvers down the dock, the way she speaks to the other people on the deck as if she, too, is an adult, an equal member of the crew. She looks my age, but is working just as hard as everyone else, helping the crew unload everything onto the docks.

She catches me watching her again and winks at me, and her mouth broadens into a wide grin as she helps the man who might be her brother heave a heavy-looking crate over the side of the ship. I blush, looking away as the rowboat bumps against the pier.

Mother has already disembarked, watching me with disapproval. "Come along, Xiang." The crew is fetching our things already, and Fen Quai is waiting patiently to help me out of the boat.

I step past him, climbing up on my own to regard the city I've been dreaming of for so long. It's dirty and messy and filled with the unknown. I think about Mother's words, the challenge she proposed to Master Feng.

I can't let this opportunity slip away. I'm going to prove to Mother that I can do this.

There are people everywhere, bodies pressed close. A million scents tangle together, the muck of unwashed skin and sweat, and the salty brine of the sea as an undercurrent. I stand with Master Feng off to one side, watching the sailors unload our ship's cargo. Captain Leung is impatiently waiting as a man inspects their manifest scroll. He is more heavily armed, but seems to carry the same air as that of the official who visited our village once every few months to collect tribute for the Daoguang Emperor and lecture us on how we could be farming more efficiently.

"These Qing leeches," Lao Ping scowls, spitting over the side of the dock. "The tariffs get higher and higher every time we get into port."

"Hush, the lady has no need to hear your whining," Lu Fen says.

"The lady could hear more," I say with interest. The villagers had often decried the emperor as well, complaining about the heavy taxes while the promised roads and opportunities for people to study in the Forbidden City went unheard and undone, but I'm curious about what these worldly sailors think as well.

Mother is now conferring with Captain Leung in hushed voices, and then Mother discreetly hands the official a small leather pouch. He coughs, rolls up his scroll, and leaves us to our business.

"Come along," Mother says, noticing me watching her.

"Leung and the others have pressing matters to tend to. I'm sure you are tired and will want to rest."

She's already moving swiftly down the dock, and I watch in awe as people step aside, clearing a path for her. Even those with heavy loads—baskets of fish or unsteady-looking bags of rice, even two men carrying a load of lumber between them—get out of her way.

I keep up with her long stride, trying not to pause and gawk at everything, but Master Feng almost treads on my heels more than a few times when I can't look away from the throngs crowding the streets. The noise is almost shocking after the steady rhythm of the ship.

There are so many different people here—people dressed in familiar hemp or cotton robes and trousers and the conical hats from my village, but also people dressed in rich silks or finely tanned leather, soft-looking linens, soldiers wearing armor of delicately quilted silk, layered so keenly it would deflect even the sharpest blade.

As we leave the docks behind, we travel through a noisy market district, filled with street vendors and billowing steam and the scent of delicious foods wafting every which way. Everyone—wealthy and poor, soldiers and merchants, nobles and farmers—is milling about and walking with purpose. There are officials in their fancy hats and robes bobbing about; young scholars carrying armloads of scrolls or studiously taking notes, their hands flecked with ink as their brushes fly across paper. One is even wearing a makeshift desk, writing on a board suspended by a piece of cloth wrapped around his shoulders. Youths in thread-bare robes weave barefoot through the crowd, laughing as they play a complicated-looking game with a ball. I catch glimpses of faces and necks adorned with the sparkle of jewels behind the red silk curtains of palanquins, lofted high above the streets on the shoulders of well-muscled men.

Rickshaws and carts abound, being pushed slowly or careening nearly out of control down the more sloped streets, their tenders holding on to the handles with a well-practiced grip. There are men transporting long stalks of polished bamboo, thick cuts of lumber, and fragrant wood, and everywhere people are carrying things, baskets stacked high on heads or dangling precariously from poles slung across shoulders.

On the corner of every street are men dressed in polished armor carved with intricate designs, layered over thick, quilted red silk tunics. They are ever present, watching, their hands on their swords, sharp eyes not missing a thing. I watch as a scuffle breaks out ahead on the street, and the guards seize a youth, whose hands are full of steaming hot bao. They grab him by the scruff of his neck, shaking him roughly as the buns fall to the ground and are immediately trampled by the crowd. I watch as he stares at the ruined food, and I can practically hear his stomach grumbling from here.

Coins. I have coins. I reach for the hidden pocket under

my jacket, but Master Feng shakes his head. "If you start handing out cash we'll be surrounded in no time. Let's keep moving."

"But—"

We've already lost sight of Mother, who has disappeared down a side street.

"Come along. I can take you to the local temple if you want to help pass out food later this week." Master Feng jerks his head, and I follow him up the street and out of the market.

The street Mother turned down is lined with smooth stones, paved flat and neat for the carriages that roll across. It seems like some sort of financial district, and my head is spinning trying to take in all the details of the people we walk past. There are dark-skinned men with elaborate turbans and long, detailed robes embroidered with fine, shining thread, speaking a language that seems to flow like a river, beautiful and smooth. Women with pale skin, wearing clothing with fitted waists and voluminous skirts and sleeves stroll along the street under colorful parasols. Their clothing looks so cumbersome I wonder how much strength it takes to keep all of that aloft and to walk properly. There are men with thick, bushy beards wearing pointed hats and helmets, negotiating in a thick accent the price of spices with a merchant.

There are so many distinct styles of hair and dress that I can't possibly keep track of all of them. The city is like a living, breathing entity filled with people from other lands, a million villages all at once clamoring together. I can't even parse out all the different languages I'm hearing. There are the familiar tones close enough to the dialect we speak in the village, and also the more formal Mandarin I've only spoken with Master Feng in my studies. Now, hearing it aloud from the city guards and the officials and so many other people walking past, I almost think it is another language at first. But as I pause to listen, the words are just familiar enough that I can understand it despite the different tone.

I stop, fully enthralled as I watch a man bargain with a merchant showing off an elaborate display of beautifully patterned rugs. The words fall from his mouth staccato quick, and I'm pleased that I can infer that he's angry the merchant isn't willing to accept his bid of thirty silver cash because of the alleged poor quality of the rug in question.

"This was woven by hand!" the merchant protests.

"Clearly that is a burn mark. This rug is used. I'll give you thirty-five for it, nothing more." He says something else that I don't understand, and then he looks at me, his mouth curling as he sneers another string of harsh words—this time directed at me. I stumble backward.

"What are you looking at?" he snarls.

"Nothing," I mumble.

Master Feng places a gentle hand on my shoulder as he

nods at the man and the merchant. "Please excuse her rudeness, she meant no harm," he says in polished Mandarin. "Come along, Xiang."

I stay close to Master Feng and try to resist reaching out like a small child to hold on to the hem of his robe. We pass a shop filled with fabrics—bolts of embroidered silk ready to be crafted into beautiful clothing, linens dyed every possible color, and shoes of multiple sizes, from sturdy cloth sandals to delicate works of art.

"The shopping district," Master Feng says with a smile. "Let's not get too distracted. You'll have plenty of time to explore once we're all settled."

I nod and take a deep breath, trying to ground myself. I'm really here, standing in this incredible city, with people of every status and possibility. I continue to hear countless dialects, and among the familiar are other tones, too. I listen to a woman bartering, her voice almost melodic the way the tones go high and low, but I can't pick out what she's saying at all.

"What language was that?" I ask.

"That of our neighbors from the kingdom of Việt Nam. There are many who speak Vietnamese here, mostly merchants and fishers. Plenty of the shopkeepers have picked up the language as well. You'll see people from numerous kingdoms here, making their fortunes. Closer to the market district there will be a delightful array of foods to try from all over the world."

I listen raptly as Master Feng rattles off a list of places from Nepal to Siam to kingdoms I have never even heard of before, trying to keep up.

All around us I see moments, fragments of peoples' lives: three youths lingering in an alley, watching the crowd; harried shopkeepers shouting out their wares; children watching wide-eyed and clapping in delight as a man plays the lute in the middle of the street.

Master Feng stops suddenly, stepping to my right and nudging me away from the center of the street, where a man with long brown hair tied back with a loose ribbon seems to be goading on two men with unnaturally curled white hair underneath elaborate black hats. I don't understand his language, but it's clear he's taunting them, and the other two men's faces are stormy with anger. The white-haired men are carrying sinister-looking weapons I have only seen in illustrations in my books—guns with long, sharp knives strapped to their ends. The angry man is armed as well, a pair of smaller guns—pistols, I remember from the texts—dangling from his belt.

"Tobacco merchant," Master Feng says. "You can tell from his fingers." He jerks his head, and as we quickly rush past the now-shouting men, I spot that the brown-haired man's fingers are stained with some sort of black grease. "I'm always forgetting the name of that island they are from. All the merchants and sailors I've met from there are overeager to prove themselves, always starting fights with the British. It's a bit strange, a kingdom without a king, but apparently they're making it work."

I turn back for another glance at the man without a king, at his long leather coat, the metal on his belt, and the expensive weapons at his side.

Master Feng shakes his head. "You would think for how far they've had to travel to get here they would have a bit more sense."

"How far away is this island?"

"Ah, I believe Zheng He discovered it in one of his expeditions during the Ming dynasty. It is several oceans away, quite a voyage."

Men with light-colored eyes and hair the color of yellowing grass, their jackets adorned with shining brass buttons and hats lined with coarse black fur of some sort, walk past us and laugh as they enter an establishment. I can see through the open doors that every table inside is full, tea and other drinks being poured constantly. A thick, cloying scent I can't identify wafts through the air, forming clouds around the people smoking within.

"Opium," Master Feng says softly. "A disgusting habit, if you ask me. But many of these foreigners love it."

At the end of the street, Mother is waiting under a lantern at the corner of the street with a cross expression on her face. "I thought you might have gotten lost," she says.

Guilt seeps through me. An excuse bubbles up in my throat, but Master Feng speaks first.

"I stopped to pick these up," he says, holding out a bag of steaming bao. I hadn't even noticed when he bought those. "I know they're your favorite."

Mother's eyes soften a bit, and she doesn't quite smile, but she nods. "We can enjoy them later. Come along, Xiang. We are almost there."

The streets widen and I am greeted by the sounds of laughter and the slurping of soup, and the scent of so many different foods being cooked over various fires. Everywhere there is the scent of liquor permeating the air, people red-faced laughing and sharing gourds with one another, awash with the flush of alcohol despite it being only early evening.

My vision dances from the people to the architecture; already on this one street is more wealth than I have ever seen in my entire village. It's all polished wood and lacquer, with intricate carvings on the pillars, doors, and window frames. Colorful banners and tapestries abound everywhere, everything from lucky prayers adorning buildings to elaborate signs enumerating the names of establishments.

I try not to let my awe show on my face; I wonder if people are looking at me, too, if they see just another village-fresh girl. The embroidered peony jacket and matching trousers I'm wearing suddenly feel rough and rustic. My whole life I thought this was finery, but compared to the fashionable people floating down the street, I feel out of touch.

A group of lovely women walk past us, and I can't look

away. Everyone on the street seems to pause, and the crowd parts around them gently, like leaves floating in a stream as a school of shimmering fish swim by. They look like goddesses who could have descended from the Heavenly Jade Emperor's court to pay a visit to the Middle Kingdom for their own amusement. Each woman's hair is styled immaculately, either combed in delicate arrangements or sculpted in variations I've only seen in paintings of courtiers modeling the latest fashion in the Forbidden City: shining black hair studded with elaborate jeweled hairpieces dripping with sparkling gems, intricate updos that must take hours to achieve.

Each one is stunning, like the petals of a rare flower blooming in the middle of the night. The woman in the center of the group is laughing with her friends. They're all lovely, but she's *beautiful*. Her face is dusted with a pale sheen of powder, her lips painted a rich, delicate plum pink, tart and full like a fruit. The sleeves of her robe trail like gossamer wings behind her with some richly spun fabric so sheer it's merely a suggestion of cloth.

"Xiang!" Mother says sharply.

"What?" I turn, but not before I collide into a stone pillar. My face smarts and my cheeks burn with embarrassment, and I catch Master Feng hiding a laugh behind his sleeve.

We make it down the rest of the street without me embarrassing myself again, but barely. Several streets later, the prosperity of the business district falls away, and smoke fills the air. The hot scent of animal fat from the torches is almost enough to make me nauseous, the coarse smell permeating the street and filling my nose. The light is flimsy, too, flickering and unsteady, leaving trails of smoky ash and long streaks of black on the buildings.

"Here we are," Mother says, a glint of pride sparkling in her eyes. She's never looked at *me* like that, and a deep hunger gnaws inside me. For her approval. For her to see me as valuable and useful as this business she's created.

She will, I tell myself.

At the end of the street, a set of fine buildings are clustered together with an elegantly carved facade that has faded over time. The entry building's double doors are open, flanked by bright red banners embroidered with scenes of the sea—long, serpentine dragons, fleets of ships, fishermen, a rich bounty of fish, and oysters brimming with pearls. The characters naming the establishment are stitched in bright yellow thread, and the long banners look like they must have taken months to embroider. I can hear laughter and the sound of singing even from where we stand in the middle of the street.

I follow Mother as she enters, expecting it to be a much larger version of the teahouse in my village, with elegant people in rich sumptuous clothing enjoying meals and drink as musicians play delicately in the background. I'd imagined it so many times, a beautiful and bright beacon of culture and prosperity . . . but nothing prepares me for the chaos inside.

Every table is crowded with people, some not even in seats, pushing forward as they shout and cheer. Mah-jongg tiles click together as players shout their challenges, wafts of smoke weaving around them in a thick haze. Men with glazed-over eyes watch three women onstage playing the lute, zither, and an instrument I don't recognize. The music is barely audible over the din of the crowd. Women carrying flagons of wine and tea and trays of dishes duck and spin deftly through the masses.

There are people whose clothes could have been expensive and luxurious once upon a time, but there's a harder air about them, as if the clothing was chosen to be intimidating rather than ornamental—a man wearing a long coat made of leather, the hide tanned a rich purple, or a woman whose long embroidered robe barely conceals the sheathed sword hanging by her side.

I try not to let my eyes go wide as I follow Mother across the crowded floor, and I attempt to take it all in—the way people move aside for her as she steps through, the men and women who come up to speak to her, whispering softly in her ear as Mother listens and gives stern instructions back. She doesn't introduce me, and I linger awkwardly, waiting with Master Feng and trying to look like I belong.

There are even city officials here, their uniform hats lying forgotten on a table. They are wearing their hair in the Manchu style, shaved in the front and gathered in a thick braid running down the back of the head. The queue isn't unfamiliar to me, but no one in the village had bothered to style their hair like that, so I can't help but watch in fascination. One official shakes dice as a woman refills his cup, and he pulls her into his lap and she laughs, whispering something in his ear. I blush, looking away; the front of her robes is undone to reveal the swell of her breasts. I realize that some of the other women on the floor are also scandalously dressed, with daring necklines or robes unlaced to reveal sheer fabric to suggest bare skin and curves underneath.

There are three girls watching me curiously, getting up from their place by the fire. As they approach I see under the makeup that they're young, maybe even my age. They bow to Mother, who gives them a nod back.

"Who's this?" the tallest one asks, gesturing to me. "I thought we weren't hiring anyone else this month."

"She looks like a country bumpkin," the one with a beauty mark penciled on her cheek says in a loud whisper to her friend.

"You were just as naive when you arrived, Yunming," Mother says.

Yunming wilts under her gaze. "It's always so busy," she says, fanning herself and pouting prettily. I wonder if it's a practiced habit; it makes the beauty mark look even more pronounced. She glances at me with a sniff. "You'll do well to help, I suppose."

I'm somewhat relieved to note that these three—who

presumably do work at the Pearl House—are wearing the usual amount of clothing and in the proper manner I would expect. Yunming is wearing a somewhat bolder look, her zhuyao visible under her sheer outer robe in the style of Ming dynasty courtiers, but the other two seem approachable. Friendly, even.

"Come along," Mother says sharply before I can introduce myself.

She waves off the other patrons and employees who approach her, and they skitter away as we walk through the dining area to the open double doors to the courtyard. Unlike the carefully tended paths and pond in the teahouse courtyard back in the village, this one is full of hedges and curtains, alcoves full of whispers.

An open-air walkway connects the second-floor landing of each of the buildings, and from the sliding doors and shadows from behind them, I see that most of them are occupied guest rooms. Another building to the left is filled with bustling movement; judging from the people carrying trays of food and drink hurrying back to the main dining area, I assume it houses the kitchens and other such storage.

From the courtyard I can see the entirety of the Pearl House, a raucous dominion of laughter and smoke.

"What do you think?" Mother asks, raising an eyebrow.

The Pearl House is nothing like the teahouse at home. It's full of character and questionable dealings and *noise*. I take a deep breath of the smoky aroma of tea and liquor and the savory spice of meals, wonder at the conversations taking place, the business being conducted under hushed whispers, the shouts and the challenges, captains interviewing prospective crew members, the reputations made and broken all in one place. I drink it all in, the stories that must be told here, the secrets kept here.

I love it.

I love the motley crowd, the unruliness of the patrons, how there are just . . . so many people who have seen so many things. I want to see what they've seen, hear their stories. I want to know where those sailors in the far corner have been, what enemies that woman with the sword has slain, what lost romances the singer on the dais is yearning for as she pours it all into her song.

I duck my head, wondering what Mother wants me to say. If I express too much eagerness, she may see it as more evidence of my naivete. If I express surprise or shock at anything I've witnessed, she'll likely believe I won't be able to stomach what happens here.

I think steel. I think calm. I keep a cool mask of careful indifference on my face.

"I think this will suit me well," I say.

Mother narrows her eyes. "We shall see."

CHAPTER FIVE

The Marketplace

My head is spinning from all the different savory aromas filling my nose. I follow the sweetest scent to one stall where a giant steaming wok stands in front of two women, their clothes of a fashion I don't recognize, embroidered with creatures that look like impossibly large horses with exaggerated noses.

I watch with fascination as one woman piles dried rice noodles onto the sizzling hot wok and ladles water directly on top; steam rises in thick clouds as the noodles cook instantly. My mouth waters as the other woman cracks eggs directly onto the hot surface, whipping them quickly into a delicate yellow froth. A thick red sauce is poured over everything and the cooked eggs and noodles are stirred together with bean sprouts and fine strips of cabbage. Everything turns a delightful shade of orange.

It smells at once both sweet and savory, and I watch as the fat prawns they add quickly turn white and then pink, plumping up before my eyes.

The women mix everything together and then deftly pile portions onto banana leaves. A third woman wraps them into parcels with a brisk hand, securing them tightly with string before handing them to paying customers. It's amazing how it all happens in the blink of an eye, so much food cooked all at once and so skillfully.

The woman nods at me. "Noodles, miss?"

"What is this sauce?" I ask. "Why does it turn such a bright color?" It reminds me of a jar of thick red paste Lan Nai Nai had back home, ground from the chilis that Mother would bring back from her trips to the south.

"It's made from tamarinds," she says. "From my kingdom, Siam, southwest from here." She nods back to her stall fluttering with colorful banners. There are open sacks behind her of dried noodles and other spices. A child is cracking open seedpods and crushing them to make the sauce, fingers stained the same bright orange.

I watch as the men in front give her a copper cash piece for each wrapped bundle, and I withdraw one from my sleeve, the pretty coin I've never had an occasion to spend in the fishing village where everything was bartered for. I take the delicately wrapped leaf bundle and give her a nod of thanks.

This morning, I had thought Mother would start my

business lessons immediately, but when I woke she was nowhere to be found. I'm not even sure which of the rooms are hers, and I could hear people snoring from behind each screen door. I didn't want to intrude on any guests, so I just figured I would find Mother later.

Master Feng had left me a pile of scrolls outside my bedroom door and a hastily written note encouraging me to continue my history lessons as usual, along with a new poetry book, a collection of Bai Juyi's work that I requested long ago. Any other day I'd be delighted with the gift and dive right into the book, but today I am here in the city I'd dreamed of, and I have every intention of being a part of my own story.

No one in the Pearl House paid me any mind as I slipped downstairs this morning. It was quiet, only two patrons quietly nursing their tea in the corner, and I stepped over sleeping people holding empty flagons of wine, toppled chairs, and even a table that had somehow been broken in two. A few of the girls I had met yesterday were sweeping up and setting the main room to rights as best they could and didn't notice as I wandered into the street.

In the light of the fresh morning it would have been easy to lose myself, and I almost couldn't decide where to go first. I tried to keep track of every turn, every banner that could help me find my way back as I followed my nose back to the vibrant street filled with stalls and food.

Now I lean against a stone wall, eating my prawn

noodles with the cheap wooden chopsticks I was given. There are others doing the same, eating quickly and discarding their chopsticks and banana leaves on the street. I'm still marveling at how plentiful the utensils are and how easily people discard them; back in the village, taking the time to cut and sand wooden utensils until they were smooth and polished was hard work that was meant to last years. These are cheaply made, splintering under my fingers, but they do the job nonetheless. Every mouthful is delicious, from the sweet and savory sauce, to the perfectly cooked prawns, eggs, and vegetables, to the hint of crushed peanuts. I eat it all before I realize it, and I toss the wrapper and chopsticks aside, feeling like a true city dweller.

I immediately regret eating my fill as I wander down the street and hawkers shout their wares.

"Roasted peanuts!"

"Dates and dried fruits!"

"Fresh bao!"

I want to eat and taste everything. I dodge vendors with piles of roasted sweet potatoes, sticky rice, and more fruits than I have ever seen before, balanced on flat baskets on their heads, ripe mangoes and oranges and others in shapes and colors I cannot place. There are piles of round flatbreads baked directly on a hot stone, sold by a man with kind eyes, a thick, curly beard, and an intricately wrapped turban. There are giant baos the size of my palm, stacked impossibly high in baskets as women yell out their various fillings. One stall is overladen with rich-looking sweets, like dates dripping with honey, and some confections I've only seen during festivals and the new year—rice cakes smothered in sweet syrup and long strips of sugar cake, glistening sticky-sweet as they are pan fried or smothered with red bean paste and baked into sweet baos.

At another stall, customers sitting on makeshift stools eat steaming bowls of noodles steeped in rich-smelling broth. I watch as one bowl is assembled with lightning-quick speed: A woman ladles thin, delicate rice noodles into the bowl, tosses in fragrant herbs and onions, and then places slivers of raw beef on top before she ladles steaming broth over everything. The meat instantly goes from pink to cooked, and my mouth waters; it must be incredibly tender. The cook and the customer who takes the bowl are both speaking the Vietnamese language I heard yesterday, and I linger, watching and inhaling the deep aroma. I want to try the dish, but my belly is already full from the savory prawn noodles.

I quickly spend multiple coppers, and I gather up a small bounty of sweets and savory bao to bring back for Mother. As I walk, the marketplace shifts from freshly cooked foods to vegetables and other produce. Merchants stand in front of their wares, their most tempting fruits displayed proudly to show what they have for sale. The sheer color and range of everything is dizzying.

"Don't just stand there in the middle of the street," some-one snarls at me in Cantonese.

I mumble a hasty apology and step to the side to more closely watch a cook assemble something; I wonder if it is the pastry Mother described. The man has hair the color of a sunset and a smattering of freckles across his cheeks, and he's making something that looks like a bao but made with a thicker, coarse flour. I watch, fascinated, as the cook grinds thick pieces of fat into the dough and then proceeds to add minced ground pork to the mixture before setting it all above an enclosed stone firepit. The cooking method is so interesting that I lose sense of time, watching until some-one jostles past me to get in line.

I blink. The sun is high in the sky; perhaps I should head back to the Pearl House.

Birds caw and the wind shifts, bringing me the salty brine of the ocean, and anticipation in me prickles; I could watch the ships from the center of it all instead of miles and miles away, hoping for just a glimpse. I could see them all right here.

I try to remember where the docks are, but Canton looks completely different in the daytime and I don't remember at all which direction I should go. Finally I just decide on heading south. I somehow make it through the food market district without purchasing anything else and enter a district that I can't quite tell the purpose of. It appears to house a mix of various shops, some food and laundry services, and unlike the previous districts, where people linger at stalls or pause to have conversations, the people in this district are all in a hurry. As I try to find my way through the crowd, I get sidetracked—watching a group of children play a game with a ball, then two elderly men at a game of chess, then a loud argument about laundry.

A thread of the savory scent of meat buns wafts through the air, coming from a tall tray balanced on a woman's head as she makes her way through the narrow street, money clinking when she pockets it after customers have selected their buns. Then there's something else—sweet, almost cloying.

Children laugh as they race past me, eyes wide with wonder and delight. At first it's a blur, but as I approach the stall I can see the sugary confections more clearly—melted sugar spun into fanciful designs: a long, winding dragon with wise whiskers; a leaping fish; a graceful rooster; a blooming lotus flower.

The man carefully drips a sugar mixture with a ladle onto a board lined with sticks. The syrup is oozing a warm golden brown as he flicks his wrist deftly, creating strands of sugar in long arcs, and I watch as a crane appears to take flight, majestic and startling. The man presses a long stick to the syrup, and in a few seconds it's cool. He scrapes it from the board with a long paddle and presents it to his next customer.

"What'll you have, miss?" he asks me with a grin.

"I don't know," I say, stepping back nervously. The children are all gone, off enjoying their treats, and I'm the only one left standing in front of his stall.

"You look like you were born in the year of the rabbit," he says, his eyes twinkling. "A curious, exploratory rabbit for you."

I watch in amazement as he creates a rabbit out of spun sugar, complete with long ears and an inquisitive nose. He hands the confection to me with a smile, and I drop a few coins into the bowl on his cart before I continue toward the docks.

I take a bite, and it crunches into my mouth, sugar dancing on my tongue. It's so sweet, a burst of tangy brightness, and I'm reaching for another mouthful when the whole confection is snatched out of my hand.

A small boy in ragged trousers disappears down the street, holding the confection aloft; he doesn't even look back as he disappears among the crowds.

I gape after him in shock.

"Didn't you know? In this area you have to be careful of thieves," an amused voice says next to me.

I whirl around to find the girl I'd seen at the docks yesterday. She's sitting atop a barrel with her arms crossed and her head tilted at a jaunty angle. A broad smile stretches across her face, lighting up her golden brown skin, and she jerks her head at a wooden sign posted on one of the shop's walls, painted carefully with the characters BEWARE THIEVES IN THE AREA. The girl crosses and uncrosses her legs playfully, and she's wearing a long coat that could have been fine once—the color's faded but it looks well taken care of—with a mismatched shirt underneath and a pair of trousers held up by a gayly colored belt.

"Oh, thank you," I say, tapping at my waist to ensure the coin purse I'd brought with me is still there. It feels considerably lighter than it was, but I did spend a lot of time wandering the market and buying sweets. I check to make sure my pendant is still tucked safely under my shirt, touching at the chain at my neck, and exhale in relief.

"Have you been to Canton before?" She speaks the dialect with a slightly pronounced accent, and I like the way her mouth lingers on the intonations.

I shake my head. "My mother has a teahouse here," I say. "But I was raised in a village much farther upriver, so I've never been here before. Is it quite obvious?"

She cocks her head, regarding me as she chuckles. "Very much. What's your name?"

"Shi Xiang," I say, nervousness bubbling in my throat.

She laughs, throwing her head back; her whole body seems to reverberate with joy. "Ha! Full family and surname? No need for a formal introduction—we aren't exactly in the Forbidden City court here. You can call me Anh."

The name suits her. It could be a nickname or a courtesy name or perhaps a name she chose for herself, but it fits her and her crooked smile.

"You should keep to the more well-lit streets. You can't really trust anyone here."

"I wanted to see the market," I say. "And the docks and

the ships and the . . ." I trail off, painfully aware of how eager I sound.

"Ah, I saw you there yesterday. But you're on the other side of the city now."

I flush, embarrassed that she remembers me. "Yes, well . . . I got distracted."

Anh jumps off the barrel and lands deftly on the street, kicking up a cloud of dust as her coat flaps behind her, and I can't help but be enthralled. Something familiar flutters in my heart, an exciting feeling that also terrifies me, and I shake it away before my mind starts to ponder what it means. There are just so many interesting people to look at in Canton; how could I blame myself for being distracted?

To my delight, Anh offers to walk with me. She accepts the sticky rice cake I offer her, taking a bite without hesitation, prompting a loud noise of approval deep in her throat. "That's pretty good. There's another stall that does them in a sweet sesame sauce—it's perfect." She unpeels more from the leaf wrapper and hands it back at me.

I look at where her lips have touched the cake, and she's watching, waiting. I throw away hesitation and take a bite, savoring the sweetness on my tongue. I blush, thinking about the taste and wondering if this one is better because she's touched it.

Her eyes are bright as she guides me toward the docks.

"So, you have the day to yourself?" Anh asks, raising her eyebrow at me. She is light on her feet as we walk, and as I try to match her pace I find myself smiling, watching the way she hops from one foot to the other, as if she can't stay still.

I nod, although I'm sure Mother expects me at some point. But she left no instruction and Master Feng knows my wandering habits. "I'm new to Canton—I would like to see the best of the city."

"Well, you have to have the sticky buns from Feng Lu's stall, and then the glass noodles over in the arts district. And the sunset of course from the top of the eastern city wall is the best. You can see the whole city and practically all the way to Macao on a clear day!"

Anh is babbling, talking excitedly and gesturing with her hands as she tells me of all her favorite places to eat in the city, where the best street performers are, how to catch the best views. I try my best to follow along, but I can't keep any of the directions straight in my head.

I sigh. Perhaps I could try to do one of those things, but I couldn't even get to the docks on my own—

"Come on!" Anh says, interrupting my thoughts.

"What?"

Anh grins at me. "You think I just wanted to *tell* you about all those places? Come on, I can show you!" She extends her hand to me, her palm open and inviting.

I take her hand, and her fingers close around mine. Her hands are warm and solid, and the roughness of the calluses on her fingers brush against my own. Our fingers tangle together, my long brown fingers against her own golden-hued skin, and my heart skips a beat.

"Let's go!" Anh dashes off, her loose hair bouncing as she runs, and I can't help but laugh as I follow along.

CHAPTER SIX

ANH

THROUGH ANH'S EYES I SEE THE CITY THE WAY SHE DOES, every shortcut and alleyway, the best food stalls tucked away in a busy corner, which teahouses where the rich spend mounds of silver on opium and other pleasures.

Ahead of me, Anh's feet are light and nimble as she weaves through the crowd. I almost miss it—as we pass a man scolding two youths carrying a heavy load of bricks, his purse open at his waist, Anh's hand dips in and out lightning quick, and then she's gone.

I find her at the end of the street, where she's buying oranges.

"Want one?" she asks, tossing one at me.

I catch it and watch as she drops a heavy stack of coins at the vendor, far more than a handful of the fruit is worth.

My hands close around the fruit. I look back, and the woman is counting her coins with a smile, two young children crawling into her lap. Far behind us, the man who Anh robbed has his hands on his hips, shouting at a crew of construction workers as they lay out the foundation for a new shop.

"You stole the money for this," I accuse her. "You're a thief."

Anh laughs and gives me a little bow. "I don't say no to opportunity. Are you telling me he'll miss a few coppers? Plus, she needed it more." She shrugs. "Life is hard, and I'm just doing my part to get by. If someone was walking around the docks with an open purse filled with coin, and they made that coin by not paying their workers enough— theft in itself—or they're collecting bribe money for the triads, then me taking the coin is really just giving opportunity back to those who didn't have it in the first place."

She peels her orange, dropping the peels on the ground and handing the naked fruit to me. I take it and hand her my orange, and she peels that, too.

We eat the fruit together, and I savor the sweetness, eating each section on its own. Back in the village, the very idea of stealing, of taking from your neighbor, was utterly despicable. I cannot even imagine anyone doing it. But every other month, an official would come to the village and leave with carts full of grain and vegetables that he didn't grow, to take back as tribute to the Daoguang Emperor. Or so he said. Old Man Lo would grumble and say it was the greedy imperial court stealing from us under the guise of the emperor's approval.

I think about the stories the people would tell, of the monstrous bandits and thieves and pirates outside our village, just waiting to prey on those too weak to defend themselves. I never thought of the officials or the emperor as thieves themselves. But the man not paying his workers surely is doing them wrong as well.

"So you're telling me if there's an opportunity, you wouldn't take it?" Anh asks me, her eyes twinkling.

"Not if it would hurt someone."

"Hm. But what if you had to? To help someone else? Or yourself?"

"I don't know. What about you?"

"Of course," Anh says. "There's nothing stopping me from going after what I want."

The sun is low behind the city skyline, and Anh grins and jerks her head for me to follow. "Come. You wanted the best views of the city, right?"

I follow her as we climb atop the city walls, laughing as she pulls me up when my foot stumbles on a loose cobblestone. We race across thatched rooftops and bamboo scaffolding, getting scolded by construction workers carrying loads of lumber and tools.

"This is incredible," I say, swinging my feet off the edge of the city wall.

Canton stretches out in front of us. Behind us, twilight has already fallen, a soft dusk sweeping across the landscape, and the city is already waking up for the night, torches blazing and lanterns being lit one by one as the sun begins its descent toward the horizon. We're close enough to the docks that we can hear sailors shouting and singing in the distance, the creak of ships as they bob in their berths, waves gently lapping against their hulls. It's better than I ever could have imagined.

"Sorry, you must be accustomed to . . ." I gesture at the expanse of beauty in front of us. "But I grew up in a small village and I've never seen anything like this."

Anh laughs. "My first time in Canton was like that, too. I got lost so many times. It can be a little overwhelming. I'm from a small fishing village, too."

"What's it like?" I ask, curious.

"Việt Nam? My village?"

I nod, biting back the tide of questions brimming behind my lips. I want to know everything.

Anh shrugs. "I guess it was just enough people to be a village. It was our family and the Diep family, just a cluster of floating homes built around the docks and traps for prawns and crabs. There would always be old fishermen yelling at boats that pass them by, and dogs, racing around the docks or just hanging out atop junks, waiting for scraps of fish." She glances away. "I was barely a child when we left. I hardly remember our house."

She closes her eyes. "It would always sway in the current, even if there was no wind. The bay was hit by a terrible storm, and everything was destroyed. We were already pretty much living on the *Huyền Vũ* then, so Mẹ packed my brother and me up and we've been sailing ever since."

I nod, listening intently.

She pauses to regard me with an inquisitive expression. "You know, most people don't care."

"I want to know everything about you," I say earnestly. "What about the rest of the kingdom? What is it like? I only know about Việt Nam from the stories and poetry I've read." I smile, thinking of one of my favorites as I cite, "The water flows, yet grief won't wash away. The grass smells sweet, yet hearts won't feel assuaged . . . we turn and look, but all has come between—green mountains and blue clouds roll on and on."

I catch myself and realize I'm not alone on my mountaintop, talking to myself about dreams and love and reading my favorite words over and over. Anh is staring at me, her eyes widening.

"What?" I say, suddenly self-conscious.

"N-nothing," Anh says, blinking furiously. "Ha!" she bursts out suddenly. "I know that one. *Chinh phụ ngâm* is one of my mother's favorites. I think poetry is pretty useless, except for making people sad."

I gasp. Poetry? *Useless?* "I think it's beautiful," I retort. "And sadness and sorrow isn't, it isn't . . ." I stumble over my words, unable to fathom how this piece could fail to stir anyone to emotion. "I think that's the point of this one, to linger in the sadness, to know you aren't alone in feeling that way. The line about her lover being at heaven's edge and being fated apart, and now they are a stream and a cloud instead of water flowing together . . ." I sigh dreamily.

Anh laughs, a bitter and sarcastic sound. "That's a clumsy translation. In Vietnamese, it's more like . . ." She brings her brown fingers to rest on her face as she thinks, and then recites in an even cadence, lovely and haunting:

> *Trong cửa này đã đành phận thiếp,*
> *Ngoài mây kia há kiếp chàng vay?*
> *Những mong cá nước vui vầy,*
> *Ai ngờ đôi ngả nước mây cách vời.*

"See?"

I'm momentarily stunned. "That *is* beautiful."

"No, it's terrible. The whole poem is about war, and loss, and men dying over and over again. She waits for her husband to return home, spinning pretty words, but he is dead and gone, and he will never return."

I remember most from the poem the yearning, the romance, the images of mountain vistas and distant deserts and the places she imagined her husband to be. I had forgotten why he was there—that he was a soldier, fighting in endless wars.

"What did you think the lines about the Han troops pitching camp and the watching eyes of the Hun were about?" Anh folds her arms, sighing. "Poetry is useless. It can't fight or catch fish or feed you. It just makes you think about things you cannot change."

"There is peace now," I say softly. "That was dynasties ago."

"Peace! Ha. What does that even mean? Sure, different emperor, different king. They're all the same to me. They want power, they want land, they want more for their empire . . . for *them*. The old fishermen in my village would talk about how soldiers would come to Hạ Long Bay and say, *This land belongs to the empire of China*. Different soldiers would insist, *This land belongs to the kingdom of Việt Nam*. They would say they would fight on our behalf, that it was for our own good, and people would leave to fight and never come back." She kicks her foot at the tiled roof of the city wall.

"Emperors and kings and officials . . . they all want the same thing from their people: constant tribute, money or grain or people for their endless wars. On the water, we aren't a part of any empire. Our home is the sea, our port wherever we choose to travel."

I watch Anh's gaze as she looks out to the horizon, thinking about how sure she sounds of something as uncertain as life on the sea. "Tell me more."

Her eyes light up when she describes the harbors of huge cities like Thăng Long, especially at night, when thousands of flickering lanterns would gleam soft and warm against the coolness of the night sky. She talks about weathering storms on her tiny ship, chasing after the current to get the best hauls, letting the winds take them where they will. Anh has been to more places than I have even read about in my stories, along the coast of

China and all of Việt Nam. She tells me about the lush river deltas and incredible temples in Bangladesh, the hot springs in the jungles of Sumatra. Even the way she talks, the cadence of her words, takes on the feel of someone who has spoken multiple languages, or at least tried them on. The confidence in the way she wears her motley set of clothing is utterly captivating.

"How old are you?" I wonder out loud.

"Seventeen."

Only a year older than myself, and she's already done so much. "I'm sixteen," I say, restlessly kicking my feet against the stone. "Until this week I've never been outside the village. I had no idea the world could even be this big. Now I want . . ."

Anh waits, watching me.

I shake my head. "It doesn't matter."

"Of course it does. Tell me. What do *you* want?"

The question stops me in the middle of discarding my own thoughts. I feel like I've been living my whole life in wait—for more books, for more stories, for Mother to recognize my abilities. I think about all the sights I've seen in the past day alone, of getting to stand witness to hundreds of these new stories happening around me.

That's what I want. It's all on the tip of my tongue, to share how I need to prove to Mother that I can manage the business. But maybe the Pearl House was just a goal I had because that's all I knew was possible. I didn't know a girl like me could sail, could travel, could see the places from the stories. I hadn't met Anh or sat on this wall with her in the glow of the setting sun. I didn't know what it felt like to be so seen and *known* in such a short amount of time.

I know now that running the Pearl House is one desire of many, despite not knowing how to say it.

"More," I admit in a soft whisper.

I have always known there was life outside the village, and now that I have traveled down the river and seen Canton, the gateway to new worlds, to people living on their own terms . . . how could I possibly return?

"I want the world," I say, my voice growing steadier as I say the words aloud. "I want to see everything, taste everything. Experience everything."

Anh looks at me, her eyes softening. She shakes her head, a few locks of hair swaying with the movement. Where she's sitting next to me, her hand almost brushes mine. I've never met someone who I felt such a connection to like this, who seemed to understand my hopes and dreams even without me having to say all of them out loud. I want to reach for her hand fully, like earlier in the market when she was leading me through town. But the moment feels too poignant with the sun dipping low on the horizon, golden light falling on the ships in luminous slants. We sit there in silence as the shadows lengthen, watching the ships come in.

Finally she looks at me with a small smile. "You're strange, Shi Xiang," she says, gently teasing.

I laugh. "I know."

"I would have thought you would say a full belly, a roof, a good harvest, a family of your own."

"Is that what you want?" I ask, curious.

Anh glances at me and then back out at the sea, a casual tilt to her shoulders. "Full nets of fish, wind in our sails, coin in my pocket, and opportunity for more. I'm not picky," she says. "We drop into ports like this often and never stay long enough to make an impression. Canton is too big for us to compete with the other traders for good prices; we're better off selling fish to smaller cities and villages along the coast. But sometimes they don't have enough coin or good-enough things to trade." She sighs, looking off into the distance.

I nod, listening. I feel like there's more she wants to say, and I want to give her the space to say it.

Anh takes a deep breath and speaks quickly, as if she doesn't want to have to think about it. "I want *peace*. To rest for a while. To not have to worry about whether the catches are going to be good, if the gods will send us a fair wind. To have enough not to worry about where our next meal is coming from or if we'll even make it to the next port."

She glances at me and then looks away, biting her lip. "But the world is just like that; you never truly know what the next day will bring, and you have to enjoy what you can." She gives herself a little shake, and then that mischievous smile is back. But it doesn't quite reach her eyes; they're still focused on something on the horizon, far away and lost in some dream.

Anh laughs, bright and merry, and she knocks her shoulder against mine playfully. "Let's go. This city comes alive at night, and I know a place that makes the best braised pork belly if you've got the silver."

I take another gulp of rice wine; our plates are scraped clean and the tiny table bears the greasy remnants of the dishes we've eaten, braised pork belly and fragrant steamed rice and spicy garlic-chives-and-scallion pancakes.

Anh's cheeks are flushed, a dusky pink sweeping prettily across her brown skin. She leans back in her chair; we're sitting close together in a crowded teahouse only a few streets down from the Pearl House. This one is just as raucous and noisy, if a bit smaller and without any musicians. But the sound of the patrons laughing around us is lively as they drink and laugh over games of dice. Everyone is crowded together, and Anh's knees brush against mine under the tiny table.

My cheeks burn, and I tell myself it is the wine, but that feeling again raises its head, making itself known, that deep unbidden yearning in my heart I have never voiced. The simple touch seems at once too much, the warmth of her, and I both want to move away from the intensity of it and to also linger here in this moment forever.

"More wine?"

I nod and Anh empties the rest of the flagon into my

cup. I feel light-headed and euphoric; I want to ask my new friend if we could meet again when she's back in port, or if she'd come back to the Pearl House sometime to visit me. But bringing it up seems like a definite end to this wonderful day. We've laughed over our food, Anh sharing stories about wrestling an overeager fish on the deck of her ship, and I regaled her with how I accidentally toppled Old Man Lo's sampan boat and was diving for his cabbage heads for hours. We've talked about everything as Anh eagerly suggested more dishes until our tiny table was crammed full. Anh deftly produces coins from her belt, and I match her with my own pieces until my purse is empty. My heart is full, and I don't want the night to end.

The stool I'm sitting on is small and unsteady, and I should be unbalanced, but between the wall and the warmth of Anh next to me, I feel comfortable enough to let my mind wander and my body relax.

"Of course I am the greatest smuggler who ever lived!" the man behind me insists, his liquored breath drifting over to where we sit.

"You couldn't smuggle a chicken over the number you've listed on your manifest," a stout woman says next to him, taking a swig of her wine. "Every time we come into port, it's *yes sir* this and *of course we have this paperwork* that."

"Because I'm sneaky!"

His companions roar in laughter.

"Stop laughing! Tell Chungxian about the time I—"

Chungxian raises her eyebrows. "Please, Wang. You can

barely handle the legal goods we bring in, let alone anything under the table," she scoffs. The other people at their table agree.

"Smuggling is not what it used to be, with all these damn Qing navy soldiers crawling everywhere," Wang growls. "Every port on this river and anywhere in the sea, I turn and see one of their damn ships."

"You know that many of the high-ranking navy captains used to be pirates," another man says, his face worn with scars. "That's how they know all the good hiding places."

"That's a silly rumor," Chungxian says, scowling.

They all break into a chorus of disagreement until another flagon of wine arrives and Wang starts boasting again, claiming his place among the best thieves and pirates.

"Zheng Yi Sao, now *that* was a pirate," Chungxian sighs.

The others at her table chorus in agreement, and they raise their cups together and drink. Anh does as well. The other table doesn't notice as she grabs a flagon of their rice wine and brings it to our table, filling both our cups and returning it. She winks at me, and I giggle as I listen to the storyteller.

Chungxian speaks with the practiced air of someone who has told many an exciting tale, and our corner of the teahouse grows quiet as she begins. "Many years ago, the South China Sea was not as it is now, patrolled by the Qing navy with their tariffs and endless nuisances. It was a time when merchants, fishers, and rogues took their own fortunes in their hands, when the laws of the empire could not touch them. And there were many fortunes to be made, in the rich bounty of the seas . . . and of course, the taking of those prizes from others.

"The Red Banner Squadron was one of the first fearsome fleets, amassing followers and striking fear into the hearts of many, including the Jiaqing Emperor himself. But it wasn't until Zheng Yi married and Zheng Yi Sao joined him at the forefront as a formidable leader that the Dragon Fleet started to become the legend we know it as today." She pours herself another cup of wine, taking a long gulp. "Zheng Yi Sao was as terrifying as she was beautiful, commanding fear and respect. She united multiple squadrons and lieutenants, delivered punishment for those who crossed her, and grew the pirates' central treasury until they were a powerful force to be reckoned with. After the death of her husband she only became more ruthless, and her true ability as a commander emerged."

"And you sailed with them, Chungxian?" one of the men asks, rapt with attention.

"Yes, I did. Many years ago. I was in the Yellow Banner Squadron, at the height of the Dragon Fleet's power. Zheng Yi Sao had an efficient manner of paying her crews—we would turn in the goods to one of her floating fortresses and take a cut for any information and the leads we brought in, and get paid generous wages for any prize we took. It was a far better living than fishing ever was."

"How big was the Yellow Banner Squadron? And the Dragon Fleet?"

"Ha! The Yellow Squadron had about fifty junks all reporting to the fleet and hundreds of pirates. Cheung Po Tsai's Red Squadron had over a thousand men reporting to him alone." Chungxian sighs.

"Can you imagine?" I whisper to Anh.

Anh rolls her eyes. "The numbers they talk about are ridiculous."

"The Dragon Fleet in all had over fifty thousand people," Chungxian says with a grin. "Over three hundred junks all sailing under the Head of the Dragon's command."

As Chungxian goes on, I am awed at the idea of such a powerful woman. Chungxian talks about a time when the Dragon Fleet was so prominent that more villages and cities paid tribute to the fleet than to the emperor for their protection. I have heard some of these stories, but they've always been of the sort to scare children from wandering, that there were bandits in the cities and life outside the village was harsh and wild. Of pirates, I'd only heard they were fearsome monsters who would steal everything you had and destroy your home. The official who passed through last month when I pressed him for details about the empire talked about the great achievements of the past twenty years, including eradicating the pirates. But I hadn't thought about how villages might want protection from the imperial court itself.

The woman serving us pauses as she refills a pitcher with wine, nodding at Chungxian thoughtfully. "My village paid tribute to the Red Banner Squadron and then the Dragon

Fleet once the other squadrons joined them; they did a better job of protecting us than any of those corrupt Qing officials."

"Aye," an older man from another table recounts. "Zheng Yi Sao's word was true. You could buy protection from any of her offices in Canton or Macao, and then you could sail and go about your business."

"Protecting you from *them!*" Another man in the corner laughs. "A bandit charging you a fee so he doesn't rob you is still a bandit."

"The pirates don't come back season after season, demanding more of my best grain. And for what? To pay tribute to an emperor who only wishes to grow his own coffers? My sons can't afford to go to the university in the Forbidden City, and yet he promises roads and protection from bandits and asks for us to capture them when they have guns and cannons and we have nothing."

The argument roars on, and I can barely make sense of it. Our village is too far inland to have any fear of bandits. Occasionally I'll hear travelers talk of such dangers, but this is all new to me.

"There was never peace," the serving woman agrees. "But at least there was order with the Dragon Fleet. We knew then the pirates would fight the navy and other kingdoms and leave us common folk be."

Chungxian raises her gourd. "And whatever your feelings about the emperor, whatever your feelings about Zheng Yi Sao, you have to agree that she was the best pirate who ever lived."

"That much is true," Anh says to me.

"You were there! For the great siege of the Tiger's Mouth!" a man says, eyes wide. "Tell us about how it all ended, the last days of the formidable Dragon Fleet."

Chungxian grins. "Now, it was . . . 1808? I remember, because the monsoon that summer went on for weeks. But that was when it all started to fall apart."

She spares no detail about how the governor-generals of Guangdong one by one in the next few years would fail to defeat the pirates, as the Dragon Fleet only grew in number and power. She lists names I've skimmed over in my history books, men who were demoted or killed in their line of duty.

"Even the Jiaqing Emperor's own personal customs commander, the once-respected Hoppo, was demoted," Chungxian crows. "The Dragon Fleet and the Red Banner Squadron at its head controlled all trade flowing in and out of every port, and no one could travel without fear for almost two years. The Chinese navy, seeing those red flags fly, would sabotage their own ships rather than take on the pirates."

An old man in the corner smoking a pipe nods. "Protection was expensive. I heard the Red Banner Squadron charged as much as fifty Spanish dollars for safe passage out of the inner sea."

"That's what they charged the *Spanish* merchants," Wang says with a guffaw. "A fishing vessel could easily get a protection certificate for a hundred pao of salt."

Chungxian continues, "After the loss of the hundreds of ships and thousands of people fighting, there was little the emperor could do. The Qing navy could not defeat the pirates, even after the navy requested the help of the British and the Portuguese. The pirates were too cunning, too quick." She sets down her gourd and shakes it, summoning a hostess to fill it with more wine.

"But what happened, if the Dragon Fleet was so powerful?" I ask, surprising myself.

Chungxian glances at her cup. Despite her experience in the fleet, her knowledge and admiration of the mighty pirate commander, it's clear she doesn't know all the details.

"Greed," Anh says quietly. "And fear. The lieutenants, those who led their own squadrons, started seeking power of their own. Mutiny. Desertion."

Chungxian nods. "The winter of 1809 dragged on as the siege outside Canton grew more and more desperate. And one of the most feared captains himself—Cheung Po Tsai—had his sights set on even conquering all of China and becoming emperor."

"Ha! The Kid!" Wang guffaws. "All his stories are great, too." He glances at his companions, eager to impress. "He was called 'The Kid' because he was kidnapped by the pirates as a boy, and then quickly rose up in the ranks."

A bearded man with a cross expression elbows Wang, rolling his eyes. "What happened next, Chungxian?"

"The hot-tempered Cheung Po Tsai led his Red Banner Squadron to challenge the Portuguese navy so he could take Macao. But he suffered heavy losses, and lost hundreds of ships in the attempt. I imagine Zheng Yi Sao was not pleased at all, especially when Cheung started negotiating for his own pardon."

"The Battle of the Tiger's Mouth," Anh says, her voice low. She shakes her head a little, watching Chungxian take another drink. "The turning point of the siege."

"And then the Dragon Fleet began to splinter, each squadron lieutenant motivated by their own fears, their own greed, and that was when Zheng Yi Sao knew it was the end. But she refused to go on anyone's terms but her own. So when the Qing settled on pardoning all the pirates, the terms of the pardon were challenged by Zheng Yi Sao. She demanded to keep her ships. In her anger, she lay siege to the city of Chuenpi, where negotiations were taking place, keeping the governor-general Pai Ling and his advisors hostage. She displayed her might for three days while her pirates waged war against the soldiers on the beach. Finally the governor-general conceded to her demands, and the Dragon Fleet was disbanded."

"What became of them?" someone asks.

"The pirate generals retired, many of the crew returning to their former lives as fishermen and sailors," the storyteller says.

"And Zheng Yi Sao?" I ask.

"She vanished. Some say she took her wealth and left the sea forever. Some say she continued to operate in secret, for not even the Qing could stop her—she did demand the right to keep a sizable fleet to continue her operations, and they had no choice but to look the other way. But there hasn't been another force like it since the Dragon Fleet was disbanded."

"I hear she died," a man in the crowd mutters.

"I hear she and Cheung Po Tsai settled in Macao and are growing old together, enjoying their wealth," another says.

"I don't think it's possible, the way she lived—ruthless, never fearing to carve out her own path," Chungxian replies. "She demanded her terms, and I think however she chose to live, that's exactly what she wanted."

"And the treasure?" a man missing his front teeth says, waggling his eyebrows. "What about all the treasure they amassed in those years, from the Qing emperor's own coffers and countless other kingdoms?"

The teahouse erupts into noise again as the people argue about what happened to the wealth, but it seems clear that no one truly knows.

"What do you think?" I ask Anh. "Do you think the treasure is still out there?"

"Of course not, it's just a story," Anh says casually. "Zheng Yi Sao likely died during that siege and the Qing seized all her possessions. People just like the idea of her, you know."

"Oh," I say, unable to hide my disappointment. "So the story, the siege, the battle—it's just a story?"

The hostess is eyeing us as new patrons come in, and Anh gets up, dusting off her multicolored coat. I follow her out into the cool night air, awash in the sounds of the city.

Anh glances at me, her eyes narrowing in consideration. "What does it matter?"

I bite my lip, thinking of the daring feats in the story, how one woman brought multiple governments to their knees and forced them to accept her terms. I think about choices and the world she defined for herself, and wonder what may be possible for me. "She just . . ."

A small, sad smile dances on the corner of Anh's lips. "Hers was one of my favorite stories growing up. I know all of them, even the more nonsensical ones. That one was pretty good. Most of it, anyway." She reaches into her jacket and then flicks something at me.

I catch it, fumbling. It's a warm, solid piece of metal, the size of a cash coin, but it doesn't bear the seal of the Daoguang Emperor. It's engraved with a dragon, its long serpentine body circling the hollow center.

Intrigued, I examine it for a moment before handing it back to her. "What's this?"

"A protection token, from the days of the Dragon Fleet. Fishers and merchants could purchase them to guarantee safe passage. Zheng Yi Sao and the Dragon Fleet were real. But that was twenty years ago. The great pirate fleets are all gone. Nothing but petty smugglers and thieves trying to make a living now. No one has heard from Zheng Yi Sao since that siege. But everyone loves a story."

"She was your favorite, but you don't believe in the treasure?" I ask. "What happened?"

"I grew up," Anh says. Her voice is curt, and she looks away quickly. "For years sailors have tried to find it and failed—including my mother. We are a small ship with limited resources and a crew with many mouths to feed. Fishing and delivering goods is all we can do to survive, and barely that. My mother—"

Anh glances at her feet. I still. For all that Anh has talked about adventures in various ports and narrowly escaping the wrath of city guards and the incredible sights of the world, this is the first time she's talked about her family.

"My mother was obsessed with the treasure when I was growing up. Convinced that it would solve all our problems. We spent years chasing every rumor, sailing to islands far out of our trade routes, taking risks we could not afford." Her eyes brim with emotion, and she sniffs quickly, a hard mask falling over her features. "We nearly lost the ship once because of this story. My mother's come to her senses since then, and so have I."

I don't know what to say. I want to reach toward her, comfort her somehow, but any words that spring to mind don't seem like enough.

She shrugs, blinking quickly and then looking at me. "It's fine. Life on the sea is like that."

"I lost my father at sea," I say quietly. "I may not understand all the hardships you and your family have gone through, but I can try."

Anh's smile is sincere and a little sad. "Thank you."

We walk down the street, and I'm unsure of where

we're going, if I'm leading the way or if I'm following her somewhere. The night sky twinkles above us, and I think of how I could have never imagined a day like this before. There's a strange lingering sense that I need to say goodbye, that Mother will be wondering where I've been all day. But I don't know how to put into words how I'm feeling, how this day spent with her has felt like something out of a dream I don't want to end.

Stars blink in the night sky, almost as if they're in conversation with the lanterns flickering throughout the city. We are alone on this empty street, and I want to reach for her hand, to embrace her like an intimate friend, and—

Anh glances toward the direction of the docks, and then back at me, and a brief thundering of my heart dares to hope that she doesn't want to say goodbye, either.

"I have to go," she says. "We leave in the morning."

"Thank you for showing me the city," I say.

Anh grins at me. "You're not bad, for a merchant girl."

"Can I . . . can I see you again? Would you come visit me, when you dock in Canton?"

"You live here? I thought you were visiting with your mother."

"I do now. My mother manages the Pearl House, and one day I will as well."

Anh raises an eyebrow at me. "That's a rough district."

"I'm learning the ways of the city," I say with more confidence.

"It's a wonderful place, filled with everything you could ever want, I'm sure. But for every kindhearted person, there are twice as many people who will only look out for themselves." She cocks her eyebrow at me and leans in closer.

I drift toward her, the space between us disappearing, my heart pounding. The day we've shared, the glances between us, the spirit in her laugh . . . I feel like meeting her was a gift. Every smile I gave her she returned in full. How she had peeled a ripe orange for me and watched me break it into sections, the bright wedges bursting with juice. I had not imagined the way her eyes had flicked to mine and then to the juice lingering on my lips.

Am I imagining it now, the way her eyes are glowing with warmth under the light of the lanterns on this lonely street?

The night air seems to come to a standstill, and I cannot look away. This girl with a warm smile and bright eyes who has seen the world is looking at me. This girl who within a moment knew me immediately and understood my yearning for more. This girl who listened to me babble about the sea and my dreams of far-off places and who had a story for each one.

I think of all the poetry I've read, the way people would talk about being thunderstruck by sudden emotion, like the wind changed course and everything was different and they understood the world in a different way. I have read so much about these feelings, but until now I had only understood on the surface. These same feelings are roiling within me now, threatening to bubble over.

I wonder if she is feeling this, too.

I want to kiss her suddenly, and the feeling is even more overwhelming than stepping into this city for the first time was.

Anh smiles, bringing her lips to my ear.

I close my eyes, not daring to breathe.

"You shouldn't trust so easily," she whispers.

For a long moment, there's nothing but silence and the rising beat of my thundering heart. When I open my eyes, I'm alone on the street, with nothing but the rush of wind and the flicker of the street lanterns.

She is gone.

CHAPTER SEVEN

THE ARRANGEMENT

I PUSH THROUGH THE DOORS OF THE PEARL HOUSE, MY hands sweating as I slip inside. It's as crowded as it was yesterday, and I make my way upstairs. I don't see Mother anywhere, but Master Feng is sitting in the corner with another man I don't recognize, surrounded by scrolls. He stands abruptly when he sees me, sending brushes scattering and knocking over his pot of ink.

"Xiang!" he gasps. He races over to the stairs, bounding up after me. "I was so worried, I was just about to alert the city guard to go find you!" He pulls me into a tight embrace like how he used to when I was a child. I breathe in the comforting scent of paper and ink and relax a little, my spinning mind starting to calm down.

Master Feng steps back, embarrassed, and I save him the trouble of acknowledging the rare expression of emotion by bowing my head guiltily instead of teasing him as I normally would. "I'm sorry, I went to explore the city and lost track of time."

"You should have left a message!" Master Feng scolds. "I had no idea where you had gone; Yunming said she saw you leave, but no one had seen you since this morning. Do you have any idea what I've been through, imagining the worst? You know Canton is a dangerous place, and I—" Master Feng shakes himself, taking a deep breath. "Your mother is not happy, and—" He turns as a door on the opposite side of the landing opens.

Mother steps out, her face hard and cold with disapproval.

It feels like the whole world comes to a standstill; the din of the open dining room below us falls away as she approaches me, her mouth a thin line.

Master Feng ducks his head at me, giving me an apologetic look. He squeezes my shoulder, a small gesture of comfort, before he turns to stand at her side.

"Where have you been?" Mother asks, her tone as sharp as a honed blade. "I arranged for a meeting with the Liu family for you, and yet you were nowhere to be found today. It did not make a good impression."

"I apologize, Mother." I look down at my feet, guilt swirling in my stomach. I should have just stayed here and studied. Now I've disappointed her, and I feel so small. "I wanted to see Canton, and I didn't see how late it was getting, and I-I—" I stutter to a halt, trying to think of excuses, of the sweets and savory treats I had picked up in the market to bring back to her; I realize in horror I must have left the bag of treats at the other teahouse, or dropped it somewhere in my wanderings with Anh. I don't even recall when I lost track of it. The guilt seeps into me deeper.

"I let Xiang know there's a grand collection of books here at the university library, and a colleague of mine would let her read and study there if she wanted," Master Feng says softly.

Mother humphs but she does not say anything, and I exhale a sigh of relief. Master Feng's excuse sounds much more palatable than the truth that I had spent the day traipsing all over the city.

"Pah! You academics and your musings," she finally says. "You can only learn so much from theory. If you want a keen understanding of business, you must practice it."

I look up to meet Mother's calculating eyes. I haven't lost this chance just yet. "Of course. I promise I will do my best."

She gives me the slightest of nods and walks past me down the stairs. Heads immediately turn toward her, and I watch her as she surveys her domain. People wait until she approaches their table, taking in what I imagine to be her counsel. I strain my ears to listen, but above the general conversation I can't pick out what she's saying.

"The business is much different from the teahouse back in the village," Master Feng says. "It's not only the number of patrons, managing the staff, providing meals and tea and liquor, but the actual business done here—the trade. All of it has roots here. People conduct business meetings here, sign on crew members for their ships, pick up leads, and trade secrets. Would you be able to handle the same?"

I watch Mother nod at Yunming as she pours another flagon of wine for a group of merry gamblers, watch her hand a scroll discreetly to another merchant and accept a pouch in return.

"I must," I say.

New determination flows through me. The day was wonderful, to be sure, but dreaming of *more* and Anh and sights unseen will do nothing for me. I have to focus on the task at hand: proving to Mother I can run the Pearl House.

It is only when I have returned to my room and am getting ready for bed that I realize my gold pendant is gone.

Panic strikes through me, multiple possibilities flitting through my head as I toss and turn, trying to fall asleep. In my mind I explore every possibility of where it could have fallen, wondering if it would be possible to retrace my steps. But as the hours pass and the teahouse quiets, I realize there is only one answer left—one that leaves me with a sick sense of betrayal curling through my stomach.

Anh must have taken it.

It isn't possible that it slipped off my neck; the clasp on

the chain was too secure for that. I'd been wearing it for years, the weight of it comfortable against my chest.

You shouldn't trust so easily, she had said. She had said something similar when we had first met as well, that thieves operated in the area. She spent the whole day with me, probably laughing in her head the whole time at my naivete, my silly dreams. I was a fool to believe she would have wanted to actually spend time with me.

I think about the moment we had on the street, and I had closed my eyes like . . . like I was awaiting a kiss . . .

I shake myself, angry at how willing I was to believe that was what was happening. Of course it was all a lie.

I can't blame her. She saw the opportunity and took it. With the life she leads, not knowing when her next meal might come, it makes sense. But it doesn't change how I feel about it. It was the only piece of my father I had, and now it's gone.

After a night of little sleep, I get dressed in the pale glow of dawn and wander over to where I saw Mother emerge yesterday; these must be her rooms. My frustration makes me bold, and I slide open the doors to find an office of sorts. Mother is speaking in an agitated tone to the people gathered in the office, one of whom I recognize as Lao Ping. Master Feng is sitting quietly at Mother's side, glancing up at her from his half-written scroll. Kang is leaning against the wall, watching with an observant eye.

Mother finishes giving Lao Ping instructions and waves

him off. Her eyes snap to me lingering in the doorway. "Come in, Xiang." She gestures for the man in front of her to approach.

Lao Ping nods and turns to leave, giving me a smile. "Little rabbit, how are you finding Canton?" he asks.

"Well," I say quietly.

"Bai Li," my mother snaps, "tell your brother for the last time if he asks to sell his tea here again I will personally pour every single cup of his disgusting brew down his throat until he understands the answer always has been and always will be no."

Bai Li scampers from the room, barely giving me a second glance as he retreats into the courtyard. I step inside, glad to be invited. Perhaps this is another lesson of sorts, to observe and learn.

"There was talk in the taverns last night," Kang says. "Talk you may be interested in. A few rowdy sailors insisted they knew the location of the map to the fabled treasure of the Dragon Fleet and were drinking like they already had it."

Master Feng sits up. "That's impossible."

"A ridiculous rumor," Mother says. "Everyone knows Zheng Yi Sao died years ago." She laughs, scoffing at the idea. "A map? For a few buried trinkets? It's all just a story. You know how these things get exaggerated."

"Perhaps," Kang says. "But the revelers got a number of people riled up. Could be bad for business."

"For the salt trade?" I ask, curious. Would it mean fewer sailors for crews if they all were more interested in hunting down a legend?

Mother glances at me, her eyes narrowing. She whispers something to Kang, who nods before slipping out the door.

I try to put together some clever words, something insightful that will show Mother I'm excited to learn more about the business. But every single possible comment seems silly in light of the question I've already asked.

Mother sighs. "Yes, it's good to keep track of the rumors around town. My trade is about knowing who is willing to do what and for what price. The salt trade can hinge on many things—the sea itself, storms, officials and their tariffs, whether people are more interested in pursuing silly rumors—"

"I don't think it's just a rumor," I interject. "There was a whole tavern yesterday filled with people—multiple people—confirming Zheng Yi Sao's legendary treasure did exist and just how much wealth the Dragon Fleet amassed during their power."

Mother turns her eye toward me. "Really, now? Are you so keen to believe every story you hear, Xiang? What of your studies?"

I shrink backward. "I—" I try to remember what I've learned of the history of the South China Sea. Master Feng had me memorize a list of names of governor-generals once when I asked about current events and recent history, but he'd always said it was boring, so I didn't press.

Mother sniffs. "I'm glad to see your day in Canton was spent well, taking every drunkard at his word." She shuffles the papers on her desk, clearly done with the conversation. "Have you eaten?" she asks, not looking up.

"I—" I bite back the sigh of disappointment rising up inside me. "I just woke up."

"There's food in the kitchens. There will be no wandering today. The girls will help you get ready, and at noon a carriage will arrive to take us to the Liu estate."

"And my lessons?"

Mother waves me off. It's as much of a dismissal as anything else.

I barely taste my breakfast. I can't even enjoy the fried youtiao, an entire pile of them crisp and shining with oil, the perfect complement when dipped in the savory congee. Yunming takes me back upstairs and helps me get dressed in a practically sheer robe belted over a dudou and long skirt. The thinly woven silk feels strange against my bare shoulders, and Yunming gives me an appraising look. "Very fashionable," she says. "I rather like a corset myself; it really emphasizes my assets." She gestures at her chest and winks at me. "Want to try?"

I shake my head, blushing. The corset garment looks like an extreme version of the Ming dynasty zhuyao, except instead of only lacing up in a few places to accentuate the waist, it looks like stiff armor, laced up and tightened to an extreme.

"Yes, perhaps too bold for a first impression for potential in-laws. But you don't want to appear stodgy or old-fashioned; the Lius are new money. I hear the son is a talented artisan. Sounds like you'd have a beautiful home."

I sigh. "It's not decided yet." I wave my arms around, shifting uncomfortably at how I can see my bare arms through the fabric.

To my relief, we aren't quite done. Yunming hands me a robe with long flowing sleeves embroidered with dragonflies, which she helps fasten over the sheer one, playing with the neckline as she crosses and uncrosses both of them until she is satisfied. Her delicate hands are slim and soft, and I can't help thinking of Anh's brown skin and calloused fingers.

"There you are," Yunming says, finally satisfied. "Modesty meets allure. Now, your hair."

Finally we are done, and Yunming turns to show me my reflection in a slightly rusted plate of silver. Her work is appealing: The embroidered robe crosses at my neck, kept in place with a delicate sash, and the sheer robe underneath reveals just a hint of skin. My face has been powdered and my hair swept up into an elegant knot, secured with a matching dragonfly hairpin. I might even call myself pretty, although next to Yunming, I am but a weak candle to her fiery features and stunning dress.

I'm already tired by the time the carriage arrives, and Mother is silent the entire ride through Canton. We pass through the inner-city walls and travel along a well-kept road through the outer city, where larger homes, artisan guild-houses, and workshops are neatly arranged. The Liu estate is quiet, tucked away behind a woodworking shop that is filled with intricately carved tables, chairs, screen doors, and more. I don't know what to expect from the family who has proposed this match, and I wonder how much of it is due to Mother's business connections. There is no matchmaker, no auspicious reading of the heavens for our compatability, just Mother and I being welcomed to the Liu home. Tea is served, and Mother and the Lius talk while I observe quietly.

The estate seems well managed and comfortable, and both elder Lius greet me warmly. I feel guilty, thinking of how many girls would feel lucky at this kindness, this opportunity for safety and security. I do not begrudge them for wanting this, even as it makes my insides churn.

I try to think if this would make Mother happy, to see me settled with the Lius. Would she be proud of me? Or would she forget me as easily as she did when I was in the village? Is it her way of just taking care of another one of her tasks?

Liu Mingbao is also quiet, a boy who seems to fade into his surroundings as our parents talk over tea. We're seated opposite each other, and he glances at me once before set-tling his gaze back into his cup. We don't talk the entirety of the dinner, just silently regard each other occasionally across the table. He has a round face, and his hair has been tidily braided back into a queue, and he eagerly looks to whoever is speaking, nodding intently.

He only speaks once, when his father asks him to share what he's been working on in the shop. "I am carving a set of doors for the Shaofan family," Mingbao says proudly. "A dragon and a phoenix, very lucky for the upcoming wedding." He gives me a shy glance before adding, "I would happily carve whatever you would like to make our future home as beautiful as you wish."

"What do you enjoy carving most?" I ask politely.

"Oh, I—" Mingbao glances at his father and then back at me, flustered. "I rather like designs with carp. Their scales, the repetition of it."

I smile at him. He seems kind, and his attention to his work could be endearing. I can't help but think of the way poets describe their lovers, the swell of emotion inspired by their first meeting, the nervousness, the excitement.

I don't feel any of that.

If my heart cannot inspire any feeling, at least my mind can use logic and reason. I could find a way to be content here, I suppose. But I think about what that life would look like, and all my imaginings pale even in comparison to what I had in the village. I would not have the freedom to wander under the scrutiny of my new in-laws and my husband.

Mother sips from her cup of tea, and her stern face has an air of satisfaction to it. This is what she wants, but surely she would be prouder of a daughter who could follow in her footsteps, take charge of her business?

I cannot picture a life with Liu Mingbao. I cannot see myself talking more with him beyond this strained script, cannot see him understanding me and my hopes and dreams.

If not for myself and any foolish ideas of romantic notions, then for Mother's respect, I must refuse this offer.

Mother is silent on the ride back to the Pearl House, and the sounds of the city envelop us. "They're a good family," she says.

I murmur in agreement, but the events of the day are starting to weigh heavily on my shoulders. The hours spent with Yunming preparing for my introduction seem wasted for the time spent in the Lius' estate. Thoughts spin through my head, each imagined future with the Lius more lackluster than the next.

"Liu Shan's own work on the Pearl House is rather outstanding, and his son is an apt apprentice," Mother says. "It would be a good life. You would be in the city, in the center of it all, with your own household. You would be safe with them."

Safe? *Safe?!* I am tired of safety, tired of Mother setting me aside. All the emotions I kept locked away for my dutiful dinner with the Lius come seething to the surface.

"And I wouldn't be safe running the Pearl House?" The anger in my voice surprises me, but it's too late to take it back. I've never spoken back to Mother before. Then again, I've never spent this much time alone with her before.

I square my shoulders and take a deep breath. I have to own it.

Mother raises an eyebrow. "After you disappeared yesterday, I thought you might not return. The city has a way of swallowing people up, and I know for a fact you were not at the university reading books, as Master Feng claims you were. I have eyes and ears everywhere."

"How can I learn if you don't let me?" She cannot both promise me a choice and then show me only one option. "I agreed to see any suitors you brought me, and you would consider my aptitude for the business. You can't have seen enough to make a decision just yet." I consider my next words carefully. "All my life, you've only had the word of others to go by about my skills, my abilities. Now you have the opportunity to see for yourself and you don't take it?"

Mother blinks at me, the mask of indifference slipping. Something like genuine surprise—and for a second, I see it, the respect I want so badly—shines in her eyes before her features settle back into the hard steel I know.

She lets out a small humph that could be a laugh. "I did promise you time. And I keep my word. Very well. We'll start by going over my ledgers tonight, and see how much you can pick up from there."

I nod, too delighted to speak.

We sit in silence as the carriage rattles on, slowly winding its way through the crowded streets of Canton. I keep looking over at Mother, wanting to bask in this new thing between us, this new burgeoning feeling of being seen.

Outside the window, a man rushes by, water sloshing in the buckets he's carrying. Two more men carrying buckets follow, shouting hoarsely.

I watch from the carriage window, wondering if it's a kitchen fire that's gotten out of control. It happened occasionally at the village, people working together to bring water from the river to snuff it out. I reach for my neck to toy with my pendant out of habit before I remember it's gone. My thoughts immediately flit to Anh.

"That's a terrible habit," Mother says disapprovingly. "Fiddling nervously for your throat like that only serves to remind thieves that you have something valuable to lose." She reaches under my collar and stops suddenly when she sees I'm not wearing the pendant. "I thought you loved that thing. When did you stop wearing it?"

I'm not ready to face Mother's disappointment yet, especially so soon after I've been given another chance. I can tell her I lost the pendant much, much later. Besides, Mother always hated the way it looked; she wouldn't search for it or ask again if I never meant to bring it in the first place. "I . . . I left it in the village. In a hiding place in my room."

Mother draws her hand back and sighs, shaking her head at me. "Good. You can't be too careful. I myself never keep any of my valuables in one place. Too many thieves in this town." She glances back out the carriage window, as if to cut short the small gesture of softness and affection.

"Yes, Mother," I say quietly, tucking the moment away to remember later.

Outside, the streets seem more chaotic than usual, and a cart whips past the carriage, filled with open barrels of water. There's another man running after it, who gasps as he spots our carriage. "Madam Shi!"

Mother glances at the water bucket. "What is it, Yu?"

Water sloshes out of his bucket when he stops. Dark spots bloom on the hard-packed earth of the street, and he gasps for breath. "The Pearl House!" he says, wide-eyed and fearful. "A fire! Started on the eastern building and spread to the main dining building!"

Mother opens the carriage door, and I see flames, gold and flickering, reflected in her eyes. A few streets away, plumes of smoke spiral toward the sky.

Yu races off with his bucket, following the cart that's already disappeared around the corner. Our bulky carriage, however, is caught in a tide of people and traffic.

"Stop," Mother commands the driver. "I'll go ahead. Take the carriage to the river and retrieve more water."

"Yes, Madam Shi."

"Xiang, follow me."

The carriage comes to an abrupt halt, and the horse neighs softly as Mother steps out. Her face has hardened to a stone mask, but I can see the vein pulsing at her throat and the white of her knuckles as she grips her trousers.

I follow Mother's stride. I have to almost break into a run—how does Mother walk so fast? Smoke is billowing up from the end of the street, and then the Pearl House comes into view. Flames are licking up one side of the building, completely consuming the eastern walls.

Mother comes to a stop at the end of the street as she stares up at the teahouse. She immediately starts barking commands at the men fighting the fire and demanding answers. Yes, everyone is outside. No, we don't know how it happened. Yes, we're trying our best, madam.

I can only stare in horror as the place I've staked my future on is engulfed by thick columns of smoke and tall, leaping flames.

CHAPTER EIGHT

A Chance Up in Smoke

THE FIRE CRACKLES AS IT BATS AT THE WOOD, GLOWING bright against the stillness of the night. The mahogany creaks and groans, and then a beam from the top floor of the front building comes crashing down with a sickening crack.

A line of people passing buckets of water has started, and I rush forward to bridge a large gap between two men. Everyone is working to put out the fire, from the musicians to the kitchen staff. In the middle of the line, Yunming and the other girls are working hard, huffing as they pass the heavy buckets down the line. I even see Master Feng at the front, his brow dampened with sweat as he heaves water onto the flames.

The bucket's handle digs into my palms, and the water

soaking through my sleeves is ice cold, but I grip it tight and pass it to the next man in line and keep going, bucket after bucket.

My robes are drenched by the time the fire is put out completely. The once-proud, bright red banner that read THE PEARL HOUSE is singed and stained with soot. The eastern wall has crumbled, and the main dining room is completely wrecked. People are rushing through, putting out any remaining embers.

I stare in shock at the remains of the teahouse and inn. The buildings housing the living quarters and guest rooms have escaped the fire, but the entry building's damage is extensive. The collapsed beam has crashed through the eastern wall, exposing the main dining area to the central courtyard. It's clear that the Pearl House won't be able to take any guests or serve meals until repairs are made.

Mother is standing unnaturally still, her eyes taking in all the damage; I know from experience that Mother holds anger close to her, like a coiled snake ready to strike.

"Mother," I say cautiously. "Are you all right?"

Kang approaches Mother, her face pinched into a grim expression.

"The office?" Mother asks quietly. "Did the fire—"

Kang shakes her head. "It's fine."

"Anything missing?"

"Some petty cash that was on your desk. They went

through everything that was in the open. The thieves likely set the fire as a distraction."

Mother's face hardens. "If we had met with the Lius yesterday, I would have been here." She glances at me. "This disaster could have easily been prevented."

Suddenly, I feel small. Any progress I have made with Mother seems to shrink in an instant.

"Mother, I—"

"Xiang, go with Master Feng. I need to discuss this with Kang."

"But—" I want to stay and hear what she plans to do next. This could be an important part of my lessons.

"Come along," Master Feng says, gently taking me by the elbow. "The living quarters are safe—the fire in the first building has been extinguished. You can go back to your room now."

I follow him reluctantly, casting Mother and Kang one last look as they confer in quiet voices.

"Every local gang knows not to trifle with the Pearl House," Mother says.

"Yunming reports some navy brats were sniffing around this afternoon."

"Imperial bastards. Let's review the bribes—"

Master Feng nudges me, and I keep going up the stairs, charred with soot. The whole building reeks of smoke. He gives me a quavering smile. "Everything will be fine."

I fall into an uneasy sleep and wake to a cacophony of hammering. I step downstairs, and from the courtyard I can see people working to repair the front building. There's been progress made already—a new support beam is being fitted in place, and carpenters and builders are scattered everywhere like ants. In the courtyard, I find a makeshift stove set up over a fire and take a chipped cup of tea from Yunming. The kitchens escaped most of the damage but they shared a wall with the main dining area, so there's much work to be done.

Broken furniture is everywhere, and now that the fire has been put out, streaks of soot line the once-fine mahogany walls, and hot sunlight and the noises from the bright, busy street stream in unfiltered.

Upstairs, Mother's voice echoes through her open office door—it was ransacked as well, the sliding door off-kilter, its paper ripped. Broken shards of wood line the hallway.

I can do this. Mother promised me lessons in the trade, and I can be useful. I quickly think of what to say, how to help. I can relay messages, I can go over the ledgers with her, I can talk with suppliers . . . I just need to learn.

I steel myself outside the open door, waiting for an opportune moment.

"We're lucky those weren't stolen as well." Master Feng's voice is tinged with worry.

Papers shuffle, and the sound of heavy scrolls being rolled up echoes through the open door.

"Don't be foolish," Mother snaps. "I had these in my

quarters in a hidden compartment. You know trade routes and maps are too important to be left just lying around."

"Do you think the robbery had anything to do with—"

Mother furls the maps on her desk. "Kang has confirmation that it was one of those poorly disguised navy boys from the wharf. Could be just youngsters causing trouble. I will have a word with the port officials and demand compensation."

"Yourself? Can you not send delegates?"

"For this? Absolutely not. The fire yesterday . . . it was made to look like an accident once they realized they could not find what they were looking for."

"Did they get close?"

The ledgers, I think. Mother's business. The salt trade, the teahouses . . .

Mother laughs. "Of course not. But this insolence cannot be tolerated. My name and presence in this town is respected, and it needs to remain so."

"You know that it isn't—"

"Madam Shi is a force to be reckoned with. Everyone knows this."

Master Feng murmurs in agreement. "But this was just an accident. You said it yourself, it could just be youngsters."

"I know, I know." Mother sighs, her voice dropping.

"This isn't the old days. You don't need to be so suspicious all the time."

"Finding these charts would be useless anyway without that last piece. Damn that man to all nine hells."

"Your baobei really ruined it all," Master Feng says with derision.

I swallow down my gasp—who could they be talking about? I had long suspected Mother and Master Feng could perhaps have been lovers once; Master Feng certainly still seems to hold Mother in that regard. But the jealousy in his tone, the nickname . . . who could have been so precious to Mother once upon a time? Could they be talking about my father?

I strain to hear more and trip over a piece of shattered wooden frame. It clatters down the hallway.

"Who's there?" Mother demands from the office.

It's too late to hide, so I compose myself. "Mother?" I call out, hoping my voice is steady and calm.

"Xiang?" I hear more shuffling of scrolls and paper-work. "The kitchens unfortunately aren't quite up to producing a meal just yet, but I can have Master Feng take you to go get some breakfast if you're hungry."

"I want to help," I say. No, I will not talk to her through the door like a frightened child. I can do this. I have ideas. "May I come in?"

"Very well," she says.

I step over the broken doorway frame and into the office. Master Feng and Mother are sitting by a low table strewn with papers. A long scroll lies open, a navigational chart of the Pearl River estuary and the inner and outer seas, the edges outlined with coasts and islands. Mother places a set of scrolls atop the map and gestures for me to come closer.

The office indeed looks as if it has been ransacked; every drawer is open and all the books and scrolls are heaped onto the table or floor in a disorganized mess.

Mother gives me a small smile. "The reality of business, I'm afraid. The fire—"

"Did you catch the culprit?" I ask. "What did the city guard say?"

Mother glances at Master Feng and then back at me. "I have my suspicions. Don't you worry, my treasure. I'm sure this is overwhelming for you. I will be quite busy these next few weeks setting things back to rights. I have a ship traveling back upriver, and Master Feng will escort you home."

I want to relish in her smile, the way she calls me her treasure like she used to when I was a child, but I can't. These past few days with Mother, watching her command the attention of the crew of the *Jīn Lǐyú* and of her employees here at the Pearl House, I know she can manipulate the reaction she wants out of anyone.

But I am not one of her employees. I will not be played like an instrument.

"I want to stay here," I say, my voice loud and clear. "I know I made a mistake the other day, leaving the Pearl House without telling you, but we had an agreement. I can help you, whatever you need me to do. I can talk to your associates, relay messages, go over your ledgers with you—"

"Absolutely not. You have seen how dangerous it is here."

"I can manage this teahouse. You said yourself you would teach me—"

"And I have said this is not the right time."

"Then when? Isn't a crisis like this important for me to know how to handle? Train me to take on your legacy. Please, Mother."

Mother's eyes glint, something wild and unrestrained behind them. "Business isn't just numbers, my treasure. This fire, this attack on my property . . . it is an attack not only on my business, but on my name. How I handle this in the next few days is crucial. How will patrons feel about conducting their business here if my name is not respected? How will merchants feel about trusting me with their goods? I must make an example of the culprits, and it must stand clear in Canton that Shi Yeung and the Pearl House are not to be trifled with."

She stands up. "Business is about commanding respect. People trust me to trade their goods, to get them good prices. The Pearl House may serve rogues and gamblers and all the unsavory parts of town that officials would like to forget, but places like this are the hub of all Canton. People do business here, trade, lose their heads and their secrets. I have to keep track of merchants, ship captains, crews, who is in favor and who is not, who is welcome at which port, and all the particular capabilities of each person I work with. My legacy, my business—you think I could entrust it to you? You would barely be able to manage this tavern, let alone the whole salt trade."

"I can learn," I insist.

Mother shakes her head. "You can go home."

Frustration rises inside me, and I can feel myself shaking, my cheeks reddening with anger—no, no, I will not cry—

Big, fat tears are welling up in my eyes, and if I wipe them away now I'll lose what little ground I have gained here.

But it is too late.

"Mother—"

I can see disappointment settling into the way Mother tenses her jaw, the way she looks away from me, her eyes downcast.

"Master Feng, make sure she gets ready. I'll have the *Jīn Lǐyú* prepared and ready to head upriver by sundown."

No amount of pleading will move Master Feng.

"I thought you believed in me!" I cry out as I watch my trunk and other crates loaded onto the carriage that will take us back to the docks.

"I do believe in you," Master Feng says quietly. "But your mother's decision is final. This is not the way to sway her."

"And you think just going home will prove to her that I could run a business like this? Why not let me *try*? Why not confide in me like she confides in you and Kang? How can I ever learn if she's always keeping me at a distance?"

"She is trying to protect you. To keep you safe," Master Feng says. "I know this too well." He swallows, his throat swollen with some emotion. "I understand."

"I thought you wanted me to be happy."

"Of course I do. But your mother expects obedience from those who listen to her."

"I've been listening to her my whole life! Even when she's never been there!"

Tears are falling down my cheeks, hot and wet, and I look away, embarrassed by the outburst of emotion. *Calm.* I must be calm. How can Mother trust me to run a business if I let my emotions carry me away like this? But it feels so final as I watch Kang oversee crates being packed and Lu Fen load a carriage full of supplies in front of the Pearl House. The sun is setting, and too soon this chapter of my life will also end.

Master Feng pulls a handkerchief out of his robes and carefully wipes my tears away. "I know. You have always done your best. But this fire, the threat . . . it's a stressful time. Trust me. I know she will see you are capable. I will stay in Canton and convince her to send for you once all of this is settled." He gives me a soft smile. "I have raised you as I would my own daughter. I know you can achieve anything you set your mind to. Your mother will change her mind. Just be patient."

I nod, taking a deep, shaky breath.

Kang gives me a cursory look. "I am waiting on a ginseng delivery from one of our merchants. I'll be back for you when the *Jīn Lǐyú* is all packed and ready to go."

I exhale. There's some time. Mother won't change her mind unless I do something drastic. But what?

CHAPTER NINE

THE MAP

I'M LEFT TO WAIT ALONE. THE GINSENG MERCHANT'S SHIP-ment must have been more delayed than expected, because night has fallen and Kang has yet to return to the Pearl House. I contemplate running away, but I don't know where I would even go. I have only the clothes I'm wearing; all my things have already been packed onto the ship. I could take some food and just escape into the city, but that won't prove anything.

The sounds of Canton rush in now with the open wall, and while I thought it would be quieter without the guests, it's somehow louder—I can hear the neighing of horses, the clack of carriages and rickshaws and constant footsteps and conversations from the street.

My hand clutches to my neck, to fiddle with my pendant

out of habit, but its absence only churns my anxiety into a writhing froth. With no instruction except to wait to depart, I have nothing to do but spin in my own thoughts. I sigh, staring at the ceiling of my bedroom.

I still haven't told anyone I lost my pendant. I can only imagine Mother's disappointment—it would not help my cause to prove myself capable at all. My first day alone in the city, and I managed to lose a precious family heirloom.

I pick up a lantern and step outside to the walkway overlooking the interior courtyard. Moonlight reflects upon the small pond, and the trees and paths are silent. Before the fire, the courtyard was full of rustling; people walking the paths, finding a quiet moment to themselves. Now the inn is silent, despite the constant noise outside. The lantern is almost out, feebly drawing from the dregs of the oil at the very bottom. The paper is flimsy and decorative, painted with cherry blossoms.

How easy I thought this would all be, to learn all the unwritten rules and intricate dances one must do to survive in this place. I could barely make sense of what was next for Mother, but it was clear there *was* a plan—people to be punished, walls to be rebuilt, business to be conducted.

I listen to the street, trying to find rhythm in the movement. I was the one who wanted to come here, and I need to prove I can stay. That this can be a place for me.

Something scuttles above me—footsteps on the rooftop. I look up to see a shadow lingering by one of the parapets.

"Who's there?" I call out in alarm. Could it be the thieves who set the fire? I grip the lantern tighter, and I feel the wooden handle snap under my fingers. But I don't move, don't give the stranger any cause to believe that I'm afraid.

A figure gracefully drops from the rooftop onto the balcony and stands up.

Anh grins at me. "Hello, Xiang."

I take a step back. "What are you doing here?"

"I wanted to see you," she says, her smile soft.

"You stole my pendant," I snap. My face is hot with what I want to believe is indignant anger, but there's something else, something warm and happy, blooming inside me. My heartbeat is betraying me with its thudding at the notion that *Anh came back to see me*. I tamp down the thought quickly, focusing on the facts: Anh is a thief who pretended to be my friend, and at an opportune moment made off with my only memento of my father.

I am *not* happy to see her again.

And yet, the way Anh deftly steps forward, her coarse hair gleaming slightly in the moonlight, the warm mischief dancing in her eyes . . .

I raise the lantern as if I'm holding a weapon, my hand shaking.

Anh throws her hands up, almost laughing. "I'm a thief. It's what I do. I told you not to trust anyone. That includes me."

"You should leave. One shout and everyone will come running." I take another step back, putting space between us.

Anh smiles. "Is that any way to treat a friend? I thought you and I had something there, hm?"

"I thought so, too. Until you stole my pendant. You didn't want to spend time with me at all, did you?" It still stings, wondering if any of what Anh had said was real.

"Habit," Anh says with a shrug. "For what it's worth, I did enjoy spending time with you. Like I said. I look out for opportunity and myself. Time spent with you was a distraction; I was having fun and taking time off, and when I saw you had something of value, I took it." She smiles back at me now. "I apologize. Here. I wish to return this to you."

The pendant glitters from her hand, swinging from the slight gold chain.

I stare at her, expecting some sort of trick.

Anh doesn't move, just steadily returns my gaze. After a long moment, she sighs. She sets it down on the walkway's wooden railing, taking a few steps away to stare down into the courtyard. "I understand. You don't trust me. I wouldn't trust me, either. I'm not going to hurt you. I'm just giving it back. Because like you said . . . we're friends."

I take the pendant, my fingers closing around the metal still warm from Anh's hand. Its familiar weight is a comfort, as are the clumsy characters etched on one side: *Forever loved.* I take a deep breath and close my eyes for a brief moment. "Thank you."

I *was* right. I *am* a good judge of character, I *can* make friends in the city, I *can* live this life here.

I *can* convince Mother to let me stay.

I put the pendant on, unclasping the chain and placing it back on my neck.

"It's a beautiful piece," Anh says. "Very unique. Tell me again how you came by such a thing?"

"It was my father's," I reply. "He was a merchant in the salt trade."

"Was he now," Anh says, sitting on the edge of the rail and swinging her legs over the side. "Did he ever tell you stories of his time at sea?"

I shake my head. "He died when my mother was with child. She's run the business on her own since then."

Anh nods, her eyes taking it all in; I see her examining the courtyard, the foundations of the inn. Even with the Pearl House's main building in ruins, it still feels impressive. "And your family has done quite well in the salt trade. Well enough to run the Pearl House and keep you hidden upriver . . ."

I stiffen, suddenly uncomfortable. "Mother always said the village was the kind of life Father wanted for me."

Anh hums, drawing out the sound thoughtfully. "In a quiet village with no name, far upriver from anyone who might know what he's kept tucked safely away."

"What do you mean?" I've stepped closer to Anh without realizing it, drawn in by her words.

"What was your father's name?" she asks, not answering my question.

"I don't know. He grew up in my village, but I think we were the first of the Shi name there."

"And was he always a merchant?"

"No one—no one speaks of him. It's a somber topic, and I don't ask, not anymore."

"I believe your father left you something far more than just a token to remember him by," Anh says.

I take the pendant in my fingers, tracing the edges of the golden piece, the shoddy workmanship. It is as it always has been—a plain piece of metal with a clumsy engraving. I'd always thought of it as unbearably intimate, the words etched there, wondering if it was intended for my mother or for me. I let go and it drops back against my chest, but I don't tuck it under my robe.

"Here." Anh's fingers graze my collarbone as she lifts the pendant up. "Have you never opened it?"

"Opened it? It's just a piece of gold."

"It's a container. Look." Anh takes the clasp where the pendant hangs on the chain and presses it. I have definitely done that before; it's just a part of the poor craftsmanship of the pendant. The little metal loop for the chain makes a satisfying little click, and I've often fidgeted with it. It doesn't do anything—

Anh presses down on the clasp and turns it to the right.

"Stop, you're going to break it—"

"It's not going to break," Anh whispers, continuing to turn it. Her calloused fingers work the clasp as it spins three times. Then there's another click, and the clasp pops open entirely, releasing the bottom of the pendant from the rest.

It comes away in Anh's hand, and she holds it aloft.

I gasp as Anh places it back in my hand, and I can see it clearly: The small pendant is hollow, and tucked inside is a tightly wound piece of paper.

I tap the pendant against my palm, and the paper falls out, almost as light as a feather, barely perceptible in the fading lantern light. I unscroll it carefully, my hands trembling.

The piece of paper has a rough edge, as if torn from a book or a thick log, and it's delicate with age. I run my finger across the lines of latitude and longitude, the curve of a coastline, and the outline of several dotted islands. One of them is marked clearly with an X. On the torn edge, there's half of an illustration, a long coil and scales, like the creatures of legend inked on maps to warn of the dangers of the sea. I turn the paper over. On the other side is a strange diagram and characters inked in a small, cramped hand.

A map . . . and a strange poem.

"Do you know what this is?" Anh asks, her eyes dark.

"Obviously a poem," I say confidently, but my mind is whirling. Why would my father have hidden this in a pendant? Mother always said it was the only thing we had left of him. Was this the reason why? Did she know this had been here the whole time? "And a piece of a map," I add, tracing the undecipherable edge of an island.

"Not just any map," Anh breathes. "Do you see this symbol here? This was the flag of the Dragon Fleet."

I trace the characters with my finger and glance back at Anh, the stories racing through my head. "You said the pirates' treasure was just a legend!"

"I used to beg my mother to tell me that story over and over. It was always my favorite, the idea that all that plunder was still out there, somewhere." Anh looks away. "I stopped believing it when I got older, but this . . . this is real. This is a piece of that very map that Zheng Yi Sao must have used to hide the treasure of the entire fleet. Imagine, all those hundreds of ships reporting to her every year, a portion of that plunder tucked away for safe-keeping, never to be seen again. My mother searched everywhere for any real clues and never found any. This pendant changes everything."

Anh pats the railing next to her, and I sit down, swinging my legs over the side like her.

"Do you have anything else of your father's?" she asks. "Anything that can place where exactly this is?"

"I—I don't," I say, still struggling with the idea.

"Did he leave you anything else? Do you have any journals or books of his—"

"He was a salt merchant," I breathe, even as I stare at what's clearly a pirate treasure map. "My mother is a salt merchant."

"He must have been a high-ranking captain, or maybe even a lieutenant of an entire squadron, to have earned the trust of Zheng Yi Sao," Anh says, her eyes bright. "She was a notoriously meticulous bookkeeper, keeping track of every ship's plunder and taking her share. Zheng Yi Sao financed the entire fleet, paid them regular wages, and kept the coffers hidden so well, even her most trusted lieutenants never knew where it was all hidden. Supposedly each lieutenant carried a piece of the map until she decided none of them were trustworthy and reclaimed them all. All but one."

We both glance at the map, the X dark on the scrap of torn paper.

"But why wouldn't Mother have told me?"

Anh laughs. "What would have been the point? I can imagine the shame; of course she pretended he was a mere merchant. A good family, a good name—especially for you.

She was protecting you, don't you see? And your father's wish for you to be raised in the village—keeping the legacy safe forever."

I take a deep breath, trying to take it all in. The facts are in front of me, the piece of the map, the pendant I've carried my whole life. I'd always imagined my father as a merchant with kind eyes. Perhaps he would have been funny, a strong and steadfast man who died too early to see his only daughter enter the world.

"I mean, with a decent map any capable captain could decipher where this is," Anh continues, "and my crew—we can get to this island." She traces a length of coastline whose shape means nothing to me, but her eyes light up in recognition. "This looks exactly like the northern side of Hainan. Which means this is the Leizhou peninsula, and then it's just a matter of figuring out which of these islands—"

She seizes me by the shoulders. I almost lose my balance, but she holds me steady.

"Don't you understand? The loot of the entire Dragon Fleet has been rumored to be hidden somewhere in the South China Sea, but there are thousands and thousands of islands and inlets and coves. People have been searching for it forever with no luck, even former members of her crew. Zheng Yi Sao disappeared, but her treasure . . . For years and years, no one has ever found it. Never even gotten an inkling of it. Until now."

She grins at me, her smile wide and a little feral, and I cannot help but return the enthusiasm. "The lost treasure of Zheng Yi Sao and the Dragon Fleet," Anh breathes.

I think about Mother's worries about the reputation of the Pearl House, of upstarts and gangs and people challenging her as a trade boss, and her attention being spread so thin. Now with the fire and the swift justice she must bring to the perpetrators, she must be struggling to reinforce her image, her reputation. I imagine returning on a ship laden with wealth, Mother's eyes sparkling with pride as I give her everything she needs to rebuild the Pearl House, all the capital to ensure the success of our trade for years to come.

"Would it be possible? What would it take to find such a treasure?" I ask, my heart in my throat.

"A ship and a crew to get you there," Anh says. "I can take care of all that. In fact, I already have. All we would need is to decipher what exactly this means." She taps the poem with her fingers.

"This is why you came back," I say, my stomach falling a little.

Anh cocks her head. "Listen, I can get to this island. The captain of my ship is capable of navigating anything, and with our charts and this detail, we can find the island. But once we're there, we don't know what we will face, what traps or hidden tricks were left to guard the treasure."

Her hand is now flat on mine, palm to palm. "We could have left," she says softly. "Gone after the treasure, thrown all chances to the wind. But I say, when there's an opportunity, you take it. Can you decipher what this means or not?"

"How can I trust you? You just told me I couldn't."

Anh's smile widens. She squeezes my hand, the piece of the map a gentle rustle between our palms. "I just came back to return this to you, didn't I? To tell you the truth about what you've been wearing around your neck all these years? Don't you want to go find out what it is? To find the *more* you've always been looking for?"

She dangles my dream in front of me like she knows me. She knows me because I let her, and I was a fool.

Suspicion dawns on me—the timing, the whispers, the robbery . . . "The fire," I whisper. "Did you or your crew have anything to do with it?"

Anh lowers her eyes. "I was with some of the crew when I opened the pendant for the first time, and I realized the enormity of what I had, a piece of Zheng Yi Sao's map. Sizhui thought it was a sure thing and started bragging before I could shut him up. The tavern we were in didn't have any hardy sailors, though, only petty thieves who thought the first thing they should do was get nautical charts. Who better to find trade routes than successful merchants?" She glances down into the courtyard at the charred gap open to the dining room below.

I jerk back, taking the piece of the map as I swing back

over the ledge and firmly onto the balcony. I roll up the paper into its tight little scroll and place it back inside the pendant, turning the clasp until it clicks securely, then tuck it under my shirt.

Anh stands up, balancing on the edge of the railing as she faces me. "If you can't trust me, trust this: The treasure is worth more than anyone has ever dreamed of. I want it. And you want it. I know that to be true."

I stare up at her, standing on the edge, her coat flapping in the wind. "It is my father's map. I am the one to decode it. It is only fair I get a double share of the treasure."

"Of course."

"And you will see me safely to the island and back to Canton. I will keep the map on me at all times."

Anh nods, rolling her eyes as if it were obvious.

"I will decipher the meaning of this poem and get you to the treasure. Without me you have nothing." I stand tall, holding my ground. "My father was a cunning man, and if he sailed with the Dragon Fleet and procured this piece of the map, then he would have made it extremely difficult for anyone who didn't know him. Traps filled with poison, hidden entrances, impossible paths . . . Only someone who knows exactly where to go and what to do would be able to find this treasure." I nod at her, and the air grows heavy with intention, a promise. "This is my word."

"And you have my word, that I, Hoa Ngọc Anh, will

ensure your safety and travel to the island where Zheng Yi Sao's treasure is hidden."

We do not have cups of liquor to clink together, but as Anh bows her head at me, I can feel the sincerity of her words.

Until tonight, I had never seen my father's handwriting before, never read any of his poems. I have no idea what ciphers he could have used and what these words may mean. But if I am to sail with Anh and her crew, I will need them to think that I do.

There's no time to lose. Mother's ship taking me back upriver is leaving at dawn, apparently. Anh saw it at the docks; they were loading crates of ginseng. I will need to be gone before they finish and Kang returns to retrieve me.

I hurry to pack, until I remember all my belongings are already on Mother's ship. My mind races as Anh lingers outside my room; how will I be able to decipher the poem's true meaning to find the treasure?

If only Father had left me more than this scrap, anything of his—

Wait.

There was never anything in our home in the village, but what about here at the Pearl House, where Mother spends most of her time? Surely she must have kept some mementos, some letters . . .

The office.

"I'll need to find some things to help me decipher the map," I say.

Anh nods at me. "Lead on."

I'm lucky that all the guests have gone; the rooms are empty and quiet, and I haven't heard Mother return from her meetings just yet. But she could arrive at any moment. We have to be quick.

The office is quiet and just as cluttered as it was this morning; the breeze shifts through the broken screen door, ruffling the papers on the desk. I crouch down, shuffling through scrolls and bound books, my eyes catching on the detailed topography of the charts underneath stacks of ledgers and receipts.

"What's all this?" Anh asks.

"Trade routes for the salt vessels," I whisper.

"These are . . . very detailed maps."

"Mother is very shrewd," I say.

I don't know what I'm looking for. I creak open a trunk to find more papers, more logbooks. None of these seem like personal effects, like letters or journals. If Father had written to Mother while he was at sea . . . maybe sending the pendant with a piece of the map was his way of saying goodbye, to send off a piece of the treasure to his wife and child.

Anh brings the lantern closer, the flickering light shining inside the trunk. I move aside books and scrolls and odds and ends, but everything just looks like regular maps and ledgers and business accounts. I reach the bottom of the heavy trunk, my hands clunking against the sides, and I sigh.

"Wait, do that again," Anh says.

"What?" I knock against the bottom of the trunk.

"It's hollow. Let me see. If your mother is as shrewd as you say, I bet there's something else there."

I step to the side, and Anh crouches down next to me. She runs her fingers along the wood, tracing a knot in the grain until her hand catches on it, popping up a panel to reveal a small compartment underneath.

A stack of letters bound with red silk ribbon is sitting there, along with a few gold pieces and other coins I don't recognize.

"Do you think she knew he was a pirate?" Anh asks.

"I don't know." I take the letters, my fingers shaking as I undo the ribbon.

My heart seizes up in anticipation and longing. I've wanted for so long to know anything about him—how did he like his tea, if he would have appreciated the view from the mountain, if he too liked poetry, and now . . .

The first page catches my eye, a hand I do not recognize forming the characters with a hasty consistency. The letter is not addressed or signed, but phrases jump out at me, and the sheer intimacy of them is overwhelming. *My love, the days at sea without you are long, and I dream of your arms* . . . I read further on, skimming letter after letter.

Each page is filled with clumsy poetry about dreams and hopes. *We will grow old together and raise children who will listen to our stories, emboldened by our daring. We who have risen far above any station given to us, the gods themselves at our mercy, no emperor could stop us . . .*

I wipe the tears threatening to fall from my eyes, and I quickly roll the letters back up and bind them, stuffing them into my dudou. "Let's go. This is enough." It might not be, but I don't want to risk spending any more time here where we could be caught.

I think about how little I know my own mother, how my whole life I've been trying to live up to what she wants. Here in these letters I see a tender side of her I never knew, someone she let my father see and love, for him to express it so effusively and miss her so much when they were apart.

I turn back to the desk, picking up a brush. I find a spare bit of paper at the end of a scroll that looks to be a receipt for five pao of salt. I turn it over as I dip the brush in ink. An unsightly spot drops from the brush onto the paper, splattering in a wide, ugly blot. It shines on the paper wet and glossy, reflecting the moonlight through the window.

"There's no time to write a letter!" Anh hisses. "We have to leave! A carriage just arrived."

Footsteps. Voices.

I write quickly, fear quickening my strokes, knowing I may very well fail in this pursuit, but I know I must try.

Dear Mother,

I have found a way for you to see I am capable of more than you think. Please do not worry. I will make you proud.

CHAPTER TEN
THE *HUYỀN VŨ*

Dawn is not yet upon us, but the sky is light with anticipation, the stars a faint glimmer as I take Anh's hand. She pulls me toward the roof, and I clamber up with her. She smiles at me and I smile back, my heart racing from the warmth of her fingers in my own before I pull my hand back, self-conscious. I try to quell the fluttering in my traitorous heart; she's a thief and we have an agreement to find the treasure, nothing more.

I follow her through the city, racing across rooftops until we drop down to the street outside the market district. The city is filled with early risers at this hour—people feeding their chickens in their courtyards, wafts of steams billowing from kitchens, street hawkers piling their wares high, ready for the day.

The docks are already bustling with activity as we approach, and I duck behind Anh as I recognize Kang and Lao Ping leaning against a barrel, smoke wafting from a pipe they pass back and forth.

We slip past, ducking behind a group of sailors hauling a stack of crates toward the street. I glance once at the *Jīn Lǐyú*, and then I keep my gaze forward as the sun rises over the forest of masts and sails filling the port.

Anh's ship is as I remember, with a jumble of nets piled high at the stern. As I approach, I take it in beyond the first few details I saw. The outdated junk has clearly seen better days, but everything looks well mended and sturdy up close. I climb aboard, my soft shoes padding against the rough-hewn deck.

"Welcome to the *Huyền Vũ*," Anh says.

She stomps on the deck several times. The noise thunders throughout the ship; then she shouts, "Hey! I'm back! I brought help since Sizhui decided our wages weren't good enough anymore."

The announcement is as casual as anything, and heads turn my way. A dark-skinned man in a red head wrap approaches us, regarding me with a curious smile as he walks down the steps from the higher deck. Two women with fair complexions are wearing only zhuyao and trousers, their lithe and muscled arms bare as they stop coiling rope. One cocks her head as she steps forward, giving me a scrutinizing look. She has the kind of delicate mouth and moonlike face that poets would write about, and I'm reminded of the women I saw in the financial district the other day. As she draws near I can see a long scar racing down across her nose and right cheek and I look away quickly, not wanting to be rude.

"This is Xiang," Anh says, gesturing at me. "We're bringing her on to cook."

"Hello." My voice comes out as a croak, and I cough. "Thank you for having me." I duck my head respectfully as more people emerge from the hold. I swallow nervously as the other woman glances at me up and down, her eyebrow raised in judgment.

"My younger brother, Thanh"—Anh nods at a tall, broad-shouldered youth with her same brown skin and thick eyebrows lifting a sack of rice. He seems to have a perpetually sour face, his eyes flitting over me in scrutiny. "That's Ling Shan and Mianmian"—the woman with the scar whispering to the judgmental freckled one. "Maheer"—the first man who acknowledged me gives me a nod with a gentle smile. "Châu "—a squat brown man lingering by the bow. "Sun"—a long-haired golden-faced youth with a sunny smile. "Arthrit"—a lean man with deep brown skin leaning over the side of the ship jerks his head up at me—"and my mother, Hoa Ngọc Hạnh. But you can just call her Captain."

Captain Hoa steps forward, a tall woman with sharp eyes and rich golden brown skin, her coat billowing out behind her. It's the same rigid style I've seen the sailors on the ships with the rectangular sails wear—an overcoat that was once a deep, rich blue, faded with sun and stained and mended,

167

but brass buttons still shining brightly. Two swords hang at her hips, curved and wicked looking, and a spyglass is tucked into her belt.

She reaches out to clap me on the shoulder. "Welcome, welcome. Anh told me all about you."

Thanh slaps the bag of rice as he heaves it over his shoulder. He has Anh's deep brown eyes, but his are narrowed in distrust. "Thought we were short on upcoming work. Didn't know we'd be adding more mouths to feed. Without Sizhui the shares would have been barely enough."

Captain Hoa hushes him. "We are more than happy to have more help."

Mianmian laughs. "Are you saying my cooking isn't good enough?"

Ling Shan groans, elbowing her playfully. "Please. If I have to eat another bowl of soggy rice—"

The crew erupts in laughter and teasing, and most of them shuffle off to their respective duties.

Thanh looks me over, crossing his arms. He laughs and says something in Vietnamese, rolling his eyes.

"Some people can't help if they're pretty," Anh says, winking at me. "He said you look like a lily from some noble's well-tended pond."

He scowls. "I'm going to check the cargo."

Châu chuckles. "We teased Arthrit for weeks because he ran away from home and was wearing these delicate silk slippers that were ruined in a day."

Arthrit laughs. "Don't worry, little lily. Whatever you're running from, that's in the past now."

I can cross the breadth of the junk in a few strides, and from bow to stern the *Huyền Vũ* is about half the size of the *Jīn Lǐyú*. There's one longboat stowed on deck, a sturdy-looking vessel with its own sails and mast stowed neatly underneath it. Sun, who looks about my age, is working with Châu as they strain to flip it upright and attach it to a pulley, readying to lower it to the water.

They speak to each other in what seems to be a combination of clipped Mandarin, Cantonese, and another language I don't recognize. Over at the helm, Captain Hoa is giving Maheer instructions in Vietnamese.

"Mostly everyone knows Canto; it's the language of trade," Anh says.

"Okay," I say awkwardly.

Arthrit says something in a language I remember hearing in Canton's market, and Châu laughs, doubling over and slapping his knees. I think about Thanh's side comment and feel a little lost. I don't want people to have to translate for me the entire time I'm here.

Anh nudges me playfully with her shoulder. "Ling Shan is fluent in Mandarin, so you can practice your fancy poetry with her if you like."

On the far side of the deck, Ling Shan is honing a

long blade. She catches my eye as I watch her sharpen the sword—it could be nothing else but a weapon, too skinny to be useful as a machete or to cut wood, too long to be used for cooking.

"Right," I say, swallowing nervously. "I'm a fast learner, and I want to be able to talk to everyone. Do you think if you have time . . . you could teach me Vietnamese?"

Anh blinks at me. "Sure. Sailing is a lot of action in bursts of time, and a lot of waiting. I could teach you, if you want."

I linger behind Anh, unsure of what to do. Everyone is focused on a task—lowering the longboat, stacking crates, or coiling lines.

"I want to see it," Captain Hoa says. She jerks her head for me to follow her.

I climb down the ladder leading into the dark hold. It takes a moment for my eyes to adjust; in the center of the lower deck is an open space with hammocks pushed to the side, tied up neatly and out of the way. At the bow, supplies are stacked and tied down; every nook and cranny is filled with tools, crates, barrels, or nets. Behind the ladder, there's a stone hearth built underneath an open grate, with a long metal shaft to direct smoke and steam outward.

Captain Hoa walks past the kitchen area and down a narrow hallway, and I have to duck as we approach the back of the ship. The ceiling is lower here, and there are three doors, one of them flimsy and swinging open, hitting the latch as the boat rocks.

"Maheer's quarters," Anh says, jerking her head at the

side of the cramped hallway with two doors. She jerks her head at the open swinging door on the right. "Châu and Arthrit."

"Private bunks are earned," Captain Hoa says, following my gaze. "Here we are. Anh, watch the door. Make sure we aren't overheard."

Anh pulls open the narrow door on the other side of the hallway and gestures inside.

The captain's quarters are small but cozy. A bed runs the length of one wall, a sturdy wooden cot stacked high with comfortable-looking linens, and on the opposite wall is a desk cluttered with nautical charts. The cabin itself is barely big enough for the three of us to stand comfortably. Every inch of space is covered with color; scarves and silks and tapestries, remnants of fine things strung together to make a bright and welcoming space.

Anh stands at the open door and turns back to us. "Have you told them?" she asks, dropping her voice to a whisper.

"No, not just yet," the captain replies. "It won't do well to stir them up so far from the prize. We'll need our wits about us to keep afloat, and we'll need to resupply at Changping. We can't risk whispers and loose tongues and the chance someone else will beat us to the island. Even if we have an edge on them." The captain sighs and turns to me.

"Sizhui was the one who was with Thanh and me when I opened the pendant," Anh says. "He was the one who ran his mouth back in Canton." She glances at me. "I'll tell Thanh not to say anything to the rest of the crew."

I wonder if his immediate disapproval of me is because he knows I am not actually here to cook.

"Those rumors in Canton will quell down soon enough," Captain Hoa says. "Leaving Sizhui behind was the right call. He was a liability. The fewer people who know, the better. Going off and chasing Zheng Yi Sao's treasure is one thing, but as long as we are the only ones who know of this—" She nods at my neck.

She seems much less intimidating than Captain Leung, and here in the rainbow light of her cabin, the warm colors softening the lines on her face, I can see how the crew would look up to her and trust her. I do not know what Anh promised her before she came to find me, but I am eager to prove myself valuable here as well. I unclasp the pendant and unfurl the scroll.

"This pendant was my father's," I say. "This poem is a clue to the specifics of how to retrieve the treasure amid the dangers on the island. I will decipher its meaning once we arrive."

"Very good," Captain Hoa says. "You're part of my crew now. Officially, you're the new cook's assistant—we generally rotate, although Mianmian probably is the least terrible. Have her show you the supplies and walk you through what we have. Once we get out on the open sea, we'll start setting nets and traps for fish to sell in Changping. I pay you when we get paid, but everyone gets an equal share. Work hard, keep to your tasks. We'll clear out the hold once we're in town and then head to Hạ Long Bay toward the island.

But until then, this is a regular fishing route. No one needs to know our true purpose and lose their head."

"Do you think anyone else is after the treasure?" I wonder aloud.

Anh laughs. "I'm sure everyone in that tavern went looking for a map the first chance they got. But there are tens of thousands of islands in that bay. Without the accurate location, they'll be lost for sure."

On deck, no one pays me any mind as I watch them curiously. Anh dashes to the upper deck as deftly as she had the rooftops, her bare feet hardly making a sound on the deck as she scurries to the helm. "Watch your head!" she calls out as she unties a line and tosses it at Sun.

All the sails operate on an elaborate pulley system, and each crew member seems to know exactly where to go and what to do as we leave the docks. I watch, fascinated, as Sun and Arthrit lower the longboat down to the water's edge. Now with it bobbing gently beside us, its mast raised, it no longer seems so small. It looks as seaworthy as the *Huyền Vũ*, especially as Mianmian and Maheer are currently pulling a line taut to set the longboat's main sail.

"Have you ever sailed before?" Captain Hoa asks me.

"I wasn't really allowed to spend much time on deck when I traveled to Canton," I say.

"As long as you're not underfoot, you're welcome to go anywhere on the ship aside from the private quarters. Ask any questions you have; you might learn something." She grins at me and tosses me a scrap of fabric. It's stained but clean, a large square of linen that has a faded bit of dragonfly embroidery. Captain Hoa gestures at her own head wrap. "First lesson—the sun is harsher out here. Better to cover your neck than to smart from a burn later."

I clumsily try to tie the fabric around my head, but I can't quite get it right. I struggle, tying and untying it several times and folding it into a shape where I can mimic the style that Ling Shan and a few of the others are wearing, but the fabric isn't cooperating with me.

I huff, glancing out at the sea. I'm reminded of my attempts at embroidery, particularly when I would get upset when the threads would tangle or the stitching wasn't coming out right and I'd have to set the entire project down and come back to it later.

Across the deck, I notice Anh watching me with an unreadable expression. Her eyes meet mine. My traitorous heart beats a bit faster. I shouldn't feel this way about her. She lied to me, and the connection we had shared that day was just—it was just me, imagining something that wasn't possible.

But she acknowledged it, my heart says.

Anh's voice lingers in my head. *"We had something, hm?"*

I think of it now as she walks over to me, some kind of hesitation slowing her step. Or maybe that's what I want to believe, that she feels guilty for leading me on when she meant to steal from me all along.

But it was just an opportunity she took, my heart reasons again. *She apologized. She returned your pendant. She brought you here because she believes you can do this.*

"Here, let me help." Anh brushes back my hair where it was gathered in a long plait, tucking it up and underneath the fabric. She winds it around my head, leaving it loose around my neck. She ties the wrap and neatly tucks the remaining fabric in so it won't get in the way. Her fingers graze my cheek, warm and light, almost lingering. "There you go."

Part of me wants to lean into the touch, to want more of this, and part of me still hasn't forgiven her for making me think she cared about me.

"Thank you."

My tone must have revealed some of what I was thinking, because Anh regards me for a long moment. "We don't need to be friends," she says. "If you don't want to be. But I meant what I said, all of it. Spending time together. I like you, Shi Xiang. And if we're going to do this, find an impossible treasure together . . . it will be easier if we get along. I don't want—" She sighs. "I mean, you are likely being far kinder than I would have been in your shoes. But I wanted to say that I understand."

"I like you, too," I say. "I just—"

Anh takes a deep breath. "Look, I'm sorry. I had a nice time with you, and if I had been anyone else—someone who could come back to the Pearl House and visit you and spend time with you again—I would. But I couldn't promise anything, and I would never see you again, and the *Huyền Vũ* needed repairs, and there's no guarantee we would catch enough fish before the next port, and I just . . . the gold piece would have been enough to keep us going a bit longer."

I nod. I don't understand completely, but I do know what it's like to go hungry. There had been one long winter where Mother did not come back to the village for four months, and no messenger, no word, nothing. There had been constant storms, and the river had flooded three times. Harvest was bad that year, and Lan Nai Nai struggled to make our stores last. There were a few days it was nothing but tea and plain rice, and when the rice ran out it had been rough.

A long moment of understanding passes between us. It's not the same as before—the easy camaraderie, the excitement of a new connection—but it feels nice. Solid. Like laying the foundation for a new friendship.

I cough delicately. "So . . . what should I . . . what should I do? Captain Hoa said I should learn something."

"Hm," Anh considers. "Navigating out of the docks is rather tricky with all this traffic, but once we're out to open sea I can show you a thing or two. Right now everyone needs to concentrate, but you're welcome to watch."

Right. Stay out from underfoot.

So I watch.

The crew labors away, everyone at their designated job. Thanh and Ling Shan work the longboat, towing us slowly out of the harbor, and then all the sails are raised as we make our way toward the sea. Dawn is truly on its way now, and as we leave Canton behind us, the river mouth widens.

And then the open ocean beckons.

I lean over the edge of the ship and close my eyes, inhaling deep. Salt air fills my lungs, and the wind cuts at my cheeks, and every part of me seems to sing with sheer joy. The stars are disappearing from sight, a few of them still twinkling weakly as light starts to fill the heavens. A sliver of moon is still barely visible. Pink is streaking across the sky, the waves softly returning the color as a sliver of orange gold peeks over the horizon.

In the village, by the time the sun crests the mountaintops it already seems so distant, hard at work. Here the sun is fiery and blazing headstrong and full as it greets the new day, unencumbered by anything in its path.

I reach out my hand, and I feel I can almost touch the sun as the ship speeds toward the new day—the swift wind, the great expanse of water ahead, and the great unknown rushing up to meet us.

"The best view is from over here," Anh whispers next to my ear.

She laughs as she quickly darts up the stairs to the upper deck. I follow, stepping carefully in my bare feet. I have only the cotton slippers I had left in, and I wish I hadn't packed the sturdier shoes away. I'm feeling overdressed in my robe, already sweating through my dudou, and my trousers feel rough and heavy.

Anh's eyes twinkle with laughter as she throws herself over the side of the ship, catching herself by the railing just before she falls to the sea. She's wearing a garment like the dudou, tied at the neck and the waist, her shoulders and back bare. I swallow as I watch her gleaming muscles ripple as she hoists herself onto the rail, and anchors herself by hooking one of her legs around the wooden railing. "Come on, sit up here. Face right into the wind."

I take a deep breath and hoist myself up, perching onto the swaying rail. *It's just like climbing a tree*, I tell myself— although no tree has ever moved so precariously underneath me like this. The combination of the moving ship and the waves and the motion of climbing up onto the rail is all very disorienting, and I am already starting to feel dizzy.

"If you keep an eye on the horizon it will help," Anh says.

I gulp and nod, seeking out the steady line where sea touches sky. I breathe in Anh's warm laughter and think of where I am, high above the ocean, the rough feel of the wooden rail firm under my palms.

Anh grins. "All right, over here." She lets go of the rail and darts ahead onto the bow of the ship, toward the farthest edge.

"Where are you going? Are you mad?" I shout into the wind.

"Come on! Do you want the best view or not? What happened to seeing *more?*"

I snort, hearing my words being thrown back at me, and I step down from the rail, ready to take on the challenge.

Anh holds her hand open to me, and I take it. She grins and pulls me toward her, and I step gingerly, one foot at a time. Behind us, I can hear red sails billow out as they catch the wind and send the ship forward. The sudden change in movement takes me by surprise, and I lose my balance, my feet slipping.

Anh catches me neatly by the waist and holds me steady. My heart pounds erratically, and I hardly dare to breathe. "Thank you," I say, trying to laugh lightly. My treacherous nerves are crackling away, my skin warm under my shirt where Anh is touching me. My heart is already forgetting that there is no future in this friendship, that Anh only sees me as a way to the treasure. That this is merely a business agreement.

I dare not dwell on it and think of what this yearning means. I don't want to think about what I thought I wanted on that street in Canton, how I'm thinking about it now, even after she betrayed me.

She came back, my heart says. *She wanted to see you.*

She wanted the information about the map, my logical head replies.

Anh doesn't seem to notice my inner turmoil as she reaches out to take my hand. "Steady now," she says. My blood is racing, hot and quick, a rapid pulse beating all the way to my fingertips.

"Have you ever seen anything so beautiful?" Anh asks, her eyes sparkling as she takes in the view. "Look. Behind us." She gestures toward the land, where Macao sparkles distantly.

Anh's hair flutters loose around her shoulders, whipping carefree in the wind. She takes a deep breath, closing her eyes, a soft smile flickering on the corners of her mouth, and she looks so much at peace standing here at the top of this boat.

My heart feels light and buoyant, watching her. "Yes," I say in a soft whisper.

I tremble with a fear that doesn't come from our precarious position on the bow, the wind buffeting us with nothing but a mere handhold keeping us from being tossed into the ocean. The waves are getting rougher now as we approach the unprotected sea.

Thanh's voice from the deck snaps me back to reality. "Đụ!" he shouts, tripping over his feet and waving at us, another string of angry words following the gesture. "Help me! What are you even doing over there?"

"Đéo biết!" Anh calls back at him. "Come on, let's go help raise the sails." She nimbly darts back over to the rail and jerks her head at me to follow.

Not trusting myself not to fall, I shimmy forward on hands and knees, holding on for dear life as I make my way back to the rail. I climb over it slowly, exhaling with relief as my feet meet the solid surface of the deck again.

Thanh shakes his head at me, scoffing.

Anh is already on one side of the pulley of the main sail, waving at me. "We're going to take this sail and pull it up," she says. "Are you ready?" She deftly hands the end of the line to me. "We pull this up, and then we'll tie the line here." Anh pulls, yanking hard on the line and taking in the slack.

I follow suit and attempt to copy her movements, but my arms start aching from the weight only a few moments after we begin. I grit my teeth and keep going, but I can barely pull for a minute before I have to rest, and it's so heavy it's already sliding back down.

"Go arm over arm, make a rhythm," Anh suggests, tying off her end already.

"What's the holdup?" Châu calls. "We're losing the wind, here!"

"Shut up, she's learning! You think you moved fast when you first signed on with us?" Anh snaps back.

I try again, going for shorter bursts before switching arms. I pull and pull, straining with all my strength.

"If you do it like that you're going to get tired quickly. Here, hold your whole body steady. Your back, your hips. Everything working together. Follow the rhythm of your breath. I've got you." Anh is a warm presence behind me, holding me steady with one arm as another joins mine on the rope. "Don't worry, you won't fall."

As I pull, she reaches over and jumps up, pulling on the line in front of me, taking in the slack. We work in a rhythm as she pulls it in, reducing the friction enough so I can get a good heave in. Across from us, Mianmian and Sun are working in tandem on the other sail, using the same method but going twice as fast as we are.

Sweat drips from my brow with the effort, and finally the sail is fully raised.

"All right, tie it off like this," Anh says, showing me a knot that I immediately forget.

I exhale in a gasp. "You do this every day?"

Anh laughs. "Multiple times."

I can feel my arms singing with exhaustion.

"Don't worry, it just takes practice," Anh says, laughing.

I rub at my arms. "If you say so."

She wipes sweat from her brow and turns around to shout something at Thanh, a challenging taunt that makes me wonder if she's telling him how well I did. Her bare back glistens in the sun, beads of sweat sliding down the curve of her spine, and her shoulders draw together as she ties off my line as well.

"Do you want one?" Anh asks, turning back to face me, stretching and yawning.

As she does, her biceps go high and round with the movement as she reaches overhead, and I can't look away.

"What?"

"A yếm," she says, picking at the ties at her neck. She unties them and untangles the long cords without even looking, letting the fabric fall to reveal her collarbones and the swell above her breasts. She reties them, her hands deftly reaching behind her neck as she ties a sturdy knot. "Mianmian has one of those old Ming dynasty–style ones, because these don't work for her."

Mianmian nods, the bun she's gathered her hair in today bouncing up and down with the movement. "Oh yes, absolutely! When I first joined the crew I tried, you know. I thought since shoulders are completely free it would be easier to do tasks, but it doesn't quite work with my—" She grabs her ample breasts, giving them a firm squeeze, and laughs. "The dudou and yếm both dig into my shoulders too much, and these are way too heavy."

Captain Hoa grunts. "Those things really only work for you small-chested folks. It's too much weight to bear."

"You can add another cloth wrap as support," Mianmian says. "My older sister used to do that all the time, but she wasn't as blessed as you."

Captain Hoa laughs. "I got this a few years ago. It's a ridiculous fashion, but I rather like it. It's good for my back." She takes off her outer robe and underneath it she's wearing a corset, a sturdier-looking one than the contraption Yunming showed me back in Canton. This one looks like armor, laced up in the front and the back. "I don't think I'm wearing it the same way the British or French women do; they like to lace these things so tight they can hardly breathe, but I like the support around the waist."

Ling Shan laughs. "Imagine wearing that with five more layers, though! Did you know those ladies also wear wire hoops under their skirts to get that shape and size?"

Mianmian shrugs. "It seems like it could be useful. No one could sneak up on you if your clothing was so large you could use it as a rowboat."

"Fashion is the worst. I am so glad I don't have to care anymore," Ling Shan says. Today she is wearing a thin robe that looks like it was once fine, embroidered with bright orange carp on a blue background. The robe is open to reveal the simple dudou-and-trousers combination she was wearing when we met.

Mianmian grabs my elbow conspiratorially and mock-whispers in my ear, loud enough for everyone to hear. "Ling Shan was a courtier in the Forbidden City," she says.

Ling Shan rolls her eyes. "It was endlessly exhausting. What power games are we going to play today? What color should I wear to express how fearful the other ladies should be of my position in court? Which suitor's gift should I adorn myself with so they each know exactly where they stand in my esteem?" She huffs. "I don't mind the undergarment without all the trappings. Robes and dresses and overrobes and sashes and waistbands, ugh. After years in the court, it's refreshing not to have your breasts strapped down every day under layers and layers of fabric. I hate it; it gets sweaty and disgusting. A corset's not so bad on its own."

Ling Shan stretches, taking off her robe. The flimsy dudou does nothing at all to disguise her figure. She's not as endowed as Captain Hoa or Mianmian, but has the slight physique of a dancer, her chest gently rising and falling as she moves. Ling Shan winks at me. "Plus, if I'm in a fight, wearing little clothing always does well as a distraction. And to remind folks that, yes, I'm a woman, and I beat you."

She punches Sun in the shoulder playfully, jostling him as he works on mending nets.

"That wasn't fair! You're the better fighter, and I—I can't help looking if you—you—" he splutters, his face a deep red in embarrassment.

Maheer laughs, a bright and joyful sound, and the rest of the crew joins in. Mianmian wipes her eyes, doubled over. I lean awkwardly against the rail as they all share this inside joke, and I wonder how long all of them have been sailing together. I think of the pervasive feeling of urgency on the *Jīn Lǐyú*, that everyone was working hard all the time, sneaking in breaks here and there. There was familiarity there, too, the way Kang and Captain Leung and the crew worked in sync with one another, but this—this feels like a family, with years and years of intimacy and affection and teasing.

An awful lot of teasing.

"You can look," Ling Shan says, her mouth curving upward in a flirtatious smile.

"I—" Sun looks back down at the pile of nets in his lap.

Ling Shan grabs the hemline of her dudou and yanks it up and over her head. "It's so warm today. I mean, Châu's already lost his shirt."

Châu nods, wiping at the sweat on his bare chest with a scrap of fabric before tying it back around his head.

"I think I'll work the rest of the day like this," she says, putting her hands on her hips. "It's so nice out." She walks away in just her trousers, back to her line on the other end of the ship.

Maheer climbs up from the hold and looks away respectfully and doesn't say anything, just walks over to the helm to adjust the tiller.

Sun, on the other hand, has completely forgotten about his task and is staring red-faced at Ling Shan.

Mianmian slaps him on the back, and he coughs, his blush deepening before he looks away.

"Does this . . . happen often?" I venture.

Mianmian laughs. "When it's hot, yes. Which is often."

Great.

Behind me, the distant mouth of the Pearl River is growing farther and farther away. The cluster that is the port city of Macao is promptly fading, and on the other side the large peninsula is just starting to take view.

There is no turning back now.

Behind us, sails move slowly, other vessels going along their trade routes. I wonder if any of them is the *Jīn Lǐyú*, in hot pursuit. No, it couldn't be. I didn't leave any identifying information of where I would be, what ship I would be on. I wonder if Mother found the letter and whether she would search for me. Guilt automatically rises up inside me, built upon a lifetime of obedience.

I think about the treasure, of returning to Canton immeasurably wealthy. Mother will marvel at my negotiation skills, how I worked with a crew of this regard and navigated the oceans to find what was thought to be impossible. We could rebuild the Pearl House, together. I wouldn't ever need to go back to the village. And then Mother will make me heir to the business, teach me everything I need to know to manage the merchants and the trade and forget all about suitors.

The letters rustle against my waist where they're tucked safely against my belt, reminding me of the task to come. I will need to decipher exactly what was Father's meaning in that riddle . . . or at least convince this crew that I can.

CHAPTER ELEVEN

LIFE AT SEA

The South China Sea

"I NEED A KNIFE!" CHÂU CALLS OUT, HIS HANDS FULL AS HE mends a patch. One of the sails is fully lowered and spread out, practically taking over the entire deck, and I step carefully around the canvas. Sun has a section in his lap, humming to himself as he works his fingers over the material, feeling for tears and weak spots.

"Here you go!" Ling Shan calls out from the hold below us.

I saw her throw a sword yesterday at a clumsily painted target Mianmian had set up after dinner, so I step away from the open grate as quickly as I can.

Captain Hoa looks up from the helm. "Don't—"

A knife sails directly up at Châu through the open grate, and he catches it with one hand.

"Thanks!" Châu says.

"Đụ má! What did I say about throwing sharp objects?!" the captain roars.

"It was sheathed!"

I linger, watching everyone work, unsure if I should look for Anh or ask Captain Hoa for a task; my only instruction so far is to not be underfoot. Mianmian said she would come find me once she was ready to show me around the kitchen, but I haven't seen her. It seems like I'm free to just watch and learn, but I have no idea where to start.

Maheer sets a bucket and a long coil of rope in front of me. "You wandering around like froth on the sea is distracting. There is always work to do—you can always ask me what needs to be done."

"I don't know how to do any of—" I gesture at where Arthrit is immersed in splicing together long strands of hemp into fine, sturdy rope.

"You'll learn," Maheer says, his gentle eyes twinkling. "One step at a time, like we all did. You can start by scrubbing the decks."

He shows me how to draw up seawater from over the side and hands me a wooden brush with long, stiff bristles. "Water. Soap. Brush. Like this." It looks so smooth and easy when he does it, but after hauling up one bucket of water, my arms are already aching and my fingers are red and angry from the rope. It takes me twice as long as Maheer did to push the heavy brush across the deck, sweeping up dirty water and the sticky remnants of fish entrails, scales, and bones.

I'm exhausted by noon, and then Sun teaches me three different knots, all of which I muddle considerably. I fumble with my little piece of practice rope, trying over and over again to get it to lie flat, but it doesn't seem right at all.

Finally Mianmian takes me to the kitchen, which is little more than a heavy stone hearth underneath an open grate in the deck. She shows me the supplies and walks me through our week's rations.

"We cook the freshest ingredients first, when we have them—we just left port, so there's plenty this week. Once we get out to sea it's rice and whatever dried meat and fish we have."

Mianmian seems satisfied as she watches me measure out rice grains from a sack, despite my insistence to her that I have been terribly incompetent at this in the past. She leaves to do another task, and it's up to me to get the fire hot enough to cook the rice. I'm unsure of what to do with the fish; I've seen Lan Nai Nai prepare fish plenty of times, but she's never trusted me to do it myself.

I stir the rice and chop the vegetables roughly, tossing them in the wok until Mianmian comes back and shows me how to gut and clean the fish. "There's only one wok and one pot, so no need to get fancy, as long as everyone gets fed. Here, you can steam it on top of the vegetables." She nods in approval as I heave the whole fish into the wok and ladle soy sauce and freshly chopped scallions atop it, adding fresh water before I place the lid on.

"Dinner's ready!" she calls out before I'm done.

"I—"

Mianmian grins at me and hands me a ladle as everyone shuffles around, getting ready for the meal. Above deck, Ling Shan and Sun produce a number of small tables that were folded and stacked neatly away and start setting them up as Arthrit and Châu bring up crates and barrels from the lower deck to be used as chairs. Maheer passes out bowls and chopsticks from a communal cupboard, and then everyone lines up as I dole out bowl after bowl of vegetables and fish over rice.

Anh meets my eyes as she holds out her bowl, and she smiles at me. "Nice job, merchant girl."

"It's delicious!" Châu roars in approval from his perch atop a barrel.

"This looks good," Captain Hoa says as she approaches.

"I saved a piece of fish for you." I ladle her the piece I set aside, a slice of the fish's belly, soft and tender with fat. I'd waited to serve this, watching carefully as I portioned out the stew. This is the best part of the fish, and I hope she appreciates the gesture.

"Oh," Captain Hoa says in surprise. "We're all equal here. No one gets better shares than anyone else." She takes her bowl and slides the meat back into the pot, breaking it up with the ladle. "I appreciate the thought, but as cook you should remember that."

I nod quickly, immediately ashamed for my mistake.

"It's not a reprimand," the captain says gently. "Just a reminder. You're doing well." She glances back at the crew, lost in their conversations and food.

"Thank you," I murmur softly, unused to praise.

"Have you eaten yet?"

I shake my head.

The captain ladles me a portion. "Go ahead."

I follow her up above deck. Under the flickering lanterns and the night sky, it seems like the rest of the world has disappeared and there's only the ten of us sprawled around a mismatched set of tables and chairs eating together.

I take the piping hot bowl to the hastily constructed table, a bare plank set atop barrels. There's a seat between Anh and Sun, but not quite enough room, and the rest of the crew is seated already. I could take the bowl back below deck, I suppose, or eat it standing—

"Xiang! What are you waiting for? Come sit here," Anh says, scooting over.

I sit down between them and begin to eat, carefully at first.

"The fermented bean paste on the fish is tasty," Captain Hoa says. "Just remember we have fresh vegetables as well. Let's use all of those first before we use the condiments that will keep."

"Oh," I say, regretting that last step. I had thought it would impress them, preparing a tasty first meal. "Of course . . . I'm sorry, I'll be sure to remember."

"No, this is fine. You did very well today."

192

She gives me a warm smile, and I nearly want to bounce out of my seat at the approval. Lan Nai Nai had always been sparse in her compliments, always rushing me out of the kitchens and begrudgingly accepting my help, knowing that I would knock over sauces and it would be more trouble than it was worth. It made her job harder, teaching me to cook.

This meal is one of the simplest ones I've ever had, but Maheer claps me on the back, telling everyone what a good job I did on the decks. As we finish eating, there isn't a rush to clean up or put away dishes and get back to work, but instead everyone lingers, sharing more stories, passing around a gourd of rice wine.

Anh teases Thanh about his sunburn, poking at his shoulder while he bats her fingers away and accuses her of stealing his hat. Then Sun asks to look at my practice knots and everyone laughs as they behold my clumsy handiwork. Ling Shan helps Mianmian comb her hair, and Arthrit lays his head on Châu's shoulder. Sun offers a roughly carved wooden flute to Châu with a hopeful expression until he laughs and takes it, playing a cheerful melody.

Music drifts around us as the ship sways in the waves, lanterns shaking and flickering. A rough wind is beginning to blow, but here in this company I feel good. I feel safe.

CHAPTER TWELVE

New Skills

THE DAYS ARE FILLED WITH WORK: BOILING WATER, CHOP-ping and peeling vegetables and cooking in the kitchen with Mianmian; and an endless amount of cleaning the deck, the hold, and the cabins, sweeping and mopping. I learn how to mend sails and splice rope to repair nets, how to tell when best to haul up a fishing net.

I wake early every morning to boil a huge pot of hot con-gee. Dinner is the only meal we tend to all eat together up on the deck; during the day everyone is on different shifts and taking their meals when they can. I can barely remem-ber the way I would eat breakfast at home, quietly eating the congee plain or with a slight sprinkle of spring onions or soy sauce. Here we fry up mounds of glistening youtiao to go with it, and the crew laughs as they break off pieces to dip in their bowls, dunking it clumsily and bringing it to their mouths, speaking as they go. Lan Nai Nai would be horrified at their manners—as I was at first—but now I eat just as gustily, spooning another mouthful without reservation or bothering to wipe my mouth.

Today's morning is gray. Maheer is on the upper deck praying, as I've noticed him do a few times every day. I take the moment to myself on the other side of the ship, watching the waves and enjoying the calmness of the ocean. In the distance I see the edge of the coastline. It's a rare moment I have to myself, when I don't see a task that immediately needs help doing, and I linger on the rail, wondering what Mother would think of me now.

Maheer rolls up his prayer rug and joins me at the rail. "There's nothing quite like it, is there," he says.

The ocean is a constant, the waves drifting and never ending. There's a peace here, and also endless possibility, the way the waters connect all the lands of the world. I sigh happily in agreement.

"This suits you," Maheer comments. "You remind me of myself the first time I sailed. I thought I had been missing something all my life."

I can't count how many times I read the accounts of Zheng He's expeditions around the world, looked at the maps in the *Wubei Zhi* and thought about the ocean. He had traveled the far west, had been the first to reach kingdoms in Africa, India, Arabia, and even farther on his voyages during the Ming dynasty. After I return to Canton with the treasure, surely Mother will be so impressed with my new-found seafaring skills. Perhaps one day I could captain my own ship.

"I don't know if I could miss something I couldn't fathom," I say, my eyes on the sea. "I knew the ocean existed, but when all your life has been rivers and mountains, this—*this*—" I gesture at the broad expanse and turn around toward the other side of the ship, where the horizon extends to infinite possibilities.

"You are lucky to have found this so early in your life," Maheer says with a smile. "Nepal was all mountains. The great Himalaya range is enough to keep you humble, to see those impossibly tall peaks reaching up toward the heavens every day." His eyes sparkle as he describes the rugged summit, still covered in ice even in the height of summer, the lush valleys in Kathmandu, and the feeling of the crisp mountain air. "Beautiful, yes, but I think I was meant for the sea."

"How long have you been sailing with Captain Hoa?"

Maheer laughs. "Longer than the years you've been on this earth, child."

"Did it take you long to learn how to—" I gesture at the helm, the bow of the ship, everything. With everyone else, there isn't a clear hierarchy on the crew, as everyone seems to be capable of doing any task. Maheer is often the one steering the *Huyền Vũ*, or by Captain Hoa's side as she describes our next step.

Maheer strokes his beard. "I forget when I officially became quartermaster, but, yes, learning all these skills takes time."

I huff.

"Come, I'll show you."

"Show me what?"

"How to steer," he says calmly. "Captain! Go take a break."

Captain Hoa yawns and gives him a jaunty jerk of her head. She claps me on the shoulder as she leaves the helm and goes below deck.

Maheer places his hands on the tiller and gestures for me to watch. "This controls the rudder and the direction the ship will move. An easy way to remember is to point the tiller toward trouble—where you point it is the opposite of where we will go."

"Tiller toward trouble," I repeat.

Maheer moves the great wooden mechanism just the slightest, more toward the coastline, and I can feel the ship almost imperceptively start to turn.

"Good job," he says. "Now keep your hands on this. Right now with a calm wind and steady waters, it'll be easy to move. During rough weather, you'll need a firmer hand, and sometimes, another member of the crew as well."

We add steering lessons to my usual duties, and soon my days are full.

I learn enough Vietnamese to understand basic commands, but mostly to curse when we play cards during the off time. Châu is a patient teacher, helping me understand the minute differences in tone for words.

"Đẹp quá," I repeat, feeling out the tones. We're practicing greetings right now, and I feel confident about my accent.

"There you go," he says. "Oh, here's Anh now. Go on."

I wave at her. "Đẹp quá!"

Anh turns bright red, a rosy flush blooming on her golden brown skin. "Châu!" she curses, shoving him over as he topples to the deck laughing.

"What? What did I say? Was it something awful?" I blink as Ling Shan and Mianmian look up from their tasks.

"Oh no, you just called her beautiful," Mianmian says, patting me gently.

Anh makes a rude gesture at Châu and huffs away, ducking out of sight behind a sail.

The laughter is steady on the *Huyền Vũ*, and everyone is teased constantly. It surprises me how quickly it feels natural, to join in on the jokes and the fun, and the first time I call Sun a spoiled brat Ling Shan roars in laughter, clapping me on the back.

The crew flow and ebb together, laughter filling the air as they trade stories. Over time I glean bits and pieces of the occasional past life. Sun will happily talk about Korea and his mother's kimchi recipe, but will grow quiet if asked about anything else. He keeps a ceramic jar filled with the delicious spiced fermented cabbage, and offered it to me once during dinner, a rare honor—he only picks it up when the *Huyền Vũ*'s route takes them north.

Châu was born in a small village just outside Thăng Long, the imperial capital of Việt Nam, right at the height of the Tây Sơn Rebellion.

"I don't know much about the Huệ Emperor's rule except that it was brief," I admit. The Tây Sơn Rebellion was over and done with before I was born, an interlude in the Nguyễn dynasty that barely made a footnote in my study of our neighboring kingdom's recent history.

Châu shakes his head. "My parents would tell me stories about how Emperor Lê Chiêu Thống would host extravagant parties, dine in luxury while his people starved. The noble lords, the Trịnh and Nguyễn families, were constantly fighting for power, back and forth."

"It is the way it is," Captain Hoa says.

"We worked the land but did not own it," Châu says bitterly. "And when the Tây Sơn brothers rose up against the Nguyễn lords, my father went to war for them, for the chance for a better Việt Nam. But there was never peace. My . . . my village was burned to the ground." A quiet sorrow fills his eyes, and Arthrit lays a gentle hand on Châu's shoulder.

I think about all the people who aren't mentioned in the history texts. Master Feng tended to gloss over anything in the past hundred years; I wonder if this history is too close for comfort, the impact of it continuing to last for generations to come.

"If it makes you feel any better," Ling Shan says, "when I left the Qing court I took as many jewels and silks as I could pack into my worthless husband's carriage."

Châu laughs, the mood lightening as he asks Ling Shan to describe the fanciful fluttering of the imperial court.

Mianmian sighs dramatically as she looks up from her mending. "You know, I don't miss working in the Forbidden City. Those courtiers always had such high demands, and never seemed to appreciate just how long it took to embroider anything."

Thanh laughs. "Well, now you know many more useful skills!"

Mianmian fixes him with a stern look. "Embroidery is incredibly useful. Who do you think sewed and tanned all these sails last year when we needed new ones?" She chuckles, holding up her needle. "Everyone should be afraid of those who can embroider. We have the patience to keep stabbing the same thing over and over again."

I had not thought about embroidery that way. Every skill is valuable, I realize. Things I thought mundane suddenly are precious: Mending is used on the sails, our clothes, rucksacks. Keeping the deck scrubbed and clean is important to prevent slips and falls; being able to keep everything organized means having items where they can be found quickly.

My body grows strong as my tasks are now routine. I work, and work, and work. Every day I tell myself I will find a moment of quiet to dig out the letters and read them slowly, to decipher the meaning of the poem waiting in the pendant around my neck. But every day I put it off—there's always something else to be done, and we still have more time.

Sun shyly presented me with a trunk of my own to stash my possessions—little things that I've been slowly collecting: a linen shirt from Ling Shan, Maheer's extra head wrap, a roughly carved bowl and spoon. Father's letters are tucked away in the clothes I arrived on the ship with—the trousers and jacket embroidered with peonies—and I haven't opened them since first reading those overwhelmingly intimate lines.

I know I'm wasting time, but every day when the captain gives me a proud smile or Anh laughs as we work side by side, I almost forget I'm here for one very particular reason. But it feels good, being on the crew—I'm not just the kitchen's assistant anymore. With such a small crew, they're always short a hand somewhere, and I find myself working on deck more often than not.

My arms, which felt like soggy rice noodles on the first day, still ache, but now I can haul a full bucket of water from one end of the ship to the other with ease. When I hear "Haul away!" I jump in line with the others, helping to yank a line taut, or to release some of the slack to make a sharp turn.

I learn how to coil a rope using just the breadth of my shoulders, keeping up a steady rhythm as I move the thick coils between my arms until it is even and tight. I know to feel for inconsistencies or weakness in the woven strands, how to splice rope together, weaving under and over until I can do it with my eyes closed.

I work side by side with everyone, including the captain, as we haul nets and baskets of fish onto the deck, sorting them into barrels to sell when we get to Changping. In the hours waiting between tasks, Captain Hoa whittles whimsical shapes out of driftwood and shows me how to coax shapes of my own, one slow shave at a time. The ship moves forward, and I work hard, keeping everyone fed. Late at night under the flickering lanterns, sometimes Arthrit will sing in Thai as Châu plays on his reed flute, the long yearning tones whistling through the night.

I find new strength in the sea, in the wind in my hair, in the way the sunlight glints off the ocean waves, in the dazzling sunsets over the water. I listen to Mianmian's stories about daring heists and how she could steal sweets off a lady's plate without her noticing. I drink rice wine and learn lewd songs in different languages. I try to carry a basic conversation in Vietnamese and Thai and Korean and Arabic, even as Arthrit and Sun keep attempting to get me to say vulgar things in each other's language.

I've felt so alone my whole life, waiting to fulfill some expectation, to perform in some way.

All my life I've been waiting, and now I'm doing.

The island of Hainan looms in the distance. Up until now we have been sailing close enough to keep the coastline of China in the distance. Captain Hoa is taking us on an indirect path, avoiding the main trade routes. As we approach the pass between Hainan and the Leizhou peninsula, the world that I've been used to seeing—the endless expanse of ocean—narrows to a singular pass of water. Dark clouds lie thick on the horizon, and the storm catches up to us right as we approach the pass.

The screeching wind is merciless.

"It's not good, Captain!" Sun calls out as his hat flies away. "We're running right into the wind!"

"What do we do?" I ask in alarm. If the storm is pushing against us we surely won't be able to sail through the pass.

Captain Hoa grips the tiller and widens her stance. "I need everyone on deck, ready to tack!"

The crew snaps to attention. Sun, Arthrit, Châu, and Ling Shan take their places on the starboard side of the

Huyền Vũ, and Mianmian, Anh, and Maheer mirror them on the port side.

"Xiang! With me!" Anh says.

I join her at her line. Every sail on each side has a team of two now.

"Ready about!" Captain Hoa roars.

I take the end of the line Anh hands me. "How are we——"

"Lee ho!"

I duck just in time as the boom sweeps across the deck; all the sails shift as the *Huyền Vũ* turns suddenly. The deck tilts dangerously enough for me to lose my balance. Everyone else has widened their stance, taking the change in stride. I right myself, watching as Mianmian and Maheer pull their line, taking in all the slack.

Anh jumps and sweats the line, dangling the end at me and I jump to it, pulling with all my worth.

On the other side of the ship, the other team is releasing the mainsheet, and we work together to bring the *Huyền Vũ* about.

"Steady," Captain Hoa says.

We do it again, and again, over and over into the wind, the ship moving forward precariously slow, turning back and forth as we sail at an angle, making precious progress over the next hour.

The storm lets loose as we are halfway through the pass, a torrent of rain emptying down on us from the heavens. The wind is relentless and cutting, and my clothes are plastered to my body. As the sky darkens it's difficult to see where we are on the roiling waves. I can hear the crew shouting beside me as we keep to the rhythm and Captain Hoa's encouragement.

We are almost through.

The pass widens as we approach the end of Hainan island, and Captain Hoa pushes the tiller. "One last stretch!" she calls. "Maheer!"

Maheer passes off his line and rushes to her side, joining her at the tiller as he adds his strength.

The force of the storm seems insurmountable.

"To port!" Maheer calls.

Anh races to the port side rail and I follow as the ship keels over, riding the last stretch at an impossible angle, so severe that the *Huyền Vũ* seems about to capsize entirely. Water crashes up over the lower edge of the ship, and anything unsecured on deck slides perilously downward.

Ling Shan grabs Sun right before he topples over the edge of the rail and hauls him back onto the deck. It's all chaos and wind and rain, and out of the corner of my eye I see Captain Hoa and Maheer struggling to keep the tiller steady.

"I need one more!" Captain Hoa shouts.

"We can't move, we're all that's keeping us from going under!" Mianmian cries.

"Hold on!" Anh calls as we struggle.

Below us, I see Captain Hoa and Maheer slide down toward the starboard side. Captain Hoa is hanging on to the tiller with one hand and holding on to Maheer with the other, outstretched as she strains to keep him from sliding into the ocean.

If we don't turn again we're all going to be lost to the sea.

I make a quick, impulsive decision.

I let go.

"*Xiang!*" Anh shouts.

I slide down the deck toward the tiller and crash into it with the full force of my body. I grab the steering mechanism and pull with all my strength.

Maheer shouts something incomprehensible, but he's nodding and I keep going.

Captain Hoa roars as she grips onto Maheer tightly and swings her arm, lending him momentum to reach back up and grab the tiller with me.

Together we turn it just enough for the ship to right itself.

Captain Hoa takes the tiller, and Maheer and I push together to heave it against the force of the storm.

"That's it," Captain Hoa says. "Almost got it!"

A whoop of celebration sounds all around the deck; the crew is soaked and exhausted, but we're all alive.

And we've made it through the pass.

Maheer picks me up and spins me about joyfully, and then I'm enveloped in warmth and praise. Captain Hoa claps me on the back, Châu ruffles my hair, and Anh beams at me, her eyes sparkling with pride.

"Nice work, little lily," Thanh says, giving me a reluctant nod.

I can't tell if the salt on my face is from the sea or exhausted, happy tears of relief. We are all weary, but the embrace seems to go on forever, and I am surrounded by the warmth of my crew as the storm rages on.

CHAPTER THIRTEEN

CHANGPING

On the other side of the pass, as we approach the tested waters and coastline that is not quite one kingdom or another, we start preparing our cargo for Changping. Fishing on the *Huyền Vũ* is an elaborate operation. I have never seen it done on such a scale as this.

"How often do you do this?" I ask in wonder the first time they set up the big nets.

"The *Huyền Vũ* is both a fishing and a merchant vessel, whichever works to our favor," Maheer says. "We unloaded all our last cargo in Canton, and didn't pick up any new shipments or contracts, so a fresh catch for Changping it is."

"Why do trade at all?" I wonder. "Wouldn't you make more money on just the bounty of the ocean alone?"

Maheer nods at me. "You might think so, but a fortune

in fishing depends on the whims of many; if current is in our favor, and if we're on our way to port to unload. We do more so in the rainy season; in the hot season it can take too long to get there, and then the whole boat stinks of fish."

I nod, but I'm not entirely sure. The hold's storage is massive, and there are all sorts of nooks and crannies built into the ship's hull to store even more items. Maheer's initial explanation for the freshness of the cargo makes sense, but they could easily salt, smoke, or dry a catch to preserve it for longer trips.

Today's haul is filled with shiny fish, flopping on deck as we wrestle them into barrels. I'm about to toss a slippery eel back into the ocean when Châu grabs it from me with a delighted grin. "These are delicious. Let's have this tonight."

"Just one, Châu! Don't keep too many," Captain Hoa warns.

"You always overcook it," Mianmian sniffs.

"We're docking in Changping tomorrow; every bit of storage space is precious," the captain says. "Don't catch anything we're not going to sell. And remember, tomorrow everyone is on their own for meals, and I mean it when I say that the ship is leaving at dawn."

The energy on deck is palpable, and even Anh is grinning wide, tolerating Thanh's rambling about spicy prawns and Sun combing and recombing his hair several times.

"What kind of city is Changping?" I ask.

Voices burst out all at once.

"It's where I lost this finger," Ling Shan says fondly.

Châu grins with delight. "I once won three caskets of fine wine in a card game!"

"My dearest love lives there," Sun sighs happily.

"Just another port," Anh says. "You're the newest, so we'll be last to shore. I'll wait with you."

The day is a calm, bright blue, the storm of a few days ago a distant memory. The water is clear and sparkling until it meets a torrent of sediment, churning from where another river meets the sea. From here, Changping looks like a cluster of rooftops amid the swaying outburst of jungle and makeshift structures lined on the beach. It takes us most of the afternoon to offload our goods, with the longboat and two small rowboats going back and forth between the shore and where we're anchored.

Mianmian and Thanh have already returned from a full afternoon in town, their faces flushed with excitement as they climb back aboard deck with baskets stuffed with delicious-smelling treats: fried scallion pancakes studded with strips of octopus, fragrant savory bao, and several gourds of wine.

I watch jealously as they laugh with Ling Shan, and Sun pries them for information about his beloved tavern musician, Yu Shen—who apparently left port last week, much to his chagrin.

The shifts are all set; there will be two of us on the *Huyền*

Vũ at all times, and Sun and Thanh will take the longest shift overnight. Captain Hoa was among the first to leave, and all afternoon I unload barrel after barrel of fish until my hands are dry and shriveled from all the salt. Finally Anh and I haul the last of the barrels into the longboat and it's our turn to take it to shore.

The docks of Changping are cluttered, ships berthed haphazardly in the bay. Unlike the clear hierarchy in Canton, here it seems almost random where people are docked. Larger ships are anchored farther out in the bay, and smaller rowboats and midsized junks are hastily tied to wooden poles or even other boats closer to shore.

The motley collection of ships bear flags from multiple kingdoms, or most commonly, no flag at all. Every ship seems just as ramshackle as the *Huyền Vũ*, and as we pull up I can see the beach is covered in tents. People lie on the sand, drinking and laughing, cooking meats over smoking fires. There's a cluttered street leading away from the beach into the trees, and I follow Anh, pushing our cart filled with barrels of fish as we come up to a warehouse where Captain Hoa is negotiating with the trade boss, a salty-looking man with a long beard.

Captain Hoa doesn't notice us as she continues arguing. "That's four fewer silver a barrel than last time. You're cheating me here."

"Seasons change, and these won't keep as fresh," the man

retorts. "Dong won't take as much, not with these winds and not being able to chance rotting cargo before he gets to Nha Trang." He scowls. "I'll give you thirty silver cash per barrel."

"The barrels themselves are worth ten! I won't accept anything lower than forty-five each."

The trade boss raises an eyebrow. "Well . . . Perhaps if you're headed toward Thăng Long, I've got an iron shipment that could use—"

"Let's talk terms in your office." Captain Hoa sighs. "Oh, there you are, Xiang." She tosses me a small leather bag filled with coins. "Your wages."

"I—" I hadn't realized I would be getting paid. I thought my share was to come from deciphering the map . . . something that is still not done. Guilt tears at me, and the money seems to grow heavier in my palm.

I stand there, frozen for a long moment until Anh closes my open palm around the bag. "Take it. Everyone gets a fair share. You're part of the crew. We sailed here together. We wouldn't have made it through that pass without you."

Captain Hoa nods, a proud grin stretching across her face. "That's right. You're a quick learner, Xiang. Go on. You deserve it."

"I—" My face feels warm, and I should say something, but I don't know how to voice my appreciation.

Anh shoulders me with a knowing smile. "Let's go."

Captain Hoa waves us off as she follows the trade boss into his office. "Now, here are my terms . . ."

Unlike Canton, where there are veneers of respectability—people from all backgrounds with government officials, the city guard, and the Qing navy interspersed everywhere—the twisting streets of Changping are wild with chaos.

"No one insults the great Shao Lin!"

"I believe I just did!"

A man whose face is streaked in dirt and blood charges headfirst at another man, fists flailing. I back away from the brawl as Anh just walks right through, ducking slightly to the side as people cheer and shout bets. We pass an open courtyard where I see Ling Shan and Sun raising tankards to each other, laughing with women giggling in robes so sheer they leave nothing to the imagination. There are barrels upon barrels of goods being loaded and unloaded everywhere without an official or clerk in sight.

Anh gestures wide. "Welcome to Changping, the last free place in the world," she says. "No official would bother even trying to bring any sort of order to this place."

I palm my wages into the width of my sleeve instead of tucking the bag into my belt and nod. "Mianmian said I should pick up supplies for the next leg of our journey. Do you know where Xi's stall is?"

"Plenty of time for that. We aren't going to be leaving at dawn if my mother agrees to take on any more shipments." Anh laughs. "We have wages to spend, and this whole town is way more fun than Canton. Come on. I bet I could double this cash by nightfall. What do you want to do?"

My stomach grumbles loudly.

"I know just the thing," she says with a wink, "and then we'll hit the tavern."

On the beach, people are hawking their wares, and tents are everywhere—some simple canvas draped over wood poles, some elaborate, covered in tapestries and more permanent looking.

"If you'd rather sleep in a bed, there's rooms for rent in town," Anh explains as she leads me through, "or the beach makes a nice change from a hammock. Thanh is always complaining about his back."

We trade a small package of salt for a pile of freshly grilled prawnlike creatures, practically as big as my palm. We plop down on the sand in the shade of a swaying tree, and I watch as Anh uses her teeth to crack the hard shell. "Just peel it like that," she says.

I take a bite and wince, unable to break the hard shell of the claw.

"Turn it sideways, bite it where it meets the—like this." Anh turns the claw, crunches down and takes it out of her mouth. She deftly peels the shell away, taking out the soft meat inside, and dips it in the sauce before pressing it to my lips.

I open my mouth and taste garlic and lime and make an unabashed noise of appreciation. Anh drops a whole pile of them in my lap.

"There you go," she says.

I flick one at her, and she laughs, wiping its juices from her cheek. We work our way through the bag of prawns until our fingers are sticky with sauce and our bellies are full. Another vendor sells us fresh coconut water, which we drink out of the husk she slices open neatly with a machete. I lie in the shade, wondering when was the last time I'd ever felt so content.

"When we're back on the ship, Mẹ will tell everyone about the next stop of the journey," Anh says. "Are you ready? How is the code breaking coming along?"

Ah.

I have not done any of it.

"I'm going to wash my hands," I say, standing up. I walk over to where the tide is starting to come in, the water sluicing up the beach. My feet sink into the wet sand, and I drop to my knees as the water rushes in all around me, scrubbing at my hands until they are raw and red.

Footsteps slosh behind me. "Xiang!"

I turn around to face Anh, ready for a confrontation. Instead I see worry twisting her eyebrows together, something like fear dancing in her eyes.

"Once they know about the map, there will be no turn-ing back," she says. "You will have to deliver us to the trea-sure, as was your word. I promise I will keep you safe, but you . . . you have to keep up your end of the bargain."

"I know, I know. I will."

I do not know what to do about the concern lining her face, or the way she pulls me to my feet, clasping my hands in her own. A wave surges around us, rising and break-ing down as it knocks into our knees, and Anh holds me steady.

There is something here in the way she's holding my hands, a feeling inside me that might be the *more* I've been yearning for all along. These weeks on the ship, Anh has worked alongside me, teaching me the ways of sailing, and I've found friendship here, yes, but there's another layer— something in the way she's listened to me ramble about my dreams and has shared her own, and now this . . . this steadfast belief in me.

Her hands are warm against the cold water, and for a long moment I can see only Anh, her luminous brown skin golden in the soft light of the setting sun. She says something that is lost in the surf, words that are drowned in the tide and fade out to sea.

"What?" I ask, my heart pounding.

Anh shakes her head, salt water dripping from her eyelashes. "These past few weeks with the crew . . . you think they are your friends, but you have to remember, it's different out here. Once they know you're not just here to help cook, that you have something that means something beyond their wildest dreams . . . *anyone* will betray you to get a better share, to get more."

I want to ask who has betrayed Anh before, why she sees the world this way.

With a pang, I think about the warmth of the crew, the way they've been patient and fun and included me in their jokes. The way it's felt like being a part of a family. Surely Anh cannot believe this of them as well?

"You can't trust anyone," Anh says bitterly. "There's no one out there who is going to save you or help you. Everyone is going to look after themselves first. There's no one who wouldn't betray you to save their own skin."

"I don't believe that's true," I say immediately. "Your mother, your brother . . . you've sailed with everyone for years, don't you—"

"I would not begrudge anyone the choices they make, however hard they might be." She shakes her head. "You've been living in a different world, Xiang. I'm sure in your village everything was perfect and everyone pitched in to help one another, right?"

I want to protest, but it is true. With so few families in the village, everyone knew one another. People had always checked on one another, asking about someone's grandfather or if they'd heard from their son from the country, or watching the children while one was out fishing. "I lived with Lan Nai Nai all my life. She and her husband have always taken care of me."

"They were servants?"

"No, Lan Nai Nai helped Mother run the teahouse." I remember vaguely Lan Nai Nai's children, two men I had called my uncles before they had moved away to find their fortunes. They visited occasionally after they had gotten married, with their children in tow, but never stayed long. "She raised me."

"Because she was paid to," Anh says.

I had always thought Lan Nai Nai's lectures had been harsher than necessary, and I had been jealous of children whose parents carried them and blanketed them with hugs and kisses, but Lan Nai Nai had never been unkind.

"You were raised by servants in a beautiful teahouse in the idyllic country," Anh says, her words cold as the seawater lapping at our feet. "You've never had to worry about where your next meal is coming from, or if your ship would be trapped without wind while you lay thirsty and aching on a dead ship. No water or food and no strength to pull the sail, but you have to if you're ever going to make it." She looks off into the distance, her eyes glimmering with an old pain.

I swallow hard. She hasn't let go of my hands as the waves crash down around us. In fact, she's holding on tighter, like I'm an anchor and she's afraid she'll float out to sea.

"I can't speak to what you've endured," I say quietly, "but my life was not perfect. You have people who care about you, a mother who respects you and your opinion, a home where you belong. I had this . . . this expectation, and it was like trying to win a race I couldn't even finish. I wish . . . I wish I was loved like you are."

Anh's mouth falls open, and she closes it quickly. "You think you can live on love? You think love will feed you or put a roof over your head? Love doesn't mean anything." She lets go of my hands now, taking a step back, staring at me as she clenches her hands into fists.

"But your crew—"

"You think any of them wouldn't turn on the captain if the price was right enough? On you?"

I think of the promises we made to each other, and I wonder why she's saying this now, why it hurts so much.

"There you are!" Mianmian waves at us from the beach. "There's only one room left at the inn and an extra bed, if you want it. And Châu won at cards—he's buying dinner and drinks! Let's go!"

Torches and lanterns blaze merrily as night settles over the town, and loud, bawdy music echoes everywhere amid the sounds of drinking and gambling. People smoke opium right out in the open, their eyes glazed over as they lazily watch spirals of smoke billow into the air.

Mianmian's cheeks are flushed and she bounces with excitement as she pulls us both along to the tavern. Sun sits up from a table, nearly toppling Arthrit over in his excitement. "There they are!"

"Xiang! I was just telling the crew of the *Zongzi* about how we made it through the Hainan-Leizhou pass," Châu exclaims and stands up, handing me a cup of amber-colored liquor. "And then this one just *lets go!*"

Sun claps my shoulders, gesturing at me with a grin. "Go on, tell the story!"

Maheer takes Châu's empty chair and offers it to me, and I'm pulled into the fray with shouts and smiles. Anh settles in across the table, her eyes not quite meeting mine. I want to spend more time with her, to talk more about what we started on the beach, but now in the tavern with everyone in such high spirits, there's no such chance.

Sun starts a song, and the others join in, singing boisterously, and I find my own voice among theirs. How can Anh speak of betrayal when everyone has been so welcoming? Perhaps she's jealous, seeing me at the center of attention. Of course I haven't figured the map's clues out yet, but I'm certain I will.

The tavern spins around me, and the drinks and food keep coming until our table is piled high. Cups clink together, and my belly is roaring with spiced rum. All around us, the tales grow wilder and more boisterous, of adventures and exploits in ports in distant kingdoms, of feats daring and bold, and then, to my amusement, the legendary cache of the Dragon Fleet.

"I heard Zheng Yi Sao once robbed an entire treasure galleon from Siam, laden with silks and pearls and fine jade, a tribute for the Jiaqing Emperor."

"Barrels and barrels of fine wine and mead . . ."

"Statues and art and antiquities . . ."

"Spanish gold . . ."

"Portuguese silver . . ."

Anh and Captain Hoa exchange knowing glances as the tavern erupts into stories and speculation of the treasure. It's familiar enough to me now that I almost don't notice it over the roar in my ears and the warmth in my blood and belly.

Arthrit sighs happily as he leans back, curling into Châu's neck, and they gaze at each other, fingers tangled together. I had thought at first they were sharing a chair because Maheer had given Châu's to me—but there are plenty of other chairs in the tavern. The affectionate gesture makes me wonder, my skin prickling with the memory of Anh's fingers in my own.

"Who's up for a game?" Anh calls out, setting down her cup on the table with a heavy clink.

A gunshot shatters the glass, the liquor exploding onto her tunic. Eyes snap toward where the shot came from. Even the music stops, the lute in the corner coming to a halt.

A man whose three-cornered hat is barely hanging on to his wild-looking curls cocks his gun again, aiming at Captain Hoa. "You conniving thief! You knew that was to be my shipment, and you took it right from under my nose!"

She laughs, standing up. "Please, Harrington. As if anyone wants you ferrying their iron on your leaky bucket of a ship."

"You and all you filthy rats on the *Huyền Vũ* all reek of—"

The last word is mumbled, and I have enough trouble understanding Harrington through his thick accented Cantonese, but the intention is clear. He raises the gun, and I stand up in alarm.

Before he can fire again, Ling Shan tosses a knife at him, knocking the gun cleanly out of his hand. Mianmian rushes forward headfirst, tackling Harrington to the ground.

And then it's all chaos.

Plates are thrown, swords are drawn and quickly tossed away as the scene descends into a squabble of punches and kicks. Someone gets me in the stomach, and I flail wildly. A woman from the other crew has me tossed on the ground, and I can't move, I don't have anything on me to use as a weapon—

I may not know how to fight, but the *Huyền Vũ* has been insulted, and I won't stand for it.

My hand closes on a broken chair leg, and I bring it down on her head. It splinters all around us, and I take advantage of the moment to bite the arm she's using to pin me to the ground. She screams and flops to the side.

I scramble to my feet, and someone pulls me up— Maheer, whose face shines with a thin sheen of sweat, his eyes glittering with amusement. At some point during the fight the musicians started playing again, lute strings twanging with delight as our brawl tumbles into the street, a mess of arms and legs and improvised weaponry. The insults get bawdier and even more nonsensical, until finally both Captain Hoa and Captain Harrington are roaring with laughter.

"Your crew has more fleas than the mangiest cur in Canton!" Harrington roars.

"That's no way to talk about your own mother!" Captain Hoa retorts.

Harrington laughs and responds in a blunt-sounding language. The words sound like heavy crates with sharp corners, unwieldy and rough.

Captain Hoa answers in the same language, and then the two are going back and forth, and I don't understand any of it.

My heart is racing with excitement, and all around me the fight seems to have stilled, but I don't want to let Harrington's crew get the upper hand. I see an opportunity and lunge for the woman whom I bit earlier, landing a clumsy punch to her shoulder.

She gives me an incredulous look. "What are you doing, child?! Clearly we're done!"

"What?"

I look around; Harrington is back in the tavern with Captain Hoa next to him, and they're raising their tankards to each other and laughing. They're still speaking that other language, and I can make out Ling Shan's name accompanied by Harrington's waggled eyebrows. Captain Hoa doubles over in laughter as Ling Shan shakes her head, grinning back up at Harrington.

The rest of the night is a blur; Harrington buys everyone a drink, and then Captain Hoa buys a round. My head spins as I accept another cup, and I knock it back as people roar in approval around me. Some sort of game starts, and I can't keep the rules right, not when they involve the bouncing of a cash coin and drinking if you fumble the rhythm. Sun pounds my back with pride when I successfully bounce the coin into Maheer's cup. He nods at Mianmian, who takes the cup and drains it in a single gulp.

"Hey! He has to drink! It's the rule!" a greasy-faced man from Harrington's crew says.

"I don't drink," Maheer says.

Captain Hoa nods. "Mianmian always drinks for him when we play this."

"And I do it well!" Mianmian bellows, standing up and tossing her empty cup on the floor.

The greasy-faced man accepts this, and it's clear that the rest of Harrington's crew is familiar with it as well. One man cuffs him on the shoulder, and the game goes on. I don't remember when Harrington's crew stopped being rivals, or maybe they never were. It seems like our crew has known them for a long while—at least from Ling Shan's perspective, whom Harrington keeps attempting and failing to woo.

I lose another round of the drinking game, and I can't seem to lift the cup to my lips; every time I reach for the table it seems to move just out of my vision.

Anh taps me on the chin, drawing me close to her as she looks into my eyes. "I'll take this one," she says, downing the contents of my cup. She hands me a flagon of water. "Here, drink this."

I take a long sip of the cool water and struggle to keep my eyes open.

"Let's get you upstairs; this party is going to go on all night," Anh says.

I nod, stumbling to my feet. It's like trying to stand on a rolling wave, and I almost fall over. Anh catches me by the waist and holds me steady.

"You all right?"

"Did we win?" I mumble.

"Yeah, we drank Harrington's crew under the table. You did a lot of it." She guides me gently up the stairs. "Mianmian snores in her sleep. Let's make sure she gets the bed closest to the door."

The three little beds crammed together should look uncomfortable, and the continued raucous noise from downstairs should make the tiny room sound anything but inviting. But after many nights in a hammock and my head still spinning with drink and the rush of the events of the evening, it feels like the height of luxury to sink into the softness of a bed that doesn't move.

"Who else is sleeping here?" I yawn, the words barely tumbling out of me.

"Mianmian and Sun," Anh says, guiding me toward the bed next to the window.

"I thought Sun had the overnight shift on the ship," I mumble.

"He changed shifts with Maheer once he was on his third round," Anh laughs. "Châu and Arthrit got the next room. Although maybe we should go back to the ship—they can be pretty loud."

My eyelids are drooping, and I struggle to keep them open as I process what Anh is saying. All I'm understanding is that there are four of us for the room and three beds. I try to sit up and somehow end up just sinking farther into the soft bed.

"Oh, that was a joke," Anh says, her voice light. "You aren't going anywhere. You're going to drink the rest of this water and then go right to sleep."

"But," I mumble, "there aren't enough beds."

"It's fine, I can sleep on the floor."

"No, I will floor!" I say, standing up and pointing. I don't know why, but it seems incredibly important to me. Also there's no floor space, really. The room is just these three beds.

"You will not," Anh says, amused.

The door opens. Mianmian is singing and Châu and Arthrit bound in, demanding a card game. I blearily lose my next week's wages to them, my head falling onto my shoulder until gentle arms tuck me into bed.

"Stay," a voice says, and it is my own, an honest thought unburdened by fear. "Stay, please," I say again, reaching for her hand.

And she does.

I'm somewhere between dreaming and awake, and I feel safe. A warm heart is beating underneath me, and an arm is holding me close. Consciousness pulls at me, and a soft voice groans in my ear, "Just a few more minutes."

I blink, the dull cannon fire at the base of my head starting to wake me up. It takes a moment for my brain to catch up to where my body is; Anh is holding me, her leg thrown over my waist and my head tucked under her chin. Her heavy coat is lying atop the both of us, and the patched linen of her shirt tickles my chin. Hot daylight streams into the open window, dirty curtains fluttering in the breeze.

"Let's go, lovebirds," Mianmian calls. A door opens and shuts. "Captain Hoa says we'll leave port at noon today. We've got a huge shipment to load, and it's going to take hours. And that's *with* everyone helping."

For a moment I think I imagine it, but Anh curls in closer before her whole body freezes, going stiff with realization. She doesn't move and neither do I, and in the space between breaths I wonder what I should do. I wonder if she can feel my heartbeat as I feel hers, rabbiting out of control.

Outside, chickens squawk and voices chatter in the streets. And then the spell is broken when Ling Shan opens the door, wrestling a bundle of cloth from underneath the next bed, startling Sun awake.

"*That's* where I left my sword!"

"Why," Sun groans pitifully, pulling the blanket back over his head.

Anh and I spring apart from each other, and she hastily scrambles to her feet, picking her coat off the floor.

I tuck my pendant back under my shirt and hastily undo my tangled plait for something to do with my hands.

"Good fight yesterday," Anh says, her voice a little stiff. "I still can't believe you bit Wen Liu; that was hilarious."

I laugh weakly. "Thank you."

She looks at me, considering. "You know, of all the skills you've learned so far, I think that's what you need next. You'll need to know how to fight."

The subject neatly changed, she looks at me with a familiar smile, and we're friends again. We don't speak of how we fell asleep embracing like it was the most natural thing in the world.

CHAPTER FOURTEEN

THE WAY
OF THE SWORD

Open waters, northern coast of Việt Nam

ANH HANDS ME A BLADE. IT'S LONG AND SLIM, WITH A wicked curve at the edge.

I gulp.

Anh shrugs. "In the event you have to defend yourself."

When I just stare open-mouthed, she adds, "Last night's fight was silly. A bit of fun. But there are people out there who would genuinely want to harm us. We've been boarded before by those with ill intentions—for us or for our cargo— and you'll need to be able to hold your own in the event there's ever a real fight."

An actual battle? Another ship boarding this one? I've only heard of such things in stories.

Anh's eyes soften, and her hands close around mine on the hilt. "Look. It's just good to have. I'll teach you how to use it." She lowers her voice to a whisper. "Having a weapon and knowing how to use it . . . it may save your life, or at least get you out of situations you don't want to be in."

I remember how some of the older patrons at the teahouse back in the village would cluck at me and make kissing noises until Lan Nai Nai slammed her tray onto their table. I remember Lo Zhan, Qian's older brother, and the way his leering eyes had followed me that afternoon when Qian and I had gone swimming in the river. I'd kicked him in the groin once when he kept persisting, but it wasn't until Mother had steadfastly refused the marriage proposal that he stopped following me around the village. I shake the memory loose and focus on the heaviness of the blade in my hand.

The rest of the crew has paused in their duties to watch us. Sun takes a seat on the rails, swinging his feet and smiling at me in encouragement. Even Maheer, keeping his hand steadily on the tiller, is watching us. Since we left Changping with the iron shipment in our hold, we've been sailing at a fast pace. Today is the first day the seas are calm enough to take a bit of a break.

Anh squeezes my hand quickly before adjusting my stance to hold the blade aloft. "Like this."

I swallow nervously.

She places another hand on my hip and guides me to move forward, pushing the blade into the air. "Step with the movement. Use your whole body, not just your arm. Watch."

Anh falls back, the warmth of her touch still lingering

on my skin, my waist tingling from where she touched me. I quickly look at my feet, trying to shake the overwhelming heat that is rising inside me; I feel like my blood is about to boil.

"Xiang-xiang," Anh says, the nickname rolling off her tongue effortlessly like she hasn't even thought about it. "Watch me!"

"I am," I say, trying not to let my breath betray how much I'm affected by all of this. The nickname itself is overwhelming; I have never had anyone say my name so intimately. *Like a lover*, an unbidden thought rises in my head, and I quickly quell it. People often have nicknames only those close to them are comfortable using. Anh folds my name into itself like a melody, and I want to keep hearing it just like that.

She holds up her own sword and cocks her head, a smirk on the corner of her lips. She moves with a sure confidence; Anh thrusts forward in one swift movement, her arm as steady as if the blade is an extension of herself.

I exhale, my heart pounding with exhilaration as the point comes to a stop a scant finger length from my lips. My mouth falls open ever so slightly.

Anh lowers her sword and arches her eyebrow at me. "Why didn't you move?"

"I—" *I didn't know I was supposed to*, I don't say, because even as the thought forms in my head, I can hear how silly it would be to say aloud. I'd been so captivated by

Anh and the way she moves, the way she carries herself, that I had completely forgotten about the point of the lesson.

"You can sidestep to avoid the attack, or bring up your own sword to block, like this." Anh gently takes my hand again and brings up my sword to cross with her own.

We run through the basics, like a complicated dance that I try to clumsily follow along. Anh adjusts my grip and stance multiple times, shaking her head each time I almost drop the blade and narrowly avoid injuring myself. She shows me how to block and how to attack, and which side of the blade is suited to which. Anh talks about how to anticipate an opponent's attack, her eyes sparkling as she rambles on about fights she's been in, how the crew narrowly avoided capture multiple times from officials.

The crew laughs as they watch my clumsy attempts at attacking. My arms ache and my mouth is dry, and I feel like we've been at this for hours.

"Again."

I'm panting, trying to catch my breath, and the thin shirt I'm wearing is soaked with sweat.

A flagon of water appears in front of me. "I think that's enough for a first lesson," an amused voice huffs. The captain has joined us, her free hand on her hip as she regards us both.

"Mẹ, she has to learn to fight," Anh grumbles.

"I don't doubt that it's a good idea, but she doesn't have to be a master by morning. Go on, take a break."

I accept the flagon, gulping down the cool water.

Captain Hoa draws her sword, stepping toward Anh.

I watch.

Anh and her mother circle each other, both of them grinning with some sort of wicked delight. The entire crew is gathered on deck now, and I hear the clink of money being exchanged.

Anh charges first, raising her sword high, and Captain Hoa blocks it with ease. Whoops and cheers abound as they fight, exchanging blows as steel clangs in rhythmic fashion. It's easy to see the captain is the one who taught her, the way Anh mimics her movements and how they clearly know each other's technique. A pang of bitterness rises up in me as I see the proud way Captain Hoa smiles when Anh catches her by surprise and flings the captain's sword to the ground.

"Nice job. You're getting good," Captain Hoa says, holding her hands up. "But remember your opponent may always have another trick—"

She reaches behind her and pulls out two shorter knives sheathed in her jacket, and uses them both to twist Anh's longsword to the ground.

Anh's mouth falls open. "Cheat!"

The captain laughs. "Just because you've never perfected that move doesn't mean someone else wouldn't have thought of it. Mainly, me."

Anh scowls as the crew laughs and claps. "What are all of you staring at?"

Captain Hoa waves her hands at them. "Go on, every-one, back to your duties."

Maheer raises his eyebrow from where he hasn't moved from the helm.

Captain Hoa laughs. "And that's why you are the best quartermaster."

Maheer nods, a small smile gracing his lips, but other-wise he doesn't acknowledge the praise. "Sun, Ling Shan, set the sails. Mianmian and Arthrit, I need you on that line. We don't want to be caught stalling in the doldrums. Let's go before these winds die down!"

Anh turns back to me, but her mother claps her hand on her shoulder. "Go ahead and help Ling Shan. I'll take it from here."

"But—"

Captain Hoa gives her a stern look, and Anh scuttles off past me. "You're going to do fine," she says, turning back and smiling.

"Thanks," I mumble back, pleased.

"All right. Anh's gone through the basics with you, but I figured it would be easier if you weren't so distracted."

"I'm focused!" I say, even as my eyes trail back to Anh.

Captain Hoa gives me a skeptical look as she follows my gaze. "Really, now."

I feel my face grow warm with embarrassment. "I just— I'm—we—" I drop my gaze to my feet, shame flooding through me. It's going to be like my friendship with Lo Qian all over again—the gossip, the heated suggestions, the judgment about going against nature.

I should have been more careful. I shouldn't have let my eyes linger on Anh's form, her smile, so much. I shouldn't have betrayed any notion that I'd had deeper thoughts about our friendship.

The truth of what I'm feeling, what I've been feeling about other girls for so long, jumps out at me. I've been pushing it back, focusing on my studies and how to make Mother proud. I'd pushed far into the back of my mind why the idea of marrying a man had always seemed loathsome to me. When Lo Qian and the other girls in the village would sigh about how handsome one of the boys in the village or a traveler passing through were, I wouldn't understand. I'd read poetry and stories about love and yearning, about this deep longing and wanting, and I couldn't place why I hadn't felt it. Or maybe I had, but recognizing it would mean naming it, speaking it aloud.

With Qian, I loved the time we spent together, and I raised my cup of rice wine just like the other villagers when Old Man Lo announced her engagement. On their wedding day, I cheered as her new husband's family marched through the streets of our village, red ribbons and banners streaming bright and colorfully everywhere as they presented the Los with food and gifts. I told myself the deep sorrow I felt that day was because I would miss Qian, because everything was changing.

But it wasn't just that. Qian lived close enough—a half day's walk. I could have visited her in her new village.

I know now what I knew then but was too afraid to admit: I had wanted her, the way the poets would write about. I wanted her steady companionship, her bright laughter as we raced through the fields together. I wanted her like a lover, to hold her face and sweep her hair out of her eyes and draw her in for a soft kiss. I knew it wasn't possible, and yet I still mourned the loss of her, mourned the idea that I was not the one presenting her family with trays of delicacies on *our* wedding day.

The image changes, and it's Anh standing there wearing red brocade, her eyes bright and laughing as she kisses me. Anh, who has come to know me in a way no one else has.

I push that yearning back deep inside me. This wanting, this way of being, has no place in the world.

"It's all right," Captain Hoa says gently. She squeezes my shoulder, and it's such a motherly embrace that I freeze, unused to the tender way she's regarding me. I expect her to scold me or to pull away immediately, but the touch remains, constant and steady.

"I don't . . . I don't know what you mean," I whisper. I haven't spoken aloud any of my thoughts. There's no way she could know.

"I think you're a good member of my crew," Captain Hoa says. "You've certainly proved yourself. You haven't complained once—and I thought you would—about the cramped quarters or long hours of work or hot sun. But you've worked hard and done more than your fair share of the work."

"Thank you," I say, unsure of where this is going.

"Anh tells me after we retrieve the treasure you intend to settle back in Canton. To run the Pearl House with your mother."

The word *after* lingers in the air. I hesitate before nodding, because it is as much as I said to Anh when we first discovered the map. I want to prove to Mother that I'm capable of running the business, that I'm worthy of her admiration, her trust, her time. I'd been hoping for her to see me for so long that it's strange to think that it's finally going to happen.

And yet after only a few weeks of working with Captain Hoa, she's already acknowledging me. My work. My heart swells with a strange new feeling. I'm not quite sure what it is.

"I've always considered my crew my family. I've seen the way you look at Anh . . . and the way she looks at you."

My breath catches. The words aren't an accusation, just a statement.

She smiles at me. "You could be happy here, if you wanted to stay. You're welcome to be a part of this crew. Continue to sail with us."

"I thought you—Anh said the crew would want to take their share of the treasure, settle down somewhere warm—"

The captain shrugs. "Some of them might. Châu and Arthrit have always wanted somewhere quiet. But most of us have never known any other life. And I can't see us being farmers or staying on land anyway. I'd want to keep sailing. With enough cash to keep going, I wouldn't have to worry about wages or keeping the nets full or selling a catch before it turns. I could just . . . sail. Get a nicer ship, keep the navy off our tails. This map of yours, it could lead to something, or it could lead to nothing. I'm taking a huge risk here. I spent years chasing this legend, with much less to go on, losing the faith of my crew, my family. I know it's best not to count your chickens before they're hatched."

"I understand."

"I haven't told the crew about the treasure yet. Not until we're close. Can't have the crew distracted or dreaming of what they'd do with their share just yet. I used to sail with the Dragon Fleet—people would spend their wages in the blink of an eye without a thought for the future."

I gasp. "You were a pirate?"

Captain Hoa grins at me. "Don't look so shocked. A small fishing vessel could only hope to make so much money, and by the time you get to port with your catch, there are taxes and bribes for officials to worry about. And you have to keep your cargo fresh, pay your crew's wages. There's not enough ways to make an honest living."

She leans over the side of the ship, gesturing for me to follow. The waves are calm today, drifting slowly, white foam caps cresting as they hit the hull. From this close to her, I notice the scars running down the captain's face, old and weathered, faded by the sun.

The lines on her face deepen as she smiles, and turns to me. "It was only a few months, and I wish we'd joined up sooner. I resisted for so long, but Anh's father thought we'd make a good run of it. The money was good, and we kept this ship sailing, right up until the Battle of the Tiger's Mouth. The Black Banner Squadron was struggling for power and was quick to mutiny against the commander. Right at the end, when Zheng Yi Sao was negotiating for pardons and the like. It all went to hell very quickly after that. The pirates argued endlessly, because no one could replace her. Lieutenants and captains squabbled, and everyone had to go their own way. Without the security of her command and her wages, there was nothing left for us there. We were better off on our own, doing petty smuggling here and there and going back to fishing."

Captain Hoa taps her fingers on the rail. "Anh's father died that day in the battle. I remember raging for days, demanding to know why the gods had taken him from me, how I could go on. And I remember not cherishing the moments we had before, anything as simple as arguing over fish scales on the ship or getting stuck in the doldrums. I didn't realize just how many sunsets and sunrises we had left."

"Do you miss him?"

"Every day. But in the next life, who knows? Perhaps we will be together again." She turns around, looking back to the deck where the crew has dispersed to their tasks.

Captain Hoa sighs. "The Qing government made

promises—that they'd build cities as grand as the Forbidden City, that no one would want for food or shelter. That there would be peace, education, vast improvement."

I nod, remembering the official that came regularly to our village. "Bureaucratic exams and opportunities for everyone, no matter where they are from. But most people in my village didn't bother because of how difficult the exams were."

"It is a system that favors heavily those who were already set to succeed," Captain Hoa says.

In my philosophy lessons with Master Feng, he had encouraged me to think critically. But all our conversations came with a warning to keep these thoughts between us and never speak them aloud to others in the village. Here with Captain Hoa and her apt encouragement, my thoughts all suddenly come tumbling out of me, thoughts I'd mulled over for years but I'd never thought I'd have an audience for.

"Yes, the emperor claims to do so much for the empire, and yet he sits and enjoys his comforts in the Forbidden City. But the tributes he demands, the scant protection he offers?"

Captain Hoa nods at me in understanding. "Did you know that it is illegal to trade rice at any port from here to Canton? It's so expensive to ship grain across the mountains to the coast, and the kingdom of Việt Nam produces plenty of rice but lacks the iron it needs to grow as a kingdom.

It would be such an efficient trade, if only the Daoguang Emperor were not so greedy." She sighs. "Smuggling iron and rice is the quickest way to make coin, and I enjoy getting things to where they need to be. If piracy is the means by which I must do it, then a pirate I am."

My hands tremble with a fierce anger that I didn't know I was carrying. "Who is more the thief: the government that preys on its own people, or those who must become thieves in order to survive?"

"Surely you would not begrudge anyone who would leave the society that turned its back on those it swore to protect?" Captain Hoa asks me.

I have no answers, only questions about why in every story I've heard, the pirates were always the ones portrayed as monsters.

Captain Hoa places a gentle hand on my shoulder, and we both look out to sea. The *Huyền Vũ* continues on her path south toward the kingdom of Việt Nam, and for a long moment it is just us quietly regarding the ocean and our course.

"Châu and Arthrit are married, you know," she says, as casually as if commenting on the weather.

I blink. I had thought they shared a cabin because they were senior members of the crew and close friends. But to hear their relationship confirmed like that is a shock. "They're—"

"Both men, I know. It's not unusual at all, out here on

241

the sea. To have a matelot to share a cabin and your wages with. The punishment in the empire is five hundred lashes for such behavior. But we follow our own laws out here on the water."

My heart pounds. "I—I did not know that." I hadn't even known of the punishment in the cities. I just knew that it was unheard of in the village, and anyone suspected of such behavior would have been ostracized.

I look back to the water and then to the ship—this ship that has quickly become home to me. I think about Captain Hoa's offer to stay, and wonder what she is and isn't saying. About a life that could be had here.

Captain Hoa trains me every day when there's a spare moment between my duties. I learn quickly not only how to wield a sword, but to use my small size to my advantage.

"People will underestimate you," she says. "You can use that."

I learn how to fight without a weapon, how to deal concentrated blows with my fists and my feet. I grow swift with practice, my body building strength from the hours spent scrubbing the decks and hauling buckets of water. When an errant wave whips upon the deck, I relish the reprieve of coolness and stand my ground. I can set lines and see when an extra hand is needed. I take my turn at the tiller, steering us toward our destination as Maheer nods in approval. I learn to cherish the moments to myself on top of the world, with only the wind and the sea to accompany my thoughts.

Anh takes me back up on sparring once the captain has deemed me passable in a fight.

"She said I could hold my own," I said. "I want to be the best."

"You'll get there," she says.

We're on the deck again, with a small cluster of the crew watching us. Maheer winks at me; he's put coin on me, and I do not intend to lose.

Anh pulls a scrap of fabric from her pocket, tying her hair back and out of her eyes. A few strands escape from the makeshift tie, whorling softly at the base of her bare, slender neck. I glance away and try to concentrate, remembering everything I've learned.

I raise my sword.

Anh attacks with sharp, staccato movements, and I block each one, meeting her every move. I strike with the same pleased exhilaration I felt when I got my first sampan and discovered I could row far from the village on my own. Birds caw ahead, and the bright, hot sun weighs down on us, the sails' shadows flitting across my face as we dart across the deck.

I laugh when Anh lunges at me and misses. She snorts at me and dashes forward, and our blades meet in a sweet clash of steel. I know all the notes and move-ments of this dance now, and to my surprise I find myself enjoying the cadence of it—the way we circle each other, anticipating each other's next move. It's like she's in my head and I'm in hers, and we move in sync, each blow met in exchange.

I see the opening and I go for it, and then I have Anh by the throat, my blade kissing her skin. She drops her own sword in yield, a gleam of surprise dancing in her eyes. And there's something else, something unreadable. Some emotion stirring underneath that I dare not hope for.

Anh's face is flushed, her brown skin warm and rosy with excitement, a sheen of sweat on her brow. I can't look away, and I feel a sudden heat in my stomach. I can't pinpoint the feeling exactly, the fight rising up in me or the hot rush of triumph. Or perhaps it's desire, surging forward to claim me where it has been tamped down for so long and now is rushing free like a river breaking loose of its banks. Unbid-den and out of control.

"You have me," Anh says, barely a whisper. Her gaze is steady, eyes warm and liquid, pupils dark with intent.

I lower my sword.

The rest of the world seems to fade away; the rough-hewn deck I'm standing on, the weapon in my hand, the sails above us, and the ocean all around.

I want her. I want to have her in every sense of the word.

I want to drink in the way she's looking at me right now, as if she's feeling the same desire I am.

"Sails! On the horizon!"

Anh looks away, the moment broken. She brushes past me to lean over the side with the others.

In the distance, a ship approaches.

CHAPTER FIFTEEN

THE ADMIRAL

I JOIN THE REST OF THE CREW BY THE RAIL. THIS ISN'T the first ship we've seen on our journey—we've passed other small fishing boats and merchant vessels. Usually the captain will nod and continue our course, and sometimes we've altered it to avoid Qing navy ships. But this far from the coastline and not on any common trade routes, well on our way south toward Việt Nam, it's highly unusual to see the crest of the Daoguang Emperor fluttering on a banner.

The captain whips out her eyeglass, considering the ship on the horizon. The red sails stand out against the dark gray clouds billowing in the distance.

"Chinese navy," she says with a sigh. "They shouldn't bother us. But if they do, we have all our paperwork in order.

Just a mere fishing vessel, heading for Thăng Long. We should lay out some more nets in case our lack of a catch seems suspicious. Let's stay close to the shoreline, out of the main trade route." She glances at Maheer. "Make sure that iron is well hidden."

I peer over the edge of the ship, watching the massive junk slowly gain speed against the foreboding gray sky. "Why would they bother us?" I ask Anh softly.

"In the old days," she replies, "my mother says they would be too afraid to approach us for fear that we were pirates. But those days are long gone. They'll stop and hassle anyone now, just because they can. We have everything in order, though. It shouldn't take too long."

I watch nervously with the others, and sure enough no one appears to be too concerned, scattering back to their posts after taking a last look at the ship.

"Out here on the seas, it's best to keep to ourselves," Anh says. "A warship like that could easily overpower us, but these days they're more looking out for foreigners and making sure no one is approaching the mainland without the proper paperwork. Merchants and fishermen they largely leave alone, but . . ."

Thanh climbs up the mainmast to get a better look at the ship as everyone watches the horizon warily. He balances himself unsteadily at the top of the mast with a makeshift rope sling while he looks through the eyeglass.

He curses, then shouts back down to us, "She's following our course!"

Captain Hoa sighs again. "Just what we need."

Maheer glances at the captain, uncertainty in his eyes. "What do you want to do?"

Thanh shimmies down the mast and drops the final few feet to the deck, his face stormy. "We can outrun them. A heavy warship like that is no match for us. We can lose them along the coast, go upriver—"

"No." Captain Hoa places her hand on the tiller. "Even if they don't give chase, our ship will be flagged as suspicious, and they could send word ahead to Thăng Long. We cannot risk being apprehended by officials with the cargo we have."

She stands tall, looking at Maheer, and then nods at Thanh and the others who have gathered. "We keep steady!"

"Don't worry," Maheer says, catching my eye. "In all likelihood it will be a quick check and we'll be on our way."

We go back to our duties apprehensively. I'm so distracted by the oncoming ship that I scrub the same portion of the deck twice before realizing it.

It only takes a few hours for the other ship to gain on us. The massive navy warship is more than three times the size of our humble junk, its bright banner with the emperor's seal proudly catching the breeze. No one is even pretending to work now, the tension heavy in the air.

The other ship pulls closer and I can see just how many gun ports line the side of the hull and how many men are aboard in their neat uniforms, swords and pistols shining at their belts.

One man shouts as the ship draws closer, his voice carrying across the water. "State your vessel, port of entry, and your cargo."

"The *Huyền Vũ* merchant vessel, trading salt and fish," Captain Hoa calls back. "Canton, Hainan, Thăng Long."

"All merchants are subject to search and seizure. Your trade from Canton is at the whim of the Daoguang Emperor. Admiral Cheung of the *Nữ Tử* will board your ship now."

Their admiral, a stern-looking man, nods at his crew while they pull closer and ready a longboat that is practically the length of our own ship. The navy men grunt as they lower it into the water and raise its sail. I can't count how many men are on the warship, but the number of grim-faced men on deck are enough to make me uneasy. With a crew of only ten, even the men boarding the longboat outnumber us.

The patchwork sails of the *Huyền Vũ* looks shabby in comparison to the new sail of the Qing longboat, let alone the five masts of the *Nữ Tử* dwarfing us from a scant distance. A long plank is thrown across the two ships, and then we are boarded.

I watch carefully from the upper deck with the rest of the crew as the newcomers take in the *Huyền Vũ*. They're all impeccably dressed, their black robes neat with embroidered red trim. They look well fed and polished, their heads half-shaved and shiny, their queues hanging down their backs in the imperial Manchu style.

The men wrinkling their noses at our ship and looking disdainfully at us from their own deck all have the air of having never wanted for a meal, their cheeks full and round and healthy. Compared now to the clean and well-groomed men striding onto our ship, we look especially haggard after weeks at sea.

The men walk right past me, and I look down at my hands. They're calloused and rough, and I realize with pride that I must look like just one of the crew, not some runaway waif. I had never been fair—much to Lan Nai Nai's chagrin. She wanted my complexion light like the beautiful moon-faced ladies in stories. But I was the same nut brown as everyone else in the village, and now my skin is an even deeper brown, darkened from days in the sun. My hair is in a rough plait, coiled and pinned underneath a head wrap. I'm wearing my borrowed clothes of trousers and tunic just as well as any fine dress I'd worn at the teahouse. I stand tall, feeling good about my rightful place on the crew.

The men pay me and the rest of the crew no mind as they approach Maheer, who hands them the ship's manifest. Captain Hoa looks on with a critical eye and crossed arms.

"Everything seems in order." A thin man sniffs disdainfully, thumbing through the paperwork before handing it to a broad-shouldered man with the largest hat. This must be the admiral.

Maheer gives them a slight nod. "Captain Hoa Ngọc Hạnh," he says, jerking his head meaningfully to his right.

Admiral Cheung turns to face Captain Hoa, and if he is surprised or taken aback that our captain is a woman, he doesn't show it. "Admiral Cheung." The answer is curt and formal, no other names or titles. He's a handsome man who's just starting to go gray, streaks of salt and pepper in his long queue. Despite the wrinkles on his face, his eyes are sharp as he glances at our crew.

I almost miss it, but a brief moment of surprise flickers over Captain Hoa's face, her eyes widening slightly as Admiral Cheung steps toward her, and then it's gone, her features cold and blank.

"Did you port in Canton?" Admiral Cheung demands.

Maheer glances at Captain Hoa, who crosses her arms. "Yes, we did. What of it?"

"I'm going to need to search your ship and look at all your logs," Admiral Cheung says.

"Why, sir?"

"You know the trade laws. I need to make sure you're

transporting only what you say you are and nothing else. Search the ship!" He signals for his men, and soon our deck is swarming with navy soldiers.

Maheer scowls, but steps aside as they begin their search.

Captain Hoa is watching Admiral Cheung, her eyebrows knitted together as she watches him.

I huddle closer to Anh. "Does this happen often?"

"Never like this," Anh whispers back. "If they board us at all, they just look at our papers and leave. This is very strange."

I still, looking at the longswords and the guns on each of the men roaming the ship. They rifle through nets and the day's paltry catch, upending a net so fish slip out and shimmy all over the deck. I can hear them going through the barrels in the hold.

One of the men opens a barrel and makes a face. "Your cargo is rotting," he says. "Despicable trawling lowlifes. Can't believe they would eat this."

I exhale; it's only a thin layer of decaying fish atop the wax sheath covering of iron bars we're bringing to Thăng Long.

The admiral arrives back on deck, a frown on his face. "I have one more question, one that pertains to imperial security. I am looking for this lady, sixteen years of age, who we believe was kidnapped by a group of rogues."

He unrolls a scroll, and to my horror it's a painting of me. It's not a terribly close likeness; the painter made my eyes too small in proportion to my head, and the outfit and hairstyle are ostentatious and completely fictional—when I posed for it I certainly wasn't wearing a headpiece dripping with beaded gems, which looks peculiar contrasted with the plain pendant sitting against my neck. Mother commissioned this when she first started looking for suitors, and I've always hated it.

"The Shi family and the Liu family are offering a sizable reward for any information that may bring about her safe return," the admiral continues.

Something about this seems strange, especially knowing Mother's dismissal of the Qing government and its navy. Why would she enlist this man to find me? It doesn't feel right.

Admiral Cheung gestures at the painting. "She was last seen in Canton. Do any of you have information?"

Sun whispers to Maheer, who glances at me before stepping forward.

"We have not seen this youth. We were docked in Canton for three days." Maheer's tone is firm and offers nothing else, nothing to betray what he's thinking.

"The reward is five hundred gold cash," Admiral Cheung says. "Do any of you have any information on the whereabouts of Shi Xiang?"

Thanh's mouth falls open and his eyes dart toward me, but he doesn't say anything.

My stomach twists and turns, and I take an involuntary step backward.

Admiral Cheung catches my eye, and for a brief

second I think he might recognize me from the painting. His gaze is cold and considering, and I think about what he's looking for. A merchant's daughter, raised in a village. Kidnapped and terrified. I raise my chin and stare defiantly back at him, like I have belonged on this crew my entire life. But then his eyes slide over to Anh and then to the captain.

"If that's all," Captain Hoa says.

The admiral stands taller and gestures at his men. In a few minutes all the navy men are gone, and gradually we manage to put a bit of distance between us and the *Nữ Tử*. They don't appear to change course, though; it seems ominous to have them in our shadow.

"What are you lot gawking at? Let's go!" Captain Hoa barks. "Full speed ahead, and we're going to keep going through the night so we can lose them. Once this storm takes hold, we'll put out the lanterns so they won't be able to see us."

Maheer makes for the tiller, but no one else moves. Châu glances at me, and then back at Cheung's ship.

Ling Shan's eyes narrow. "That was *you*. Why is the navy looking for you?"

"It *is* your name, is it not?" Mianmian says. "I didn't know the Shi family had such strong imperial connections. I didn't even know Madame Shi had a child."

"I . . ." My stomach sinks. I don't know what to say.

"I don't think Cheung believed us," Thanh says. "He'll be back. Maybe with more ships. The *Huyền Vũ* will be placed

254

under suspicion. We won't be able to dock in Thăng Long if he sends word ahead to have officials arrest us there. And with the damn iron in our hold . . ." He curses.

A new kind of confused fear ripples through me—I had come to think of these people as my friends, and now they are all looking at me with suspicion and distrust in their eyes.

"The reputation of the *Huyền Vũ* still stands strong—*my* reputation," Captain Hoa snaps. "I always will get the goods to where they need to go. "Our problem is not the damn imperial navy on our tail, it's that we aren't moving fast enough, especially when we know we can get to Thăng Long before they do!"

"On our tail? They're on *her* tail!" Thanh stands up, pointing directly at me with a scowl. "I knew you were trouble. Runaway indeed. If the navy is looking for you, they're not going to stop. We'd be better off turning her over to Admiral Cheung and collecting the reward! Why don't we do that?"

The crew bursts into murmurs, and everyone is looking at me. I meet the eyes of the people whom I've shared meals with, who've taught me how to be one of them.

Anh's voice echoes in my mind. *You can't trust anyone.*

Ling Shan elbows Thanh in the stomach and glares at everyone, her eyes sharp. "We all came on this ship for our own reasons. The past is the past. Whatever Xiang's past is, she came to us for this chance at a greater future. Like many of us once did."

I give her a small, grateful smile, and she nods at me in solidarity.

Châu shifts uncomfortably, and Arthrit whispers something in his ear. Châu's gaze softens as he looks at me and then at his feet, chagrined.

A rain has started, drenching everyone on the boat with a steady, dreary mist.

"Everyone shut up and get to work!" Captain Hoa snarls. "There's a storm on the horizon, and we're sailing right through it. Let's hope the navy decides to moor somewhere safe and forget all about us. Keep steady the course!"

The storm is ferocious, and sailing without lanterns is miserable. There's no moon, just an endless onslaught of heavy rain. I go to light the hearth to cook as usual, but Mianmian stays my hand. "It's too risky with the oncoming storm," she says.

I nod in understanding as she lays out an array of pickled vegetables, dried meats, and yesterday's cold rice. Without my usual task, I feel untethered.

Mianmian eats quickly and goes back above deck, and I'm left wondering if I should as well. My stomach grumbles, and if it were any other day I would eat my share and then go up and see if anyone needed help on a line. I don't want to overstep, and I don't know what my place is on this crew anymore. Everyone seems to be avoiding me, giving me strange looks that range from curious to suspicious. I wonder what they're thinking—if they're measuring up how little I've contributed to the work on the ship, if they'd rather have the reward. Surely it would be worth far more than an untrained fool like myself.

Ling Shan and Sun eat quickly without talking to each other or to me, and I can't take the silence. I move to the ladder going up to the deck when the grate cover opens and rain splatters in. Anh drops down to the lower deck, shaking her wet hair. She takes in my sad, drawn face and asks, "Did you eat?"

I shake my head, and I look at Ling Shan and Sun. "I'll eat later."

Anh grabs me by the elbow before I get to the ladder. "Now's as good a time as any. We do this for all storms. Half the crew stays below to rest so we're fresh when we need to relieve the rest up top. You have to eat. Come on."

I follow her back to the food and watch as she prepares a bowl for herself and then for me.

Ling Shan and Sun finish eating quickly and wipe down their bowls before returning to their hammocks.

"It's the imperial association," Anh mutters to me under her breath. "The fact that your family has the ear of such a high-ranking officer makes them nervous."

"My mother runs a teahouse," I whisper back, incredulous.

"Imperial officers dine there?"

Of course I'd seen officials and clerks there, but that didn't mean Mother could have the influence to search for me this far.

Anh is silent for a moment.

"Ling Shan thinks you're a runaway, like she was," she says quietly. "The others assumed as much. It's not so much the *what* you're running from, you know. I think they're just upset you didn't warn us. That an admiral of the Qing navy himself would be searching for you."

"I didn't know," I plead. "I had no idea that would happen."

Anh exhales.

"You believe me . . ." I trail off, not daring it to be a question.

"I believe you had no idea what you were wearing around your neck your whole life," Anh says. "I believe you put the work into sailing, into being a part of this crew." The rain has slicked her hair to her face, and I cannot see her expression aside from the gleam of her eyes reflecting back at me. "I also know you haven't opened those letters since we started sailing. I know you have no more idea than I what that poem means and how to get to the treasure."

Captain Hoa said that she would tell the crew when the time was right. But that was before she took the iron shipment in Changping, before Admiral Cheung revealed that painting of me and changed everything. When does she plan to tell them now? After we speed to Thăng Long and offload the iron? What if we are arrested there and we never have this chance to find Zheng Yi Sao's treasure? If I never get to prove myself?

My hands close around the cold bowl, the brittle chopsticks in my hand. "I could—if I talk to the captain—"

"My mother has a plan. You cannot sway her." Anh glances at the not-sleeping forms of Ling Shan and Sun in their hammocks and then back at me. "If she plans to take the iron to Thăng Long first, then that is her decision. Plus, that will give you more time to decipher the riddles."

"But . . . you believe me. You know I will get us there."

Anh leans in close as if to say something, and then at the last moment hesitates, hovering. "Yes. I know you will." She takes a step back. "I'll talk to Thanh. He's just protective, that's all. With my mother, the *Huyền Vũ* . . . all of us."

I nod, grateful for the affirmation, but it doesn't instill much confidence in me with all the cool distance from everyone else. I eat in silence, quickly wiping my dish clean and setting it down. A stray crate clatters across the floor as the ship careens back and forth. I am technically alone for the first time in weeks.

Ling Shan and Sun both appear to be asleep, their breaths even and spaced. Sun is snoring ever so slightly, shuddering as his dream shakes him.

In my trunk, I find the letters untouched, still bound in the red silk ribbon, wrapped in the clothes I wore when I first arrived. I undo the ribbon with trembling fingers, and I read the words of my father for the first time.

The letters are clumsy, the words of affection merely attempting poetry, but the sentiment is sincere. They had loved each other, and he missed her dearly when he was at sea. I cannot discern if they were on different ships and exchanged letters when they were apart, or if this was when Mother managed the teahouse while Father was abroad. But the letters are not the hive of information I thought them to be. They're mundane and conversational and occasionally go off on long tangents like *I listened to the song of the nightingale, and the melody does not compare to your voice*, and I do not have the time to ponder ciphers or intricate codes.

I hold each of the letters up to a lantern to see if there is any hidden ink to be revealed, but there is none. There are no references to the treasure or the island or any of the lines in the poem scrawled on the map piece, nothing to go off of. I read them again and again, and I wish I had started sooner. I wish I had stolen away moments to ponder them better, because I do not have the time now, and I cannot admit to this crew that I do not know the way.

Footsteps sound as rain enters the hold before the grate is shut again. I slip farther behind the hammocks, tucking my feet under me and hoping that the darkness is full enough that no one can see me. The sound echoes as wet shoes make their way across to the kitchen area. Two bowls are being prepared and hastily eaten.

"We're pushing the ship too far; I don't like our odds in this storm," Thanh mutters.

"The captain has steered us through worse." Maheer's voice is calm and steady.

Thanh scoffs. "You put too much faith in her."

"You don't believe in your own mother?"

"I think she is risking all our lives to prove something. I'm not sure what or why. We can easily just approach the *Nữ Tử* and make a fine profit by turning Xiang in to the imperials."

"It's strange, isn't it?" Maheer ponders. "A navy ship being enlisted to help a merchant find her daughter?"

More footsteps. "Maheer, I need you up top," Captain Hoa says, her voice gruff.

After Maheer leaves, Thanh glances around the lower deck, confirming that both Ling Shan and Sun are asleep. Then he speaks again, his voice low and angry.

"You can't be serious about going after the treasure," Thanh says.

Oh. He knows, I remember. *He's known this whole time.* Suddenly it all makes sense—Thanh was with Anh when she opened the pendant for the first time. It explains the disdainful way he has regarded me the whole time I've been on the ship, the suspicion he's held toward me, the snide comments he's made. He thinks I've been leading his mother on a wild chase after a legend. After what Anh has told me about their previous experiences, I can understand why he wants to protect his family.

Thanh speaks again, his voice filled with urgency. "A sure thing versus one full of risks. Mẹ, you can't—"

"Oh, but I *am* sure," the captain says. "The admiral . . . I recognized him. He wasn't always a navy lapdog, you know. That was Cheung Po Tsai himself."

"You mean . . ."

"One of those pardoned from the Red Banner Squadron of the Dragon Fleet and placed directly in the emperor's imperial navy. He was always thirsty for power, and wasn't satisfied being Zheng Yi Sao's second in command."

I almost drop the letter. The admiral was—is—a pirate? What does this mean?

"It explains exactly why he would go to this trouble to find a lost girl," Captain Hoa explains. "The navy doesn't care about the personal affairs of random merchants— unless it would also suit their own ends. The fact that Cheung Po Tsai is here . . . he must have followed the whispers here from Canton. Thanh, you were there when Anh found the map in Xiang's pendant in that tavern. Who else was there?"

"I didn't think anyone was paying us much mind. And Sizhui had a reputation for tall tales. There were a few navy men in the corner drinking."

"Did you recognize any of them from Cheung's crew?" Captain Hoa asks.

"It's possible." Thanh sighs. "People in the tavern may have gathered that it was a map that had resurfaced. As soon as we knew what we had, Anh hid it away and didn't mention it again. Sizhui, of course, ran his mouth. I made sure to plant several rumors to throw any rival crews off our track, but no one knew anything about that pendant."

"He must have known," Captain Hoa mutters. "Of course he would have known. If the navy is sniffing about for that map, then Cheung Po Tsai must have put the information together once he saw that painting of Xiang and thought he would get it first. But no matter. The fact that Cheung Po Tsai is here, searching for the pendant, too . . . it only confirms that the map is real."

Thanh exhales. "If you're sure . . ."

"I've already changed our course. We are on our way to the treasure now. Once we get to the island, we can move it, give Cheung Po Tsai the map he seeks, and be on our way."

"And the girl?"

I do not hear what is whispered next; they continue their conversation as they climb the ladder back up to the deck.

Once I am alone, I remove the map from my pendant and compare the poem written on the scrap to the letters. I'm startled to realize they were made by a different hand. But of course, that would make sense; perhaps this is the fabled Zheng Yi Sao's own hand who wrote this.

When sunset clouds fall into the deep ocean blue

The place where the spider-lilies bloom longing for distant vistas

Weary traveler, for what aspiration do you come?

The tiger's tears shine brightly at the second watch of night.

I read it again and again. Perhaps I've been thinking about it too metaphorically, looking for meaning behind each literary reference, wondering if the Head of the Dragon or one of her pirate captains had a poet's heart. Perhaps it is exactly what it is—a set of instructions to pay heed to once there.

I carefully take one of the letters and onto it copy the map itself, with the charts and the coastline but without the words. I ruin three letters because my hand won't stop shaking. It doesn't help that the storm is tossing the ship from side to side. Or perhaps it is because my tears have smudged the ink.

Finally I have one that's a respectable copy, and I hope the ship stays steady enough for the ink to dry. It won't pass for an original without the seal, but that won't be the point.

I commit the poem to memory, the diagram and the strange X and the squiggle of coastline. Then I dip the scrap of parchment into the lantern's flickering flame, watching it burn to embers. The edges of the map fade, and the crisp outlines of the island go red hot and then crumble to ash. Then I do the same to the rest of the letters.

I'm tired of others deciding my fate for me. I won't be a pawn in anyone's game. Now, there won't be a way to take this information from me.

CHAPTER SIXTEEN
THE TRUTH

I CLIMB ABOVE DECK, INTENDING TO TALK TO CAPTAIN HOA. She's at the helm with Maheer, shouting something against the wind. He nods and heads back down below.

The wind howls and rain pummels the deck; within moments my clothes are completely drenched and I'm shivering. I sweep my hair out of my eyes and approach the upper deck, keeping my pace even as an errant wave sends the ship careening to the right.

Châu shouts as he holds the line steady with Mianmian as they pull it taut. On the other side of the ship, Thanh is watching me from where he's taking in the slack on the other line.

"Captain," I venture. "I need to—"

Captain Hoa nods. "Yes. I know."

Does she? My heart pounds as Maheer, Ling Shan, and Sun climb back onto the deck.

"Shift change already?" Ling Shan asks.

Captain Hoa approaches the center of the ship as all eyes turn toward her. "I needed everyone on deck," she says.

The wind ruffles through the thick canvas sails, and everyone gathers. The tension is thick, Thanh glancing at me, his eyebrows knitted together.

"What's all this about?" Mianmian asks. "Are you going to explain why we're pushing through this storm instead of mooring somewhere safer up the coast?"

"We need to put a considerable distance between us and Cheung," Captain Hoa says.

Ling Shan frowns. "Do you think he knows we have Xiang? That he'd come after us?"

"I am certain he is aware we know far more than we gave him," Captain Hoa says. "But we have what he does not expect, and we will use this to our advantage."

"What are you talking about?" Sun asks.

Maheer steeples his fingers together. There is no surprise on his face; he just nods for the captain to continue. I wonder how many voyages they have sailed together, to know each other so, to build a loyalty like that. "I am sure Captain Hoa has had her reasons she has kept the true nature of this course to herself," he says.

Captain Hoa grins. A flash of lightning illuminates the gleam of her broad smile, the determined set of her jaw.

Her long coat billows in the wind, and she stands tall as she takes to the center of the watching crew. "My family of the *Huyền Vũ*. You all put your faith in me, to keep you safe, to bring you to sunny shores, to keep the wind at our back, to keep sailing."

She paces back and forth, and not for the first time, I can feel how her very presence hums with energy and strength, how everyone is drawn to her every word. Her commanding stance widens, and she gestures around at each and every one of us.

"You all are here for a reason—whether it be your blood cast you out, your emperor did not do as he promised, or your king found you lacking—well, I did not! The sea cares not of your status, of whom you love! On this ship we work hard, and no emperor, no king, no navy lapdog could tell us what to do!"

Châu nods, his face intent as Arthrit lays his head on his shoulder. Ling Shan looks to me and back toward Captain Hoa.

"For years we have struggled to fill our nets even as tariffs rose. We smuggled goods right under the watchful eye of any government, but did our coffers grow?"

Thanh shakes his head.

"No," the captain continues. "With each passing year, the storms got rougher. And you all held steady, even in those times when it seemed *Huyền Vũ* would not sail again. We banded together, scraped what we could. It was all we could do just to survive." She closes her eyes. "Those who knew me in my younger years know my history, that I once sailed with the Dragon Fleet. That I knew Zheng Yi Sao had hidden a treasure beyond anyone's wildest dreams. The plunder of a thousand ports."

Ling Shan inhales sharply.

"I chased this treasure for years. Every rumor. Every possibility. You see, when the Head of the Dragon first hid her massive wealth, she kept the secret location on a map that was separated into many pieces. No one lieutenant could hope to find it on their own. But as the years passed, Zheng Yi Sao grew paranoid. One by one she hunted them down, killed them to protect the final resting place, gathered the pieces of the map that she once entrusted them with. Even her second in command." Captain Hoa holds her gaze steady. "I used to report directly to him. Cheung Po Tsai. I know his face. I know she left him for dead when she realized he had stolen a piece of the map, hidden it somewhere. And I know that he, too, lost it, many years ago."

Captain Hoa strides over to me, taking my hand and holding it aloft. "Shi Xiang is the answer. Her father took that piece and sent it away back to his village where she kept it safe, hidden, not knowing its true nature. Upon learning the truth, Xiang chose us—the *Huyền Vũ*—to find the fabled treasure."

Thanh crosses his arms. Whatever direction he thought they were going after his conversation with his mother, this likely wasn't it.

"How do you know it's the real map?" Arthrit asks.

Captain Hoa claps me on the shoulder. "Because Cheung Po Tsai boarded our ship today. Up until now this could have been another rumor, another story. But I saw his face and recognized immediately who he was. The one who rose to power as Zheng Yi Sao's chosen favorite. You see, the rumors in Canton were just that: Rumors of the map resurfacing. But Cheung wasn't looking for Xiang . . . he was looking for *this*."

Captain Hoa flicks my pendant out from under my shirt and nods at me.

My fingers tremble to unclasp it in the rain, and I pull out the copy of the map as everyone turns to look at me. I widen my eyes, playing the naive fool they think I am. "I've been grateful to have a place here. All my life I thought I was suitable only to be married off, and you all . . . you all taught me I could be more." I look to Ling Shan and find her nodding along with me. "The truth is, I ran away from a betrothal, and—" I take a deep breath, and this is the part that hurts the most, because it is true. "I've found a home here. I hope you will want to keep me." I unfurl the map and present it to Captain Hoa.

She looks at me, and I can see she knows it's a fake. And yet with all the eyes of the crew on us, she holds it aloft. "My family of the *Huyền Vũ*! I hold in my hands the last legacy of the legendary Zheng Yi Sao, in her own words the location where the plunder of a thousand ports lies hidden.

We will sail through this storm, find the island, and take the treasure for our own, and Shi Xiang will have brought us there!"

A great cheer erupts, and Anh catches my eye as if to say, *I hope you know what you're doing.*

The next morning the storm is behind us, and Cheung Po Tsai's ship is nowhere to be seen. As we move farther south, the stormy blue waters turn a frothy, verdant green, speaking to the lush shallows below with their underwater forests and strange drifting animals, translucent as ghosts.

"Welcome to Hạ Long Bay," Thanh says, his eyes misting over in wonder. The waters are calm as we drift between two impossibly tall structures, a rocky outcrop that seems to have split in two.

There are islands everywhere, as far as I can see. They rise out of the water like the coils of a great serpent's back. I can see where the bay gets the name, the way it looks like a dragon sleeping in the water. Great mountains rise up in the distance, and everything is green, the dense jungle slowly climbing up the cliffs and the deep emerald of the waters. We sail past a tumble of rocks lying in the bay, a scar on the cliff face above as if the gods had reached out and struck the mountain. The smaller islands on the outskirts of the bay are worn rough by the harsh batter of waves and storms long past, and as we drift closer to the bay, a huge land mass appears to the south.

"That's an island?" I gasp. "It looks like another kingdom."

Captain Hoa grins, a new light in her eyes. "Cát Bà. It is the largest island in this area, with a port. We aren't going to stop there. Too many tongues wagging now."

We sail past Cát Bà and its busy port, until we enter a strange sort of quiet, broken only by the rustle of trees and the cries of birds and other creatures I cannot identify. Two massive rocks rise like guard towers, a small copse of trees swaying in the wind as they grow stubbornly atop the stone. We pass by a few smaller boats and sampans in the coves and beaches, and occasionally see fishermen draw their nets, but for the most part, we are alone.

Ahead we see a shrine on a lonely beach, its colors faded and its offering stand empty.

"Let's drop anchor here for a moment," Captain Hoa says. "It doesn't hurt to pay our respects."

Maheer smiles at me before I follow the others to the rowboat. He and Ling Shan linger on the deck, observing quietly as we approach the shore.

My feet sink into the soft sand, and the captain produces a few sticks of incense. She lights them, offering a silent prayer.

I close my eyes and wonder if the gods are displeased with me for leaving the village, for wanting more, for getting to this place. Perhaps they would understand.

The shrine is adorned with a worn statue of Guanyin.

I begin the usual prayer, but as a sense of peace washes over me, I find myself not asking for forgiveness. Perhaps my soul has lived in the wrong place this whole time, and I've always been meant to be at sea. The time spent with the crew on the water, the work we do . . . I feel my mind sharpening each morning when I wake, my arms sore and tired, but every day bringing new strength as I hoist the sails or pull the nets or cook the day's food. I'm good at this, and the Goddess would understand.

There's a peace here in the journey, and I find all I wish for is for it to never end.

Once we find the treasure—if my plan succeeds, and it must—and we return to Canton, what then? I could manage the Pearl House, for sure. But would I be satisfied merely listening to travelers' stories now that I've had a taste of the world?

Hạ Long Bay is quiet.

The *Huyền Vũ* drifts through the waters as Captain Hoa steers us toward our destination, a thick tension lying over all of us instead of the usual boisterous conversation and song.

The island is a crooked, scraggly thing, with a winding stretch of rock fallen in a near-perfect circle, as eerie and strange as if the gods had left it there themselves. From afar it looks like a mess of dark rock shrouded with trees and undergrowth, its mountains reaching for the heavens, and as we approach along the southern edge it's all cragged rock and rough waves, broken masts and the derelict wrecks of ships that have been dashed to pieces in the dangerous shallows.

Captain Hoa looks at the map copy and then back at me, her eyes steely as she guides us around the island. It's a mass of overgrown jungle and deep, dense mangroves, and in silence we drop anchor in the inset cove from the map, a calmer bit of water protected by an atoll. We set up camp on the beach as night falls and the forest rustles with ominous quiet. The fire flickers, but this isn't a celebration tonight. No drinks are passed around, and wary eyes follow me when I get up to refill my water flagon.

Arthrit comes back from scouting the island with Mianmian. "I have bad news. Admiral Cheung and his men are here."

"What?" Captain Hoa straightens her belt, her hands twitching toward her sword.

"They've just anchored on the far side of the island and are setting up camp on the northern beach."

Whispers break out, and Sun wrings his hands anxiously. "Did you see all those cannons? They could absolutely destroy us."

Thanh stands. "I say we give them Xiang." As I begin to protest, he pats me on the back and gives me a patronizing smile. "You'll be safe. He'll return you back to your mother and you can eat sticky buns and grow old as your heart desires, hm?"

"What's a paltry five hundred gold when we could have all the treasure of the Dragon Fleet?" Ling Shan demands. "We keep her with us, divide the shares equally."

"The navy will be after all of us if we do," Thanh retorts. "Even if we went after the treasure first, the *Nữ Tử* could overpower us and take it. What use is finding the treasure if we don't get to keep it?"

"If you forfeit Xiang to Cheung Po Tsai, he will have the ability to find it on his own," Maheer says. "Unless you have other plans for her map."

Thanh's eyes flicker to my throat. "We could—"

"No," Anh says immediately.

"What if we find the treasure, and then drop off Xiang at Changping with her share?" Sun suggests. "Then we all just go our separate ways."

"Does the treasure even really exist?" Mianmian wonders.

The argument gets louder until Captain Hoa empties a flagon of water onto the fire. It sizzles out, smoke billowing everywhere. It flies into her face but she doesn't move, and the soot leaves long smoky marks on her skin as she glares at all of us. "Quiet!" Captain Hoa roars.

"You're not an emperor," Thanh says, folding his arms across his chest. "We accept your guidance because you are captain. But as we have always done—anything that affects all of us this way—we decide as a crew. I vote we collect the reward and get off this island!"

Ling Shan frowns, and Mianmian looks at her feet.

Captain Hoa glances at me, and all other eyes follow.

I reach for the pendant at my neck. I turn the mechanism until it unlocks, and I pull out the copy of the map and drop it to the ground. "You want the map? Go ahead."

No one moves.

"The map leads us to this island, and Captain Hoa got us here, but the rest of it—the riddles, the instructions— they're all in here." I stand tall, tapping my temple. "I give you my word I will lead you to the treasure, but you need me. We will retrieve the treasure together, and I will take my fair share back to Canton. You can't just hand me off to Cheung and take the map for yourself. *I* am the map now."

The fire flickers, and behind the flames the crew murmurs agreement.

Captain Hoa picks up the copy of the map and hands it back to me. I reroll the scroll and place it back in the pendant—it's useless now, but on the letter on the back are still my father's words, and it is still important to me.

The captain regards the crew. "Xiang will guide us to the treasure. We will move it, as planned. We know Cheung Po Tsai is here. They know we're likely on the island, but they don't know where we are just yet. They don't know we have the map and we have Xiang. We must be ready to fight his men. We'll lay traps, and we will be prepared."

We get to work.

Long wooden poles we picked up in Changping are brought out—I had thought them for repairs on this ship, but instead the crew is sharpening their ends into pikes to be laid in ditches or used as weapons. It comes together beside the dying embers of the fire, and I carve my own pike alongside Anh. I can't find a good rhythm, but I try to match Anh's long, sure strokes. I am pleased to discover my grip is better, and that there are calluses on my fingers to help hold the wood in place.

While everyone is settling down on the beach to sleep, setting out mats or blankets, an unease seems to drift over the camp. There's no music tonight, just the unsettling squawk and occasional strange laughter from the jungle.

"Monkeys," Mianmian says with a shudder. "Terrifying creatures."

"I'll take first watch," Thanh says. "But I want to know where we're headed in the morning."

I meet his gaze and muster all the confidence I have. "You'll have to wait until morning, then."

I'm dreaming, floating in that awful space where I know it's a dream but I'm helpless to leave. Everything is a blur—Anh's warm smile, the ship being tossed about like a child's plaything in a turbulent storm, Mother looming above me, her face twisted in disapproval.

I'm jolted awake by a sudden shaking. A cold hand claps over my mouth, and in the dark my vision adjusts to see Anh's sparkling eyes in front of me.

She jerks her head at me to follow, and I sit up on the hard sand, following her lead as we carefully make our way around the sleeping forms of the crew. Captain Hoa's hand twitches on her sword. Châu murmurs and snuggles closer to Arthrit, his arm curling around his partner's waist. Sun's head droops as he snores, and he yawns for a terrifying moment, his eyelids fluttering, until his head falls back to his chest.

A crescent moon casts long, midnight-blue shadows on the dark shoreline. The sea is calm tonight, the ship protected by the island's rocky atoll.

Once we're far enough away from the camp I dare to whisper, "What? Why did you wake me?"

"We must leave. I waited until my watch and everyone was asleep." Anh glares at me. "You think you're so clever, but you know now with the navy breathing down our backs there's nothing stopping anyone from killing you once they have the treasure in hand!"

"But—"

"You're a fool, Shi Xiang. Brave, but a fool nonetheless." She pushes the longboat out to the shore, tossing the lantern and a small rucksack inside. The mast is still lying lengthwise across the bottom of the boat, and the sails folded and stored neatly at the helm. "Maybe if we had gotten here well ahead of the navy and had more time, I could have convinced the crew of your intentions, to share the treasure equally as you proposed. But the lure of the gold, the fear of the navy chasing us . . . now there is too much to leave to chance."

She glances at me. "Besides. What will you do at dawn when they discover you do not know what any of the map riddles mean?"

"I would have figured it out," I insist, but can't quite force enough confidence into my voice.

Anh laughs as she hops in the longboat and I push it into the water. She pulls at the oars and then offers me her hand; I climb in after her. Something in my heart swells. "Thank you."

"This doesn't mean anything," Anh says, rowing fiercely. "I'm only keeping my word. I'm protecting my interests, because I'm not going to miss out on my share of the treasure just because my cowardly brother wants to convince everyone to take the easier route." She scowls. "I overheard him talking to Sun and a few others after you fell asleep. He would only need three more votes, and by sunrise, after learning you have no idea where you are leading us, he would have even convinced the captain."

I take the other oar, and we row the longboat out of the bay. I swallow hard, thinking of what all this means. We travel in silence for a while, with nothing but the stars to guide us.

"So what is your plan?" I ask.

"Get you to safety first. We can reach one of the other islands, and by keeping to the shallows it might take a week to sail all the way to Cát Bà in the longboat, but we could do it."

"You have no plan!" I crow at her, unable to help but laugh.

So many possibilities ahead of us, and yet all of them seem to lead back to one thing. "Well, then," I say. "Let us find the treasure first, and solve these riddles together, and then we will have all the leverage we need to get out of here."

CHAPTER SEVENTEEN

SUNSET CLOUDS

WE ROW THROUGH THE NIGHT, KEEPING QUIET AS WE CIR-
cle the cove and put as much distance between us and the
crew as possible. The still night protects us as we make our
way around to the rocky shore; I forget my exhaustion and
focus on the task at hand. We keep to the shallows until I
can hear the bottom of the boat scraping along the sharp
rocks.

The crescent moon climbs higher, and my arms grow
tired and my eyelids droop. We row until we are too tired
to keep going, finally tying the boat off in a cluster of mangroves.

I don't remember falling asleep, but suddenly I'm jerking
awake. The sun is warm on my face, and my back aches from
some part of the boat digging into my side. But I also feel
incredibly comfortable and warm, like I've been wrapped

in a secure blanket. Still in that lovely place between asleep and awake, I blink my eyes open.

It's a bit past dawn, the coolness of the night still clinging to the beach, and Anh is draped over me, her head resting on my shoulder. Her jacket is lying a few feet away at the end of the rowboat, scattered by either the wind or kicked away while she slept.

I barely breathe. This isn't like the night at the tavern in Changping, when I awoke with my head pounding and liquor still in my veins. It was easy then to excuse how we fell asleep that night as camaraderie. But last night we must have reached for each other in our sleep. I want to turn over to ease the annoyance of the oar now digging into my ribs, but I still myself. One of Anh's arms is curled around the small of my back.

The cluster of trees where our longboat is tied grows right into the water, long leaves dipping with the current. I can see from the way the dappled sunlight is hitting my face that soon we will be sitting in full sun.

But for now, the shade is cool and Anh is warm. In sleep, her face loses the tough edge she tries to maintain. A slight smile graces her lips, and she curls in closer, her face pressing into my shoulder, her arm wrapping tighter around me.

Something about this moment is precious, the way Anh seems small and vulnerable here—such a contrast to the loud, boisterous energy she usually brings to the world. I see the confident and nonchalant way she appears not to care, but beneath that I also see the softness—the way she loves her crew, her family, the way she reaches out with a helping hand when Sun struggles with a heavy load, or how she makes sure to bring Mianmian a bowl at mealtimes. I think about her laugh and how full of joy it is, the way her eyes shine when she's talking about seeing the fish jump or the luminescence along the shoreline.

Anh protected me, even when she said that she only brought me along to look for the treasure, that we weren't friends. Everything she's done seems to imply the opposite. She protected me from her brother and fought for me to be on the ship in the first place, believed me when I said I knew what I was doing when I knew anything but.

I wonder at the way Anh is curled up close, the trusting way she is leaning toward me. I breathe in the warmth of her, as if to promise back, *Yes, I will keep you safe.*

Something rustles in the bushes—a small animal, per-haps, but the sudden movement is enough to startle Anh awake. Her eyes snap open, and she blinks at me for a moment, our faces impossibly close. She sits up abruptly, brushing sand off herself and looking pointedly into the jungle.

The events of the night all come back in a rush. We've stolen a boat and escaped to find the treasure on our own. We won't be able to go back until we have the information we need.

Anh hands me a flagon of water, and I gulp it down, my throat parched.

"Careful with that," she says. "I wasn't able to sneak away many supplies, just what is on the longboat. We have enough for two days, maybe three."

The waters around us are a deep, brilliant greenish blue, and where we are, I can see to the grains of sand beneath us and the spectacular array of shells and fish swimming by.

There's something else, too—bulbous, translucent oddities in the water, like gossamer silk sleeves with long threads trailing behind them. I tug on Anh's elbow and gesture to the water. The creatures float all around us, bobbing in the current as they drift back and forth. Some are circular and some are long, and the biggest one I see is as large as my face. As I look closer, I see they're not completely translucent, some of them radiating opaque colors, lines of pink and purple and—

I gasp. "Sunset clouds."

"What?"

"The first part of the riddle. *When sunset clouds fall into the deep ocean blue . . .*" I laugh. "It's clever, because at first I thought it meant for us to look for a specific cloud formation at sunset, or watch the sun setting over the horizon, but I think this is it!" I follow the creatures as they drift by. "It must be the current that we must follow."

"I thought Zheng Yi Sao was a master at tricks and traps," Anh says. "I'm sure these aren't just pretty words. They have to be a warning of some kind." She frowns, poking one with her oar. "But these are just jellyfish. They sometimes get tangled up in our nets in the warmer waters. Pretty tasty when cooked with chili oil, or pickled. Why would it be important enough to mention?"

"Have you ever seen any this big?" They are indeed cloudlike, floating in the water with no discernible direction, but they do not seem to mind. I watch them as the current carries them along the edge of the rocks, and then the clouds of pink disappear suddenly from my vision.

"Good point. Let's bring some with us to cook later." Anh reaches for the water, and I seize her arm.

"Wait! Look!"

Horrified, I point—ahead of us is something the size of a small child rotting in the water, some sort of animal covered in coarse, black fur.

"It's a monkey," Anh says. "It's dead, it won't hurt you."

As the dead monkey drifts past us, I see it more clearly— its bloodied and matted fur . . . and how it's ensnared in the slinky silver-pink threads, the bodies of the pink jellyfish fluttering alongside it.

I let out a high-pitched shriek. "They're—they're eating it!"

Anh stares, a discomforting quiet settling in around us. "You know, they always did have some sort of sharp, numbing sting. These must be poisonous."

"They must have been in the poem for that reason," I mutter. "Come on, let's see what's up ahead."

We follow the current alongside the mangroves where their thick roots tangle in the water, and there I see the jellyfish weren't just disappearing—the current is drawing them through the mangroves. I stand, the boat rocking back and forth as I unsheathe my sword and start hacking away at the branches.

"What are you doing?" Anh asks. "You're going to dull the blade. Here." She hands me a machete.

It's a bit easier going with the thicker and sturdier blade. "The current goes into here. I think there's a cove or something just beyond—yes!"

I push the branches aside, revealing a huge lagoon on the other side of the thicket.

"It would be easier if we just got into the water and cut," Anh grumbles as she joins me, finally resorting to breaking branches with her arms.

"And get eaten alive by the jellyfish? No, thank you!"

"Obviously it would take them longer to eat us than for us to eat them," Anh snaps back.

"That doesn't even make sense!"

"Well, I guess if we were poisoned then we couldn't move," she mutters.

I shake my head and keep cutting. The branches scratch at my arms, and my forehead is dripping with sweat. My throat is dry again already, but I keep going. Finally we clear enough of the brush to guide the rowboat through. The water easily slips between the roots, and the jellyfish glide lazily through to the open lagoon. It's massive, a quiet emerald pool amid the rising mountains with a small protected beach on the other side.

"All right, so that's the first clue," Anh says. "What's next?"

"*The place where the spider-lilies bloom longing for distant vistas,*" I recite. "*Weary traveler, for what aspiration do you come?*"

Anh blinks at me. "I'm sorry I asked. What does that even mean? Spider-lilies?"

"Like the ones that bloom only in the underworld," I say. "On the banks of the river that washes away memories."

"So forget all chance of finding this place," she grumbles.

"No, no, it has to be more than that. The first time I read it, it didn't make sense, but it was still lovely, you know? Like the first line, using the phrase *yuān yáng*—because the writer could have just said *shuǐorhǎi* to mean the water, but they chose *yuān yáng.*"

"Which means . . . ?"

Right, Anh doesn't read or speak Mandarin. "Ducks!"

"This is ridiculous."

"No, it's poetry. Ducks are known for bonding for life. They're a symbol of everlasting love." My father etched the same promise onto the pendant, and now I wonder if these are his words, if he was the one entrusted to encode the treasure's location for Zheng Yi Sao. I feel so connected to his spirit, his love of the poetic form.

"Why not just *say* that?" Anh grumbles as the rowboat

grounds into the sandy beach. She leaps out, trudging toward the dry sand as she drags it forward.

I huff at her. "It's a poem! You know, figures of speech? Words used for other words?"

Anh laughs at me. "Poetry. What use would I have for beautiful words? Can words fill your stomach or your sails?"

I want to say something smart and witty, recite some lines of my favorite poem to impress her about how valuable beautiful words can really be, but my memory blanks.

Ahead of me, Anh yanks the rope with a huff. "Don't just sit in the boat—either get out and help or get out and make this easier!"

"Of course, I'm sorry," I say sheepishly, jumping out into the shallows. I've been lost in my thoughts about poetry, trying to think of a poem Anh would appreciate, and share some of my favorites with her. But the task at hand is here—we've made it to the island, and now we have to find the treasure before anyone else does.

The cool water splashes on my face, bringing me back to my senses, more water sluicing into my already damp clothes. The rough hemp grows coarser on my skin, sagging against my hips.

"That should do it for now. Looks like we're at high tide, so no need to worry about it drifting away."

Poetry, tides, the sun, the stars, something beautiful to say . . .

I wipe the salt from my eyes and blink. Anh is

shrugging out of her wet things, flinging her jacket at a nearby boulder, where it joins her trousers with a loud, wet *thwap*. Her bare shoulders gleam in the sunlight, her thin cotton undergarments clinging to her lithe body underneath two crossed belts of leather. She undoes these carefully, unsheathing several knives and laying them out on top of her jacket to dry. I look away, heat rushing to my face.

"Let's rest here and figure out what we're going to do," she calls back over her shoulder. "I bet we have some time; Mẹ won't leave yet because that would surely draw attention from the navy. They know they need the map to find the treasure, and the most they can do now is ward off attack." Anh jerks her head at my own clothing. "You should take the chance to dry off."

It sounds like a wise plan, and I don't have a better alternative, so I undo the ties on my own tunic, my clumsy fingers stumbling.

Anh laughs. "Here, let me help."

Her deft brown fingers meet mine as they make quick work of the fastener. Her hands are calloused and rough, and cold at first, but then comes a brief touch of warmth. Her fingers brush my hands before she drops to the next knot. For a brief moment her eyes flick up to mine, a deep, warm brown that's almost golden. The moment feels like it both lasts forever and is gone in a second as she steps away, looking up at the gray crags climbing skyward.

I shift out of the heavy jacket and my own set of trousers and set them carefully next to hers to dry in the hot morning sun.

My heart pounds. Did she see me looking at her? Would she know what I'm thinking and be angry at me for having these feelings? I can't risk it. I can't risk her leaving me when there's so much at stake. We're here together, and we're going to have to rely on each other to get through this. We're barely even friends; I can't be fantasizing when she's made it abundantly clear she's only interested in her share of the treasure and a life on the seas, the ability to go anywhere she wants.

I'd spun a future with the thought of my own share—running the Pearl House, or perhaps my own teahouse with a view of the port—and I wonder if that's what I really desire from life. Maybe I never even thought about what might be possible.

The sunlight sparkles high above us, and we make a simple meal of salted fish and rice. I look out toward the length of the lagoon and the expanse of Hạ Long Bay beyond it, the countless islands rising up in the distance. The water is impossibly clear here.

"So you burned the map," Anh says.

I nod and take up a stick, tracing in the sand as if it were a brush. I recreate the detailed map of the island from memory, a rough half circle pierced by an X. It doesn't make sense, not without any indication of north or lines of latitude or longitude. It must be its own clue, one that won't make sense until we solve the next one.

"Are you sure this was a good idea?" I ask nervously.

The pendant is cold against my chest. It's empty now, the information only in my head. I feel guilty, thinking about Captain Hoa and what she must have thought to see us gone that morning. After the weeks we spent on the boat, her comforting smile, the warm way she'd made sure I was taken care of, as if I were her own daughter. The way she'd been careful to teach me about navigating by the stars, the way she praised me each time I helped hoist the sails correctly. I'd felt for the first time I was a part of something.

"Trust me, you'll always need a contingency plan," Anh says. "Without the information that was in the pendant, our crew—or Cheung Po Tsai's crew—could search forever. And from all the stories of Zheng Yi Sao, she was every bit as cunning as she was ruthless. She wouldn't have just buried it neatly. The collected treasure of the entire Dragon Fleet? It's going to be hidden somewhere extremely well."

"We'll need the *Huyền Vũ* to get it all out of here."

Anh shrugs, jerking her head at the longboat. If we set up the mast and the sails, it would be fit for the sea. It did well enough on the coastal journey here, and its empty hull has a few flagons of water, rice and cooking implements. I suppose we could gather more for a longer journey, but there are so many ifs tied to that. If we solve the riddles. If we find the treasure.

Anh glances back at me. "Don't worry. It's all going to work out."

"*Longing for distant vistas*," I repeat to myself. I look around at where we are. The jellyfish led us to this lagoon for a reason. It must have to do with the riddles somehow. Like one must do the first to understand the second. The word choice used for *traveler* makes me think about the legend of Sun Wukong, and I wonder if that reference was deliberate.

Above the jungle, the mountain rises tall above us. It reminds me of how I'd climb to the highest peak outside the village just to be able to get a glimpse of a distant port.

That must be it.

I grin at Anh and point to the mountain. "That's our answer. We have to get to the top to see what's next."

CHAPTER EIGHTEEN

THE CAVE

"I HARDLY THINK THE TREASURE WILL BE SITTING ON TOP OF a mountain," Anh grumbles.

"It's part of the poem. Likely we're only able to see what's coming next from up there."

Anh stretches, her shirt riding up to reveal a smooth expanse of skin at her navel, and I look away quickly. I rifle through the pack of food and toss a strip of salted meat to her. I miss the warm bowl of congee we would have every day, but there's no point in wishing.

We make our way through the jungle, slowly climbing upward. Anh slices with the machete, trying to cut a path through the thick foliage of trees, and I follow closely behind. It's hard going with no trail, and I think fondly of even the rocky path up to the peak outside my village.

"Do you think anyone from the *Huyền Vũ* will come after us?" I wonder.

Anh shakes her head. "With no clue where to start, no," she says. "We have some time."

And indeed we need it.

The climb takes hours, and several times we lose track of the highest peak—a crag of sharp gray rock—but we keep making our way through the treacherous jungle, higher and higher.

Anh's face is sweaty as she leans back against a rock, scowling. "Everything here is sharp," she complains.

I agree. The rocks and dense greenery here are strange, leaves swaying in the hot, humid air. Somewhere near us a shrill, inhuman call sounds.

Anh looks around us in alarm. "Was there anything in the poem that could be a warning for what's next?"

I shake my head. "I'm not sure. The last line references tiger's tears, but I don't think we're there yet. We are the travelers seeking aspiration."

"Must be something underneath the meaning," Anh says. "Poetry is like that, right?"

"Aha! I knew you've read some!"

Anh ignores my triumphant laugh. "I haven't seen any other people on the island. What kind of travelers do you think it meant?"

Something moves in the canopy above us, a quick shadow with a long tail.

"Monkeys!" Anh shouts.

I take a step back. "Are they dangerous?"

She nods. "They can get quite vicious, attacking people for their food or shiny things. I've seen them on other islands before."

One pauses on the branch above us, and it's covered in sparse orange and brown hair, a deep red coloring at its throat. The monkey bares its teeth at us in a wide grimace.

I back up hastily, my fingers grasping around me for something to use as a weapon if needed.

Anh unsheathes her knife and slashes it warily at the monkey, which only hisses and steps forward. Behind it, three more monkeys appear in the trees, darting forward with more and more boldness. She lunges forward, but the first monkey is too quick, leaping agilely along the branch and hissing again. Another leaps up from behind me, pawing at the satchel at my waist. More and more monkeys surround us, their eyes flashing with malice.

The biggest one lunges for me, right for the shining gold pendant at my throat.

"No!" Anh gasps.

It breaks the chain and is already scampering away, chittering to its pack with glee.

The map may be in my head, but that pendant is *mine*, and anger surges through me. My fingers close around a rock, and I throw it with all my might into the trees.

The monkey yowls, dropping the pendant in the underbrush below, and I quickly reach down and grab another rock, hurling it at the vengeful pack.

The monkeys scatter, their tails raised high as they flee, scattering birds from the trees. I watch the movement rustle through the canopy until they're gone. Birds slowly start squawking again as I catch my breath.

Anh picks up the pendant and hands it back to me. "That was incredible," she says. "Makes me wonder who would have won our sparring bouts had I not been going easy on you."

"I won that fight fairly! I had you!"

"Mm-hmm," she teases. "We could always do a rematch if you like."

"Maybe after all this," I say. "Let's go."

Finally we seem to come across a footpath of some sort, long overgrown with shrubbery, and we continue upward. My legs ache and my mouth is parched, and the sun is beating down on us relentlessly. Sweat sticks my hair to my brow, and we pause to take a break.

At the top of the peak, the trees give way to tall spires of rock, which nip at our hands as we carefully make our way forward. Going up takes a perilously long time, and we take care as we scramble up the sharp outcrops of rock, finding handholds and footholds along the way.

I push myself past a particularly difficult corner and find Anh waiting for me.

"Oh good," she says, visibly relieved. "I was about to come back and see if you were all right. Here, this next part is tricky. You can come down here and then climb up."

I carefully lower myself down to the ledge where Anh is standing, holding herself with a hand to the rock face. Anh props her leg up by the rock, bending her knee, and smiles at me. "Come on, you can use me to get up."

"Are you sure?"

"Yeah, this is a solid spot. Go ahead."

I step carefully and reach the top of the crag, hauling myself over the edge. I turn back and offer a hand to Anh, pulling her up behind me. I tug a little too hard, though, and Anh falls right into me. We tumble to the ground, laughing.

"Thanks," Anh says. "Look, we're almost there!"

We push through more trees to get to the peak, and then we step onto the last crag. It is indeed the highest point of the island, a spindly and sharp peak; there's barely enough room for the two of us to stand together. The entire island is an expanse of dense green jungle and unforgiving rock spires. To the west is the bay encircled by cliffs, and in the far distance we can see the *Huyền Vũ* anchored in the bay.

"We can see the entire island from here—the bay, all the cliffs, everything," I say in wonder. "The map of the island, it's the view from here."

"And the X?"

"Where we're standing now. I think it means to show where we stand to look and find the last line."

The bay is almost a perfect circle, the way the mountain edges encircle a crater, the water still and bright blue.

Gentle waves lap at the shoreline, but the center of the bay is undisturbed by the waves outside.

The rock face directly in front of us—the sheer cliff on the north side of the bay—looks like a tiger leaning down to drink at the water's edge; one side of the rock has cracked to look like a great and fearsome eye. Where the other eye would be is covered in green and trailing vines down to the water.

The tiger's tears . . .

"*The tiger's tears shine brightly at the second watch of night,*" I murmur.

"Second watch," Anh says. "So we wait until dark, when the stars have risen."

"*The second watch* is the first meaning," I say. "But it also means the second in the twelve earthly branches, so . . ."

"Open twice a day. The tides," Anh says, her eyes widening.

"A cave," I say. "That's where the treasure is hidden. It must only be accessible at low tide."

That has to be it. The mouth of the cave is open at low tide, when it isn't flooded with water. And I know exactly where it is. We could climb back down and make our way along the shore and all of this—all the stories, everything I've been searching for—is right there.

"We've found it," Anh says, her voice trembling with emotion.

I look back at Anh, who catches my gaze with an intensity

that I can't quantify. My heart pounds, and it has nothing to do with the real possibility that we've found the treasure.

Hope, unbidden and unwelcome, bubbles up in my throat. The way she is looking at me, soft and fond and proud . . . I can't be imagining it now.

A small smile dances on the corner of Anh's lips.

The moment builds in a strange, unfathomable way, my heart thundering as I look back into Anh's eyes.

"What?" I finally say, breaking the silence.

"Nothing," Anh says quickly, looking away. "I just . . . the way you were looking at the island . . . I understand. When you said you wanted more."

I look back at the bay, admiring how calm the waters are. It is lovely, and incomparable to what I had imagined looking at paintings, the brushwork suggesting the idea of these islands. I'd imagined then what it might be like to stand here.

I couldn't have imagined Anh.

"Thank you," I whisper. "For helping me get here. For believing in me."

"Not bad for a merchant girl," Anh teases. "You truly ran away and gave up everything you knew, worked with a crew, sailed to an island no one could find. And I'm not saying I didn't help you, because I did, because I'm great, but you . . ." She takes a deep breath, looking right at me, as if she's truly seeing me in a way no one else *can* see me. "You did this. You were the one who pushed to come along. You were the one who stole those letters, burned that map, and figured out the way to get here."

I can't look away, not from the steady way Anh is holding my shoulders—we were providing each other balance, providing a steady place to hold each other. I step closer on the uneven rock ledge, not daring to breathe. "After all of this . . . what are you going to do? Where are you going to go with your share of the treasure?"

Anh laughs, a bright and joyful chime. "I hadn't thought of it, really. I'd have all the food and drink I could want, sail into any port . . . but I don't know. I mean, that's what the crew talks about whenever they have wages; some of them send money back to their families, but most of us are on our own. Mianmian wants to settle down, go back to her village, take care of her aging parents. My mother—she might want to find a quiet place where she'd always be comfortable. It's a hard life, fishing and smuggling and thieving."

"I think you mean, 'seeing opportunities,'" I say with a smile.

I think back to our first conversation, sitting on that wall in Canton, looking out into the harbor. "You said you wanted . . . peace. If you didn't have to worry about how good the next catch was or if you'd have enough to eat—even a share of that treasure will set you up for life. What would you want then?"

"You remembered that," Anh says, surprised.

"Of course I did. You're not the grand mystery you think you are. I know you."

Anh looks at me, taking a deep breath. "What would I want then, if I had everything already? Riches, comforts, food and drink . . . What more could I possibly want?"

My heart skips a beat. "A lifetime of sailing the seas, then. Seeing the impossible. The 'more' you couldn't dream of before because you always had to think of the present."

Anh smiles and drops her gaze. "And you? Do you still yearn for more?"

I have always thought my heart's yearning was for where I hadn't gone yet, what I hadn't seen yet. Now I think of waking up in Anh's arms, the warmth of her smile, the way she would always reach out her hand to offer me support, the way we've come to know each other. With Anh, I don't have to pretend to be anyone else but myself, and that's all right. It's more than all right, and Anh still teases me and laughs with me and still seeks out my company.

I want to be with Anh.

My mind goes to Châu and Arthrit, who are married, who share a cabin and a life together. I have read so many poems about love and have always thought them beautiful. But I'd never quite understood what it meant to feel that myself, to want someone else to be so happy and safe.

"I do," I say, my words unable to even scratch the surface of the depths of what I feel, what I want. Because it isn't possible. Our paths crossed in this lifetime; perhaps we knew each other in another. Perhaps we were lovers then, and in this life . . .

Anh smiles; it doesn't quite reach her eyes this time, like

she's holding back some deep sadness. "You're going to get it. I truly believe that. We will find the treasure and sail away from here. You'll return to Canton and rebuild the Pearl House, and your mother will be so impressed. And she should be, because you're clever and brave and beautiful and . . ."

She trails off as if catching herself midfall. "Perhaps I could visit you. Or when you captain your own ship, trading salt for your business . . . perhaps if there's room on your crew—"

"I want more than that," I say, the honesty raw in my throat. "I want you by my side always."

I have been carrying this feeling for so long that even just to admit it, say it aloud, is a relief. Now that it's out there, I feel like I am holding my heart out to Anh, raw and throbbing, and I feel free.

Perhaps she will laugh at me, not understanding my meaning. Or perhaps she'd be disgusted, or scornful. Or worse . . . she could pity me.

Anh's eyes widen, her mouth falling open. "I—"

She hasn't let go of me this whole time, and her fingers tighten on my sleeve, holding me close. My words hang over us, becoming more solid and real by the heartbeat.

Anh speaks again, this time her voice dropping to a whisper. "Xiang," she says, soft and reverent, full of awe.

I have never heard my name spoken like that, as if it's a precious thing to be adored.

"Xiang-xiang," she says, this time the intimate nickname, slow and deliberate. She hasn't said it again since that day she first taught me how to hold a sword, like she hadn't meant to let it slip and was careful not to do it again. But she says it now, soft and full of intention, like she wants to be mine.

My hand has not left Anh's waist, even though where we are standing is secure now and we have not moved in some time. I can feel my heartbeat in every pulse of my body, in my fingertips against the fabric of Anh's shirt, the warmth of her skin emanating from underneath it, the slight shiver there when my fingers brush against her arm.

My thoughts flit so fast, but Anh's words are enough for me, enough to know she wants this, too, whatever that life may be. I would be happy with any of it—to see her once in a blue moon, drifting in and out of port, even just knowing she was safe and happy. I want her to have all the comforts she dreams of, full sails and delicious food and for her eyes to light up when she sees a sunset. I want to be the one to bring her that joy, who finds those delectable treats for her, who keeps her warm and safe.

Oh, she deserves so many good things, and I want to be one of them.

The way our bodies move closer grows heavy and potent with possibility. I want to draw her near and hold tight. I reach for Anh now, bringing my hand up to stroke her cheek. She leans into the touch, closing her eyes, and I trace the curve of her face to her chin, my fingers resting there gently.

Anh dips her head, her lips meeting my fingers, and she open her eyes to gaze up at me with steady intent.

I'm not sure who moves first. I reach for Anh, and she is moving forward to close the scant space between us, and then, and then—*oh*—our lips meet.

The kiss is soft and questioning, the lightest press of lips, and I can't help the gasp of longing that escapes me.

I answer the question in kind. I kiss back even though I don't know how to express how much I want this. Anh's arms wrap tighter around me, her hands softly stroking my back and pulling me closer, as if she doesn't want to let me go, either.

I have felt untethered all my life, drifting endlessly, and here, finally, is a safe place to land, a quiet harbor to protect me from the turbulence of the sea.

Anh laughs when we catch our breath, and the way our lips brush against each other is euphoric, and I can't help but smile, too. She presses her forehead to mine, and I close my eyes and catch my breath, my heart pounding with the impossibility of it all.

"I feel the same," Anh says finally. "I could never have imagined you might have . . . I thought you would have wanted to leave immediately after and I'd never see you again, or perhaps I'd see you at a distance—"

"After we return to Canton—would you want me if I—if I wanted to stay with the crew? With you?" I ask.

She laughs. "Of course. I'll have to knock some sense into Thanh, after he apologizes to you. And you know how everyone is—"

"Opportunity." I laugh. "There's nothing to forgive."

"You're a good addition to the crew. Of course, everyone will be so rich they may not want to sail anymore, but who knows since they don't know how to do anything else. Perhaps they will want to become farmers or work the land or just keep going, have ships of their own. But we could be together."

A laugh bubbles out of me, a desperate excitement I could never have hoped for, that a life I had never imagined could be mine is within reach. Anh laughs with me, and then pulls me forward in an embrace, and I rest my head on her shoulder. I'm feeling too much at once, and I try to get my thoughts to settle on the present, on what we need to do.

"So the next step is to—"

Anh suddenly steps back, her mouth falling open. "Sails," she says. "On the horizon."

"Another ship? How is it possible so many people know where this island is?" I squint, shading my eyes to see better. I hand my spyglass to Anh, my heart still pounding from the kiss.

"That can't be," she gasps.

"What is it?"

"That's the flag of the Dragon Fleet."

I take the spyglass she offers and look for myself. What

I thought was another sail is in fact the symbol that has haunted me ever since I saw it on the map.

The symbol of Zheng Yi Sao's mighty pirate army, thought to have disappeared so many years ago.

The Head of the Dragon has returned.

CHAPTER NINETEEN

THE HEAD
OF THE DRAGON

"ARE YOU SURE?"

Anh pulls something out of her pocket and hands it to me. It's the same token she showed me on the day we met: the marker of protection the Dragon Fleet would give to fishing boats and merchants in the South China Sea. I turn the coin between my fingers and look back at the sail on the horizon. There's no mistake. It's the same emblem.

A chill runs down my spine. "Do you think they're back for their treasure? Do you think—"

"The Head of the Dragon is alive and well and would defend her treasure to her very last breath? Absolutely. Let's go. We have to warn my mother."

We don't speak at all the whole urgent trek down the mountain. It's almost as if we never kissed, and I could have

307

simply imagined our moment together on that mountain-top.

"We'll have to explain why we left," I say, breaking the uncomfortable silence.

"I'm sure they'll understand. I—"

"Not everyone wanted me on the crew anymore," I mutter. "I was in danger, and you—" I glance at Anh's back in horror, watching her shoulders tense. "I'll say it was my idea, that I forced you to come with me. That way you wouldn't be a deserter and they wouldn't—"

"It doesn't matter, Xiang. They know I chose you. They know I left. But it doesn't mean I don't care what happens to them. We can move forward with the plan now, but . . ."

She doesn't say what might happen if Zheng Yi Sao beats us to the treasure first.

"In any case, we were the ones to solve the riddles on the map and we know where the final location of the treasure is," I say. "She must have known that piece of the map had gone missing. She might not be able to find the treasure without it."

"Or it could have been someone else's riddle, who wanted their own way back to the treasure," Anh says.

The climb down the mountain takes just as long as the climb up because we have to carefully pick our way down the sharp crags. By the time we get to the bottom. The sun is dipping low on the horizon as we row all the way across the lagoon and back to the outer edge of the island.

"Let's leave the boat here," I say, shoving it into a thicket of mangroves.

Anh nods, and neither of us voice what we're afraid of—that the Head of the Dragon may arrive on shore before we do.

We make slow progress along the beach, our feet sinking into the wet sand, and I'm relieved to see that the *Huyền Vũ* is still anchored in the cove.

We're spotted well before we approach the camp, and Thanh comes out to meet us, his sword drawn.

"Well, well, look who's back," he sneers.

I raise my hands. "It was my idea! I thought I needed to know exactly where the treasure was before I returned, and now I do."

Anh nods. "She's right. We know where it is."

Châu approaches, and Ling Shan and Sun bring up the rear, all looking skeptical.

"I can't believe you left us with the navy just a mile away!" Sun cries.

"Have they—"

"Done nothing but sniff around their own butts. We've captured one scout." Ling Shan jerks her head at a nearby tree, where a man is tied up, his naval uniform disheveled and dirty.

"You'll all be hanged!" he shouts, struggling against his bonds. "Piracy! Lunacy! Admiral Cheung will have all your heads!"

Captain Hoa slaps him across the face, and he quiets. She regards us with a long look. "Well, then. I suppose you have a good answer for why you left your watch, Anh?"

"She was making sure I was telling the truth about the treasure," I say. "I couldn't risk you giving me up to Cheung before I could find it."

"*Did* you find it?" the captain asks.

"Of course." Anh winks at me and tosses something gold and shining through the air.

The captain catches it, and I realize it's my pendant— Anh must have slipped it off me at some point.

Captain Hoa closes her hand around it and grins at me. Then she turns to look at the crew. "Empty the hold! Tomorrow, we will be filling it with the plunder of the Dragon Fleet!"

A chorus of shouts rises in the air, and I elbow Anh expectantly. She shakes her head.

"Shouldn't we tell them?" I hiss. "About the other ship?"

"Let the crew celebrate," she whispers back. "They have to trust you again. We'll tell my mother alone."

But it's too late.

Maheer approaches, clapping me on the back fondly before he looks up at the captain. "Another ship is approaching. Red banners flying from their mast. The old symbol."

Captain Hoa stares at him before snapping her spyglass to the horizon. The red sails aren't as visible from here, but she must see something that confirms Maheer's information.

"Come with me," she says, taking me by the elbow. "You, too, my conspiring and clever daughter. Let's see if there's a way out of this."

Captain Hoa paces back and forth in front of the fire. "After all this time, why now? Why would she return?"

"Are you certain it's her?" I ask. "The Head of the Dragon?"

"Who else would dare fly that flag?" Captain Hoa mutters.

"Did she know you when you sailed with the Red Banner Squadron?" Anh asks.

The captain shakes her head. "Me? No, I only reported directly to my squadron lieutenant. I saw Zheng Yi Sao once, watching from the deck of her great warship, but I never met her in person."

"Do you still have that copy of the map I made you?" I ask.

Captain Hoa pulls it from her belt and presents it to me. I fold it into quarters and roll it up like a tiny scroll, and then hold out my hand. She gets my meaning and presses the pendant into my waiting palm. I twist the clasp until it clicks open, then tuck the map copy inside, close it, and loop it back around my neck.

"Here's what we're going to do," I say. "If she approaches us, demand all the goods she has on her ship, everything of value for this map. Then we'll sail away."

Anh looks at me. "What about the treasure?"

"If everything I've heard about Zheng Yi Sao is true, she will be as ruthless as she is cunning. We can't risk our lives here and now." I glance at Anh, and then Captain Hoa. "I bet the reason why Zheng Yi Sao disappeared for all these years is that she never had access to her little nest egg. That my father stole this piece of the map and sent it to me, and she has no idea what was written on it." I tap the pendant. "By the time she realizes it doesn't have the information she needs, we'll be long gone."

Captain Hoa nods, her eyes sparkling with glee. "And we'll be free to come back with the real location of the treasure whenever we please."

"Perhaps the navy would be interested in capturing the most notorious pirate of the South China Sea," Anh says.

"Perfect. Once they have taken care of one another, we will return and claim our riches." Captain Hoa turns to face the oncoming threat on the horizon.

It's as good a plan as any.

As we settle ourselves back in the camp for dinner, Captain Hoa approaches the crew gathered around the firepit.

"Thank you for your patience," she says, raising a flagon. "We are very close now. What say you to waiting a bit longer, until the navy takes care of this rival ship that may seek to take what is ours?"

I lean back, enjoying my hot meal and the warmth of Anh beside me. "Were you really going to maroon me in Changping?" I ask Thanh.

He scowls. "Do you know what imperial association would do to our reputation?"

Ling Shan laughs, elbowing him. "Please. I was a courtier in the Forbidden City. We can all remake ourselves."

The mood isn't quite as lighthearted as the Dragon Fleet ship approaches, riding a brisk wind. The crew's trepidation only grows stronger as the shadow of its hulking mass looms closer and closer.

"Are they coming to this cove? Do they see our ship?" Mianmian asks.

The *Huyền Vũ* isn't hidden well, but the darkness does give us some cover. I watch as the massive junk approaches and veers away from the cove, making its way farther down the coast.

I exhale a breath of relief. "The navy warship is sure to draw more attention; the pirates will find them first."

"Perhaps everything will work out after all," Anh says, throwing her arm around my shoulders.

I expect a great battle to rage through the night—a massive navy warship stocked with cannons and soldiers against the might of the most famed of all pirates back from the dead surely would be a good match.

But the night is quiet, free of cannon fire. Soon clouds roll in and we cannot see where Zheng Yi Sao's ship has gone. The silence is an awkward and nervous thing. No monkeys screech from the jungle, no birds caw. It's as if the island itself is waiting.

Maheer and Arthrit have not returned from their scouting mission, and the crew slowly falls into an uneasy sleep. Thanh has the first watch, but I cannot sleep, either. I watch as he paces back and forth, keeping his eyes to the horizon.

"It doesn't feel right," he says.

I can't help but agree.

Something is moving in the dark, and I think I glimpse a flicker of light. "Did you see that?"

"I don't see anything." He raises his lantern and moves to light it.

"Wait, don't—"

The darkness is all we have keeping us from view, and whatever is happening on the other side of the island, we are only safe as long as they do not know we're also here.

The flame at the bottom of Thanh's paper lantern

flickers to life, and it glows softly, illuminating his wary face. He holds it out, and I rush over to blow out the flame.

"You have been nothing but annoying since you've arrived," he growls. "We're too far from the navy's camp; one small lantern won't go amiss."

"Anyone in the bay could see that," I insist.

A thunderous *boom* explodes in the air, and the cove itself seems to reverberate with the noise.

Captain Hoa snaps awake. "The ship," she gasps.

In the cove, the Dragon Fleet ship shoots another cannon at the *Huyền Vũ*, and then a volley of flaming arrows. The cove lights up with the flickering remains of the humble fishing vessel—and our only means of escape.

The crew watches in horror as the *Huyền Vũ* burns. The red sails catch fire, flames consuming them entirely as the ship, heavy with our illicit iron cargo, begins to sink into the bay.

We can only watch in stunned silence, shock and sorrow flashing across everyone's faces. Captain Hoa can't seem to look away, her eyes brimming with unshed tears.

Unfortunately we don't have time to sit with our grief.

The pirate warship has dropped anchor now, and a rowboat approaches our cove.

Sun screams. "What do we do?!"

Captain Hoa draws her sword as the rowboat approaches. "What we must," she says. "Fight."

The pirates have already seen us; there's no point in hiding now. We light the lanterns on the beach, and we wait as the first rowboat approaches. There's another behind them, and who knows how many armed people wait on the ship.

Anh glances at me. "We could still bargain," she says. "Use your plan."

"And leave the island how?" I mutter, drawing my own sword.

One of the pirates lights a lantern, and I count at least ten of them in each rowboat.

Our crew grows still as we take in the figure standing at the front of the first boat. It's clear she's a woman, her hair coiffed in a graceful yet intimidating fashion; it's an older style from the Ming dynasty, echoing tradition and intimidation.

She doesn't wait for the rowboat to reach the shore, but jumps out of it with years of practiced skill, the waves rushing in around her knees as she approaches us.

The Head of the Dragon. Zheng Yi Sao. It could only be.

A quiet mist rolls into the cove as all the heavily armed pirates make their way to shore. They linger back, waiting, as all of us hold our weapons tighter, anticipating an attack.

They hold fast, like water surging behind a dam, building into a tidal wave as the Head of the Dragon approaches us.

"Hello there," she says, her voice cool and collected . . . and very familiar. "I believe you have something of mine."

My eyes widen, and my lungs seize inside my chest as if I have suddenly been thrown into the sea. It is all I can do to gasp out a single word in my shock:

"Mother?"

CHAPTER TWENTY
The Gambit

Mother strides across the sand, her head held high; she's wearing a brocade I have never seen before, a bright yellow jacket—a color reserved for royalty—embroidered with regal dragons and the curves of ocean waves. A sword hangs proudly at her side; multiple belts bear sharp knives and twin pistols, elaborately wrought with silver and inlaid with mahogany, a European design that must have been taken as a trophy. A single sparkling ornament rests in her hair—a golden dragon, serpentine and twisting, its eyes inlaid with emeralds.

Mother looks more at home standing at the head of this group of brigands than she ever has in the village teahouse, at the helm of the merchant ships, or discussing trade in the Pearl House. Or perhaps she has always worn this air at home, this quietly burning rage, manifested in the precision and rigidity she wields with her business. With me.

My whole life spins into focus, and Mother, with all her disappearances and keeping me at bay . . . This is what she had been hiding from me.

I don't know how to feel, a discordant rush of emotions making their way through me. It's a heady mix of betrayal, fear, and a dazzling sense of awe.

Mother takes in each and every one of the *Huyền Vũ* crew, and her eyes fall on me. There's no surprise written on her face, no anger or disappointment.

She smiles.

It's a genuine one, one that I would dare to say contains a hint of pride.

"There you are, my treasure. I have been looking for you." She chuckles, her slight amusement dancing across the beach. "You were so excited to prove yourself that you ran off after my lost prize on your own." She holds out her hand. "Come along, Xiang. We have much to discuss."

I blink.

Ling Shan gasps. "It's you. The Head of the Dragon."

I'm still trying to equate the Mother I know—the distant merchant, a salt trader, cold and unforgiving, sparing with her praise and approval—with the greatest pirate legend of all time.

Mother's smile widens, broad and threatening; she gives a mere nod, as if acknowledging Ling Shan and all of us standing here are far beneath her.

One of the pirates steps forward, and I gasp. It's Master Feng. The old scholar wears a pistol at his side, but otherwise he looks the same. He's known this whole time as well?

One by one I recognize the people behind Mother, including Kang and Captain Leung; I wonder if all of them knew Mother more than I ever did. I feel hollow and strange. This journey to prove myself has just been one wide circle.

"Xiang, come here."

My hands shake. The Shi Xiang who had never left the village would have obeyed in a heartbeat.

I don't move.

"I know this may be a shock to you, but I've only ever wanted you to be safe," Mother says. "Why do you think I had you tucked away in that tiny village? *You* are my greatest treasure. To know you wanted to see the world, to see Canton . . . I was so afraid. I was so afraid I'd lose you, my dear."

She opens her arms to me, her smile full of affection. There's a part of me that wants it so badly, that wants to run into her embrace like I've always imagined.

The two crews stand on the beach, a scant expanse of sand between us as I look at Mother and she looks at me.

Captain Hoa stiffens, her hand on her sword, and I can see a cord of tension bulging in her neck. I look at Anh, whose mouth has fallen open, her expression unreadable. I'm not sure how I feel, either, but my first instinct is to reassure her.

"I didn't know," I whisper. "How could I have known?"

Anh doesn't move, her eyes looking at me like she's seeing me anew, like I'm a stranger to her.

"Xiang, come along," Mother says. "The treasure is my legacy, and you needn't have worried yourself and gotten involved with this pitiful crew." She gives Captain Hoa and the rest of the crew a condescending glance.

"They are my friends, Mother," I say, finally finding my voice. "They kept me safe on my journey here." I raise my head higher. I can do this. I can keep the crew safe. I can keep *Anh* safe. I hold all the cards here.

Mother looks at the ragtag crew behind me and cocks her head, considering. Everyone waits with bated breath, and then she raises her hand.

Someone grabs me from behind, cold steel sharp against my throat. I can feel it pressing to my pulse.

"You can have her back after we retrieve the treasure," Thanh spits vehemently. "We will retrieve it first, and then—"

"Wait, Thanh, don't—"

Through my shock, I can barely process what is happening. For a moment, time seems to stop, everyone tensing around me. I struggle to form the words to bargain with Mother, but—

The moment breaks.

Mother draws the long weapon from her belt and fires directly at us. A loud shot whizzes right past my ear, and Thanh is falling backward, his grip loosening all at once.

Blood pools from his shoulder as he hits the ground, and the tang of gunpowder is sharp in the air. I can't move, can't comprehend—should I press something to the wound—

Another gunshot fires. It's Mother, shooting into the air, a vindictive gleam in her eyes. "Get my daughter back to the *Lóng Zhī Ào*!" She faces Captain Hoa, her lip curling into a snarl. "Kill the rest."

The pirates race forward, and Mother draws her sword, the sharp metal singing in the air.

I stumble backward as the night erupts in a chorus of steel. Everywhere there are shouts and battle cries as swords meet one another. This is no tavern brawl. This is going to be a fight to the death, and the crew of the *Huyền Vũ* is outnumbered and outmatched.

Captain Hoa grits her teeth and charges directly at Mother. Their swords flash in the air as they fight, blow after blow, captain against captain, mother against mother.

The pirates seem to be toying with us—after the first gunshot no one else has opened fire, like they know they already have the upper hand. Not even everyone is engaged—only a handful of Mother's crew have drawn their weapons; the rest of them stand on the shore, lingering with smirks and knowing looks with one another. Master Feng and Kang hover off to the side, watching and waiting.

"Captain!" Maheer shouts. "What—"

"To the jungle!" Captain Hoa bellows. I see Sun already

running for the trees, Mianmian on his heels. The pirates don't give chase just yet, and a few of them laugh viciously.

My crew, my friends—I need to help, I need to fight. My hand twitches against the hilt of my sword, and I look quickly to see where I might most be needed.

Ling Shan stabs one of Mother's men in the stomach and kicks him away, snarling and ready for more.

Arthrit's blade is on the ground, and he flails wildly at the man above him until Châu punches the assailant across the face.

Maheer ducks a blow and parries another with his sword, sweat dripping from his brow.

Anh is holding her own against Captain Leung, whipping her blade back and forth as the taller woman grins, barely exerting any effort.

These are the people I've lived with the past few weeks; I've come to know them, eaten with them, drank with them, sang with them, worked with them—

"Stop!" I call out. No one pays me any mind, focused on their own survival.

"*No!*" Anh screams.

I turn to see Mother stab her sword clean through Captain Hoa's shoulder; blood seeps bright red through her tunic.

Anh yells a hoarse battle cry, plunging her sword deep into Leung's side and shoving her away. Chest heaving, blood drips from the blade as she charges directly at Mother.

Mother knocks Anh's blade aside carelessly, parrying every one of her blows as if she were merely an annoying fly. Without even breaking a sweat she disarms Anh easily, and then her arm swings in a menacing arc.

I move without thinking.

"I said *stop*," I snarl, blocking the blow with my own sword.

Mother's eyes meet mine as my blade braces against hers—mine shoddy steel, rusted with use; hers, a long, curved piece honed by decades of skill. I struggle, bracing with all my strength.

I do not back down.

Mother raises her eyebrow and steps forward, her blade rising to slice at me. She swings with one hand with the assured confidence of someone who has bent violence to her whim for years, and I am only just starting to understand.

I block and circle around, and Mother tilts her head, a calculating smile on her face.

She raises her blade again and sends another cutting blow my way. She is no less forceful than in her fight with Captain Hoa or Anh, but with me, there's something else. Another edge. Like she's testing me, watching to see how much I know.

I show her.

I thrust forward, lunging for the opening I see, using everything I've learned. The sharp sounds of battle die down around us. I don't dare look away, but I can hear the sound of people catching their breath. I don't know who is still here, who is injured—and I do not dare think if anyone is dead.

Mother knocks my sword away with a particularly fierce blow, and it falls to the sand with a dull thud. She raises her eyebrow at me and sets down her sword.

"Not terrible form. I could teach you better."

"Why didn't you?" I spit out, years of anger unleashed with my words. I scrabble at the sand and grab at my blade to slash back at her.

Mother humphs at me but doesn't answer. She lets out a sharp whistle, and all around us, her pirates stop where they are, lowering their weapons.

I leave the question where it is but don't sheathe my sword, even as Mother sheathes hers to regard me. "Leave them be," I demand.

"And why is that? I have traveled across the outer seas to find you."

"They are my friends, Mother," I say, raising my head higher. "You destroyed their ship, thinking they've done me harm, but I—I was the one who led them here. With this." With my free hand I take the pendant from my neck and dangle it in the air. Lantern light glints off the tarnished piece of gold.

Mother regards me and the pendant. "That trinket of your father's?" she scoffs. "What an ugly thing. He stole from me; I ripped that from his neck the day he betrayed me. Then I left him to die on this very beach."

I close my fingers around the gold pendant like I have

so many times before. How often have I wondered about Father, what he might have been like? If I had any of the courage or strength or wits he did?

I don't know the man Mother speaks of. He's as faceless as he ever was, perhaps even more so than in all the times I imagined him.

Mother laughs. "You always were so stubborn with your questions. It was a joke, at first, letting you have the pendant. I think he would have liked the idea that you wore it, some sort of legacy of his. I could have finished it clean, his death. But I wanted him to suffer. To struggle and bleed, alone on this beach. To think about what he did, how he failed. Some might say he did not die, that his blood survives. But the truth is, he has no claim on you. I am your mother, the only parent you will ever need."

My blood surges inside me.

My blood is my own. My fate is my own.

I twist open the cap and pry free the scroll. I unroll it, shaking it out, the copied map on one side and the words of the love letter on the other.

Mother's eyes narrow, a brief look of surprise crossing her face before a mask slips over it. She smiles, victory in her eyes. "So that's where my baobei hid his stolen piece of the map," she mutters.

I raise my sword and step forward, putting myself between her and Anh and Captain Hoa. "They go free. All of them."

"Very well," Mother says.

I reroll the map, place it back in the pendant, and slip it under my shirt.

Mother holds out her hand to me, and I take it.

I follow her into the water, the cold seeping into my skin as we wade toward the rowboats, Mother's crew following close behind. I look back once to see Anh watching me, tears flowing from her eyes before she turns away and runs for the tree line. The rest of the crew is gone already, and all that is left is blood on the sand.

CHAPTER TWENTY-ONE

THE DRAGON'S PRIDE

THE LÓNG ZHĪ ÀO IS FAR GRANDER THAN THE MERCHANT vessel that bore me to Canton, twice as long and with three times as many sails. It's filled with more people who regard Mother with reverence as we climb aboard. Captain Leung and a few of the others head off to see the ship's doctor to tend to their injuries—I'm proud to see that my friends put up a good fight.

The beach is empty; from the ship I cannot see any smoke at the camp or any movement from the trees. My heart twists with worry for my crew. My impulsive move bought all of them time. I can only hope they are safe and recovering from their wounds.

"You must be tired," Mother says. "You may rest in my chambers."

"Come with me," I say, tired of balancing on the edge, carving and choosing every word carefully for her approval. "Like you said, we have much to discuss."

In her cabin, I see the truth of who she is. The paltry trinkets I had thought the reminder of her worldly demeanor in the cabin of the *Jīn Lǐyú* pale in comparison to these effects. The furniture is finely carved, but worn with scratches that can only have been caused by battle. Expensive-looking trunks, covered in ancient, fading bloodstains, and weapons of every sort imaginable line the walls. There's a small statuette of Guanyin carved with words I now recognize as Thai, and I flash back to the story of Zheng Yi Sao taking an entire treasure galleon headed for Siam.

"Why?" I demand.

"Why what?" she says, sinking into a chair. It's a Song dynasty heirloom, carved with the seal of the emperor and decorated with a brocaded cushion.

I set my jaw and do not answer. I have been asking her questions my whole life, and she knows exactly what I mean. I don't understand why she would not have trusted me with the truth. Why she did not tell me from the beginning, why she always left me behind in the village.

Mother cocks her head at me. "My treasure, I am tired, and we have been through much today. Give me the map, and I shall put it away for safekeeping. We can talk about this in the morning when we are far from here."

"Tell me why you left me in the village," I insist.

"I was keeping you safe," Mother says, her mouth hardened into a smooth line.

"Were you really?" I retort. "Why not teach me, then? Everything I learned in the past few weeks, about sailing, about fighting——"

"I wanted what was best for you," Mother says. "A life where you would not have to struggle. You could have all the books you've ever wanted, all your stories. You like those things." She reaches out and gently strokes my face.

I close my eyes, trying to enjoy the small bit of intimate affection that once would have made my heart soar. But I can't. I lean away from the touch, from the mother that I do not know.

"I never just wanted the stories!" I cry out. "I wanted to *go* to those places and *do* those things! And you let me believe it would never be possible when all this time you were——you *are*——the Head of the Dragon. Leader of the most famed pirate fleet ever to sail these waters. The commander so feared, multiple kingdoms could not defeat you and your army. Even when the fleet was crumbling underneath you, you still forced your enemies to negotiate to your terms. You . . . you . . ." I close my eyes, wiping furiously at the salty tears streaking down my cheeks.

Mother laughs. "That is a great story. It warms my heart that it is still told." She sits up and regards me with her familiar scrutinizing gaze. "Do you have any idea what I've had to do to get where I am?" She taps the beautiful, expensive desk, littered with maps. "Even as

Madam Shi Yeung, I still command respect. Because I am who I am, and I have built an empire of pirates when no one else could.

"Zheng's Red Banner Squadron, oh, they were mighty indeed. But unorganized, filled with greed and corruption. I was the one who saw the potential, and I was the one who united the Yellow, Black, Blue, and Green Banner Squadrons to the mighty confederation that the Qing Emperor himself could not challenge—the Dragon Fleet. And yes, my achievements were mighty. But my greatest treasure, my darling—you—" She leans forward and caresses my face again.

This time I let her. I want it so much, her love and approval.

"Can't you see? It was all out of love. I did not want my child to suffer as I did. Your father loved that village. We had spent some time there, away from it all. It was a soft, idyllic place."

"You said you killed him."

Mother flicks a hand dismissively. "Perhaps. The man on the beach could have died. It matters not to me, only that he suffered. And when I say 'your father,' well, one can never be sure. It doesn't matter to me. I had several lovers at the time, and you were a surprise. It was at the height of the negotiations when I realized I would bear a child, and bringing you into the world would be the most beautiful gift of all." She beams at me, a bright smile on her face that doesn't seem quite right.

How many times have I longed for her to look at me like this, her face warm and full of affection? For her to hold me and tell me how proud she was of me?

Is it truly me she is seeing?

Mother sighs, lost in nostalgia. "You, the village—it was all so lovely and peaceful. It was perfect. A simple, quiet life. And to protect you, I had to keep some semblance of the business, for you to be comfortable. Smuggling is so easy when you have the ships and connections for it. And the village, my dear, well . . . it just wasn't for me."

I swallow, thinking of Lan Nai Nai's comment once about Mother thinking of us like a pond of carp, stopping to admire us whenever she felt like it.

Mother is still looking off into the distance, wrapped in some memory. "I could have easily married you off earlier, but Feng Zhanli convinced me to give you a choice. You wanted to see Canton; you wanted to run the teahouse. I thought bringing you to the city would cure you of these notions, and yet you ran away at the first opportunity."

"To prove myself to *you*! Because you wanted to send me back to the village!"

"Do you think I had not heard the whispers that the map had resurfaced?" Mother glances at me. "I knew Cheung Po Tsai had survived. I should have stayed to make sure the job was finished, but affection stayed my hand. I kept watch over my treasure all these years, and he never touched it. I figured I destroyed his piece of the map that day when I set his ship ablaze."

She laughs, wiping at her eyes, a mirthful tear almost dripping down her face—perhaps the first real emotion I've seen since we've stepped into the cabin. "It was years later when I learned he had taken the position offered by the emperor. Using all the tricks he learned under my tutelage and his time with the fleet to now capture petty thieves and smugglers. Of course, he went looking for me and the map. But by then I was already secure as Madame Shi Yeung, salt merchant."

She leans forward and taps the pendant at my neck. "It's funny just how many years it took him to put the pieces together, and even then, he never came to the Pearl House. That is, until that day you spent on your own in Canton, and someone somewhere must have seen the pendant and reported back to him. He sent his agents to set fire to my teahouse, search for it that very night."

She smiles now, and I can feel her eyes at my neck, at the pendant. "I suppose he'll never know now that I had the last piece of my map all along, and it was never in any danger at all."

Mother laughs again, and she stands up with a triumphant grin. "You have done well, my treasure. When we return to Canton, I will teach you the trade. All of it. How to run ships right under any official's nose, how to make a business deal, how to fight. And we will carve out our own empire together."

She embraces me, wrapping her arms tight around me, and presses a kiss to the top of my head.

I stiffen like a board in her arms. It's everything I ever wanted . . . wasn't it? Then why does my stomach churn with unhappiness? Why doesn't it feel *right*?

She pulls away and gives me a fond smile. "Now get some rest, my dear. There is much to be done."

She closes the door behind her—and locks it.

CHAPTER TWENTY-TWO

A Father's Last Stand

THE DOOR DOES NOT BUDGE, AND THERE ARE NO WINDOWS, no way out of this cabin. Outside I can hear the crew get to work, and I worry about Anh. Does she think I've abandoned her?

I rattle the door. "Let me out!"

It's solid wood, with no screen, giving me no way of knowing what is happening on the rest of the ship.

"Shh, it's all right, Xiang." Master Feng's voice comes from the other side of the door.

"You knew all this time," I growl.

"Yes. You know I would have told you, but your mother—"

"She's your commander. I know. I know everything now." I want to cry, but I have no tears left. "Where are we going?"

"We're going home, Xiang."

I don't even know where that is anymore.

Master Feng's voice is as I remember: steady, soothing. "Everything is going to be all right. You're safe now, and you—" His voice softens. "I'm so proud of you."

Any other day my heart would be filled with happiness—Master Feng's praise, although intermittent, was something that always made me feel better. But Mother has locked me in here; after all her pretty words about building a new life with me, she again is leaving me without a choice.

There's a moment of silence so long I thought Master Feng might have left, until he sighs.

"What?"

Another pause. "I want to tell you—"

The ship suddenly lurches to the left as a cannon blast rips through the air.

I stumble as the entire ship shakes. I catch my balance and pound at the door. "What's happening?"

"I don't—I don't know," Master Feng says. "Give me a minute."

I wait nervously as there's a thundering of footsteps and shouting from above deck. I look up, trying to listen, but it's all chaos. I strain my ears, and through the cursing I can barely hear Mother's voice.

"These imperial dogs never stop! Fire! Where is everyone? Captain Leung! Ready the cannons!"

It must be Cheung and the *Nǔ Tiě*. I reach for the door

again, and this time it opens to reveal Master Feng crouching and holding a set of lock picks.

I blink at him. "You can pick locks?"

"When the occasion calls for it—" He steps inside the cabin and closes the door behind him.

"Don't worry." He looks at me, lowering his voice to a whisper. "Your mother will take care of the navy. They'll regret boarding us quite soon. We'll just be quiet—"

The noise on the deck comes to a halt. No more cannons. No footsteps, no voices.

I wait with Master Feng, holding my breath.

Thud. Thud. Thud.

Someone with heavy boots paces right above me.

"Is that everyone?" a familiar voice demands.

Admiral Cheung.

"Yes, sir. An excellent plan, to wait for these rats to attack the rival pirates ashore. The men we captured aboard the *Lóng Zhī Ào* are still secure in their own hold, and we have the rest subdued here on deck."

"Very good. Did any of them go below deck?"

"Just the captain, before we launched the attack. We have her here."

"Don't touch me!"

It's not Mother's voice. Hadn't I heard her earlier, demanding her crew to fire? Is she still above deck, or hidden somewhere? If she realized her crew was incapacitated, surely she would have a plan.

"Who are you?"

"Captain Leung, of the *Jīn Lǐyú*."

"This is not your warship. I know this impossible beauty. How did you come by the *Lóng Zhī Ào*?"

I don't hear what comes next, but it must be some sort of rude gesture because the next sound is a hearty slap.

"Answer me. How did you come by this ship?"

Captain Leung is silent.

"Why are you flying the emblem of the Dragon Fleet? A foolhardy decision, especially for a weak captain like you. Did you hear the rumors of the treasure as well? Chase down every ship that left Canton in the past week? What did the crew of the *Huyền Vũ* know?"

More silence.

"I will know soon enough. If they are still on that beach, I will find them. We watched you and your men go to shore—a great show of intimidation for such a small prize. Capturing the *Lóng Zhī Ào* may have been the easiest thing I have ever done." Cheung laughs. "I didn't even have to blow too many holes in it. It'll make a nice addition to my fleet."

More pacing.

"That banner . . . ," Cheung muses. "Bold, but foolish. There's only one person who could fly that flag, and she would kill you all for the disrespect—"

Something heavy thuds onto the deck, like a body falling over.

"Did you miss me, Cheung Po Tsai?" Mother asks, her voice filled with scorn.

338

Next to me, Master Feng gasps. "Cheung Po Tsai! He's alive!"

"Surely you knew that," I whisper. "He had my painting. He said he was searching for me under Mother's orders."

"Shi Yeung would have nothing to do with the navy," he says. "But if Cheung Po Tsai knew who she really was this whole time . . . He would know her connection to the Pearl House . . ."

"He set the fire," I say softly.

"Your mother—she told you? She knew he was alive?"

"Yes."

A sad shadow passes over Master Feng's eyes, but he shakes himself. "She has her secrets. It doesn't matter. I am sure she has a plan . . . but if Cheung Po Tsai is involved, it may cloud her judgment. We must go."

I groan, closing my eyes. "Go where? Cheung has everyone captured, and even if Mother is free, she's one against however many men—"

Master Feng coughs.

I turn around. My old tutor is standing behind the desk, where he presses a hidden panel on what I thought was a cabinet. The door swivels open to reveal a small porthole carved into the hull of the ship.

"How did you know that was there?"

He grins wryly. "I used to sneak through this window all the time. Come, I'll help you through. Whatever happens out there, it won't be good. We have to leave before Cheung Po Tsai finds you."

Master Feng gives me a boost out the window, and we climb out onto the ledge. I'm not sure where he means to go—perhaps to one of the rowboats? He edges himself along the side of the ship slowly, gesturing for me to follow.

I push forward up toward the rail. I have to see what's going on.

The crew of the *Lóng Zhī Ào* are all bound in chains. Admiral Cheung is laughing as Mother glares at him. She's standing in the center of the deck, surrounded by raised guns. And still she looks like she is holding court.

I hardly dare to breathe, unable to look away.

"So it is you," Admiral Cheung says. "Isn't this just like the old days? Except clearly I have you in a stalemate. I followed the *Huyền Vũ* here. They knew where they were going, the only ship in the outer seas that had left Chang-ping with a true purpose. And they were so surprised when I dangled the reward for the girl in front of them. Of course, the girl is unimportant. It's my map that's the—"

Mother laughs. "*Your* map? You parasitic sap, *you* don't have anything. You have soldiers who are underpaid, their wages unable to settle their debts, their families waiting ashore. You think they are loyal to you? You think my people, even bound, aren't a threat to you?" She glances at Captain Leung, at all the bound crew members. "Even with a gun to my head, I have more power than you ever will."

This seems to strike a chord with the admiral. "I've made a name for myself. Admiral Cheung has the ear of the emperor, and a fleet of ships—"

"Then prove it. A duel. Captain to captain. No guns, no tricks. Just me and you."

The admiral strokes his chin. "And?"

Mother smiles. "And I would let you see your daughter."

"My—my—"

"You think I disappeared all those years for no reason? Come now, if you knew I was pregnant we both know you would have followed me to the ends of the earth. You were always a possessive, jealous fool. I've kept her well and safe. The poor dear always thought you died at sea. She has this pendant, you know. A last reminder of you. And you thought your little trick would keep me from my treasure—"

"*My* treasure! *My* daughter!" Admiral Cheung roars. "I will duel you, and I will take what is mine."

They circle each other on the deck.

Cheung takes the first swing, but each of his blows is easily matched by Mother. With every parry, her crew bound in chains roars in approval, cheering her on, as Cheung's own crew seems to grow more nervous.

Mother is the first to draw blood with a vicious swing that cuts into Cheung's shoulder.

"You would be nothing without me," Cheung hisses in pain, attempting to cut deep with his words when he's clearly no match for her blade. "A widow playing at being a commander."

She blocks his strike with a ferocious laugh. "You think you would have risen up in the ranks so quickly if I hadn't chosen you? Placed mentors in your path and made sure you learned only from the best?"

"Zheng Yi was the leader you thought you were! He taught me everything! You're just some whore he picked up from a floating brothel."

Their blades clash, sharp steel grating as she pushes forward. Mother has the upper hand, and Cheung knows it. He stumbles backward, losing his footing.

"Zheng led a scattered group of pirates with no sense of ambition or cunning," she snarls, bearing down. "*I'm* the one who grew our coffers. *I'm* the one whom everyone fears. *I'm* the one who had every settlement from Changping to Macao swearing fealty."

"Xiang!" Master Feng whispers from below me on the ledge. "We must go!"

I look back once more. Dawn is breaking, and in the pale light I can see Mother fighting the man who could be my father, their swords locked as they circle each other. The crew is shouting, and all I can see are feet and the quick blur of movement from the duel.

"Now! Before they know you're gone!" Master Feng hisses at me.

I drop into the ocean. Water fills my nose, and I struggle

to find my balance. There's another splash and a flurry of robes—Master Feng has jumped in alongside me, and we push our way up to air.

I tread water, trying to see what is happening on the ship, but I can't.

"Let's go," Master Feng says.

"What now?" I ask.

"We swim to the beach and wait."

I collapse on the shore, tired and aching. I haven't slept, and the fatigue is catching up with me. Beside me, Master Feng is watching the two ships in the bay, a pensive expression on his face.

The beach is empty, the sand still streaked with blood. There's no sign of Anh, or Captain Hoa, or any of the crew. The camp is abandoned; a few pitiful tents and sleeping rolls remain, along with the sooty remnants of the fire. I wonder where they've gone, if they're all right.

"Are you hurt?" Master Feng asks, reaching to brush a tendril of hair out of my face.

"Don't fuss over me!" I smack his hand away and sit up, ignoring the way my body is screaming at me to rest. "I need to find Anh."

I look to the tree line and then back to the beach, the muddle of footprints. What hasn't been washed away is almost impossible to decipher. But despite the amount of blood in the sand, the fact that no one's body is here gives me hope. They all survived. They must be hiding somewhere on the island.

I look up. Master Feng looks so forlorn and wet and sad I immediately feel guilty. I haven't seen his face in so long, but it was easy to fall back into old patterns and dismiss his overprotective nature. "I'm sorry," I say. "I'm just tired. And I'm worried about my friends."

I look back at the two ships in the bay. I'm still angry at Mother, but that doesn't mean I don't care what happens to her. "Do you think Mother will be all right?"

"She'll be fine."

Something falls over the side of Mother's warship with a loud splash, and a cheer rises up from the deck. I can't quite tell what is happening from here. There's a great deal of movement, and then people are rushing over the gangplank to the *Nü Tiě*.

Master Feng unclips a spyglass from his waist and hands it to me. "See?"

On the navy warship, a red banner is hoisted above the sails and flutters proudly in the wind.

He collapses on the sand next to me, coughing. "We should light a fire so your mother knows you're all right. She'll send a boat out to get us."

I stand up. "I need to go find Anh and the rest of the crew."

Master Feng sighs and rubs salt from his eyes. "To what end? I'm surprised your mother called off the attack to begin with."

"I need to find her!" Tears prickle my eyes. "You didn't see how she was looking at me when we left. She thinks I've abandoned her, and I can't . . . I can't . . ."

Master Feng's eyes soften, and he pats the ground next to him. "Tell me more."

The story comes out in bits and pieces, and then all at once. I tell him how Anh discovered the map, and I left with her crew to find the treasure, to make Mother proud. I tell him about learning how to sail, how to fight, and feeling like a part of the crew. I choke up as I explain Admiral Cheung's reward and the crew's suspicions and how I needed to find the treasure first, but then Mother's arrival changed everything. I'm aware of how I sound, so overcome with emotion, especially when I talk about Anh and how important she is to me.

Master Feng listens, and pulls me into a soft embrace. I bury my face into his shoulder. I haven't been held like this since I was a child; he wraps his arms around me, smoothing my hair, nodding and making sympathetic noises as I relay the events of the past few weeks.

"I feel like I should be surprised, but I'm not," he says. "You've always been quite resourceful, determined to learn anything you set your mind to. It was rather frustrating for me as your tutor, as you would only want to study what you liked. But it sounds like you've truly made a place for yourself on this crew." He smiles at me, his eyes as gentle as I remember them.

I spent years wondering about my father, and knowing now that Cheung Po Tsai could be him—I hate the very idea that his cruelty, his anger, may have passed on to me. Why not Feng Zhanli's kindness and ingenuity? I would be proud to call him my father.

He squeezes my shoulder. "They are important to you, so they are important to me. I'm sure your mother will understand. We will go search for them, and then I will help you convince her to escort all your friends safely off the island."

My heart swells with relief. "Thank you."

Although there is much to do, I take a minute to rest here, to draw comfort from this moment.

Master Feng's eyes twinkle. "So this Anh . . ."

I blink and squirm, embarrassed. "I, um, she has become a . . . dear friend."

Master Feng hums. "I understand."

I barely understand it myself, and so much has happened since that moment between Anh and me at the top of that mountain. I realize now that of the entire story I've just shared, most of it was about Anh.

Then comes the realization that's been standing in front of me all along.

I love her.

I don't know how to say this to Master Feng, not when it

is so new to me—and it is a new, beautiful, precious thing that has just begun to blossom. I don't want to think about what he might say to cause this new thing to wilt before it has had a chance to bloom in my heart.

"We should go, before she and the others get very far," I say quietly. "I just hope she knows how I . . . I mean, when I left with Mother, that it wasn't because I didn't—that I'm not leaving her. I just wanted her to be safe, and—"

"She knows," Master Feng says, patting my back. "I'm glad you've found each other. She sounds like a good soul."

I sniffle, and he offers me a handkerchief from his sleeve. "It's wet, I'm afraid. I mean, everything is wet, but it is clean."

I laugh and take the drenched bit of fabric and wipe my face with it.

"May I see it?" Master Feng asks after a moment. "The map?"

"Of course." I take the pendant and unclasp it, pulling out the tiny scroll. "It isn't the real one. I memorized the original and then destroyed it. This is a copy that I wrote over one of Mother's old love letters."

Master Feng exhales as I hand it to him. He flips it over, ignoring the clumsily copied map entirely, instead reading and rereading the love letter, tracing his fingers over the words almost tenderly.

"I can't believe Cheung Po Tsai wrote these," I say. "He

seems so awful. I don't like to think of him as my father." I shudder a little.

"He didn't write these letters," Master Feng says quietly.

I frown at him. "They're from a lover, aren't they? I had thought they were from my father when he was out to sea for the salt trade, sending them to Mother back home. But if she was also at sea the whole time . . ."

Master Feng brings the letter to his lips and kisses it before bringing it to his heart with a sigh. "She kept these," he says, almost to himself. "She always laughed at me. Called me a romantic fool, said my poetry was clumsy. I think she was a little embarrassed, but I wanted her to always know how I felt."

"You—?"

"I wrote these. Sometimes we wouldn't be on the same ship for months at a time. I was never a great pirate. I was the accountant—hers at first, and then for the entire Red Banner Squadron, and then for the entire fleet. I often had to travel and spend time with each lieutenant to keep everything in order. Once the Dragon Fleet amassed enough wealth where it became necessary for a central place to hide it, I was the one who wrote the poem that went with the map of the island. I thought the poetry would go over most of the pirates' heads, and it would be too difficult to figure out the directions. Especially since each lieutenant only got a portion of it."

The literary nature of the directions, the beauty in each

word choice, the references to Sun Wukong . . . "I knew the voice sounded familiar to me!"

Master Feng smiles. "So you and the *Huyền Vũ* landed first, I presume? Did you find the treasure? What did you think of my directions?"

"I made it to the top of the vista," I say proudly.

"That's my Xiang," Master Feng says, ruffling my hair. He smiles, looking back toward the ship.

"Wait, wait—" I snort. "Did she build that secret port-hole in her cabin for you?"

He smiles. "I like to think so. I know I wasn't as . . ." He gestures at himself. "Appealing as a consort. Cheung Po Tsai fit that role well, and naming him as her second, her husband, her equal—it was for the good of the fleet. After they married, I didn't get to see her as often, but Cheung was still incredibly jealous. He would make sure I was assigned to other ships, and I would miss your mother terribly. I adored her beyond reason."

He sighs. "Shi Yeung. When we met she was already Zheng's widow, famed and feared. Only I knew her by her real name. She trusted me with her heart, her secrets. There was a time when I thought we could . . ." He glances at me, his gaze softening. "I thought we could be a family. But she was always leaving. I suppose I wasn't enough. But it means something that she kept my letters, right? That she sees me—perhaps even loves me—still?"

I stare at him, unable to look away.

Master Feng sighs again, handing the letter back to me. "You should keep that safe, if no one knows it's not the real map just yet. Your memory is far likely better than my own." He laughs a little. "What say we find your friends, and then the treasure together?"

I nod, and he tucks a strand of my hair behind my ear. I must look like a bedraggled mess, but he's looking at me like I'm the brightest star in the sky.

"In the end, it doesn't matter. We found you, and you're safe. I couldn't ask for anything else."

"I could," says a voice from the sea.

A dripping figure approaches us, wincing and clutching his side. "You," Cheung Po Tsai says, pointing at Master Feng. "And you," he says, giving me a cursory glance. "I saw you on that smuggling ship. It's you, isn't it? I thought perhaps something in your eyes reminded me of her that day, but the name Shi Xiang meant nothing to me. I didn't know what happened to my pendant after she tore it from my throat and left me to die. I was only looking for the map. I didn't know you existed. If I had known . . ."

Cheung spits on the ground. He winces in pain, reaching for his side again; I can see red seeping into his robes. "Feng Zhanli, I want to thank you for finding my daughter. Now that I've found you, my blood, my heir, there is nothing that can stop us."

I shuffle backward. Master Feng gets to his feet and steps

in front of me, raising his arms protectively. "Don't you touch her."

"Daughter, give me the map." Cheung reaches forward, his outstretched hand twitching. He smiles, his handsome face tilting. "I did not know about you all these years. If I did, I would have rushed to your side. You could come live in my manor in the Fuijian province, have everything you could ever desire. Rich silks, perfumed baths, delicacies from all over the world, servants to wait on you hand and foot. I could secure you a marriage to a high-ranking captain in the navy. You would never want for anything."

"You did not raise her! I did!" Master Feng says, his eyes glittering as he turns to me. "He only wants the treasure. He already betrayed your mother once. He would take the treasure for himself, or pay tribute back to the emperor in bribes and—"

Cheung scoffs. "Please. You know as well as I that plunder was collected over years, from multiple kingdoms and governments." He glances at me. "Daughter. This poor accountant knows nothing. Come with me and we will use the treasure far more than your miserly mother ever would, leaving riches to rot in a dank cave—"

Master Feng bristles. "You see? He does not love her! This man only cares for himself, for riches." He looks back at me and smiles. "You have always been my daughter. I love your mother. Cheung Po Tsai only married her for status, to ascertain his position in the fleet. I know her for who she is. Forget him. After we find the treasure, we can go home, Xiang, back to the village. We can be a family. Safe, together—"

"Safe?" Cheung laughs harshly. "Like your mother kept you *safe*? Secret, more like. Daughter, I would never lie to you—"

"*I* have never lied to you—"

"Be quiet, you fool—"

Cheung Po Tsai draws his sword, but not before Master Feng does the same. Sharp steel glints in the sunlight as the two men stare at each other, faces hardened with hatred.

I back away, my heart pounding. I don't want Master Feng to get hurt, and, shockingly, I realize I don't want Cheung to be hurt, either. I have no wish to see more blood spilled.

I scramble to my feet. The odds aren't good. Cheung is injured, but surely he is the more skilled swordsman. Desperation shines in Master Feng's eyes. I don't have a weapon. I want to do something, but then I remember what they're fighting about.

Me.

It's not just about the map. Both of these men, in their own way, want my acceptance as their daughter—to somehow prove to Mother that they're worthy of her. And as much as Master Feng means to me—his comment about going back to the village, about a safe little life there—it is not what I want. It is what *he* wants.

I'm tired of others deciding my story for me.

I'm done.

I do not want to go back to Canton and run a smuggling empire with Mother. I do not want to live in a mountain village with Master Feng and read books and only dream about places I cannot visit. I certainly do not want to be waited on hand and foot in Fuijian, a pretty decoration for some man to marry.

I do not want the lives they've promised me. All these dreams are for an idea of a daughter—not actually me, who I am, as I am right now.

The family I want is here, on this island, and they need me.

I turn toward the tree line and run.

"Xiang!"

I ignore Master Feng's and Cheung's calls and dive into the expanse of jungle. My eyes adjust, but it's hard going to pick my way through the dense thicket of undergrowth. I trip over an exposed root and tumble to the ground. I bite my lip to keep from crying out in pain and struggle to stand back up. Exhaustion is catching up with me.

I look back to see if I'm being pursued. On the shore, Cheung is huffing toward me, and Master Feng tackles him to the ground.

"Leave her be!" he snaps.

"You are annoying and weak, and I don't know what the Head of the Dragon ever saw in you!" Cheung swings his sword angrily, scrambling to his feet.

I look away from the two men squabbling in the sand and see a rowboat approaching the shore. Mother disembarks the boat alone, prowling across the beach like a storm.

"Where is Xiang?" she demands.

Master Feng and Cheung both point toward the jungle. I sink farther into cover of the underbrush.

Get up, I tell myself. My ankle throbs where I hit the root.

"Enough."

Mother strides toward the men, pushing between their blades. Cheung and Master Feng immediately lower their weapons, tracking her movement.

"Xiang is *my* daughter. Neither of you has any say in matters that concern her."

Mother steps past them and sees me in the trees. She fixes her steely gaze on me. "Come, ignore these fools. Give me the map, and we will go home and keep it safe."

"Yes, Xiang!" Master Feng nods at her. "I was just talking with her, my love. We could go find—"

Cheung laughs. "You hopeless sycophant."

Mother ignores him and jerks her head toward the rowboat waiting at shore. "Get in the boat, Xiang."

Cheung steps forward. "She is my daughter, and that is my map—"

Mother draws her sword on Cheung. "You will leave. Otherwise I may actually kill you for once."

"You could never. Even in an evenly matched fight, you had to resort to trickery—"

Mother plunges her sword into his shoulder, pinning him to the ground.

Blood blossoms onto the fabric of his open jacket, and he lies there, spluttering and twitching. He watches her for a long moment in disbelief before he coughs, struggling.

"Please . . . finish it." Cheung jerks his head at the pistol at her belt.

She leans toward him, close enough to hear the rattling gulps of his breath. "What is it they call me?"

". . . the Head of the Dragon."

"And am I known for being merciful?"

Cheung gulps, his eyes wide and wet with pain, as if he cannot bring himself to say the answer he already knows.

Mother straightens, holding her head as high as the title she's earned. "I said get in the boat, Xiang."

"No."

"What did you say to me?"

I get to my feet. "No," I repeat. "I need to look for the crew of the *Huyền Vũ*." I look at Master Feng, who nods at me, and I go on. It may not be as eloquent a speech as he might have made, but it is the truth. "Then we can find the treasure, and give them a fair share as I promised them, and we can all be on our way."

Mother sighs. "I'm not sharing my treasure with some petty smugglers. It stays where it is. Hidden."

Master Feng reaches toward her. "Darling, listen, they're important to her—"

Mother presses her fingers to her temples and looks at

me once more. A strand of hair has escaped her carefully coiffed bun, and the hair pin is drooping, the golden dragon almost falling from its resting place. There's a fire in her eyes that I recognize: It's the same fire that drives me, and I understand.

"Mother, please."

She walks toward me, Master Feng beside her, and reaches out to me. "My treasure, come along. We will go home and forget all of this."

When I still don't move, she grows impatient. "Are you still upset I kept all of this a secret?" she asks.

"Yes," I reply. "Did you think I would love you less if I knew the truth?"

Mother looks toward the sea, her eyes dark with heavy thoughts. "I wanted you safe. I knew I could not be a mother the way you might have wished. I did not think you would understand."

Tears well up in my eyes. "I *do* understand. I've only ever wanted to make you proud."

Mother smiles at me now, real and true, and opens her arms again. "I am, Xiang. I am."

I close the remaining distance between us and sink into her embrace, feeling Mother's arms wrap around me tightly, holding me like she hasn't since I was a young child.

She fiddles with the pendant at my throat. "You did well, keeping this safeguarded on your journey here. I always knew that piece was out there." She taps my chin with amusement. "You gave us a merry chase indeed. Then again, it did set me back a week behind you, going back to the village—"

I pull back from her. "You went back to the village?"

"Of course. Once I heard the talk that people were searching for my treasure, I had to confirm that my other pieces of the map were safe."

"I thought you . . . You said you went looking for me first." A dreadful cold seeps into my bones. "You said you were worried about me."

Mother blinks. "Your letter told me not to worry."

I take another step back. "You said you went to make sure *your treasure* was safe first. It was never me, was it? You had no idea I was on this island. You had no idea what was in the pendant this whole time. Cheung Po Tsai knew—that's why he fixated on that painting of me, because he was the one who stashed the piece of the map in the pendant. You . . . you were just looking for the map the entire time!"

Mother shakes her head. "That's neither here nor there."

The tears fall now, hot and angry. I should have known better. I should have known Mother would always put the business first, as she always had.

I pull the pendant from my neck, snapping the chain, and toss it at her feet. "Take it. It doesn't matter."

She unclasps it and pulls out the scroll. Her eyebrows knit together as she looks over the shoddy copy, and she turns it over to see the love letter on the other side. "Where is the real piece?"

"I burned it," I say coldly.

"You did . . . what?'

"It's gone. The last piece of your map. The only one who knows how exactly to get to the treasure now is me."

"Good," Mother says after a moment. "So no one will be able to find it unless you tell them."

"Surely you—"

"When I was building my empire, I thought it would bolster my lieutenants' esteem to have a piece of the map, to know where it might be hidden, to think that they mattered in the grand scheme of things. But once it was out there, I saw greed and envy twist even the most loyal of my lieutenants. After the Battle of the Tiger's Mouth, I saw how willing they were to accept the pardon of anyone who would have them."

Mother's eyes flash with anger. "A pardon! From the Chinese empire? Pah! The Portuguese king? The British? The Spanish? These kingdoms feared us. They feared *me* most of all. They trembled in their palaces, with their riches, lording over the people they promised to help. They offered me a pardon because they were afraid. Afraid of what I had built, a kingdom of my own, people who followed me indiscriminately into war."

Mother flexes her fingers, making a fist, clenching and unclenching so her knuckles turn white against her skin. "They wanted me to disappear, they wanted to run their country without being made a laughingstock everytime they needed to leave the sea. The sun was setting on the Dragon

Fleet, I knew it. One by one, all of my lieutenants feared for their lives and were only too willing to accept the terms set by that pitiful governor-general Pai Ling."

"Why did you want everyone to think you were dead?" My body is aching, and I am trying to think of a plan. I am unarmed and exhausted to the bone, but as Mother has talked, I've regained a little strength, recovered just enough to maybe make a break for it into the underbrush. Or grab for Master Feng's sword. He's too busy watching Mother with wide eyes.

She cocks her head. "To preserve my legacy. The stories. The fear my name and my banner would strike in the hearts of anyone who would see it. The idea that I—the Head of the Dragon—would accept a pardon was utterly ridiculous. I had to go out on my own terms, and I did. I kept my ships. Kept my smuggling business. Nothing in the Canton underworld happens without me knowing. I am still the Head of the Dragon. And it is even better, to run my world from the shadows. My legacy, my treasure, all of it is mine still."

Then she laughs, looking askance at me. "It's *my* treasure. *I* hid it. You think I can't find it again without some lovelorn poetry to remind me? My whole life I've just needed to keep my legacy safe. Now that I've collected the last of the map pieces, there's really only one thing left to do to ensure that no one else ever finds it again."

Mother raises her pistol and aims directly at my heart.

"Anyone who wishes to find the treasure needs you, my dear. But I do not."

The shot fires before I can think to move. There's a blur of motion, a weight slams into me, and I find myself tumbling to the sand. Blood spurts all over me, seeping into my shirt, but it isn't mine. I've been knocked clear of the bullet's path.

Master Feng lies on top of me, wheezing as the wound blossoms in his chest. His blood seeps onto me in a torrent of crimson.

"Don't move," he whispers. The words are barely audible.

I am still. I let my eyes go wide and unfocused.

There's a long pause, and I can see only the tangle of branches above me, the sunlight filtering through the jungle canopy. Somewhere far away, a bird warbles.

Footsteps approach in the dirt, and then stop.

I imagine what Mother sees: her daughter and her lover, dead at her own hand. Or grievously injured, at least. If she would only bother to check.

"What a waste," Mother finally says.

Her footsteps fade away. I don't dare move until I hear the splash of the rowboat leaving.

"Master Feng," I whisper, afraid that he won't answer. "Master Feng . . ."

He groans.

I carefully try to turn him to his side. Blood is trickling from his mouth, and he looks at me, his fingers trembling as he reaches for my face.

I do not know anything of medicine, and I press my fingers to the wound, but hot blood still spurts from his chest. I sit up, trying to hold him—my tutor, my . . . my father. "Please, how can I—"

"I will be fine," he says. "Everything will be fine . . . my daughter."

He wheezes and splutters.

I press harder, trying to stop the flow.

"Xiang," he coughs.

"Shh, just rest," I say. "You need your strength. Close your eyes, and just . . . just go to sleep."

There's a small smile on his lips—he knows I'm humoring him. But he closes his eyes all the same, and I can feel him relaxing in my arms.

I do not know what comfort I can give. So I give him the only thing I can think of—my words.

"The village . . . that's where you grew up, isn't it? Before you became an accountant for the Dragon Fleet?"

He nods weakly, and I try to find the truth in all the stories I've been told. "It's a beautiful village, soft and peaceful."

His smile widens, and I cannot stop, even as his breathing goes more and more shallow. "I grew up there, just the way you wanted. And you got to take care of me, and we had all the time in the world to spend together. And it was wonderful."

His hand finds my own, and I squeeze it.

"When you wake up, we'll go find the treasure, and

361

everything will be all right. We'll go back to the village and buy as many books as you want. I'll tease you every day for being old and grumpy. We'll talk about philosophy and history, and you'll find me new stories, and I'll love every one of them. We'll climb to the top of the mountain, and I won't run, I promise, and I'll walk slow because you're old and your back will hurt. And we'll eat oranges and watch the sun set over the terraced fields. Together."

His grip goes slack, and his agonized breathing ceases.

I don't know how long I hold him, but it's long enough for the tide to change, the water slowly rising to shore.

He deserves a proper burial. A shrine with his name. But I do not have a shovel.

I instead grab him under his arms and slowly drag his body into the surf, until each retreating wave pulls at him, drawing him back to the ocean. I hold on as long as I can, wading in deeper. Then I take a deep breath and let go of his body, and watch the waves carry him out to sea.

I do not have any incense to burn, and I don't know the proper rites, but I offer a small prayer to each of the gods of the underworld to see him well into the next life.

"Feng Zhanli," I say, standing there in the waves, watching them carry my father's body toward the horizon. "Be at peace."

CHAPTER TWENTY-THREE

Alone

I FORCE MYSELF BACK TO THE REMNANTS OF THE CAMP AND collapse there in a heap. I don't remember falling asleep, but my dreams are restless, full of fear. Faces swim in front of me: Anh's, Captain Hoa's, Mother's. My father dies in my arms again and again, and I scream.

I rub my face blearily and sit up, hugging my knees to my blood-soaked chest. I wonder if Master Feng's spirit is on his way to the underworld, or if he's trapped here. Is his ghost watching me, growing hungrier and hungrier with every passing moment?

He gave his life for mine.

My lip wobbles and I want to cry, but I have nothing left.

The two warships are still anchored in the bay.

What is Mother waiting for? The safety of her treasure

is ensured, or so she believes. Why didn't she take Cheung's ship and go?

But as I look closer, I can see the damage to her ship. There are several holes in the hull, and from the movement on the deck I see people furiously pouring water out from the breaches.

The repairs needed must be intensive. I'm lucky they haven't camped out on the shore yet. I'll need to hide, and quickly.

I stumble to my feet.

. . . *Wait.*

I scan the beach, but Cheung is nowhere to be seen. Where he lay is a bloodied, sandy mess, but I cannot tell which way he could have gone.

Maybe Mother should have finished him after all.

I wonder if I could have done it. If it had been Anh who betrayed me, could I ever leave her to die?

No. Anh would never, and I would never.

I bury my face in my hands.

Captain Hoa doesn't have the map, but she's seen enough of it to know the layout of the island. And Anh may not have memorized the poem like I did, but I'm certain she could retrace our steps to look for the final resting spot of the treasure.

That's where I would go. With the *Huyền Vũ* destroyed and an enemy in the bay, the next best asset to secure would be the treasure itself.

There are a few scant supplies left at the camp, and I eat cold rice and the last of the preserved fish I find before I make my way along the shoreline. The longboat Anh and I stole to find the treasure ourselves is still where we left it when we returned. It has drifted slightly, stuck in a tuft of mangrove roots, but I manage to yank it free.

I row to the sheer cliff face I'd seen from the peak. It's low tide now.

"The tiger's tears . . . ," I mutter to myself. I look to the mountain peak and back to the cliff, trying to determine where the tiger's face must be.

The dense green foliage looks impenetrable the way it's covering the cliff face, but it must be here. I know it.

I row my boat carefully to the eye and press forward.

The vines give way to a soft darkness, and I grin.

The cave is long and dark, in some places as wide as a great hall. All is quiet except for the slight sound of my oar hitting the water and the echoes of it dripping. I light a lantern and grip my paddle tighter, taking on the darkness ahead. I am not afraid; I want to see what all this blood has been spilled for. How many lives have been destroyed to amass this wealth?

I vaguely remember the fanciful dreaming about what I would do with my share. A life I thought I wanted.

Now, all I want is to take this treasure away from the woman who wanted it so badly she defied empires and was willing to kill everyone whom she claimed to love. I want Mother to reckon with what she has created, and what she cast aside.

I want revenge. I want justice for Master Feng. I want the Head of the Dragon to pay for what she has done.

I follow the twisting labyrinth, and my lantern flickers, the tiny flame shuddering in the pool of oil. Bulbous pillars of rock grow down from the ceiling, and every so often I have to duck to avoid them. I pause to touch one, its smooth surface cold in my hands.

The darkness ahead is thick and full, almost alive, like a monster lurking just out of sight waiting to devour me. The space between the water level and the top of the cave gets so low, sometimes I have to press myself to the bottom of the boat to avoid them. My oar scrapes gravel, and I wonder if this would be passable by foot.

"Hello?" I call out. My voice reverberates eerily. "Anh? Captain Hoa?"

Only my echo answers.

I cannot tell if anyone else has been here. Would Anh have come here on her own, seeking the treasure? Or waited until she found the rest of the crew to work together to recover it?

With no sun to tell the passing of time, there's only the slowly growing pool of melting wax in the lantern, the candle burning to a small stub. I fumble in the bag for another. There isn't one.

I turn around and try to find the light, but I've come so far through the twisting tunnel there's only more darkness behind me.

Logic says I should turn around, but I feel like I'm drawing closer to something, and I have to see what lies at the end of this cave. My arms are beginning to ache, but I keep paddling, settled into a rhythm echoed by the beating of my own heart.

I let out a soft curse as the candle goes out. My eyes adjust to the dark, and I can make out some movement, but it must be my imagination, thinking there are spirits flickering around me.

I dip the oar back in the water and blink again. I jab tentatively at the water with my oar, swirling it in a circle. A path of light follows my oar, in an enchanting cloud of blue green. It looks like it could very well be from the spirit world, and I watch with amazement. I turn around, and behind the boat there is a slight trail as well, rippling behind me.

As my eyes adjust further, I see the cloud in the water and on the sides of the cave, too, in slightly different colors and intensity of brightness. In the water, the lights disappear as quickly as they appear, like dust particles floating lazily in the afternoon light, but as soon as I dip my oar again, a soft cloud of luminescence blooms. It's just enough to get a sense of where I am, and it's comforting in a strange way. I wonder if the gods are speaking to me, letting me know I'm on the right path. I say a silent prayer of thanks.

The cavern widens and the boat runs aground again. I clamber out of it and wedge it free where it's caught between the rocks, and then move on ahead. I swirl my oar in the water again and pause; there are two long tunnels ahead of me, almost identical. I consider them both. There are no more riddles to solve, nothing left but my instincts.

I touch the cave surface and try to imagine if I were Mother. Would I have gone here by boat, at first? Or would she have explored this by foot at the lowest tide? I use my hands to examine the sides of both tunnels, and then on the one to the right I feel it—sharp grooves in the rock, worn over from water, but clearly there.

Like someone had walked by with a heavy iron trunk and it scraped against the tunnel.

I get back in and paddle to the right.

A few moments later, the boat comes to an abrupt halt, and I swish my oar in the water. The luminescence swirls forward and then stops, as if it's hit the end of the cave.

I am here.

CHAPTER TWENTY-FOUR

The Treasure of the Dragon

I CLAMBER OUT OF MY BOAT AND FEEL AROUND; I FIND SOFT sand and step forward. There are hard things all around me, and some soft ones. In one small oiled sack I find a stash of candles, and I relight my lantern with relish.

I raise the light and survey where I am, lifting it higher, and still I cannot see the end of the tunnel. It's crammed full of trunks and barrels, all of them sealed by wax and damp to the touch. This entire cache must get flooded at high tide.

I open the chests closest to me one by one. They're all different in fashion; some rough hewn and some elaborately made, some foreign and some familiar, elaborate brass hinges or sturdy iron, all revealing some marvel within. There's a trunk filled with Spanish coins, silver and gold glittering softly under my lantern. A smaller chest is filled with elegantly carved pieces of jade, lustrous and green and shining. There are barrels of Portuguese silver. Casks of sumptuous freshwater pearls.

I close each one and sit back on the wet sand with a sigh. What use do I have for this treasure now? So much blood has been spilled for this gold and jade, so many lives lost.

I have the longboat. It's sturdy enough. It would take time, but I am strong now; I could raise the sail and make it all the way to Changping if I wanted to, use the riches here to buy my own ship. I could lead the life I want to, knowing that wherever I go now I don't have to prove anything to anyone.

Maybe I never did. I set out on this journey to find the treasure, all to prove that I was capable.

I have the answer to my question. It took me leaving home and running after what everyone had thought was impossible to know it.

I've always been taught that blood was everything—that family, where you came from, defined who you could be. Mother claimed she cared about me, but she was only ever looking after her own ends.

I want to cry, but my body is tired and my eyes are dry.

I've cried enough.

I've found the treasure, and I could have a life of my own,

one I've always wanted, with the *more* I've dreamed of just within reach.

But what would it mean without Anh by my side?

I open the trunk next to me and run my hand through the precious jewels within, the strands of pearls, the carved pieces of jade, and the gold coins stamped with words in a language I cannot read.

I do not care about any of this.

I take the rucksack that once held the candles and sweep handfuls of precious things inside until it is full. I shove it back into the boat's storage compartment and look at the meager cooking supplies. I could empty the small hold and fill it with treasure, but then I remember the narrow passageway, how the longboat scraped the bottom of the cave with just my weight.

No, this will do for now. I just need enough to prove I found the treasure.

I go to close the trunk and see a jade pendant, plain and unassuming against the other intricate pieces of jewelry. It's a dark, lush green—the color of vitality, of longevity—a plain gold band affixing the jade circle to a simple chain. I pick it up, and the stone is cool against my skin. It's a bit dull from its time in the trunk, but with time it could be lustrous and shining again.

I pocket the piece and shut the trunk with a heavy finality.

Anh must be somewhere on this island still.

I have to find her.

I pick my way back to the longboat and paddle out of the cave. It's harder leaving than it was entering, with the current against me now—I realize with a pang of terror that the tide is coming in. My arms are burning with effort, and I have to hop out of the boat a few times to guide it through the narrow passage, my feet scrambling to find purchase on the slippery ground beneath me. I finally give up and swim, holding my breath as I push the boat along with me in the close darkness.

At long last, I push my way out through the vines, my head barely above water as I blink in the astonishing brightness of the day. I climb back into the boat and collapse there, exhausted.

If I were Anh, where would I go? What was the last piece of the riddle she would remember, if she didn't make it to the tiger's eye?

My vision adjusts to the bright blue sky, and my gaze falls to the highest peak on the island.

Of course.

I row back to the camp, keeping to the shadows. Mother's ship is now beached, its hulking monstrosity supported by fallen trees and makeshift scaffolding as her crew works on the repairs. The damage looks even worse up close, multiple gaping holes on the side of the hull open to the lower decks within. Our old camp has been completely taken over by Mother's crew, a hustling hive of activity.

I wait until nightfall to row past them. There's one man keeping watch, and I count twelve more on the beach. I wonder how many of Mother's crew is left after Cheung's attack. There aren't any lantern lights coming from the *Nù Tử*.

I shake off the thought. I have to find Anh.

I follow the path we took around the island that night we stole away. I tie the rowboat off in the same cluster of mangroves where we fell asleep in each other's arms.

In the morning I wake alone, but with fresh determination. I follow the jellyfish to the hidden lagoon and row my way across it. On the other side, I set off into the jungle. It's easy enough to follow where Anh and I have trodden before, marked by the shorn branches from my machete clearing the initial path and the litter of brush and debris on the ground.

It is almost midday by the time I find my way to the topmost crag. There's no reason for her to be here—nothing except a feeling that I have, that she may want to find the highest point on the island to gather her thoughts and to try to find the treasure on her own, or to use the vantage point to look for the others. After all, if she had gotten separated from her crew in the confusion, it would be the most logical thing to do.

An illogical part of my heart suggests that it is because I want to believe that this place meant something to her, too.

The last maneuver at the top is difficult to do on my own without someone to give me a boost, but I manage it—barely—my heart heaving as I hoist myself to the top.

Anh is here.

She's sitting alone at the small peak, hugging her knees and sobbing quietly.

"Anh!"

Her head whips up, her eyes red, widening with surprise when she sees me. "Xiang! Are you—"

I shake my head and look down at the dried blood all over my shirt. "It's not mine, I—I'm fine."

"Oh, you—" Her features harden into a scowl, as if she's remembering she's angry with me. "What are you doing here?" she huffs.

"Looking for you," I say.

"Leave me alone. It's your fault we're stuck here, without a ship, with nothing to show for this venture. I can't believe I ever trusted you."

"But . . . there's nothing on the beach. I didn't see Thanh, or your mother, any of the crew—"

Anh buries her face back into her hands. "I haven't seen anyone. No fires, nothing. You didn't see how much she was—she was bleeding so much, and she could be—"

"We can look for them," I say gently, sitting down next to her.

"What do you care?! They're not your family! They're *mine*!" Anh shakes, sobs convulsing through her. "I've lost everything, all because of you! I should have believed Thanh from the start. You must have orchestrated this all along, you and your mother, the Head of the Dragon—" She stops to gasp for air.

I offer her a flagon of water. Anh accepts it, takes a long drink and then glares at me. "I'm drinking this because I'm thirsty, not because I trust you or forgive you."

We sit there in silence for a long moment. "I didn't know my mother was the Head of the Dragon until that moment on the beach. You know I didn't." *You know me*, I don't say, the words unbidden in my throat. Anh seems so far away from where we were the last time we stood on this peak.

She looks up at me for a moment that seems to stretch to infinity. Ever since I've met her she's always been so confident, so composed, treating everything as cavalier and casually as she can. And yet from that very first day we spent together, she saw me, the real me—the way she's seeing me now.

"Then why did you leave?" she asks, her voice gone soft and vulnerable.

"It was the only thing I could think of to let you all go free."

"Free!" Anh scoffs. "We were ready to fight to the death. I should have died on that beach with my family, fighting for

375

our lives." She looks at me. "You would have fought, too. You raised your sword against your own mother."

"I did. I—*you're* my family, Anh," I say. "She . . . she is my blood, yes. But that's all I am to her. She always called me her treasure." I look down toward the cliff face, at the shape of the tiger looming there. "She wanted to keep me safe. Like a doll. Like a story. She didn't see me as a person, just . . . something else she could control. At the end of the day, the treasure was more important to her than I was."

Anh regards me, some of her old curiosity returning in her eyes. "What do you mean?"

I laugh, but there's no mirth in it. I quickly recount my time on Mother's ship and my escape. "She tried to kill me. To protect the location of her last legacy. But my father protected me."

"Your father . . . the one who died at sea?"

"He died on that beach, Anh," I say softly, a painful lump in my throat. "The man who raised me, protected me, encouraged me to follow my heart. He told me I should find you. Because that is where my heart is."

"Your tutor . . . your father . . . I'm so sorry, Xiang." Anh rests a gentle hand on my shoulder.

"Thank you. Your mother . . . have you seen any signs of her? Any of the crew?" I try to remember when I saw each of them during the frenzied battle, who was still fighting and who got away.

Anh shakes her head. "I was too afraid to look. Afraid of what I might find, or not find. I should have—I ran in a completely different direction, then I heard cannon fire. I wasn't sure what was happening in the bay, and if the navy showed up . . . ."

She shudders, then looks back down to the island below us, the sweeping view of the coves and inlets and beaches. It's a breathtaking place, ruggedly beautiful.

Anh suddenly sits up a bit straighter. "Smoke . . . there. Do you see it?"

A small trickle drifts up from the trees on the western side of the island. "Yes, I see it. Over there." I pull the spyglass I took from the longboat and hand it to Anh.

She takes it and gives that side of the island a long, calculating look. "It's barely visible against that cloud formation. But it's smoke!"

I take the spyglass and look to where she's pointing. I discern a fire on the western beach, and if I strain my eyes, just a bit of movement. Impossible to tell who, but at least three people. "It could be your mother, or anyone from the crew!"

"Could be the navy soldiers. Or the Dragon Fleet crew."

I shake my head. "They fought each other." I look back to the cove, where red banners are still flying from the two ships, Mother's and the navy warship. "Cheung Po Tsai's men attacked Mother's after I boarded. Apparently while the Dragon Fleet was on the beach, Cheung's men took the remaining crew hostage and lay in wait for them to return. Once I was below deck, the attack began."

"I thought as much."

"It'll take her time to repair the boat, and knowing her pride, she won't just take Cheung's ship and leave. Besides, it's still a Qing imperial ship, easily recognizable." I narrow my eyes. "I only saw her crew on the beach. I assume Mother would have killed most if not all the soldiers before claiming Cheung's ship. She won't have enough people to keep watch on both ships, and I rowed past them on my way here. That's their camp, there. Right where we set up the first night."

Anh follows my gaze. "There could be a way out of here yet," she says, sitting upright. "Zheng Yi Sao believes herself to have won. She won't be expecting another attack. She only has one good ship remaining and not enough people to keep watch on the *Nù Tie* while making the repairs." Something like hope flickers in her eyes.

"And—" I reach into my pocket and offer her the jade pendant. "I know exactly where the treasure is. We steal the ship, rescue the rest of our crew, and snatch the treasure right from under the Dragon's nose. Then we make our escape."

Anh gets to her feet. She looks at the necklace in my outstretched hand, her eyes widening. Her gaze drop to my lips, and I wonder if she's thinking about the last time we were here.

Her hand closes around the pendant, and around my own. "Well, then. What are we waiting for?"

We stash the longboat in the cluster of mangroves, swimming back to spy on the Dragon Fleet camp.

They're celebrating, sitting on the beach and drinking around a roaring fire, clearly unconcerned with anyone seeing them. Saws have been brought out, and people are hard at work felling more trees to acquire lumber for repairs. An elaborate tent has been constructed since I last saw the camp, and two burly guards are stationed in front of it. That must be Mother's.

We count heads three times to make sure of the exact number of crew and watch them take shifts. There's one rowboat that goes from the bay to shore every three hours. I was right—it's a skeleton crew on the ship. There's never more than two guards on the *Nù Tiể*. They must be feeling incredibly safe.

The moon is high when the shift changes again. Over the rush of the waves, I can barely hear the two men laugh as they struggle to keep time to their drinking song.

We're just two shadows in the night, and the men in the boat don't even take notice as we trail behind them. Anh's already ahead of me, swimming quickly, her arms strong and steady as she works against the current.

I keep my head above water, the night as dark as the ocean around me. The moonlight glinting off the shifting pulse of the waves is barely distinguishable from the stars above. I almost lose sight of the hulking shadow of the ship ahead of us, but the mast rising tall cuts a clean line through the moonlit sky and I'm able to keep a steady course.

The two men call out to the crew on board, and a rope ladder is thrown down.

"Come on!" Anh mouths to me.

We finally reach the side of the ship and watch the pirates climb aboard. The plan is to wait until the two men relieved from their shift get in the rowboat and go back to shore before we climb up the anchor chain . . . but no one climbs down the ladder.

I point to it, and Anh nods. The men must all be taking a break.

Water drips noisily from my wet clothes, and every tap and scrape against the wooden hull of the ship seems to echo loudly as the ladder thumps against it. But with the sound of the waves granting us cover, I know we won't be heard.

We slip through an open gun port and onto the lower deck, watching for the shift change to be completed, but nothing happens.

Something doesn't feel right. I shake my head, tugging on Anh's sleeve.

"They're probably just having a drink together or something," she whispers. "Come on. We can take them by surprise."

They can't hear us above the sounds of the ship slowly rocking back and forth on the waves, so the sailors on the shore or the others on the ship deck surely won't hear them call for help, either. As long as we don't set off any of the cannons, we should be all right.

The gun deck is quiet. I want to light a lantern to see if we can find a weapon, but Anh is already climbing up to the deck. She gestures to me, pulling me up behind her. All is quiet. There isn't anyone to be seen, not any soldiers drinking together or standing watch. There is no one at all.

"Anh, I don't think—"

I turn around and come face-to-face with a bare sword.

CHAPTER TWENTY-FIVE
THE PLAN

"Captain—Captain Hoa?" I splutter.

"Xiang! Anh!" Captain Hoa gasps, dropping her sword her sword. She envelops her daughter in a close embrace, tears brimming in her eyes. "When I didn't see you with the others, I thought . . . I thought . . . you're alive!"

I back away, uncomfortable with the outpouring of love.

"Come here, you clever girl!" Captain Hoa pulls me in and hugs me tightly as well. I stiffen and then relax, letting the affection wash over me.

"I thought the Head of the Dragon would have eaten you alive," she mutters, pulling back and regarding me and then Anh. "I didn't know what to think, I just—when I saw the Dragon Fleet setting up camp, I knew Zheng Yi Sao had defeated the navy and would need time to repair—"

Anh laughs. "You had the same idea we did: Steal the navy warship."

We catch up with one another in bits and pieces, and Captain Hoa recounts the crew's time in the jungle. She had found Thanh first, then Ling Shan and Maheer, and later they had met up with Châu and Arthrit, who had set up a makeshift camp. Thanh is injured but he'll survive, and Châu may never see out of his right eye again.

"The spirit of the *Huyền Vũ* cannot be defeated!" Captain Hoa says, pumping her fist in the air triumphantly. "Zheng Yi Sao underestimated us, toyed with us on that beach, but her pride will be her downfall. They may have destroyed our ship, but revenge is sweet—their ship is in pieces, and we have a far better one to show for it!"

Behind Captain Hoa, I see Maheer and Thanh climb up from the hold, approaching us. Thanh rushes over and seizes his sister in a hug, wincing when she squeezes him back in return. "Hey, hey, easy."

"It's good to see you, Xiang," Maheer says.

My eyes brim over with unshed tears. "And you," I say, and I rush forward to hug him. He pats me gently before stepping back, regarding me with a smile.

Thanh looks at me, biting his lip. "Yeah," he says awkwardly. "It is. I, uh—"

Anh rests her head on his shoulder.

Thanh looks between his sister and me and opens his other arm. "You're a part of this family, if you want to be,

Xiang. I—I'm sorry. I was only trying to protect it, and I couldn't see you were also doing the same."

"I should have told you all the truth from the start," I say, stepping forward. The embrace is a little stiff, and I'm careful not to jostle Thanh's bandaged shoulder. I pat him carefully as the three of us break apart. "You were right to be suspicious of me."

"It's all in the past," Thanh says with a smile. "Now you're the youngest, Mei-Mei." He ruffles my hair, and I laugh.

Anh grins. "Xiang gave herself up so we could get away. And then she escaped to find us." She pulls the jade pendant I gave her from her neck and holds it aloft.

Captain Hoa inhales sharply.

"I found the treasure of the Dragon Fleet. I know exactly where it is." I step forward, looking to our captain. "We can wait until low tide and go back and fill this ship's hold with everything and leave Zheng Yi Sao here on this island with nothing but her empty legacy."

Thanh whoops in the air, a fierce delight sparkling in his eyes.

Captain Hoa claps me on the back. "Yes—"

"Quiet!" Maheer snaps. He glances at each of us, horror dawning on his face. "We're drawing attention to ourselves. Let's get back below deck and come up with a plan, out of sight."

Captain Hoa looks over the deck. "We have the upper hand. If they board us, we can fight them off—"

"We don't have enough people to run the cannons or to fight off Zheng Yi Sao's entire crew, even what's left of it," Maheer says. "Half of us are injured. We barely have enough people to sail this massive warship."

"What about the guards?" I ask.

"We were planning to dump the bodies once we were far enough away."

I look back at the shoreline, where the outline of a row-boat is making its way toward us. "Duck! There's only four men on this ship, remember!" I gesture to Anh, and she drops to the deck. "It's perfectly reasonable they stopped to have a drink with one another."

But it may be too late. They could have already seen all of our silhouettes.

My mind races through the possibilities.

There's the pirate army on the beach slowly making their way toward us.

There's the treasure.

There's Anh and her crew—my new family that I swore to protect.

For so long I've dreamed of impossible destinies, of adventure. These past few weeks I've had all of that and more. I've found love where I wasn't looking, and a crew that cares for me as if I were their own. I found my father and lost him.

I found myself.

I don't need to prove anything to anyone.

I know who I am, and I know what I'm capable of.

"Anh," I say, pulling her close.

"What are you doing?" She looks to me as I glance back to shore.

"You have to leave. Leave with the captain, your crew. Make sure the ship sets sail. I'm going to go back and tell them where to find the treasure. It's the only leverage I have left."

"What?" Shock drains the color from her face, and she grows still. "You can't! We can do it, we'll all get away now. Forget the treasure! We're all here, we have the ship, we can just go!"

I shake my head. "It's not enough. Mother won't stop until everyone who knows about the treasure is dead. You think she won't hunt you and your ship down? If you leave and take this warship, you'll at least get a fair start."

A plan starts to form in my head. "I will distract them long enough for you to be able to get away."

"Xiang, you don't have to leave—" Anh protests.

"It is the only way you'll be safe." I pull her close. "I wanted to always be by your side, but I can't do that if you're dead. Live, Anh. I love you."

She kisses me then, her mouth soft and filled with promise. I can taste the salt of her tears, or perhaps it's just the spray of the sea.

"Stay," Anh begs.

I push her away and jump off the side of the ship.

I am no stranger to the cold water, and I swim back toward shore without difficulty, passing the rowboat undetected.

When I reach the beach, I stumble onto the sand, then stand tall and give a wordless shout. The sailors on watch whip their heads toward me, reaching for their weapons.

"Who the—"

I feel as powerful as a water spirit, the moonlight shining down on me, determination flowing through my veins. I have nothing to lose and everything to gain. "I am Shi Xiang, daughter of Shi Yeung—who you know as Zheng Yi Sao, the Head of the Dragon."

The grand tent flaps open, and Mother strides out. "What is the meaning of this?"

Her gaze falls to me.

I cock my head in defiance, staring directly back at her.

If she is surprised to see me alive, she doesn't show it. "Xiang. I thought as much." She glares at me, folding her arms over her chest. "Well, what are you waiting for? Kill her."

"But she's your—"

"Don't you want to—"

Mother scoffs. "Do as I command."

The men in front of me, I notice, aren't carrying guns, just swords. "Tell me, has she ever shared her plans with you?" I say to them. "Her treasure? She keeps the location all to herself, trusting none of you despite the many years you've worked with her! And what do you have to show for it? Even the most loyal of her people feel the cold of her indifference. Master Feng, a bullet to the heart. Cheung Po Tsai, stabbed and left on the beach to die."

I gesture at the island. "She brings you here with nothing but her word. But *I* know where the treasure is, and I can take you there. And you can all have a fair share." I reach into my pocket and toss a few gold coins at them.

One man bites one with his teeth and then marvels at it. "It's real. This is—this is from the Siamese job." He turns back toward Mother. "You said you never recovered the loot from that prize!"

Roars of discontent rise up from the pirates on the beach. Behind me, I see the sails drop on the warship.

"Follow me and I will take you to—"

Something cold and heavy presses against my temple.

"Hello, daughter," Cheung Po Tsai's voice hisses in my ear. "What's this I hear about you leading others to *my* treasure?"

CHAPTER TWENTY-SIX
THE TIGER'S TEARS

THE GUN COCKS RIGHT BY MY EAR, AND I GULP.

Mother crosses her arms. "This is too dramatic, even for you, baobei."

Cheung flinches. "Don't you dare call me that! I'll shoot her!"

"Go ahead," Mother says. "I'm going back to sleep." She whirls around, her robes fluttering around her.

Cheung laughs, and I can see where his clothes have been stained with blood, his face drawn and hollow. I don't know how he hasn't succumbed to the elements or his wounds. Perhaps it's just sheer spite that sustains him.

The men pause, unsure of what to do. They look at me, their fingers twitching. I can practically feel their greed in the air.

"I can take you to the treasure," I say again.

One pirate looks at his companion and shrugs, and he charges at Cheung.

Cheung keeps his gun on me and draws his sword, parrying the thrust quickly. "You are exactly your mother's daughter," he hisses. "Why would you do this?!"

He stabs the man in the stomach and kicks him aside, and his companion makes his move, wary. The battle is short, the amateur's moves unsteady as Cheung dispatches him easily even despite his injuries.

The warship is nothing but a shadow on the horizon now, and I exhale in relief.

The tent flap ruffles again, and Mother emerges, her sword at her side and her belts clinking with guns. She gives me a steely glare, and then turns her gaze to Cheung. She jerks her head, and behind her the rest of the pirates fall in line. I recognize some of the faces of people who used to eat in the teahouse. Kang is at Mother's right hand, watching me, an unreadable expression across her face.

Mother smiles sweetly at me. "Very well then, Xiang. It can never be said that Zheng Yi Sao is not fair. Lead us to the treasure, and I'll make sure all of us are compensated fairly." Her voice turns cold. "Traitors excluded. You and Cheung Po Tsai will come along because I want you to see it. And then I will kill you there and let you bleed out slowly."

I watch the tides as we shuffle into Mother's rowboats, and we row our way along to the cliffside. I lead the way to the tiger's eye, and Mother smiles as she reaches out and lets the vines brush against her fingers like she's greeting an old friend. Lanterns are lit, and we paddle through the labyrinthine caves in silence. This time, there is no wonder, no lights from the spirit world to guide our way. Just the flicker of multiple lanterns, the sound of water dripping, and our oars hitting the water.

The treasure is even more impressive in the full light of a dozen lanterns, and everyone is stunned into silence. Even Cheung doesn't say anything as Mother steps from the boat, stroking each of the chests fondly. "Go on," she says indulgently to her crew.

One by one the pirates leave the rowboats, and Cheung is pushed roughly onto the pile as Kang lazily keeps him at gunpoint. Each trunk is uncovered, and soon the cave is filled with sighs of awe and whoops of adoration.

No one is watching me.

I slink into the water, the sound muffled by the clinking of gold and the babbling of the crew. I watch them as I inch farther and farther past the two boats.

Cheung is eyeing a jeweled saber in one of the open trunks. Mother picks up an elaborate headdress from another, a beautiful circlet fit for an empress, studded with jade and delicate pearls. She places it on her head with a serene smile just as Cheung picks up the saber and charges.

Mother meets his sword with her own, snarling.

I take this moment to turn away . . . and I bump into someone warm and solid.

Anh.

I gasp, and Anh claps her hand over my mouth. She gestures at the ensuing fight, and I jerk my head toward the end of the cave. She puts her hand on one of the boats, questioning.

I shake my head. "Let's go," I mouth at her.

The water is well past my waist now. We swim as the current floods in to meet us, and this is ten times worse than the first time I found myself on the wrong end of the tide. Screams and hoarse shouts begin to sound behind us, and I press forward, even as the cave twists and turns. The water rises to my chin.

Anh gasps for breath. "I'm sorry, I thought—"

"You came back for me."

She nods, laughing almost hysterically. "Of course I did. I saw them surrounding you on the beach. I couldn't bear it. I want"—she gulps—"I want what you want. To be by your side. To make you smile every day. To have a life together."

The words fill the drowning air around us. She means it. Anh, who always skips three times around admitting what she's truly wanted, who hides her feelings with bubbly jokes and sheer confidence, who confessed her fears to me under a starry night sky.

Anh is here, and she wants me in return.

She pulls me close, and despite the desperate moment, I take the time to return the embrace. Anh rests her head on my shoulders, and I feel the solid relief of her body against mine as we hold each other close. The lantern Anh is struggling to keep above the water sizzles and goes out, and it's just us and the darkness.

"However short it might be," Anh says. Her hand finds mine in the darkness, and the water rises even higher.

"I love you," she gasps.

It's raw and honest and I can *feel* it, in the way that I have longed to understand in all the poetry, in all the stories I read, how some say soulmates can find each other in every lifetime. Perhaps they were ducks who shared a nest together, or a weaver goddess and a cowherd, or just two girls who looked at the world and wanted more.

I feel it now—this connection, this love, this truth. I hold it close, this precious vulnerability, laid bare in front of the rest of the universe.

Our kiss is soft at first, but unlike our first kiss that was all question and hope and wonder and hesitation, or the second, filled with desperation and goodbye, this—this is an answer, one I didn't even know I was hoping for.

"Do you trust me?" I ask her.

Anh blinks at me, as if she can't tell if she wants to laugh or cry.

"Can you live on love?" I ask her.

This time she does cry, a tear leaking down from her eyes, and she laughs as well.

"Of course," she says.

I take a deep breath, and her hand, and I plunge into the water.

At first all is darkness, but I know Anh is by my side. Even as the world collapses into just the suffocating dark, I keep my eyes open. I pull her forward, thrashing in the water, opening my palm wide to mimic an oar.

There.

A flicker of light.

Anh's hair billows up around her face, and her eyes are open, and she's seeing it, too. Bubbles stream from her nose as she looks around us, at the flickers of light motes glowing faintly from the movement.

I jerk my head for her to follow.

We swim, following the flooded tunnel, occasionally finding a pocket of air, trusting the trail of light. I don't know how long it takes for us to find our way through the darkness, and I grow light-headed and dizzy in long stretches where we can't find a spot to breathe. Finally we push through to the open sky and gasp for air.

We find our way to the rocks, and I collapse on the nearest

one, Anh beside me. She coughs, spluttering as she turns over and stares at me in wonder. "Do you trust me?" she echoes. "I thought—don't laugh at me! I thought we were going to die! I thought I would have to love you in the next life!"

I laugh because there's nothing else I can do. I laugh, and then Anh laughs with me, and it feels like the sheer incredibility of being alive is going to eat us whole. Anh pushes me playfully, and I fall in the water. I pull her down with me as we roll to the shore, wheezing with relief. I can barely breathe; all the impossibilities, the life I never could have dreamed of for myself, everything I want is right here. For the first time, I can see that we *can* do it. That we can get away from everyone who expects us to be what we aren't, to be pawns in someone else's game, to be used as bargaining chips or to be made in someone else's image.

Anh rests her forehead against mine. We breathe together, inhaling and exhaling and falling into a rhythm. I marvel at how well Anh fits in my arms, how my hand rests just so in the curve of her upper arm where it's rounded with muscle, as if that curve was made for me to rest my hand on.

Anh turns to look at me, her expression soft with wonder. She carefully wipes the tears from my cheek, and lets out a soft, desperate laugh. "So this is where we are," she says. "I suppose I wouldn't rather be stuck on this island with anyone but you." She laughs again as if trying to register the absurdity of the situation.

She glances at the entrance to the cave, hidden now by the water. One could never tell inside this cliff lay an unknowable amount of riches. "Do you think they survived?"

I shake my head. "I don't know."

There's a part of me that does know, a sinking realization that will catch up to me later, and the grief that will come with it—an unwieldy, uncomfortable thing, to mourn for the loss of someone who you never really knew.

In many ways, I understand my mother better. If she had told me the truth from the start, would I have wanted her acknowledgment in the same way? If she had loved me for who I was from the very beginning, would it have turned out this way?

I let the tears fall, hot and wet, streaking through the salt water on my cheeks. I don't know if I'm mourning Mother, or who I used to be.

The water has risen well above the tiger's eye, shrouding the hoard of the Dragon Fleet, the untold spoils within. Mother's fight to keep her legacy.

I close my eyes. She got what she wanted, in the end. To have her treasure. To have her name, her story, her reputation unmarred, unfettered, the unparalleled Head of the Dragon.

Well.

That's her story.

Mine is just beginning.

I sit up and look to the sky. "You know what? I don't think we have to be stuck here if we don't want to be."

"What do you mean? If we wait for low tide again we could fetch those rowboats, but we'd have to tend with whatever's inside. Alive or not." Anh reaches out for me. "I know at the end of it, it wasn't . . . it wasn't what you wanted. But she's still your mother."

Something twists inside my heart, something I will deal with later.

"Well, there is one more seaworthy vessel."

CHAPTER TWENTY-SEVEN

THE HORIZON

MY HAIR FLIES FREE IN THE WIND, AND I LAUGH AS IT BLOWS in my face. The air is tangy with salt, and in the distance, dawn is breaking, soft and golden along the horizon.

The longboat was where I had left it among the mangroves, and we pulled it out without any difficulty. It'll take time to sail all the way to Changping, but we can do it. From there we'll keep a look out for the *Nù Tiě* and find Captain Hoa and the crew.

And then . . . anywhere we like.

Anh takes a flyaway strand and tucks it behind my ear, grinning wildly. "Look," she says.

Behind us, the island stands in its glory, all unkempt jungle and jagged rock. The *Lóng Zhī Ǎo* lies on the beach, a spindly, sad-looking thing now. As we row away, the ship disappears from view, and one could almost pretend that this is just another island, a wild place with no memory.

I think about the coins and the jewels, the sumptuous bolts of silk, the gold and the jade, the treasure succumbing to the high tide. I think about the blood spilled to get here. What it cost for everyone to find this place. The lengths Mother had taken to keep the treasure hidden, the way she had trusted her lieutenant, her lover, who had betrayed her in turn.

"I'm sorry we weren't able to get any of the treasure," Anh says.

I take Anh's hands in my own and smile, knowing what is stored in the hold of the longboat. It isn't all the riches of the Dragon Fleet, but it's more than enough to get us started on our new life. "Are you sure we didn't?" I ask, my heart light with joy.

"Why are you laughing?" Anh teases.

It's pure joy and relief bubbling out of me. The tension and fear I've felt since we set foot on the island is gone.

Anh is here by my side now, and we have a lifetime to spend together.

Our sails catch the wind, and our vessel speeds toward the unknown, toward a new beginning.

"I think what we have here is worth far, far more," I say.

Anh interlaces her fingers with my own, and together we face the beckoning horizon.

Author's Note

My mother left Vietnam during the fall of Saigon in 1975. She was a schoolteacher, one of the many people who lived and worked in the city.

My mother recalls the bombs that fell on the city, the constant terror of both the Viet Cong and American attacks, and the helplessness she felt. She and many other civilians fled the country, refugees who would then be known as "Boat People," leaving a war-torn conflict raged by powers beyond her comprehension and people caught in the middle. My mother bought passage for herself, my sixteen-year-old aunt, and my five-year-old cousin on a fishing boat by pawning my grandmother's jewelry. As I grew up, she would often tell me how small it was, the length of it barely the size of our living room, and yet it would hold more than fifty people crammed together, all of whom were holding on to a desperate hope for a life beyond the constant attacks.

One night in a terrible storm, the fishing vessel paused as another vessel pulled alongside it. Pirates. My mother and my aunt were stricken with fear, for they had heard terrible stories of the pirates who would raid the refugee ships. But the dangers of the sea were far preferable to the dangers on land, and she knew the risk she was taking. The pirates led all the men off the boat and then proceeded to search for valuables, taking what cash and jewelry they could find.

My mother had sewn her last piece of jewelry—a gold pendant—into the hem of her coat, hidden along with handwritten addresses of family members and friends who had already escaped.

After an hour, the men returned, and the pirate ship sailed off, leaving the refugees to their escape. The men had been provided a warm meal during the siege. Not all the men had returned. Some had chosen to go with the pirates.

I grew up with this story, remembering not just the fear but also the desperation. From the refugees on the ship, from the pirates themselves. My mother would say it was both clever and cruel, to trick the men into not fighting. There were other pirates, stories of refugee ships that never made it to shore, pirates who seized vessels and destroyed lives. There were also ships that towed those to safety, ships with people who had nothing and spared what they could to help others. The pirates who boarded my mother's refugee ship were confusing to me as a child. Weren't they the bad guys? Why did some of the men choose to go with them if they were? If the pirates had food to spare, why did they not feed all the refugees?

These were questions that stayed at the back of my mind as a child and a youth beginning to voraciously read stories. I thrived on adventure, consuming every bit of action, science fiction, and fantasy. As a teen, I was obsessed with Keira Knightley as Elizabeth Swann in the *Pirates of the Caribbean* series when the movies debuted. Like many young people, I read a fair number of classic literary texts, including *Treasure Island*. I remember being captivated by the story, the adventure, the image of seafaring rogues, and the legends that captured imaginations all over the world: Blackbeard, Anne Bonny, Mary Read. It wasn't until I was in college that I learned of Zheng Yi Sao, or as she is more commonly known in Western vernacular, Ching Shih. At the height of her career, Zheng Yi Sao commanded multiple squadrons with lieutenants under her command, hundreds of ships and thousands of pirates to form a formidable army that struck fear into multiple governments. She is regarded as the most successful pirate in history. And I wondered, why were there not more stories about her?

My mother spent years in a refugee camp on a beach in Cambodia, surviving and working with other refugees to distribute supplies and take care of my aunt and cousin. Her skill as a schoolteacher and knowledge of English led her to a job working with the UN, and eventually a sponsorship and asylum status in the United States. In 1979, she found work as a waitress in Los Angeles while going to school. Her network of addresses of family and friends abroad kept her in touch with the auntie network: who escaped where, who needed help when, who knew who in what city. My mother's closest friends would be those she lived in the refugee camp with, people who I know as aunties and uncles and as family, who she would translate for and help understand the asylum process. My mother would reunite families, connect people with others who knew the language, encourage new immigrants to go to school, help them find jobs, and give them resources on how to naturalize.

One day the auntie network surfaced a new piece of information: Did you know a boy from your village—before you moved to Saigon for work—is also in Los Angeles? My father, who ended up in a refugee camp in Malaysia after the war, also had made it to the United States. He and my mother reconnected and decided to build a new life together.

My parents speak little of the time during the war, even less so during the refugee camps, but slowly I would learn. Our history is complicated; on both sides of the family are Chinese and Vietnamese roots, tangled together in past generations in conflict and trauma, brought together by love and the desire to build something new. It is my own history, the complicated juxtaposition of who I am—a descendant of hope, of a desire for freedom from oppression—that informs all of my writing.

As a storyteller, I want readers to question history, question why a classic is a classic, and who gets to determine what stories are told and what stories are deemed important. Who determines why a story is valuable? Who determines what becomes a legacy?

Treasure Island is, at first, a story about stories. Jim Hawkins and the tale of Flint's treasure, the legacy of the riches and the possibility are what drive him to pursue it to save his mother's inn.

It is an honor to be writing for the Remixed Classics series and to work with this particular story, one whose call to adventure has always been important to me. I hope you have enjoyed this work, and getting to know Xiang and Anh and this particular time in history, in all the complicated in betweens of war and piracy and the choices people make to survive and sometimes, to thrive.

I want to say I see you, and you are valuable because you exist. You exist in the past, you exist in the present, and you exist in the future.

This story is for you, and all your new horizons.

Language Notes

I believe as a storyteller we have a choice in not just the stories we tell but how we choose to tell them. I have chosen with care how words in Chinese and Vietnamese appear in this novel with respect to the culture and heritage of these languages.

The spelling and romanization of Chinese names and places is one that has been inherently tied to a colonial and Western lens. There have been many spellings and variations used by traders, explorers, and colonizers as they encountered places and people they needed to document. The translation of Chinese sounds to roman letters in the English language was difficult and could vary wildly. You have likely encountered the names of the historical figures and places that appear in this story in various other forms. I have included these spellings in the pronunciation guide for your reference.

In the nineteenth century, romanized spellings of the Nanjing dialect were quite common until the Wade-Giles system set a precedent in 1892 with the publication of the *Chinese-English Dictionary*, which was based on Herbert A. Giles's translation of Thomas Francis Wade's system to romanize the Beijing dialect. This system became the standard throughout the nineteenth century, and the spellings of names and places became solidified in the English-speaking world with this system through to the twentieth century.

In the 1950s, Zhou Gouyang created the Hanyu Pinyin system in mainland China. After widespread national literacy campaigns from the Chinese government and decades of use, it was established as the national standard in 1979.

Vietnam's written language was historically written in the Chữ Nôm script, a combination of Chinese characters with local characters. During French colonial rule in the nineteenth century, the Latin alphabet was adopted with diacritics to signify tone and punctuation. While the written system was not in place at the time of the story, I used these romanizations in the novel as this written system for Vietnamese is still used today and is the national standard.

I have used Canton as the capital of the Guangdong province and not the more modern romanization, as it was more historically accurate and also reflected the cosmopolitan nature of it as a major city and international port. Other Chinese names, places, and words are spelled with respect to their origins, whether they be Cantonese or Mandarin. Xiang, who grew up in the Guangdong province, would be most familiar with Cantonese, and so all dialogue unless indicated otherwise would be spoken in that dialect. She would also be familiar with Mandarin through her formal education with her tutor. Since the novel is told from her perspective, I chose to keep Vietnamese words as she would hear them, and did not translate words in languages she would not know, such as English. The romanizations I have chosen reflect Xiang's Cantonese perspective. Despite the historical inaccuracy of the usage of the Hanyu Pinyin system, I have occasionally chosen to use these spellings instead of the Wade-Giles spellings in the cases where I did not choose the Cantonese spelling.

Pronunciation Guide

People

Name (spelling in novel)	Variations	Chinese	Phonetic Pronunciation
Cheung Po Tsai	Cheung Po, Chang Pao, Quan Apon Chay (Portuguese), Zhang Baozi	張保仔	jhANG bow sEYE
Hoa Ngọc Anh			hwa nock hahng
Hoa Ngọc Hanh			hwa nock AHnh
Feng Zhanli		馮棶立	fung jAN- lee
Shi Xiang		石香	shEE shANG
Shi Yeung	Shi Yang	石阳 (simplified) 石陽 (traditional)	shEE yung
Zheng Yi	Cheng Yud, Cheng I, Ching I, Chang I, Zhang I, Zheng Wenxian (birth name), Youyi (courtesy name)	鄭一	jUNG yee
Zheng Yi Sao	Ching I Sao, Chang Sao, Ching Shih, Cheng Yud Sao, Zhang Yi Sao	鄭一嫂	jUNG yee sow

Places

Place	Variations	Phonetic Pronunciation
Beijing	Peking	bay- JING
Changping	Chi'angping, Giangbing, Chingpang	chANG- pING
Canton	Guangzhou (present day official), Kwangchow, Cantão (Portuegese misprounounciation of Guangzhou, which led to the English spelling of Canton)	gong- tun
Guangdong	Kwangtung	gwang- dooNG
Hạ Long		hAH long
Macao		ma- kOW
Nha Trang		nAH trang
Thăng Long	Long Biên, Tống Bình, Long Đỗ, Đại La, Đông Đô, Đông Quan, Đông Kinh, Bắc Thành, Hà Nội (present day official)	tan long
Việt Nam		vEE- it nam

Ships

Name	Chinese	Meaning	Phonetic Pronunciation
Huyền Vũ		Black Tortoise	hween- fu
Jīn Lǐyú	金鯉魚	Golden Carp	jin lee- YOO
Lóng Zhī Ào	龍之傲	Dragon's Pride	loong gee- OW
Nù Tiě	怒鐵	Iron Wrath	nOO tee

Historical Notes

Zheng Yi Sao lived and breathed and loved more than two hundred years ago. When I was first approached with the concept of reimagining a classic—not just any classic, but *Treasure Island*, a pivotal piece of literature that captured the imagination of countless readers across the world, including my own, I knew immediately that this formidable woman was where I wanted to start.

She was born in 1775 in the Guangdong province as Shi Yeung and worked as a prostitute in a floating brothel until marrying Zheng Yi in 1801. History remembers her as Zheng Yi Sao, Zheng's widow whose leadership unified squabbling pirate squadrons into a formidable fleet. At the height of her power, Zheng Yi Sao commanded over 70,000 pirates and over 1,200 vessels.

Zheng Yi Sao's rise to power begins with the origins of piracy itself in the South China Sea. In the eighteenth century and early nineteenth century, sea bandits and pirates were common but uncoordinated, without any serious unification, and did not pose a significant threat to governments. However, during the Tây Sơn rebellion in Vietnam, many pirate commanders were enlisted in the war effort and gained tactical and military experience, growing their fleets in numbers and strength.

Despite the loss of their titles and rankings after the collapse of the Tây Sơn reign, the valuable military experience and political acumen gained during their decade fighting as mercenaries would provide the opportunity for the pirates to do what they previously could not: unite under a common goal. After Zheng Yi Sao's marriage to Zheng Yi in 1801, with her leadership and financial savvy the two commanders united the Red, Yellow, Black, Blue, and White Squadrons to a formidable confederation that would be known as the Red Banner Fleet. The names "Head of the Dragon" and "Dragon Fleet" were created solely for the purpose of the novel. Zheng Yi Sao has been most commonly referred to as a "pirate queen" and I wanted to create a title that reflected her Chinese heritage, as well as differentiate the Red Squadron and the Red Banner Fleet.

Cheung Po Tsai was born in 1783 and joined the Red Squadron at the age of fifteen, rising up in the ranks and becoming Zheng Yi's protégé and lover. After Zheng Yi's sudden death in 1807, Zheng Yi Sao secured her position by marrying the formidable commander. Born Cheung Po, he would become known as Cheung Po Tsai with the nickname "The Kid" and as Quan Apon Chay to the Portuguese.

Zheng Yi Sao and Cheung Po Tsai brought the Red Banner Fleet to its full might, ushering in a golden age of piracy together with their united squadrons. However, rising discontent among the squadron leaders and Cheung Po Tsai's own ambitions to become emperor, as well as increased clashes with the Portuguese, British, and the Qing empire's attention to eradicating piracy all led to the inevitable collapse of the Red Banner Fleet. After the Battle of the Tiger's Mouth, the governor-general Pai Ling, eager to end the threat of piracy, negotiated with Zheng Yi Sao and offered amnesty if the Red Banner Fleet ceased all pirate activity. Zheng Yi Sao, dissatisfied with the terms to surrender all her ships, demanded to retain eighty junks and five thousand crew members for the salt trade. Pai Ling yielded and Zheng Yi Sao and many other commanders accepted the pardon.

Cheung Po Tsai went on to have a successful career in the Qing navy capturing other pirates until he died at sea in 1822. Zheng Yi Sao settled near Canton, continuing to run her smuggling operations, working the salt trade, and running a successful gambling house.

Cheung Po Tsai maintained several hiding places throughout his life in the vast network of underwater caves on various islands. Cheung Chau, one of Hong Kong's outlying islands, today boasts a popular tourist attraction to view one of the legendary caves where Cheung Po Tsai was rumored to hide his loot.

No treasure has ever been recovered from any of these known locations. It is likely that the secrets of the Red Banner Fleet died with Zheng Yi Sao. She lived to the age of sixty-five and died of old age after a life on her own terms, arguably the most successful pirate who ever lived.

Recommended Reading

Anthony, Robert J. *Like Froth Floating on the Sea: The World of Pirates and Seafarers in Late Imperial South China.* Berkeley: Institute of East Asian Studies, University of California, Berkeley, 2003.

Choi, Byung Wook. *Southern Vietnam under the Reign of Minh Mang (1820–1841): Central Policies and Local Response.* New York: Southeast Asia Program Publications, 2004.

Menzies, Gavin. *1421: The Year China Discovered America.* New York: HarperCollins, 2002.

Murray, Dian H. *Pirates of the South China Coast 1790–1810.* Stanford: Stanford University Press, 1987.

Wang, Wensheng. *White Lotus Rebels and South China Pirates: Crisis and Reform in the Qing Empire.* Cambridge: Harvard University Press, 2014.

For a full bibliography, extended historical notes, discussion questions for educators, and other extra content, please visit cb-lee.com.

Acknowledgments

Thank you to my agent, Thao Le: Your unwavering support and enthusiasm for my stories means the world. Thank you for being an incredible champion for marginalized writers and for being the incredible person you are. I am looking forward to making more waves with you.

To Emily Settle, my incredible editor, whose assurances to "make it as gay as you want" and delightful notes throughout the drafting process made this journey truly wonderful. Thank you for all your support through years that felt like a decade, and for launching the Remixed Classics series and bringing so many stories into the world. I can't wait to read them all.

Thank you to the team at Feiwel and Friends and everyone at Macmillan who have made this possible. Feifei Ruan, your cover illustration truly brought Xiang and Anh to life and the spirit of *A Clash of Steel* with such breathtaking beauty, and I was so truly honored to have your art grace this novel. Thank you, Rich Deas, for the cover and absolutely lovely book design.

My heartfelt appreciation and thanks to Alyzia Liu, who worked with me to write the incredible poem that leads to Zheng Yi Sao's legendary map in this novel. Her literary sense truly elevated this poem to give it the classic literary feeling that Feng Zhanli would have been proud of.

Jeanette Wu, thank you for the translations of historical Chinese texts and maps, your keen eye for detail, your passion for history, and your initiative; I could not have finished this endless research without you.

I am humbled and honored by the work of beta readers Teresa Tran and Grace Li, whose notes on the first draft truly helped elevate the story in respect to the cultural and historical perspectives in the novel. Thank you, Karuna Riazi, for your thoughtful and wise notes and quick attention to detail, and to Alex Polish for reading the very first chapter and whose endless encouragement and steadfast friendship kept me going to finish the story that was in my heart.

I could not have written this novel without the sailing expertise of Abby Gavit, practical and historical. Thank you for your steadfast encouragement, your stick figure drawings, your patience for my endless questions, and all your excitement for these disaster gays. I look forward to sailing with you in the future.

Thank you to dear friends TingTing Li and Lisa Ou, for the years of rock climbing and adventures in the woods, fandom shenanigans, for the hours of *Minecraft* and *Stardew Valley*, to staying up late to chat about adolescent lycanthropes and sad gamer boys and Chinese dramas. May the TLC house live forever in spirit.

Thank you to Lanchi, for helping me craft the epigraph and work with me on the Vietnamese that appears in the novel, and TingTing for always being up to chat about names and pronunciations and helping me with my incredibly basic Mandarin.

To the wonderful team at Interlude Press—Annie, Candy, and Choi—for believing in queer books and publishing queer stories, for believing in me as a writer, for giving the Sidekick Squad a home and a place to grow. I am incredibly honored and inspired always to work with you.

Thank you to Malinda Lo and Cindy Pon for your mentorship, for your support, and for writing such incredible and meaningful works to me. I am so glad to have met you both and appreciate your time and friendship.

I am truly thankful to Kate Johnston, Charlie Jane Anders, Courtney Milan, Sarah Kuhn, and Rebekah Weatherspoon, for being some of the first wonderful people I've met in publishing and being incredibly awesome on this journey. Thank you to wonderful writers and friends: Nilah Magruder, Julian Winters, Amy Spalding, Dhonielle Clayton, Zoraida Cordova, Ashley Poston, Tara Sim, Julia Ember, Katherine Locke, Sam Maggs, Erika Turner, Nita Tyndall, Jackie Ball, Nina Varela, Margaret Owen, Adib Khorram, Mark Oshiro, Addie Tsai, Kay Ulanday Barrett, and so many more who I hope to see again, write with again, and laugh with and spend time with at many a festival and convention in the future. Thank you to all the wonderful writers in the community whose kindness, joy, and friendship inspire my heart and whose stories inspire my soul.

To my fellow Remixed Classics authors—Bethany C. Morrow, Aminah Mae Safi, Tasha Suri, Anna-Marie McLemore, and Caleb Roehrig: Thank you for the slack and shenanigans and support. I am looking forward to everything to come and all of your incredible stories, and to all the new authors to join on this adventure.

To the Kidlit Alliance, CAPE, Viet in Entertainment, and the Asian Author Alliance, thank you for creating spaces for support and uplifting writers and creatives to be their best selves. Thank you to inspiring creators, motivators, and forces of nature—Osric Chau, Jes Vũ, Andrea Walter, Chantal Thuy: endlessly thankful for you and your energy in this world. Thank you to the Ripped Bodice of Culver City, Mysterious Galaxy of San Diego, and Skylight Books of Hollywood for being lights in the darkness, to bookstores and indie shop owners and managers and dedicated booksellers for curating and creating events and supporting authors and uplifting books in certain and uncertain times.

Thank you to librarians, teachers, educators, book bloggers, book sellers, and everyone in the book community for their enthusiasium, support, and creativity.

To my parents: Thank you for your time, your experiences, your wisdom, your dreams and perseverance and endurance. I hope that the legacy of surviving can become living, in all senses of the word, in joys and laughter and bright things to come.

I couldn't have made it through any of the tough times, celebrated the joyful times, the exhilarating, the mundane, without my friends whose chatter and memes and livestreams I've always looked forward to: Procrastination

Zone, Inkwell, Yellow Gardens, Introverts Unite, and Tomodachi Cuties. Thank you for making every day better.

My friends, my anchors—Michelle, Katrina, Freck, Sylvia, Angela, Jessie, Kate, Chloe—thank you for being there from the very beginning, to seeing it through, to being dear and near. Here's to a reunion that's been long overdue, with an abundance of baked goods and wine and laughter endlessly flowing.

Keely and Matt—my safe harbor. Thank you.

They will face first love, health struggles, heartbreak, and new horizons. But they will face it all together.

In a lyrical celebration of Black love and sisterhood, this remix of *Little Women* takes the iconic March family and reimagines them as a family of Black women building a home and future for themselves in the Freedpeople's Colony of Roanoke Island in 1863.

Thank you for reading this Feiwel & Friends book. The friends who made *A Clash of Steel: A Treasure Island Remix* possible are:

Jean Feiwel, Publisher

Liz Szabla, Associate Publisher

Rich Deas, Senior Creative Director

Holly West, Senior Editor

Anna Roberto, Senior Editor

Kat Brzozowski, Senior Editor

Dawn Ryan, Senior Managing Editor

Celeste Cass, Assistant Production Manager

Emily Settle, Associate Editor

Erin Siu, Associate Editor

Rachel Diebel, Assistant Editor

Foyinsi Adegbonmire, Editorial Assistant

Ilana Worrell, Senior Production Editor

Follow us on Facebook
or visit us online at mackids.com.
Our books are friends for life.